A Dateless Bargain

A Dateless Bargain

Bargain

Catherine Louisa Pirkis

MINT EDITIONS

A Dateless Bargain was first published in 1887.

This edition published by Mint Editions 2021.

ISBN 9781513281957 | E-ISBN 9781513286976

Published by Mint Editions®

 MINT
EDITIONS

minteditionbooks.com

Publishing Director: Jennifer Newens
Design & Production: Rachel Lopez Metzger
Project Manager: Micaela Clark
Typesetting: Westchester Publishing Services

Contents

I

"L ock the door, Mab, then we can begin to turn things upside down in comfort. Now what room in the house is most unlike a study?"

"Is it a conundrum," laughed Mab; "or do you wish for a straightforward answer? It wants thinking over. A housekeeper's room, perhaps, or a kitchen—"

"Oh, what unrefined notions you have! If you had asked me, I should have said a lady's boudoir. You get your inspiration from your brown holland sleeves and apron. Look at yourself in the glass. What a splendid housemaid was lost in you!"

These two young people gossiping so gaily on a bright May morning were Mabel and Joscelyn Shenstone, only children of Irving Shenstone, one of the largest landowners in the county of Gloucestershire. He was expected home on this day from a ten days' visit to London, and his daughters were preparing a welcome for him in his sanctum by turning things generally upside down.

"We want to leave the mark of our presence in the room," Joscelyn had informed her mother over the breakfast-table that morning, "so that when father sits down and kicks off his boots—as he always does in his study—he will say, 'Mab did that, I'll swear, and Joyce made that other lovely arrangement.'"

These sisters, in appearance, were like and unlike each other as only sisters can be. They were each of them tall, slender girls, with well-shaped heads, a profusion of dark brown hair, and large hazel-gray eyes. But here all likeness ended; for the truth must be told, Joyce was one of the handsomest girls the county could boast of, while Mab stood close upon the border of plainness. Joyce's complexion was that of a brilliant brunette, while Mab was unmistakably sallow. Joyce had the straightest and prettiest of Grecian noses, a small mouth all dimples and curves; Mab's nose was somewhat aquiline, her mouth wide and innocent of dimples and curves. Joyce's general expression was one of buoyant happiness; Mab, as a rule, wore so deep a look of intellectual thought as to amount almost to melancholy, or, to speak exactly, of anxious apprehension.

It was characteristic of these sisters that while Mab was attired in the neatest of black gowns, which she had furthermore essayed to protect from dust by thoroughly congruous holland apron and housemaid's sleeves, Joyce's sole preparation for her morning's mimic housewifery had been to pin back her pretty cambric skirt into one graceful fold behind, thereby disclosing in front her dainty slippers and slender ankles.

Mab took a long, steady look at herself in the mirror.

"I think I must be a born housemaid; I always feel so thoroughly at home with a dusting-brush in my hand," she began, musingly.

But Joyce was not at all in a mood for either musing or attitudinizing that morning.

"Well, then, begin and use it, my dear, as if you were 'to the manner born,'" she replied, laughingly, giving Mab a little push in the direction of the writing-table, which stood at right-angles to the glass. "You set to work on the ink-bottles; empty them every one—you know I'm going to turn them all into flower-vases—while I attack the book-shelves."

Mab made a little demur.

"It doesn't seem the right thing to do with ink-bottles, and where—where shall I throw the ink?"

"Oh, you want so much telling! You a housemaid, indeed! Why, out of the window, of course; never mind about the flowers underneath. Now, a clever maid would have jumped at that idea before I could have spoken."

Mab made another demur, muttering something to the effect "that it wasn't exactly the sort of work a housemaid would have given to her." It was, however, a very little demur, for, although Joyce was nearly two years younger than Mab, she invariably acted the elder sister, and Mab was, so to speak, completely "under her thumb."

So splash, splash, went bottle after bottle of ink from the window on the flower-bed beneath.

"It will dye those pansies a magnificent blue-black," laughed Joyce, hard at work at her book-shelves. "Old Donovan will throw up his hands in admiration when he comes round next with his watering-pot. Look here, Mab, here's a whole row of books on farming, cattle-rearing, and such like nonsense. Shall I turn them all the wrong way—upside down, that is—or with their backs to the wall?"

"I think you might let the books alone, Joyce."

"Good gracious! What for? Why, books are the first thing to be thought of in a study. If I let the books alone, what may I touch? Ah, I've an idea! I'll rummage about for some poetry-books; there are sure to be a lot behind somewhere, or on the upper shelves, and I'll push back all the dreadfully useful books and put all the poetry in front. Now, won't that be splendid? Oh, good gracious, good gracious!" This in an utterly surprised tone. "Here are heaps upon heaps of poetry-books! Why, there's Shelley, Keats, Coleridge, Shakespeare! Oh, no end of Shakespeare; a dozen volumes at least. Who would have thought that father had ever in his whole life been an admirer of the poets? These books have every one of them his name on the fly-leaf in his own writing!"

Mab left her writing-table all in a hurry.

"I thought it! I knew it!" she said, excitedly. "I felt certain father had been all but a poet before he went in so much for farming and that sort of thing; and I know I'm right in never opening a book of poetry—" she stopped herself abruptly.

Joyce turned upon her amazed.

"Why—why shouldn't you read poetry, if you like?" she cried. "That's it! I know you're acting up to some funny notion you've taken into your head. You've given up music, you've given up painting, you are always doing plain needlework, or poring over housekeeping books. What does it mean? What's the idea, Mab?"

Mab went back to her writing-table.

"Look, Joyce," she said, quietly, "I've emptied all the ink-bottles. Now, don't you think we ought to begin getting the flowers? Shall I go and ask Donovan to cut a basket-full?" Which remark, it will be seen, was in no sort an answer to Joyce's question.

It served, however, to divert her attention.

"Ask Donovan?" she cried. "Are you out of your mind? Why, if we went down on our knees to him he wouldn't give us more than a handful of the commonest garden-flowers and just a few very full-blown azaleas, with very short stalks, out of one of the hot-houses. No, thank you; I'm going out to help myself this time, and I shall come back with armfuls of everything—tulips, hyacinths—everything that's spring-like and delicious. Oh, the dust!" Here a fit of sneezing prevented further exclamation.

Whereupon Mab volunteered her services.

"Let me finish those book-shelves while you get the flowers. You only want all the poetry in front, and the farming-books pushed back, so that father won't be able to lay his hand upon anything he wants. Isn't that it?" she asked, setting to work briskly on the volumes.

A door opening off this little study led, by a flight of steps, straight into the garden, now, thanks to a singularly sunny month of May, in the full glory of its spring blossoming.

Down these steps went Joyce with the biggest pair of scissors she could find. Back again in something under five minutes she came, with a nosegay so huge she was compelled to hold her dress-skirt in either hand to help carry it into the room.

She deposited the flowers in a heap on the floor—snowy hawthorn boughs, "deep tulips dashed with fiery dew, laburnums, dropping-wells of fire."

"There's a lot more coming," she cried, gleefully. "I came upon Kathleen just now, and told her to bring all the hyacinths in pots she could lay her hands upon. Ah, here she is!" This added as a remarkably pretty and, for her station, daintily-attired damsel appeared upon the scene burdened with two full-flowering hyacinths in pots.

This was Kathleen Donovan, the gardener's daughter, who acted as maid to the two young ladies. Hers was a face that in another sphere of life might have won for her a ducal coronet, or at least a dangerous reputation as a successful beauty. Not a faultlessly beautiful face, but a face so full of sparkle, of betwitching brightness, and changeful coquetry that one looked at it, and looked again, without having the remotest notion of what shape or size were the features, what color were eyes and hair. It was a typical Irish face, not the face one is accustomed to associate with orange baskets and green-and-red shawls, but rather with the harps and the Irish melodies, the breeze-blown Norah Creinas, and the sweet vales "where the bright waters meet." Her manner was Irish too—soft, arch, betwitching—though with an English veneer upon it, caught from constant daily contact with her young mistresses.

"Ever so many more, Kathleen," cried Joyce. "I am going to fill the fireplace with hyacinths. I want this room to be as unlike a study and as much like a bower as we can make it. Never mind what your father says, bring everything you can get hold of that has leaves and flowers."

Off went Kathleen; down went the two girls on their knees, breaking branchlets from the boughs of laburnum and hawthorn, arranging the big, yellow tulips against a plumed background of lilac, doing, in fact, their very utmost to convert this chosen seat of Minerva into a shrine fit for Flora herself.

"It's like desecration," murmured Mab, looking remorsefully toward the book-shelves, where the topsy-turvied volumes showed mournfully through a bowery arrangement of bright-tinted posies.

"It's consecration, you mean," cried Joyce. "These dry old walls have never held so much beauty before;" and on went her fingers faster than ever.

Her eyes sparkled, her curly hair strayed across her forehead, she sang merry little snatches of old-world ballads which a modern fashion has revived. Assuredly the May sun, after climbing the Mendips that morning, turning the forgotten battle-fields of old Gloucestershire into fields of "cloth of gold" with buttercups and celandine, could find no daintier work for its mid-day hours than throwing its light and its shadow on this blithe picture of Joyce Shenstone on the floor amid her bright, spring flowers.

Mab lifted up a finger.

"Hush! There's a step on the gravel," she said, not inaptly, in the middle of Joyce's carol that—

> "Every fair has a sweetheart there,
> And the fiddler's standing by."

Down went all Joyce's posies in a moment.

"It's Frank!" she cried, jumping to her feet.

And, before Mab could have counted ten on her fingers, she had flung down the garden steps, and might have been seen out there in the sunshine talking and laughing with a tall, dark young man of about six or eight-and-twenty. Now looking up into his face, now looking down at the pebbles at her feet, with bright, quick, happy glances and smiles that left no doubt as to the footing on which the two stood toward each other,

For of course she had a lover—this gay, beautiful girl—and of course (equally as beseemed a gay, beautiful girl) he paired well with her. He was tall, dark-haired, dark-eyed, and, if a little thin, yet withal it was not a thinness that implied want of bodily vigor, but rather an extreme of nervous energy, and a sufficiency of muscle.

Joyce dashed at once into a glowing description of her morning's performance.

"We have had such a delightful morning, Mab and I," she began; "no end of fun in father's study."

"Fun in a study? Oh!" This in a voice of comic horror.

"Well, why not? We've only turned everything as nearly upside down as possible. If you'd been there we should have done it in half the time."

"Is it likely I should have aided and abetted? I'm only surprised that Mab should have allowed such iniquity to be perpetrated."

"She couldn't help it. You know I'm the ruling spirit in the house. Come in at once, Frank, and pronounce an opinion on our handiwork. From your first exclamation we shall be able to judge what father's will be when he walks into the room."

But Frank demurred vigorously to this proposal.

"You know it's my last day with you. I'm off to London by the first train tomorrow morning. I've no end to say to you. Two are company; three, begging Mab's pardon, are not. Come into the orchard, and let us see how the fruit-blossoms are getting on!"

Meantime, Mab and Kathleen, indoors, were bringing their work of decoration to a close, Mab, with a sudden diminution of energy, which told either of a decrease of interest in her task now that the ruling spirit had departed, or else of headache and languor, brought on probably by the heavy odor of the masses of sweet-scented flowers they had packed into such a small space. An atmosphere compounded of the scents of hyacinth, hawthorn, narcissus, and lilac would be assuredly more likely to suit the organs of bee or butterfly than those of a supersensitive human being.

More than once Mab put her hand to her head. Kathleen, flitting in and out of the garden, could not possibly have felt overpowered by the fragrance, but, nevertheless, she had suddenly grown silent, and an expression somewhat akin to sullenness had chased away the smiles and sunshine from her pretty face.

At the foot of the garden-steps, with a final pair of hyacinth-pots in her arms, she stood still, looking after Joyce and her lover on their way toward the orchard-gate.

"You're no prettier than I am; you're taller, maybe—a trifle, that's all—but that's no reason why—" she began muttering.

"Kathleen, I'm waiting," called Mab from within. "Put those two flower-pots just within the fireplace—so. Now, I don't believe we could find room for any more, if we tried our hardest. Don't go away, I want to ask you about your brother. Has he really made up his mind to go to London—will nothing make him give up the idea?"

"Nothing, Miss Mab, I'm sure. He has as good as said goodbye to all of us, and means, I know, to set off some time today," answered Kathleen, evidently with an effort bringing back her thoughts to answer her young mistress's questions.

"But he has not said good-bye to me, Kathleen. He must come in and see me, I've something special to say to him."

"I told him so, miss, only this morning. I told him how good you had been to him, lending him books and all that; but he said he shouldn't dream of coming up to the house, unless you sent for him."

"Well, then, I'll send for him. You must go down to the cottage, and tell him I'm waiting in here to see him. I want to know exactly what he is going to do in London, and I want to make him give me a solemn promise that he won't join any of those dreadful secret societies."

Kathleen's face brightened.

"Ah, if you could make him do that, miss, it's a heavy load you'd be lifting from mother's heart," she said, in her excitement unconsciously drifting into her father's brogue—a feat she did not often accomplish, for her mother, being a thoroughbred cockney, had impressed upon her daughter from her earliest years that all such eccentricities of speech were to be avoided, as indicative of kinship with an inferior race of people.

Mab began to fear she had been indiscreet.

"Don't tell Ned what I want him here for," she said, "or perhaps he won't come. Only say I want to say good-bye to him."

"Do you think he'd refuse anything to you, Miss Mab?" cried Kathleen, as she departed on her mission, "why he worships the very ground you walk on."

Kathleen shut the glass door as she went down the steps into the garden. The room seem to grow more and more stifling. Mab's head went round. She sank into her father's easy-chair beside his writing-table, feeling drowsy and stupid. Her eyes closed, she would get up in a minute, she thought, unlock the door leading into the hall, open the opposite window and let a full current of fresh air sweep through the room, and then straightway her head dropped upon her hand, she leaned backward in her chair, falling into a deep, dreamless sleep.

Five, ten, fifteen minutes passed, and there came the sound of a foot-fall on the garden steps, a face looked in through the glass door, the handle turned, and a man entered the room.

It was Ned Donovan, the gardener's son. His face, like his sister's, proclaimed his nationality. He was the beau-ideal of an Irishman of the heroic, enthusiastic type, the type one can not bear to think of as priest-ridden or demagogue-driven, and yet which so frequently falls into the trammels of either priest or demagogue. He had the bluest of eyes, curly chestnut hair, a woman's mouth and chin, and a carriage of head and shoulders such as one sees in the soldier-Irishman, and in no one else. Under his arm he carried a couple of volumes of Carlyle's "Frederick the Great," and, if one had opened the first volume, Mab's name would have been seen on the title-page.

He gave a great start of surprise when he caught sight of the sleeping girl. Then he too became conscious of the oppressive atmosphere.

"It's enough to suffocate her," he muttered, doing what Mab had proposed to do, opening both doors and letting a free current of air pass through.

Mab stirred in her sleep as the sweet, feesh breeze swept over her face. Something of color came into her pale cheeks, her lips half parted, as though about to smile. In sleep Mab always looked an idealized likeness of the Mab who went about the house with cupboard keys, or else knitting-pins, in her fingers. It was so now. The look of anxious, troubled thought had disappeared, in its stead there was an expression of serenity and peace, which brought out a latent beauty never seen in the Mab of waking life.

Ned's expression as he gazed down upon her was first one of admiration, next one of sharp, sudden pain.

"Those cursed walls which rank and wealth set up!" he muttered, breathing hard and clenching his big strong fingers into the palms of his hands till naught but nerve and muscle showed in them.

He stood for a few moments looking down on her irresolutely. Should he make some slight stir in the room, rouse her from her sleep, and say his good-bye?

"I should like to have heard her sweet voice once again," he said to himself; "Heaven only knows when and how I may hear it next."

But at this very moment there came the sound of another voice, and this not a sweet one, from the other side of the door.

"Mab! Joyce! where are you hidden?" It asked once, twice, and again. It was a weak, tinkling little voice, all head-notes, and those out of tune. And it was a voice Ned knew he should never forget, since he had heard it assert one day, all heedless of his presence, "Mab, really you carry things too far. The idea of lending Herbert Spencer to a gardener's boy! You had much better send him a spelling-book."

So with one more look and one more sigh, and a muttered "God bless you, Miss Mab," the handsome Irishman departed, closing behind him the glass door leading into the garden exactly at the moment that Mrs. Shenstone turned the handle and entered the room from the hall.

"Mab, Joyce, are you here?" she queried for the last time, as she crossed the threshold. Then she stood still, looking round her incredulously. Was it daughters of hers who had wrought this havoc in the quiet, neat little study?

"Dear me, dear me!" she soliloquized, "where do they get their notions from? Some unheard-of preposterous idea is forever coming into their heads. One day one thing, another day something else equally far-fetched and ridiculous."

It may be noted in passing that for the past twenty years of her life two complaints had been perpetually on Mrs. Shenstone's lips. The first had reference to her husband: "He spends the whole of his time in his study; except at meals I never see him," it had run. The second related to her daughters, the number and variety of their ideas.

"Where do they get them from? Certainly not from me," had been her all but daily question and answer, as first Mab and then Joyce would startle her into wonder.

It was certainly not from her that the two girls derived their individuality. Her nature was too superficial, too slightly cut, as it were, to impress itself upon anything, even her own children.

Physically, even, they were at opposite poles. Their one point of resemblance to her was their long, slender figures. Her face might have been molded in another planet for all likeness it bore to theirs. It was colorless, trifling in feature, devoid of expression. Any child with four pricks of a pencil within a round O might have drawn it on a slate. But, trivial and uninteresting though it might be, to its possessor it was a mine of wealth, for it gave her subject for thought, and occupation for every one of her waking hours. Only her looking-glass could have rendered an account of the number of admiring glances Mrs. Shenstone bestowed upon herself between sunrise and sunset. Now, after her first hasty look round the transformed study and exclamation of surprise, she walked as naturally to the mirror above the fireplace as the duck walks to the pond. Midway, however, between the door and the mantel-piece, she came upon Mab asleep in the easy-chair, and stopped with another exclamation upon her lips.

"How extraordinary! Another whim, is it! Are they going to turn this room into a sleeping-apartment, or what have they in their heads now?"

She broke off for a moment, then her thoughts went zigzagging into exclamations of surprise as before.

"Dear me, dear me! How remarkably plain and odd-looking the child is getting! I declare, she looks years older than I do! Now, if she were only a little more like me in the face" (here a complacent side-glance toward the mirror) "people might think she was my elder sister! Oh, dear, what's this on the floor?"

The last sentence was added with a little accession of energy as her foot caught in the volumes which Ned Donovan, in his haste to open door and windows, had deposited on the floor at Mab's feet.

Mab opened her eyes with a start. For an instant she looked about her confusedly, then an expression of amazement went sweeping over her face.

"Why—why," she stammered, looking well over Mrs. Shenstone's head with wide-opened yet unseeing eyes, "when did you come home, papa? Why didn't I hear you come in?"

She jumped up from her chair, then suddenly paused, passing her hand vaguely over her forehead and eyes.

"Oh—h, what is it? Where has he gone?" she asked, in a bewildered tone, looking about her uncertainly.

Mrs. Shenstone went to her and took her hand.

"Why, Mab, you must be dreaming!" she cried. "Wake up! you look uncanny and bewildered."

Mab drew the deep breath of an awakening sleeper.

"I suppose I must have been dreaming," she said, slowly, "but I could have declared that my father stood there just in front of me, looking, oh, so terribly sad."

Mrs. Shenstone pointed to the clock.

"Five minutes to twelve," she said, "your father has just a minute ago stepped out of the train onto the platform, and, I should imagine, was looking anything but sad at the prospect of seeing us all again."

II

We measure time by its loss. Two years out of the very middle of a girl's girlhood, looked forward to with the girl's eyes, seems, no doubt, to fall but little short of an eternity; looked back upon, which, after all, must be the only way to gauge its minutes, it seems but a wave-beat on a shore, the flight of a bird from north to south across the sky—nothing more.

So at least it seemed to Mab and Joyce, as, exactly two years from the day on which, with blithe hearts, they had decorated and generally turned upside-down their father's study, they stood in the same room talking over what had been, what was, what was to be.

Not with such light-tripping tongues as heretofore, for this quiet, unpretending little room has grown to seem—to Mab, at any rate—a solemn and holy place; a place, that is, sacred to solemn and holy memories, ever since that terrible day on which, as she stood on the threshold awaiting her father's return, his dead body had been brought past her into the house and laid upon the sofa in this room.

Mr. Shenstone's sudden and awful death had been a great shock to his family. He was in the very prime of his manhood, his health, his wealth; he might have said with the fool of old time, had he been in the habit of indulging in frivolous soliloquies: "Soul, thou has much goods laid up for many years, take thine ease, eat, drink, and be merry," when lo! on a sudden, alighting from his train, at the end of a short, pleasant journey, he took a false step, he fell heavily upon the platform, he struck his temple against an iron pillar as he fell, and headlong into eternity he went.

Mrs. Shenstone's grief was of the vehement, hysteric kind. Its outward form of expression was the insistance upon the constant daily attendance of a local doctor, the constant daily communication with a London or Parisian dressmaker, an increased subscription to Mudie's library, and incessant appeals for sympathy to everyone who went near her.

Mab's grief was of the silent, undemonstrative kind. Its outward expression was *nil.*

Joyce's grief was of the healthy, vigorous kind common to girls of a healthy, vigorous nature, who know that fate, as it crosses their path, will come to them with both hands full—one of sorrows, one of joys—and are prepared to take heartily whichever hand she offers; to weep with a will if she holds out her left, to laugh with a will if she holds out her right. Joyce knew nothing of half measures; "thorough or nothing" had ever been her motto. Only next to her sunny good temper was her aptitude for deciding momentous questions at a glance. "That is why they are called 'momentous,' they are to be decided in a moment," she had once quaintly informed Frank Ledyard, when he had on one occasion slightly demurred to her rapid decision on a matter of importance.

Somehow this habit of Joyce's inspired people with confidence, not only in her capacity for arranging mundane affairs, but also in the mundane affairs, but also in the mundane affairs themselves. Things certainly could not be in a very desperate state, so people were apt to reason, when they admitted of such simple and easy solutions.

Even now, as she and Mab stood together in the dead father's study discussing a serious question, Mab's nervous frown slightly relaxed and her deep-set eyes looked less cavernous under the influence of Joyce's cheery decisiveness of voice and manner.

"It can't be helped, Mab, so we'll just make the best of it. Mother's heart is set upon going to London, and getting into the vortex—whatever that means—and go she will. You have tried your hardest to keep her here, so also has Uncle Archie, so also Aunt Bell; very well, you see it can't be prevented. So we must just look the thing well in the face, and make the best of it."

Mab sighed heavily.

"If papa were here—" she began, but broke off abruptly.

"If papa were here he would hold the reins and keep things straight," said Joyce, taking up the broken sentence and completing it. "He is not here"—here her voice hushed reverently—"so I will hold the reins instead, and keep mother out of mischief."

"Oh, Joyce!"

"I mean it. I know what I'm saying. Some one must do it. You think it beyond your capabilities; I don't feel it beyond mine—"

At this moment the door opened, and Uncle Archie entered. He was elder brother to Joyce's and Mab's father—a small, thin, wiry-looking old gentleman on the down side of sixty. He had a perpetual frown on his forehead, and a perpetual grumble in his eye; his voice was grating, irritating. It recalled the sense of grains of sand under the eyelids, thorns up the side of one's finger-nail, or the stinging nettle-rash of one's juvenile legs.

CATHERINE LOUISA PIRKIS

"If there's one thing in the world I detest more than another," he said, raspingly, "it's the overweening confidence of very young people—of very young people." The last sentence repeated with a pointed emphasis.

Joyce looked up at him saucily.

"Poor Uncle Archie," she said, pityingly, "what has put you out now?"

"What has put me out! Is there anything in this house that doesn't put me out, I should like to know? First one thing, then another. Nothing goes as it ought. I've been talking with your mother for the last half-hour."

"Ah—h—h!"

"Reasoning with her, I should have said, if anyone in this house had been capable of such a thing as reasoning; but, at any rate, talking to her of her folly in breaking up her home here and setting up an establishment in London, where she knows no one with an ounce of common-sense in their heads."

"But, Uncle Archie, no one has more than a pinch of that precious quality here. You know you said so only yesterday."

"No one, in fact, who can put two and two together with a certain result," went on Uncle Archie, heedless of the interruption. "But there, I might as well have tried to reason with a skein of silk. Anything more limp, more tangly than a woman's brain I can't imagine."

"Poor old Uncle Archie!" again exclaimed Joyce, softly. "What a life Aunt Bell must have of it sometimes!"

"I repeat—"

"Oh, don't!"

"Anything more limp and tangly than a skein of silk—"

"You said a woman's brain just now."

"Than a skein of silk and a woman's brain is beyond my conception. And now, on top of it all, comes this letter still further to worry me."

Here the old gentleman put his hand into his pocket and drew out a letter.

"Why, that's from Frank! Give it me, uncle," cried Joyce.

"Don't be in such a hurry; it's addressed to me. But I want to talk it over with you. Come, sit down at this table."

Here Uncle Archie drew a chair close to the table, and sat down. Mab crept out of her corner, and left the room without a word. Uncle Archie had taken the dead father's chair. To her way of thinking, it should be kept empty and sacred to his memory for ever more.

But Joyce, without demur, kneeled on the floor beside the old gentleman, looking up in his face.

"What can Frank have to say to you? Really, he might have told me beforehand that he was going to write to you."

"Really, I see no necessity for his so doing," said Uncle Archie, snappishly. "This letter comes in consequence of a remark made by your mother in Mr. Ledyard's presence."

"Addressed to Frank, was it?"

This was asked with a little show of nervous apprehension.

"Really, I'm not prepared to say to whom the remark was addressed. Your mother is in the habit—you may have noticed it before now—of speaking out whatever comes into her mind, irrespective of the person or persons she may be addressing. No doubt it is a charmingly ingenuous and juvenile habit, and worthy of cultivation; at the same time it is apt to be slightly embarrassing to those on whose behalf it is exercised."

"Uncle Archie, please tell me, word for word, what my mother said to Frank about me."

"No, I couldn't undertake to tax my memory so far; I will give you the general idea of her meaning. My own words you must allow me to use."

"Oh, don't take a hundred years over it."

To this remark Uncle Archie only raised his eyebrows. It hurried him on, though, a little.

"Your mother intended to imply that you two girls were a very great anxiety to her (what she said doesn't in the least matter). She was confident Mab would some day degrade the family, by starting a school for cookery at Shadwell—as though they had anything to cook there beyond red herrings!—or teach domestic economy in one of the Board Schools. And, as for you, you were bound to make shipwreck of your life by some undesirable marriage, when, with your fortune and good looks, you might be a reigning beauty for a season, and a duchess at the end of it."

"Did my mother say that? And before Frank? Two nights ago, I suppose; when he was staying here!"

"Do you imagine I'm telling lies, young lady?"

"And did he hear her? Do you think he could have heard her, Uncle Archie?"

"Not a doubt. To make sure that he should hear her, she said it twice over, and I dare say would have gone over to his side, and said it a third time right in his ear, if he had not shown he had heard it, by taking his hat and saying good-by at once."

"That was why, then, he went off in such a hurry that night to Cheltenham—and that is why he has written such short, unusual letters, I suppose! Uncle Archie, let me have that letter, and read it all to myself, will you?"

Here Joyce made a desperate effort to get possession of the letter.

"Stop a bit, stop a bit!" said Uncle Archie, laying his hand flat upon the paper. "I don't hand over my correspondence unanswered in that fashion. I'll give you the gist of it. In the letters of a young fellow at his time of life there's always a lot to leave out that won't be missed. Now, don't jog my elbow like that; you'll give me the jumps. I'm coming to it fast enough."

Uncle Archie adjusted his glasses, spread the letter in front of him, humm'd and haw'd a little bit more, and then proceeded to condense and expound it for Joyce's benefit. It may be remarked in passing that Joyce contrived to secure a bird's-eye-view for herself of the said letter between the lapel of the old gentleman's coat and the inside curve of his elbow, scrupulously verifying his condensations sentence by sentence as he read them.

"'Trusts I will pardon'—h'm, h'm—'with respect to the remark made by Mrs. Shenstone the other evening. Is quite willing to admit she had a perfect right to make it, that in fact it is a remark that nine mothers out of ten might, in the circumstances, feel disposed to make; but nevertheless it is a remark which he can not with dignity pass over.' H'm, yes, dignity is the word he uses. On his high horse, do you see, Joyce."

"Go on Uncle Archie, I'm taking it all in."

"Don't be in a hurry. I shall get paralysis in my elbow-joint if you lean on me in that way—nine stone on a few inches of muscle is a little too much. Yes, well, 'with dignity,' as I said before, 'he would like to direct my attention to the fact that his engagement to my niece had Mr. Shenstone's entire approval, that there was a distinct understanding between him and Mr. Shenstone that so soon as he' (Frank, that is) 'could secure by his profession an income of five hundred pounds per annum, Mr. Shenstone was to add another five hundred pounds to it, and the marriage was to take place.' Is that true, Joyce?"

"Perfectly so. Go on."

"I am not a locomotive! Well, 'this arrangement he is perfectly willing to consider annulled by Mr. Shenstone's death; he is also willing to admit that you are now through your father's death in a very different position to what you were in when this arrangement was made.' Well, of course, there he's right. I suppose you and Mab will have each of you a steady income of a thousand a-year when some of the leases fall in next year?"

Joyce left off jogging his elbow to utter an exclamation of astonishment.

"You don't mean to say Frank suggests our waiting till he earns a thousand a-year by his profession?" she asked, jumping to the conclusion, which showed on the upturned side of the paper.

"That is exactly what he does suggest, and he puts it on grounds which makes it difficult for us to resist. He says 'he makes this proposal not alone on the score of personal dignity' (high horse again!) but because he conceives that by deferring the marriage till he can double your income with his own, he best carries out the spirit of the arrangement made with your father at the time he was accepted by him as your future husband.'"

Joyce drew a long breath, and got up from her knees.

"It's preposterous; it's ridiculous; it's Quixotic!" she cried, her face flushing crimson.

"Hump. I call it sensible, matter-of-fact, judicious. I shall tell the young man when I answer his letter that I thoroughly approve the idea."

"And I shall tell him, when I write, exactly what I think of it! Why, he won't earn a thousand a year at his profession for another ten years to come at the earliest. And now I'm twenty-one—why, that would make me thirty-one! Fancy a bride at thirty-one! Oh, how dreadful!"

"How's this, young lady? I'd no idea you were in such a tremendous hurry to get married!"

"I'm not the least bit in a hurry to get married, and if I were turned thirty-one I should be still less in a hurry; in fact, I wouldn't marry at all at that ridiculous age. But I'm surprised at you, Uncle Archie, encouraging any one in such far-fetched, high-flown folly; I should have thought you would have put your foot at once on anything in the shape of romance."

"In my young days young women were not in the habit of throwing themselves at the heads of young men," said Uncle Archie, pursing his lips and looking as sour as possible. Defense with him always took the form of aggression.

"You had post-horses and Gretna Green, notwithstanding."

"I'm not an antediluvian. That was twenty years before my time."

CATHERINE LOUISA PIRKIS

"As if twenty years, more or less, mattered on the other side of sixty! Good-bye for the present, Uncle Archie, I want to save this post. It is not of the least consequence what you say to Frank, I shall tell him right out what I think of the whole thing."

Uncle Archie wheeled round in his chair and faced her.

"This is the young lady who felt confident she could hold the reins and keep others out of mischief," he said, taking off his glasses so that she might feel the irony of his eye as well as of his tongue.

Joyce paused with her hand on the door-handle.

"Exactly, Uncle Archie; that is what I'm bent on doing now. I won't let you, or Mab, or mother, or Frank, make yourselves ridiculous—any one of you—try as hard as you will."

III

Mrs. Shenstone laid down a letter just received from the Countess of Cranbury.

"To think," she said, looking round the breakfast-table appealingly for sympathy, "that the friend in whom I trusted should fail me in this way!"

"Countesses are not to be caught with chaff any more than jackdaws," said Uncle Archie, gruffly, from behind his newspaper. "You should bait your trap according to your bird."

"What is it Lady Cranbury won't do, mother?" asked Joyce, good-naturedly desirous of putting up an umbrella between her mother and the hail of Uncle Archie's aphorisms.

Mab looked up nervously.

"Oh, what a pity to ask favors of an almost stranger—" she began, then checked herself.

"An almost stranger! What are you talking about child? Why, I met her and sat next her at supper at the county ball ten years ago!" cried Mrs. Shenstone, in mild astonishment. "And such a small favor, too, that I asked of her! I put it so sweetly to her, reminded her of our pleasant meeting—now, alas! so long ago—and asked, as a special kindness, that she would assist me with her experience as to the choice of a locality for our London house; whether she thought we could be comfortable in a furnished house; whether we had better take up our horses and carriages, or trust to the London livery-stables; whether we should require a large staff of servants; whether—but there, I've forgotten the half of what I wrote to her. And this is her reply."

Here Mrs. Shenstone held up to view the countess's letter, and read as follows:

"'The Countess of Cranbury presents her compliments to Mrs. Shenstone, and begs to suggest that at any respectable house-agent's office she can obtain answers to her queries upon the matter of house-hiring.'"

"My lady was afraid you meant to float yourself into society on her satin skirts, so she very wisely tucked them up," chuckled Uncle Archie.

"My lady needn't have been so easily frightened," cried Joyce, indignantly, "Never mind, mother dear, consult with us; we'll answer all your questions, no matter how many you may ask."

"In future I will have nothing—nothing to do with 'society!'" began Mrs. Shenstone, semi-hysterically.

"Don't, except with the society you have a right to command," interjected Uncle Archie.

"There is an aristocracy of intellect, I'll cultivate that; I'll gather about me the *élite* of the worlds of art and literature. My house in London shall be renowned as the meeting-place of art, science, and letters. I'll choose its locality, irrespective of rank and fashion."

"Oh, the locality must be close to the British Museum; of course that must be the seat of the Muses," said Joyce, with a merry laugh, and throwing a saucy, challenging look at Uncle Archie, meant to be interpreted.

He was quick enough to catch its meaning.

"Let me see," he cogitated, rubbing his chin, "isn't it in close proximity to the British Museum that a certain young barrister has his quarters?"

"Ah, Frank has my letter by this time. Such a letter!" laughed Joyce, accepting the counter challenge with alacrity.

"Mother," said Mab, abruptly rising from the table, "will you mind going through the housekeeping books with me this morning? There are one or two items I can't quite make out."

Mrs. Shenstone sighed.

"I am so tired of housekeeping," she said, plaintively.

To hear her speak one might think her days were passed in the supervision of her establishment—her nights made wakeful by plans for the comfort of her family. The fact of the matter was that Mab was the Atlas of the household, and bore its burden on her shoulders.

For once, however, she deemed it necessary to insist that her mother's shoulders should bear an ounce or two of the weight; so the two left the room together, to spend a happy half-hour over account-books.

Uncle Archie dropped his banter, and turned to Joyce directly he found himself alone with her.

"I want you to explain that sister of yours to me, Joyce," he said. "You I can understand easily enough—any one can understand you—but she is always a mystery to me. I can't penetrate her."

Joyce grew serious in a moment.

"She is a mystery to me, too, in some things," she answered, gravely. "Here we are always together; we read each other's letters; we haven't a secret from each other; yet sometimes I feel as though, slowly but surely, a brick wall were being built up between us, and that, by-and-by, I should only hear her voice far away on the other side of it."

"Is she over-studying, do you think—going in for philosophy or mathematics? Girls often muddle their brains by attempting things they've no real capacity for."

"I'm certain she is not. She never opens a book, unless it is a cookery-book, or one of dear papa's old 'Farmers' Guides' or 'Agricultural Gazettes.' She is dropping all her accomplishments, too—never touches a pencil nor opens the piano."

"She played decently, too, didn't she?"

"Decently! Brilliantly, you mean," cried Joyce, with enthusiasm. "Yet she hasn't touched a note since one day—about six months ago—I went into the drawing-room, to listen to her playing one of Beethoven's sonatas. It was between the lights—too dark to see the keyboard even, much less the music. Yet she was playing deliciously, as though she had every one of the modulations by heart. I knew she hadn't had the piece long enough to be playing from memory, and, when I went close to her, I saw that her eyes, though wide open, seemed looking nowhere, seeing nothing. Of course I spoke to her, and asked if she wouldn't like candles, and she jumped up with such a terrified start, and clutched at me. 'I am so thankful you have come in, Joyce,' she said; 'the room seemed full of shadows.' And from that day she has never touched a note."

Uncle Archie frowned heavily, and shook his head.

"Your mother ought to have advice for her—something must be wrong with her nerves. It's just as well, after all, that you're going up to London; the best of medical advice can only be had in the big cities. I remember your father—"

He stopped short, as though his reminiscences were not of the sort or kind for the daughter's ear.

But Joyce caught at his meaning—snapped at it, like a spaniel at flies.

"Uncle Archie," she queried, peremptorily, "was my father at any time like Mab in his ways?"

"What do you mean? Afraid to sit alone in a room after dark, or for ever bringing out his words with a jerk, or stopping short in the middle of every other sentence he uttered?"

"No. I mean, did he seem to be like Mab, always forcing himself to act up to some preconceived ideas? Of course, I mean as a young man, I know very well what he was later on in life."

CATHERINE LOUISA PIRKIS

"He was very fond of poetry at one time—used to sit reading Shakespeare, Milton, and that other fellow—what's his name? Shelley—all day long. Then he suddenly dropped it all, took to farming as a science, settled down here and married."

"Ah—h!" said Joyce, "I see."

But she did not say what she saw. How could she? when the fact suddenly made intelligible to her understanding was how her father with his strong, clear intellect came to marry a woman whose brains might have been put into a nutshell without the slightest inconvenience to the kernel. "Here am I—I shall drown in the Ideal, only the rock Common-place can keep me high and dry," must have been the cry of his heart when he did the deed.

Uncle Archie possibly followed in the track of her thoughts.

"The truth of it is," he said, with the air of a man accustomed to deal out panaceas to the women of a previous generation, "Mab ought to be married. She is old enough—three-and-twenty nearly—nothing gets the maggots out of a girl's brain so effectually as marriage."

Joyce begged the question.

"I like that, Uncle Archie! You would like to marry Mab right off at once, but me you would keep single for another ten years, if you could!"

"You and Mab are two different beings. If you were an old maid for another twenty years you'd developed no eccentricities. You'd just be comfortable and commonplace, and—and—help to keep other people the same."

But it was not unlovingly said.

"Thank you, Uncle Archie. I'm sure you mean it for a compliment though it is not a remarkably well-turned one. Well, I promise you, when mother's establishment in London is set up—somewhere in the vicinity of the British Museum it will be, I'm confident—I'll look out for a husband for Mab. I daresay there will be plenty of young men about the house—mother always did like young men about, didn't she?"

"Ay, there's the mischief," groaned Uncle Archie, bringing his hand down on the table with an energy that made Joyce start, "you'll get young fools about the house in swarms—impecunious idiots, incapable of making their way in life, anxious to tack themselves to a woman's skirts and be dragged into competence. There's your mother not pastmarrying—large income—Mab—you! all with independent fortunes, and no one to look after you."

"You come up and do the jailor, why not? Take it in turns with me; turn and turn about."

"In turns with you! Great Heavens!" exclaimed Uncle Archie, with a keen upward look over his glasses, taking stock of Joyce's exceedingly youthful graces. "Why, Mab would do the chaperon better than you, or might if she chose to exert herself. What's the world coming to?"

"Why, to common-sense, I hope, now that young ladies of one-and-twenty are so well able to take care of themselves and other people also," laughed Joyce. "As if you didn't know I had chaperoned my mother and Mab ever since I was out of the nursery. Why, Uncle Archie, you dear old thing"—here she went up to the old gentleman and gave him one, two, three good kisses—"I'd chaperon you if you were a bachelor and had no one to look after you!"

IV

U ncle Archie was right when he said that any one could read and understand Joyce Shenstone's character. Truly there were no hieroglyphics in it, although many contradictions met there. For instance, her sunny good-humor was a thing not often found in company with keen powers of observation and a quick sense of the ludicrous. How, too, it was that her frank plain-speaking ran in couples with her power to make and keep friends was a puzzle to not a few. "If I see a spade I feel bound to say it's a spade and not a teaspoon," she had often said to Mab, when the latter had stood open-eyed at her sister's combined fearlessness and truthfulness.

Joyce had plenty of opportunities for saying spades were spades and teaspoons teaspoons, as likewise had Mab of standing open-eyed and admiring when, in due course, Mrs. Shenstone's London establishment was set up.

It was not until the season was well advanced that Mrs. Shenstone succeeded in finding a house to her liking. Eventually one of the roomy, comfortable houses in Eaton Square fixed her fancy.

Joyce wrote saucily enough to Uncle Archie from the hotel where they were temporarily located.

"I allowed mother to decide upon Eaton Square instead of the vicinity of the British Museum, because I knew it really didn't matter two straws, for wherever we went Frank would be sure to repitch his tent within a stone's-throw of us. He has already made preparations for so doing, and next week we may be able to kiss the tips of our fingers to each other across the mews at the back of the house. The thought is an inspiring one for both of us to carry about, and may serve to enliven our ten years' penal servitude."

"Ten years' penal servitude," was the form of expression she frequently adopted to designate her matrimonial engagement, since it had become a received notion in the family that no marriage was to be thought of until Frank's income equaled her own.

The phrase jarred terribly upon Frank's ears at times.

"It is too near the truth to be pleasant hearing," he would occasionally say to her, when he called at Eaton Square in the evening, looking white and tired from a heavy day's work in the Law Courts. "Do you know, Joyce, sometimes I feel I am doing you a positive wrong in keeping you tied down to a poor beggar like me, when not a doubt, from a worldly point of view, you might do so much better?"

But this would be only after a very hard day's work at some insignificant and unprofitable case, when it seemed as though the harder he wooed Fortune, the colder her face grew toward him.

At other times, when Fortune showed in a little better temper, it would be—

"I don't believe there ever was such a lucky fellow—no one ever had such an incentive to hard work as I have. Everything is going on oiled wheels now. I shall soon be—well, if not on the top step of the ladder, at least half-way up, and then—and then—"

Joyce knew how to be cheery and comforting to the first mood, merry and teasing to the second.

"'And then and then,'" she finished his sentence for him. "People will say what an intolerably conceited, altogether insufferable young man that Frank Leydard is! How he plumes himself on his success, and looks down on every one who comes near him! and what a dear, patient girl that Joyce Shenstone must be to put up with him as she does, falling in with his whims and humoring his pride!"

"Joyce, if you had not humored my pride in this way I don't know what would have become of me."

"It was Uncle Archie who insisted that your pride should be humored, not I."

"You were *'particeps criminis'*—"

"Oh, keep that for the Law Courts!"

"Joyce," Frank went on, speaking as seriously as though he were already seated on that bench toward which his ambition tended, "when your mother spoke those careless words that night, all in a flash I seemed to see myself as I stood before the eyes of the world, and to hear the verdict which the world would pass on me."

"Law Courts again!" murmured Joyce, "but why lay so much stress on mother's words? No one—" she broke off all in a hurry.

If she had finished her sentence it would have been:

"No one ever pays any attention to what mother says. If Mab and I did so, we should be in perpetual hot water."

But there are certain things one can not in good taste say, even to one's lover, second self though he may be.

Frank seemed to read her unspoken thoughts easily enough.

"There are some words which a man can not pass over with dignity," he said, somewhat doggedly.

"Dignity! I have heard that word before. If I hear it often I shall fall into the habit of adopting it for my own personal use. I wonder how much you thought of my dignity when you wrote so bluntly to Uncle Archie: 'Whatever you say, I'm not going to marry that niece of yours for another ten years.'"

"Did I make use of that expression? But you see, Joyce, a lady with an independent income of a thousand a-year does not need to lay the stress upon her dignity that a poor beggar with less than half that sum does."

"I wish you would forget the thousand a-year."

"I wish I could. But somehow it seems before my eyes and in my thoughts all day long. I say to myself when I get up in the morning—"

Joyce laid her finger on his lips.

"I don't in the least want to hear what you say when you get up in the morning. Spoken thoughts always sound so ridiculous when they're repeated—like dreams, which bore other people to listen to. Do you know, Mab has lately taken to speaking her thoughts out loud? It sounds so funny."

She was evidently in a great hurry to lead the talk away from her thousand a-year.

"Mab's soliloquies ought to be worth hearing. She opens her mouth so seldom to the outer world, her brain must be packed with ideas," said Frank, following the decoy simply enough.

"If you could hear them! She comes out of her room in the morning counting on her fingers all the things she has to get through before lunch. 'Let me see,' she says, touching finger number one, 'there is Mrs. Gibbs's baby wants new flannel! and Smith, the chimney-sweep, burnt his brush last week, and must have a new one,' and so on till she gets to finger number five. I must tell you that Mab, the last few days, has not been quite so keen about her housekeeping duties, but has taken up with 'Practical Beneficence,' as the newspaper biographies say."

"Does that mean she has turned Ritualist, and goes about visiting the slums in company with a fellow in a black night-gown, with a cord round his waist?"

"As if I would let her! No; it simply means that she is working very hard at schools and district-visiting, and has given up the parish church to attend a Non-conformist chapel."

"Good heavens! I hope she won't be taking up with concertinas and the Salvation Army, or those semi-hysterical things called revivals! The truth of it is, Mab ought to get married."

"There! Exactly what Uncle Archie said! You men seem to think marriage is the cure for all earthly ills. If a girl goes in for high art, and dresses like a saint in a church window, you say immediately, 'She ought to get married.' If she takes up with horses, and talks like a groom, you repeat the same thing; and here, because poor Mab, as I said just now, has 'embarked upon a career of practical beneficence,' you pull a face like a consulting doctor, and say, 'She ought to get married!' I've no patience."

Frank grew grave—people generally grew grave in talking of Mab.

"You don't understand, dear. It's not with Mab's practical beneficence I'm finding fault; I honor her for it. But, you see, these are self-imposed duties, and can be laid down at any time. Before another month is over our heads, she may have found another outlet for herself not quite so desirable."

"Do you mean that before another month is over our heads I am to find an outlet for Mab's eccentricities in the shape of a matrimonial engagement?"

"I did not even hint at such a thing," began Frank, indignantly.

But Joyce was bent on teasing, and rattled on inconsequently.

"Oh, the awful responsibility! Oh, the crowds of young men I shall gather about me so soon as I make known the fact that one of the family is wanting a husband!"

"Well, let it be clearly known which of the family is wanting a husband, or I may be called upon to enter a protest."

"Could you, 'with dignity?'" laughed Joyce. "Well, come in next Friday evening when we shall be 'at home' to our friends, and you shall see me set the ball rolling. By-the-by, did I tell you that Friday evenings are to be an institution weekly throughout the season? Such Fridays they will be! Something quite—quite out of the common! They will have to be seen to be appreciated!"

CATHERINE LOUISA PIRKIS

V

Frank was too quick-witted not to know what Joyce meant when she said, with that look of fun in her eyes, that her mother's receptions "must be seen to be appreciated." To him, with his knowledge of Mrs. Shenstone's weakness of character, and its inherent silliness, but one inference was possible, viz., that she had thrown open her doors to all sorts and conditions of men, without criticising their passports to respectable society, probably without so much as inquiring whether they had passports to criticise.

It filled him with apprehension, most of all on Mab's account. Joyce, he naturally felt, was safe enough. He had a right, to say a word as to her comings and goings, her sayings and doings, the friendships she accepted or refused. But Mab, with her odd, reserved ways, her sudden, unaccountable impulses, seemed to him beset with pitfalls right and left.

In his apprehension, he wrote a long letter to Uncle Archie, outlining the "situation" as delicately as possible, but stating most emphatically his own opinion that, if the old gentleman could make his annual visit to London tally with Mrs. Shenstone's stay in the metropolis, it would be an amazingly good thing for all persons concerned.

Uncle Archie, though at one with the young man in spirit on the matter, was yet disposed to resent his out-spoken frankness as something of an impertinence. Accordingly he wrote curtly enough in reply:

"I rely upon the common-sense and discretion of my younger niece to keep me informed of any matters that may require my presence in town. My investments do not need looking after just now (a likelihood you so kindly suggest), and—I have the gout."

Frank groaned over this letter.

"Talk about the emancipation of women," he said; "nine-tenths of them want protection, not emancipation."

By a coincidence, the word he used so disparagingly was just then more frequently on Mrs. Shenstone's lips than any other. She said it to herself very often in those days. Every time, in fact, she took out her check-book, and enjoyed the privilege she had never tasted in her husband's life-time, of drawing large sums of money for foolish or unnecessary purposes; whenever she selected her youthful and ultra-fashionable costumes from her Parisian dressmaker; and lastly, but not least emphatically, when she gave carte blanche to her acquaintances in London to bring to her house anyone upon whom was set a seal of distinction, no matter of what sort or kind.

"For I am determined to gather about me the notabilities of my time," she confidentially informed Joyce, as she planned her first evening reception. "My house shall be a representative house, so far as I can make it one; the meeting-place of the leading spirits of art, literature, and science."

Ever since the one snub Mrs. Shenstone had received from the aristocratic hand of the Countess of Cranbury, this had been her ambition.

"Ah," murmured Joyce, in response, "I hope it won't be a case of Glendower calling 'spirits from the vasty deep.'"

Mrs. Shenstone wisely passed over the allusion.

"These Friday evenings will be a momentous undertaking. I expect to sink or swim by them. I am told that any one can give afternoons in London, and make them 'go' passably; but to fill your rooms one evening every week requires talent of a high order."

Joyce pursed her lips and said nothing.

"I rely upon you and Mab to act as my coadjutors. You are handsome, and will make the house attractive; Mab, though plain, might be picturesque if she chose—"

Like flame to tinder was this slighting allusion to Mab's appearance.

"Mab plain!" Joyce cried. "Why, she has a beauty all her own if people had only eyes to see it."

"Yes, so your father used to say, but I never had eyes to see it. Don't look at me like that, Joyce; there is nothing to get red and excited over. The one thing I want to do is to make my rooms picturesque and attractive, and I rely upon you two girls to help me."

"Oh, I'll help you, mother!" answered Joyce, catching scent of the fun of the thing, and ready to run it down. "We must do the thing well, or not at all. We must give thought, time, energy to the work."

"Exactly, Joyce," exclaimed Mrs. Shenstone, delighted at the prospect of sympathetic help. "Thought, as you say, must be given to the undertaking. Very well, I have given endless thought to the manner in which people entertain in London, and it seems to me that the first thing to do is to make the house distinguished. In every house, if you notice it, there is a feature—"

"Two, three, more I should say."

"Well, no, not as a rule. In some houses religion is a feature, in some politics, in some science, in some art, in some beauty—"

"Oh, mother, let's go in for beauty here! You, I, Mab! Let's make our features a feature, and the thing's done."

Mrs. Shenstone shook her head.

"You and I would do, Joyce," she said, complacently, "but Mab would spoil it all. No; I have thought it well over, and have come to the conclusion that picturesqueness is the thing we can best accomplish. As I said before, Mab can be made to look picturesque, though beautiful, never. As for you and me, it is quite unimportant which *rôle* we adopt."

The bland manner in which she, a woman on the other side of forty, with colorless face and expressionless features, bracketed herself with the youthful and handsome Joyce, was proof of vanity swollen almost to the verge of fatuity.

Joyce, ruffled by the second allusion to Mab's unloveliness, made no reply.

"Now I was reading the other day in one of the Society journals—I forget which—the description of some celebrated literary family—I forget the name—at home to their friends. Great stress was laid upon the picturesqueness of the rooms and the people."

"Were they got up in war-paint and feathers like Choctaw Indians, and were the rooms stuffed with pampas-grass and emu eggs?"

"Ah, now I've forgotten that too. Pampas-grass would of course be most effective introduced in sufficient quantities. But if I remember rightly these people got their effects by tasteful arrangements of chair-backs, antimacassars that is, of brilliant colors, red here, olive-green there, or old gold."

"Chair-backs, antimacassars, how deliciously simple," cried Joyce; "a walk down Regent Street and the thing is done."

"Ah, then there's the arrangement of them in their right places, and the people—you, me, Mab—to be set off to the best advantage against them. The dark corners of the room must be lighted up with scarlet or old gold satin—"

"Mother, I've a splendid idea; there's nothing so scarlet as tomatoes nor so golden as oranges. Wouldn't big, piled-up baskets of tomatoes and oranges do better than anything in the dark corners, and be so delightfully original and distinctive into the bargain."

"We'll try the effect. Yes, we must be original, whatever else we are not. Mrs. Farran—you know she is artistic, and literary, and musical, and theatrical, and has her rooms always full—said to me only yesterday, when I was calling and talking these things over with her, 'Mrs. Shenstone, be original at any cost, and don't allow yourself to be swamped by the multitude.'"

"Oh, we'll be original enough, never fear," cried Joyce, with a comical little twist of one corner of her mouth, "and, as for the multitude, we'll swamp them altogether, deluge and drown them with our originality. I'll set off for Covent Garden this very minute, mother, and buy tomatoes and oranges by the hundredweight, and rosy-cheeked apples, a lemon or two, pine-apples, and a carrot, and if we can't light up our dark corners with originality I should amazingly like to see the person who can."

Joyce's purchases, however, successful as they might be from a culinary point of view, were, so far as decoration were concerned, a profitless investment.

Only two days before her first reception took place, Mrs. Shenstone came driving home from her morning calls at a tremendous pace, breathless in her eagerness to consult with Joyce over another form of display for the originality that was in her, and which was destined shortly to dazzle the eyes of the world.

"I have just been calling on Mrs. O'Halloran," she began, going hurriedly into the room where Joyce, at the piano, was getting through some storms and whirlwinds of preludes and scales. "She is the wife of the Irish member, you know, whom we met at Bournemouth last year, and she said to me, with that lovely, rolling accent of hers, 'And it's in the fashion you ought to be, Mrs. Shenstone; whatever else you're out of, be in that. You ought to catch what's in the air, ride on the top of the times, if you'd like to be one of the women of the day.' Well, Joyce, I stayed with her nearly two hours, and all that time people came in and out, and they talked of nothing, absolutely nothing, but Irish politics, and the dreadful manner in which Ireland had been ground to the dust by the Saxons."

"Oh, my poor tomatoes!" sighed Joyce, feeling they would be doomed to the saucepan now, and the dark corners of the drawing room be begrudged to them.

"And, by-the-way, Joyce, there were, among others, two such charming people calling, a brother and sister. He was a splendid-looking man, tall, with fine features, and a grand defiant air, between forty and fifty years of age, I should think;—and the sister—oh, so sweet and gentle, and soft-speaking, all smiles and curls."

"Irish both?"

"No, American. His name is George Ritchie Buckingham. Captain Buckingham, I think they called him. He writes for the press, and does ever so many things besides. I asked them both a great many questions about themselves; they answered every one."

Joyce could fancy her mother asking a great many questions.

"And you should have heard him talk about poor Ireland's wrongs. It was grand beyond anything. He was defiant, furious. I never heard finer declamation."

Joyce shrugged her shoulders.

"I suppose he forgot he was addressing an English lady?"

"No; that was the point of it all. He kept repeating over and over again, 'I don't forget, madam, that you are a daughter of the conquering race, of the race that delights to quench nationalities, to uproot trees of liberty.' No, I think it was standards he said."

"It doesn't matter which. Trees often are standards—rose-trees, that is. Have a cup of tea, mother?"

Mrs. Shenstone was thankful for a cup of tea. Her lips were dry, and there was yet a good deal remaining for them to do.

She nibbled a biscuit, and went on with her talk at intervals.

"So I was thinking, Joyce, as the topic of Ireland's wrongs is on every one's lips just now, we might as well take up with the Irish question hotly, and—"

"Combining originality with fashion," suggested Joyce.

"Exactly—gather about us distinguished politicians and men of letters of all nationalities."

"In rooms appropriately decorated with shamrocks, infernal machines, floating banners with stars and stripes upon them," continued Joyce.

"Become at once envied and popular among our friends—"

"And end with seeing our names mentioned with due honor in the police reports of the daily papers." And here Joyce, with a right-down merry laugh, sank back in her chair, hiding her face in her hands.

The laugh disconcerted Mrs. Shenstone a little.

"I thought you were going to help me, Joyce. I relied upon you. You know I always do," she began, complainingly.

The real plaintiveness in her voice recalled Joyce to seriousness.

"So I will help you, mother. Choose your dress for you if you like. Of course you'll be all in green, with Limerick lace!"

"Yes; green is becoming to delicate complexions. But the lace! I can't endure Limerick lace. We'll think over that. And the shamrocks! they'll be the difficulty. Now, where can we get shamrocks in London—in large quantities, I mean, of course, for I should want big bunches all over the house?"

"Wouldn't clover do? it's wonderfully like shamrock."

"Ah, it might! That's a 'good idea. Now there's something else. That little maid of yours, Kathleen, will come in most usefully. She has a thoroughly Irish face and manner, and, if we dress her up and impress it upon her that she must try and pick up her father's way of speaking and drop her mother's Cockney twang, we can make a feature of her in the entertainment. She can hand refreshments, or wait on the ladies."

"Oh, we can easily get features of that sort, mother, if you want them. In Covent Garden, the other day, every other woman I met with a basket was Irish to the backbone."

"And there's Ned, too! I wonder what has become of him? He is a fine Irish-looking fellow. He might slip into livery and open the door."

"Green, with silver harps on the collar. The theatrical costumers in the Strand might supply it for the evening."

"Ring the bell, Joyce, and send for Kathleen, and we'll see if we can get Ned here as footman. It was ridiculous of him to be in such a hurry to quit our service. My own belief is that Mab half turned his brain with the books she would persist in lending him, and quite unfitted him for his station in life."

Kathleen, summoned and interrogated by Mrs. Shenstone, stated rather doggedly that she felt certain Ned would never consent to act as footman, even for an evening—"No, not even if Miss Mab were to ask him to."

The easy familiar way in which the girl spoke her last sentence made Joyce turn round and look at her.

Mrs. Shenstone, not quick in detecting shades of expression, went on calmly putting her questions.

"Where was Ned now? What was he doing? Earning so much money she supposed that he could afford to scorn the idea of service?"

Mab, coming into the room at this moment, stood an interested listener waiting for the answer.

"He is at Woolwich, ma'am, working at the Arsenal. He gets a pound a week; I don't suppose he saves on that."

"How long has he been there?" asked Mab, in surprise. "When he wrote to me last, about three months ago, he was just starting for

America. He said he had an offer of steady work over there in some factory at New York."

"He altered his mind, miss, and took other work that offered."

"Kathleen," interrupted Mrs. Shenstone, "how is it you've dropped your pretty brogue? you talked just now exactly like an English girl."

"You should roll your 'r's' along for a yard-and-a-half before you let them go, Kathleen," interposed Joyce.

"Tell Ned to write to me," said Mab, "and tell me what he does with himself on Sundays."

Then Mrs. Shenstone took possession of the girl.

"Come up into my dressing-room at once, Kathleen," she said; "I want to try on your head a little arrangement in lace and velvet I bought for you coming home."

"Mab," asked Joyce, when the two girls found themselves *tête-à-tête* over the afternoon tea-tray, "will you mind telling me why you take such a deep interest in Ned Donovan, and insist on keeping up a correspondence with him?"

Mab's fingers trifled nervously with her tea-spoon.

"I suppose it is from pure sympathy and fellow feeling," she answered, in a low voice. "I am trying to save him from himself."

Joyce looked at her, for the moment puzzled and silenced.

"You see," Mab went on, in an apologetic and explanatory voice, "most of us are dual—half good, half bad, and it is hard work at times to keep our bad half in chains."

Joyce's reply, given with an almost defiant energy, was full of a mystic meaning for Mab.

It was: "Better rouse your bad half, fight it out, and be done with it. A foe in chains is a living, not a slain foe."

VI

"That's me twenty years hence," whispered Joyce to Frank Ledyard, regardless of grammar, intent only on fun; her quick sense of humor catching glimpse of and exaggerating a subtle likeness which existed between her mother and herself.

It was the last of Mrs. Shenstone's receptions, which had been continued with more or less success throughout the season.

The above remark had been drawn forth by a question put by the hostess to a spinster lady in the fifties, and severely marked with small-pox, as to why she had not adopted the latest Parisian fashion in hair-dressing, "It threw the features into such bold relief."

Frank winced under the allusion to a possible kinship between Joyce's frank speaking and her mother's affectation of ingenuousness.

He bit his lip to keep back a reply which must have been one of two.

Either "a carricature is as much like a portrait as you are like your mother."

Or, "If I thought even in fifty years' time you would grow into your mother's counterpart, I should put a bullet through my brain at once."

Mrs. Shenstone had not succeeded in filling her rooms to overflowing, as she had purposed when she first started her weekly gatherings. So far her evenings were to be pronounced failures. But she had certainly succeeded in collecting, in that small sprinkling of people who surrounded her, enough of eccentricity, if not of originality, to have kept the comic journals supplied with models for their character sketches for a whole year.

Everyone in the room, it was evident, was some one, and did something, or had been some one, and had done something. Here, in a corner near the window, sat a fair, moderately young woman, dressed in cœrulean blue, with a silver cresent worn above her left ear, and a châtelaine of silver stars hanging from her right side. Under the *nom de guerre* of "Incuba," she had published a bulky volume of poems addressed to "earth's green fields and heaven's radiant blue." In converse with her sat an ancient demoiselle, powder-puffed, rouged, bewigged, befrilled, who had once been a *prima donna,* but who had been compelled, after a short season, now some forty years past, to subside into obscurity on account of the sudden failure of her voice. She delighted to expatiate on that one season, the bouquets, the bracelets that had been showered upon her, the eager eyes that used to follow her up the steps of the orchestra, the distinguished arms that had assisted her down.

Replicas of this type, with deviations, abounded in the room. The men, also speaking generally, were of much the same caliber. The drama was represented by some half-dozen inferior actors; politics by about as many youthful scribblers for the lower-class press. There was no mistaking them. A trifle *débonnair*, a trifle jaunty they were, and thoroughly good-natured every one, with any amount of "rattling good stories" oozing from their finger-tips.

Thoroughly at home among these, yet standing out distinctly from them, like a cray-fish among prawns, was the Captain Buckingham whom Mrs. Shenstone had painted in such glowing colors to Joyce. He stood half-a-head taller than most men there, his self-assertiveness and generally lofty bearing possibly giving him credit for three-quarters of an inch beyond what Nature had endowed him with. Fancy a dark, handsome, lawless bandit, with a square jaw, piercing eyes, a thick wave of gray hair pushed back from his brow, compelled, from stress of circumstances, to lay aside his lawlessness for a time, and act the gentleman in a lady's drawing-room. A more vivid picture than this of George Ritchie Buckingham could not be given.

Irish politics were rampant in the room. Buckingham's deep-chested tones rang to the door, and outside it, where Frank was having a farewell five minutes with Joyce.

"I'm not forgetting the least of Ireland's wrongs when I say let your reformation, though sweeping, be judicious. A high-handed thoroughness, combined with a fine judgment, is what is needed at this crisis."

"Which way will you read that wise sentence?" said Frank, irritably. "Joyce, take my word for it, that man is one of the biggest wind-bags that ever breathed. I've had a little to do, off and on, with unmasking scoundrels; I should amazingly enjoy unmasking this one. I wonder how much of all that grand talk about a 'fine judgment' is let off, like smoke, to hide the fire—"

"Hush!" whispered Joyce, looking nervously over her shoulder toward a lady who, at that moment, came out of an ante-room, adjusting her opera-cloak as she went along.

She was a tall, fair woman of about eight-and-twenty, with a great deal of fluffy, light hair disposed *à l'Americaine* over her forehead, a very pale complexion, a minute mouth, and large, steely-blue eyes.

"George wasn't willing to stir, so I leave him behind. I'm overdone with gayety," she said to Joyce, as she swept past.

"That was Sylvia Buckingham," said Joyce, after bowing a good-night. "You put my heart in my mouth. I'm sure she heard you."

"No fear! Good-by, Joyce. I've my leader to write for the *St. George's Gazette*. I shall have the imp round for copy before I'm ready for him. Be moderate! Yes, of course I shall. I've got a good start to begin with tonight: 'Reformation sweeping, combined with a fine judgment, etc., etc.' Good-night, darling, goodnight."

In order to help him more quickly up that ladder, for whose top step his feet were tingling, Frank had of late taken to writing for the press; among other journals, for the *St. George's Gazette*, a weekly high-class Conservative paper, of "the candle, the bell, and the book" order. It presented to its readers, on the following morning, a biting article on the Irish question, in which the fingers of American agitators, who dipped them unasked into this far from savory squab-pie, were freely rapped.

VII

A foe in chains is a living, not a slain foe." These words which Joyce, with her dangerous aptitude for swift, trenchant speech, had uttered so lightly kept persistently repeating themselves in Mab's ears. They paraphrased themselves in her mind somewhat as follows: "Here you are content to have got your enemy into chains—chains, by-the-way, whose links might snap at any moment—when you might wrestle it out with him, and put your foot upon his neck at once and forever."

The words grew to be a sort of war-cry in her ears at last—a fanfaronade of trumpets calling her to her duty. Mab had ever been a slave to her sense of duty. Convince her that duty called upon her to give her life inch by inch, and she would take good care never to give two at a time. So now, when conscience took to playing the echo to Joyce's haphazard words, she did not try to silence it with other voices having less of iron in them, but met it with the simply-put question:

"How, where, when, shall I begin the tussle?"

A straightforward question enough, one would think, and bound to have a point-blank answer given to it. Yet a circumstance occurring at this time not only at once and forever put it unanswered to silence, but forced upon her the unwelcome conviction that her sense of duty must have been warped, her conscience perverted, to have so much as whispered it into her ear.

In this fashion. She had been, according to her custom, acting the perambulating librarian among her poor people one afternoon; she came in hot and tired with a big packet of books under her arm, ran straight up into the drawing-room, hoping to find there two refreshing stimulants—Joyce and a cup of tea—and discovered instead Captain Buckingham alone, seated in an arm-chair.

"Mrs. Shenstone has not yet come in—I am waiting to see her," he explained, as he shook hands; "and Miss Joyce has, I was sorry to hear, gone up-stairs to lie down, with a bad headache."

Mab wondered whether Joyce's headache was born of Captain Buckingham's afternoon call. Joyce had never, from the first day of their intimacy with the Buckingham's, attempted to throw more than the flimsiest veil of politeness over her dislike for brother and sister.

Mab's feelings were something less defined toward the pair. They were antipathetic to her senses, rather than to her feelings. Silvia's semi-satirical smile, her low-toned, sleepy drawl, the brother's bold stare and loud, domineering voice equally jarred upon her, and, so to speak, set her teeth on edge; but given certain conditions—close companionship, favors conferred—it might have been possible for her teeth to lose the sense of a rough acidity.

"Let me relieve you of your books, Miss Shenstone," Buckingham went on, as he noted how heavily Mab was laden; "ah, this is the good work your mother was telling me about. May I read the titles of your lending library? "History of England," "The Jews in Spain," "Lectures for the People," "Sanitation and Health." Why these are not the books for the hard-working classes. You would give toil to the toilers, mental labor to those who know not mental ease. You should deal out fiction to them, bright, sparkling, merry fiction, and deal it out right liberally too."

Of course he must lay down the law on every subject, small or great, that came within his cognizance. The words, "Don't you think," or "It seems to me," would have come strangely from his lips.

Mab rang the bell for the tea-tray.

"I haven't a single volume of fiction among my books," she said, and the minute after regretted she had said so. Question and controversy must follow now. She was very tired with her tramp through the by-ways of Westminster. She wished the man would go and let her enjoy her tea and talk up-stairs with Joyce in peace.

"Not a volume of fiction!" he repeated; "are you afraid of fiction? Does that mean that poetry is a *terra incognita* to you? Shakespeare, Milton, Shelley, Swinburne, names to you and nothing more."

"I never read poetry."

Then she threw off her light summer mantle and busied herself over the tea-table; fussed over the sugar, the tea, the urn, the cream, all the time feeling that Buckingham's large dark eyes were fixed full upon her face with that, bold questioning, searching stare, which, as a rule, affronted her, but which now seemed rather to disconcert her. She made the servant stay in the room, handing the tea, the cake, the biscuits; kept him with excuses waiting at her elbow, then, when there could be no further possible reason for the man to remain, walked to the window, raised the blind, wondered what had detained her mother so long, made jerky little tirades against the uncomfortable weather, the scorching heat, the blinding dust.

Captain Buckingham's eyes followed her round the room.

"Miss Shenstone," he said, in the same loud dogmatic tone as before, "you are resisting influence."

Mab gave a great start. These were the words she had felt through long years past would some day be spoken to her by some one's lips, and now they had been spoken by this man's.

She answered calmly enough, though with an effort:

"If influence is bad, it is well to resist it."

"But if good, what then? Do you know the first day I saw you I detected in you a something that cut you off from the rest of the world, but I could not tell what it was. I see it now; the 'something' is organic, therefore permanent and unalterable. You are made of the stuff of which the seers of old times were made, the augurs, the prophets, the poets, if you like. Pound yourself in a mortar, you won't get rid of it. Go atom by atom to dust, it will cry aloud in the ashes."

Fancy burying a secret a hundred feet deep in the earth, putting a marble slab over it, building a wall round it, with an iron door, a bolt, a bar, and then imagine it to be suddenly shouted aloud from the house-tops!

Mab's face went from white to red, from red to white. She clasped her hands tightly together, and turned facing him, staring blankly.

He went on calmly, yet loudly as before:

"In all my life I have only met one person at all to compare with you. She was a young Vermont girl of French parentage, Marie St. Clair by name, a born seer, clairvoyante, and of the finest susceptibilities. And her parents had sent her to sell stockings and calico in a draper's shop! Her sense of touch was so fine she could distinguish the quality and price of any article by the touch of her finger-tip. Ah," here his voice dropped a note or two, "through want of knowledge one may burn oil in an Aladdin's lamp!"

"What became of her?" asked Mab under her breath, and drawing a step nearer.

"I rescued her. I induced her to throw up the miserable drudgery in the draper's shop, and put herself under tutelage at Boston. She developed rapidly enough, had a brilliant career; in fact, at one time was more talked about than any other person in the States. The odd part with her was that, though she could do some remarkable things in a state of trance, her best moment was the moment of awaking from deep sleep, before her senses were aroused. Then it was all in a flash that she saw the person, or had the thing revealed to her, on which her mind was set."

Mab gave a painful start. Her memory flew back to that bright spring morning, when, to her fancy, her dead father had stood before her.

"You seem interested," Buckingham went on. "I'll lend you her autobiography, if you like. All the Boston people went mad over her. Three years of a most brilliant career she had."

"And then?" asked Mab, again under her breath, and drawing another step nearer to him.

"Oh, she died—at twenty-six years of age. Overdid it, lost control over herself, and died in an asylum."

"Ah—h!"

"But it doesn't follow from that that other people are to go and do likewise. Supposing that I, an English nobleman, defrauded of my rights, were to claim and get back my birthright, and then run riot in my inheritance, and die a pauper! Would you argue from that fact that therefore no one to the end of time is to venture to claim a lost birthright?"

Mab yet stood silent, and with clasped hands, before him, her thoughts all one surging, storm-tossed mass. Had any one asked her afterward to give a detailed account of her conversation with Buckingham, all she could have said succinctly would have been: "He told me to claim my birthright. Nothing else."

It was a relief at this moment to hear a voice outside the door, which suggested common-place morning calls, evening receptions, tea-gowns, and small talk in a pre-eminent degree.

It said, evidently addressing a servant:

"I am tired to death, absolutely; with listening, nothing else. I haven't opened my lips since I left the house two hours ago!"

Then the door opened, and Mrs. Shenstone, in a costume that might have suited a modern youthful Lydia Languish, made her appearance.

"I knew you were here, Captain Buckingham," she said, smiling affably, "before I was told. I heard your voice all the way up-stairs. Now will you tell me why it is that you and your sister do not talk the least bit in the world like any other Americans I have ever heard?"

"It is because we are cosmopolitan, I suppose," laughed Buckingham. "Nevertheless, you mustn't imagine that the English accent is a monopoly for which you've taken out a patent. Some of us Yankees talk every whit as broad as your Englishmen!"

VIII

Joyce's headache turned out a more serious affair than was expected. The next day found her in bed with a crimson face and ice-cold hands. The day after found the doctor in the house, with his watch in his hand and the terrible word "typhoid" on his lips.

"Is it catching, doctor?" moaned Mrs. Shenstone. "Shall we all take it one after the other? Oh, dear, dear! Just as we were all going to start for Dieppe, like the rest of the world! This comes of Mab diving into all the holes and corners of London. She has brought it into the house, somehow or other, depend upon it."

The doctor stared at her.

"Well, I've seen women blessed with next to no sense, but this one beats all!" he thought. Aloud he said: "In which case it is rather remarkable that Miss Mab was not the first to fall victim. You had better look for the cause within your own four walls, madam, and see to your drains and water-pipes."

It may be conjectured that he had but the slenderest acquaintance with Mrs. Shenstone. The old family doctor down in Gloucestershire would have nodded to her complacently and said nothing.

Three weeks packed with anxiety, with alternating hopes and fears, followed.

During those three weeks all the household wheels ran down. Mrs. Shenstone was ordered out of the house by the doctor, and rooms were found for her within easy distance.

"She'll just frighten herself into the fever and double your trouble," he explained to Mab. And, to himself, he added: "And if it's all the same to every one else, I would rather not have such a patient as that on my hands."

"My poor, darling Joyce," Mrs. Shenstone said, as she sobbed a good-by on Mab's shoulder, "such a mercy it isn't small-pox! such a mercy, too, that you are such a thoughtful, careful nurse, Mab. If you had been a beauty instead of a dear, domestic treasure you wouldn't have done half so much good in the world. Good-by, darling; I wish I could be of use to you."

Mab, as might have been expected, at once took up her post in the sick-room as head nurse. Helter-skelter out of her head went all thoughts of claiming any birthright save that of watching over her fever-stricken sister, morning, noon, and night. No one knew when she slept nor when she had her meals. Other nurses were there in attendance from the hospital; but no matter, Mab must superintend them and the general routine of the sick-room, so that her darling Joyce should lack nothing.

Up came Uncle Archie from the wilds of Gloucestershire, with fat, placid Aunt Bell in attendance. The old gentleman was still suffering sharp twinges of intermittent gout, and his views of the situation were colored accordingly.

He attacked the doctor first.

"Typhoid," he said, "I don't believe in such a thing. There was no typhoid when I was a boy. We called a thing typhus—a disease every one could understand, or we called a thing gastric fever, something quite different. Now, I don't believe she has what you are pleased to called typhoid fever, and if you let her die through improper treatment you'll be guilty of manslaughter, sir, manslaughter."

The doctor was at first naturally enough disposed to grow irate, and to stand upon his dignity under such treatment; but, when he heard the old gentleman go into the next room and rate Mab in precisely the same fashion, he shrugged his shoulders, and came to the conclusion that after all it was nothing more than family idiosyncracies coming to the front again.

"Look here, Mab," said Uncle Archie, "you've undertaken the sick-nursing. Very well, you'll break down under it; any one can see you'll break down—your face is like a sheet, and you're shivering and shaking like an aspen; you'd better have in a sister to superintend the nurses from the hospital, and take turn and turn about with her. If you break down, Joyce will get neglected—it'll be a case of manslaughter," etc., etc.

He stormed at Frank, too, in much the same fashion; or rather, he began to, but Frank turned upon him in a way he was unprepared to meet.

"Don't, don't, Mr. Shenstone," he implored, "my nerves are all gone, I can't stand it. If anything happens to her—" But here he broke off brusquely, his own words seeming to choke him.

Uncle Archie stared at him a moment, blinking his eyes very hard. Then he took to stamping up and down the room, muttering to himself and making his stick do a great deal of work.

Aunt Bell came in and carried him off to a neighboring hotel, where he was laid up in bed for a fortnight, with the worst attack of gout he had ever had.

Frank almost lived in the house for that fortnight during which Joyce was at her worst. He and Mab seemed drawn more closely to each other in those days than ever they had been in their lives before. Mab was less of a living enigma to him, he a more defined and conceivable bit of humanity to her. Joyce's extremity was, so to speak, the light which made them see each other's faces.

"If she lives, Mab, I shall say you have saved her," Frank would say sometimes, as he crept away from the house at day-dawn with face gray and ashen as that of the misty morning itself.

And Mab's answer, given with a look clear and straightforward as Joyce's own, would be, "I would give my life for hers, if God would but take it."

Frank seemed all made of nerves just then. His work was almost an impossibility to him. His leader-writing was suspended. One moment he would be all irritable excitement, the next all depressed misery. He seemed somehow to have let himself slip through his own fingers, and to have lost all power of self-control. He despised himself heartily for his weakness, fancied he could read unmitigated scorn and ridicule in every face he looked into—in Captain Buckingham's especially, when by chance they met on Mrs. Shenstone's doorstep, or within the house making inquiries for the invalid.

These meetings were not frequent. It was a subject for congratulation that they were not. There was a smoldering fire of antagonism between these two men, which frequent intercourse must have stirred into flame.

"Why is he here at all? What concern is it of his whether Joyce is better or worse?" Frank once asked savagely of Mab.

"He comes on my mother's account. He takes her a report of Joyce three times a day," was Mab's reply.

"Good heavens!" cried Frank, "I forgot all about your mother. Now, Mab, I can undertake that mission, and give this man to understand that his services are not required."

Mab, anxious to keep the peace, shook her head.

"It wouldn't do at all," she explained. "My mother has asked him to do it. Don't you see she likes him? and—"

"Doesn't like me," finished Frank. "I know it. I only hope—"

But here he broke off. Naturally enough he felt shy of hoping to Mab that her mother "wasn't going to make a fool of herself over the man Buckingham."

The day of crisis came at length. They all knew what the doctor meant when, after staying in the sick-room about double the usual time, he came out, saying:

"Come, cheer up, my young friends, she has everything in her favor—youth, a strong constitution, good nursing. We must hope for the best."

And when he announced his intention of coming in again at midnight, and resuming his watch, they all knew that day-dawn most probably meant life or death for their darling.

Joyce's dressing-room, opening off her bedroom, had been improvised into a temporary sitting-room, and here Frank passed the whole of that lagging night of suspense, getting about every quarter-of-an-hour a brief report from Mab through the half-opened door, and feeling his heart go up and down with a bound every time he heard her touch upon the handle.

The feverish mutterings and tossings of the patient came to him through the thin partition. The sounds of London night-life died down in the street, giving place to those of the young day. Frank felt his hopes sinking low, lower, like that flame of his night-lamp just burning itself out. A great numbness and stillness seemed to fall upon him. He sank upon his knees beside the table, hiding his face in his cold, trembling hands. He felt as though he were wrestling with death for her.

"God," he moaned, "be merciful, be merciful!" They were all the words he had at command, and even these seemed to freeze and die upon his lips of their own despair and agony.

Five o'clock of that August morning found the cool daylight flowing into the little room through the half-turned Venetian blinds. Mab, opening softly the door of the inner room, let out a stream of lurid light which met and quenched it. Frank started, and lifted up his wan face inquiringly.

"She sleeps; she has taken a turn. The doctor says all will be well now," was all she found voice to say. And then their hands clasped, their tears flowed together, and their hearts sent up the thanksgiving their lips lacked power to utter.

Some one came tapping at the door—a sleepy servant saying a person was below wishing to see Miss Mab.

Mab, all tottering from excess of grateful joy, went down-stairs to find Ned Donovan standing in the hall.

　　　　　　　　CATHERINE LOUISA PIRKIS

He started back when he saw her.

"They told me it was Miss Joyce who was ill, but surely—" he began, hesitatingly.

Mab could see in his startled gaze the reflection of her own ghastly, haggard face.

"It was Miss Joyce," she answered. "It is, rather, for she is not yet out of danger. It is very good of you to come. Oh, it is only anxiety that has made me look so wretched. I shall soon be all right again, now she has taken a turn."

Ned's eyes seemed riveted.

"Miss Mab, you will be ill if you don't take care. Is any one looking after you? I only heard late last night of Miss Joyce's illness. I could only get a train one station up the line. I've walked the rest of the way. No, thank you, Miss Mab; I'm not tired now I've seen you and know the worst of your trouble is over."

Mab made him come into the dining-room, and fetched him wine and biscuits from the sideboard, making him eat and drink, and asking him questions meantime of himself, of his work, and how he liked it.

"I have only five minutes to give you," she said. "I must get back quickly to the sick-room. But you must tell me all you can about yourself. Now, why is it you so seldom write to me?"

If the light had not been so gray and uncertain, she might have seen his face flush a deep red.

"I've no time for writing, Miss Mab. It was best to leave it off," he answered a little unsteadily.

"No time? Not even to me?" exclaimed Mab, in a pained voice. "I asked you so many questions in my last letter. What you did with yourself on Sundays? Why you never came near the house—not even to see your sister?"

Ned's face flushed deeper and deeper crimson, his hand holding his wine-glass trembled noticeably.

Mab, seeing his perturbation, not unnaturally misinterpreted it.

"Is anything wrong?" she asked, kindly, "are not things going smoothly with you?"

Ned jumped to his feet.

"Wrong—anything wrong?" he repeated, "what is there right in the world? God has gone to sleep, the Devil reigns everywhere." He checked himself suddenly. Possibly his thoughts would not translate into words choice enough for a young lady's ear.

Poor fellow! He was only three-and-twenty years of age; he was defiantly, yet despairingly, in love with a woman as much beyond the reach of his human arms as the stars in heaven, and so it seemed to him that God had gone to sleep and the Devil reigned paramount.

Mab looked at him in silent wonder for a moment. Then those dreadful Fenian societies suggested themselves to her mind.

"What books are you reading, Ned?" she asked. "I hope you are not taking in those insurrectionary papers—I've forgotten their names—you gave up two or three years ago to please me?"

Now in all these kindly speeches Mab was actuated by the simplest, the loftiest of desires to help a man whom she had always looked upon as one of the most hot-headed of a hot-headed race, and liable at any moment to catch the fever of the Irish demagogues, and to catch it fatally too.

Ned was born in England of an English mother; he had had an English education in English schools, and brogue was a thing unknown to him; but for all that he was, as she had so often told him, "more Irish than his Irish father." Her attitude throughout their intercourse had been that of kindly, unostentatious patronage, such as any lady might extend to any working man. Yet as she stood there waiting for an answer to her question, a something crept into his face—a sudden light into his deep blue eyes, a change of expression about the mouth—which startled her, and made her think of her sick-room duties, and that the sooner she got back to them the better.

She made a step toward the door.

"I must go—I am sure I must be wanted up-stairs," she began. Then she came back irresolutely. After all the interest she had taken in this man she did not feel inclined to let him go down the hill, when a word from her might perhaps save him. "Ned," she said, speaking up bravely, "I want you to make me a promise—a very solemn promise."

Ned hesitated.

"If it's about any of our national societies, Miss Mab, I would rather not make it," he answered, slowly.

"I will have nothing to do with you to the end of time if you join any one of those societies," she interrupted, dashing nervously into the very middle of her subject. "They are secret, detestable, formed only for murder and assassination."

A noise of door opening at that moment made her turn her head. It was the sleepy servant who had announced Ned, showing in Captain

Buckingham. There seemed an amused look in his eye as he looked from Mab to Ned. Of course he must have heard her concluding words.

"I have come for my morning's report. I promised Mrs. Shenstone she should have it before six," he said, blandly enough.

Mab gleefully gave him the glad news.

Ned, with a respectful "Good-morning, Miss Mab," took up his hat and left the room.

Mab went one step over the threshold, bent on making a final effort.

"You must think over what I have said. Pray, pray do not forget what I have asked of you," she said, gently.

"Miss Mab," was Ned's reply, as respectfully as before, "I am not likely to forget one single word you have ever spoken to me." Then he went.

Buckingham cross-questioned her as to who was Ned, what were his surroundings, what was his occupation?

"Irish of course, he is," he said, "although his brogue is fairly enough hidden. I could swear to the Irish blue eye among a thousand."

Mab, with her foot on the first step of the stairs, all anxiety to get back to the sick-room, answered him briefly as to the man's parentage and present occupation.

Had any one watched Buckingham take his departure down the house steps that morning, they might have seen his lips forming to the words: "Irish—no brogue—works at the Arsenal," and his forehead knotting into a thoughtful frown.

The cold daylight had quickened into rosy dawn as Mab passed the staircase windows. A figure glided along the landing from the small room a little hurriedly at her approach. It was Kathleen, with a tray in her hand. It did not strike Mab as strange that the girl should be dressed, and smartly dressed, as she had been on the previous night; just then no one's *toilette* was much criticised. They washed and dressed when they could, and wore evening dress in the morning, or cotton gowns at night, just as it happened. What, however, did strike her as strange was the brilliant flush and look of confusion on the girl's face as she explained that she had been taking Mr. Ledyard some hot coffee. She had thought he must be tired with his night's watching.

"It was kind and thoughtful of you," was Mab's comment as she went hurriedly into the room, trying to dismiss the matter from her mind as one of no moment.

Later on, events brought it back to her and gave it possibly a magnified importance.

IX

Frank Ledyard during the night watches of Joyce's illness asked himself a few questions.

Cut a man off from his work, shut him up within four walls, give him his sleep in snatches, make him eat his food without appetite, and the chances are his brain will swarm with questions.

Frank's did, at any rate. Irritating, importunate questions they were, one as like another as grains of sand, all eventually resolving themselves into a final and pointed one, running somewhat as follows:

"If Joyce's happiness were, as he was asserting to himself all day long, his one and only object in life, was he in reality consulting it when he had insisted upon the postponement of their marriage?"

Of course the question could be put in a hundred different fashions. As thus: "Was not the sacrifice he had made to his pride compounded in part of her happiness?"

Or thus: "Was it not rather like straining at a gnat and swallowing a camel, in the circumstances, to sacrifice to his pride at all? Supposing even by dint of strenuous exertion he could match Joyce's income in a few year's time with his own, he certainly could not hope to the end of his life, let him work as he might, to accumulate an equivalent to the large fortune that would accrue to her on her mother's death, when the whole of Mr. Shenstone's property came to be divided between her and Mab."

A man of Frank Ledyard's energetic temperament can not admit into his career anything that savors of ambiguity or vacillation of purpose. "If you have got into the wrong path the sooner you get out of it the better," is the decision with which such men generally cut sharply enough all knotty points.

This was the conclusion at which Frank, in due course, was to arrive. In his character, as in Joyce's, all sorts of contradictions met. An old school-fellow of Frank's, describing him about this time, had said, "He is the most impetuous plodder that ever came into the world. He was so at Eton. See him begin a foot-race, no one would bet on him, unless they knew him. He'd start with a spurt, and every one would say, with a chuckle, "that fellow won't keep up that pace long." But, hang it! he would, and did, and always came in the first and the freshest at the end.

The anecdote was typical of Frank's conduct of life. In early youth he had been given to understand that his future was in his own hands to make or mar, that, from economic and other reasons, the Bar was the only career open to him, and his proclivities in other directions were sharply nipped in the bud. His father had been a man of fair fortune, had died young, leaving his property at the sole disposal of his widow. She soon wearied of the widowed state, entered the bonds of matrimony again, and in her turn died, leaving the boy Frank on his step-father's hands. The step-father repeated his wife's career—with a difference; he speedily re-married, but, instead of dying, brought into the world a large family. In these circumstances, it was not surprising that Frank's patrimony had dwindled. Land had to be mortgaged to cover his school and college expenses, and, to meet the mortgage, had eventually to be sold. Subsequently the wreck of the property had been handed over to him, a sum amounting to something under two thousand pounds. On this, he was duly informed, he was expected to thrive, and be content, or else to build up for himself a fortune in life. He chose to attempt the latter, and set to work at the mill with a vast energy. No incentive to hard striving was needed by a man of his large ambitions and strong will; but naturally, when he came upon his fate in the form of Joyce Shenstone, his interest in his work doubled and trebled itself, and straight ahead of other men he went with a sure-footed swiftness that was bound to win the race.

"That is a rising man," had been the comment freely passed upon him by his seniors in the profession, as they noted the steady grasp of his intellect, his clear eye for an outline, legal or otherwise.

And "he'll make himself a name before he has done," had been more than once said of him by his colleagues on the press, as they marked the sure-handed vehemence with which he struck at his nails, and the straight, steady fashion in which every one of them went home.

But, coupled with these essentially masculine traits were others, which some would consider of less robust growth—a sense of honor so fine as to be superfine, a pride so wire-drawn as to be all but attenuated. Under the dictates of this pride, he had taken fire at foolish Mrs. Shenstone's foolish words, and had done his utmost to retard Joyce's happiness and his own. The pride, however, temporarily quenched by a stronger, deeper feeling—a terror lest, by retarding his happiness, he had lost his chance of it altogether—he saw matters in a clearer light, and lost no time in coming to a new resolution upon them.

He took the first opportunity that presented itself to explain to Mab the change which had come over his views; how that instead of wishing to postpone his marriage with Joyce he hoped he might now be allowed to press matters forward as much as possible.

"Of course it costs me something to put my pride into my pocket, I won't say it doesn't, and I expect (and deserve) to be made to eat humble pie all round," he went on to say; "but you will understand, I know, Mab, whoever else makes mistakes on the matter, that Joyce's happiness is my first thought; that if I thought I could not make her happiness for her, I would step out of her path at once and make way for some one who could."

Mab was deliciously sympathetic.

"Of course it will be a terrible wrench for me to part with Joyce," she said, with a sigh, "but I know it will be for her happiness. I am going round to mamma's rooms this afternoon; I will tell her, if you like, what you have said to me."

"Thank you, Mab, that is kind; I am afraid your mother, however, will not take my petition quite so graciously as you have," said Frank, a little doubtfully.

"Oh, but I am sure she will," was Mab's ready reply; "only yesterday she said to me, 'I shan't believe in Frank's devotion to Joyce if he prolongs their engagement much longer.' I'll undertake to manage mother right enough if you can undertake Uncle Archie. He'll be the one to give you trouble, I'm afraid."

Frank in silent wonder apostrophised his own folly that he had ever attached the slightest importance to words spoken by so feather-brained a woman as Mrs. Shenstone.

He took the earliest opportunity also of hinting to Joyce from which quarter blew the wind of his wishes now.

Joyce, looking fragile enough from her sharp illness, but withal as coquettishly beautiful as ever, turned her deep shining eyes upon him. At heart she was triumphantly glad, but she did not intend yet awhile to show him the gladness, only the triumph.

"Ah," she said, smiling up at him from the pillows of the couch whereon she rested, "this is the man who meant to serve ten years of Egyptian bondage before he entered Canaan, and he hasn't had the courage to serve out one!"

CATHERINE LOUISA PIRKIS

"I know I deserve to be laughed at," said Frank, humbly; "and I don't mind your laughing at me one bit, dear. But oh, what will Uncle Archie say?"

"What will you say to Uncle Archie?"

"That's the point, I think," laughed Joyce. "How will you begin your letter, how end it? What will you put in the middle of it?"

"You shall see it, Joyce; you shall dictate it, if you like—you shall tell me word for word what to put down."

"Shall I? Then take out your pencil and begin to write at once." Frank obeyed her immediately.

"Now begin: 'Dear Mr. Shenstone, I feel so small as to be absolutely microscopic, and I sincerely hope you won't overlook me together with the request *I* have to make.' That is to be by way of making a beginning. Your request is to be sent when you get Uncle Archie's reply; that is, if you dare send it at all after the crushing answer you will be sure to get."

"I deserve 'crushing,' I admit," said Frank, sharply rapping his knuckles with his pencil. "But I don't believe any reply of Uncle Archie's will crush me, let it be never so ponderous. Just now, with you given back to me, dear, I am in the seventh heaven, and it would take an army of Uncle Archies to bring me down from it!"

"Ah, but fancy such an answer as this: 'Sir, remain the infinitesimal atom that you are, and keep your request unspoken.' I assure you, I have known Uncle Archie go farther even than that in a letter."

Strange to say, when Uncle Archie's answer to Frank's petition for an early wedding-day came, it was something quite other than Joyce or Frank could have pictured in their most sanguine moments. It was the heartiest of complacent consents given with the most thorough good-will.

"To say truth," wrote the old gentleman, "I have been very ill since my trip to London, though I have not liked to lay stress upon my illness for fear of causing you all needless anxiety. I am, however, beginning to feel I am getting near the end of the race, and I should like to see my dead brother's children in safe keeping before I drop out of it. What you told me when you wrote some little time ago, and what I have heard from other friends in London as to the sort of people my sister-in-law is gathering about her, has filled me with anxiety on my nieces' behalf. Joyce married to you is safe, of course (you are made of sterling stuff, though you have your whims and your cranks like other people), and there will be always a haven for Mab should anything arise to make her feel the need of one. So, my dear fellow, all I say to you is, make all arrangements for as early a date as is admissible, and the sooner it is the better I shall be pleased."

X

After her illness, Joyce, accompanied by Mab, went for a month of sea air to some old friends in Wales; Mrs. Shenstone, for reasons best known to herself, refusing just then to take flight anywhere. Her quarters seemed very much to her liking, and she appeared extremely loth to be dislodged from them. It was possible that alone in rooms she was able to claim a freedom of action for herself which her daughters occasionally begrudged her.

The house in Eaton Square was meantime thoroughly cleansed and disinfected by her orders. Some one must have suggested this sanitary measure to her, for common-sense on the matters of health or comfort she utterly lacked. It might have been the Buckinghams, who, during the absence of her daughters, passed a great deal of time in her society.

Joyce and Mab, returning from their sea-side trip at the end of September, to their surprise found Sylvia Buckingham installed in their home as something of a major-domo, that is to say, she held the household keys, and appeared to be keeper of the privy purse.

Joyce came back in altogether redundant health and spirits, intending to make brisk preparations for her wedding-day, and to wind up generally the household clocks. In straightforward fashion she took her mother to task on this matter.

"Is Miss Buckingham going tomorrow, mother?" she asked, trying to be as sunshiny as possible; "if she stays over another twenty-four hours, you may be sure I shall snub her frightfully."

Mrs. Shenstone begged the question.

"How can you speak so rudely of my friends?" she said, querulously. "I can't tell you how kind the Buckinghams have been to me while I have been so lonely and wretched. Sylvia and George—"

"Who? who?" exclaimed Joyce, aghast at her mother's easy and familiar mention of this man, with his doubtful captaincy and objectionable personality.

Mrs. Shenstone turned her head toward the looking-glass to see if she had a girlish blush on her face.

"Well, Joyce," she said, deprecatingly, "you know I never could adopt your stiff and formal way of speaking of intimate friends."

"Friends! Mother, get upon stilts as soon as you can if you can't keep out of the mud any other way."

"Mud! Stilts! That is always the way you and Mab talk when I want to have a little rational conversation."

"Ah, then we're of one mind now," cried Joyce, brightly. "I only want a rational answer to my very rational question—how much longer is Miss Buckingham going to inflict her presence upon us?"

The door opened at this moment and Miss Buckingham entered. There was nothing possibly to give the impression that she had heard Joyce's last sentence, for her small mouth always wore that semi-satirical smile; but, nevertheless, Joyce felt sure that she had done so, and that, in due course, she would acknowledge her indebtedness for it.

Mrs. Shenstone gave a sigh of relief. There could be no more cross-questionings from Joyce so long as Sylvia remained in the room. She would do her best to keep her there.

"Sylvia darling," she began, "what do you advise about that black lace dress of mine? Must I condemn it, or shall I get it retrimmed with blush-rose tints?"

But "Sylvia darling" had something else on her mind at that moment. "In a minute, Tiny," she answered.

Joyce looked up at her. Her mother s name was Ernestine, but even her father had never made a diminutive of it.

Miss Buckingham laid a bunch of keys on the table.

"I have much pleasure in resigning my post, now you have returned; but it has been an equally great pleasure to keep the keys in your absence, and so lighten Mrs. Shenstone's housekeeping cares," she said, addressing Joyce in that patronizingly amiable manner of hers, which Joyce said always made her want to open the windows to avoid suffocation.

"It was more than kind of you," answered Joyce, getting on her stilts at once, and laying a conspicuous emphasis on the word "more."

But, though Sylvia resigned the keys, she did not bring her visit to a close, and the privy purse still remained in her keeping.

So at least Joyce surmised, from the manner in which Mrs. Shenstone constantly appealed to her on various matters of expenditure. "Was she running ahead in dress expenses? Could she afford this or that luxury or piece of extravagance?"

It was very irritating: but an even more potent cause for annoyance was to follow. Captain Buckingham, who had been on a few days' visit to Ireland, returning, made himself quite as much at home in the house as his sister.

Joyce flew for sympathy to Mab, and, for the very first time in her life, strange to say, did not get it.

Mab, scratching away with her pen at answers to a pile of her mother's letters which had been left unattended to, looked up nervously for a moment.

"I don't like to hear you call them adventurers, Joyce. I think you are rather hard upon Captain Buckingham. I'm sure he's honest and straightforward." Then her face drooped over her notepaper again.

Joyce for one moment thought her ears must have deceived her.

"What!" she exclaimed, staring blankly at her sister. "'Honest and straightforward,' did you say?"

Mab grew confused. She never seemed able to stick to her opinions if Joyce stared her full in the face and asked her to repeat them.

"I mean," she began, hesitatingly, "he has ideas, and does not mind giving other people the benefit of them."

To this Joyce agreed with a nod.

"And the ideas are always worth listening to."

Here Joyce shook her head vehemently.

"Well, at any rate, they are opinions that have been well thought over. I should say he never speaks until he has given careful thought to what he has to say."

"What of that?" cried Joyce, scornfully. "Heaps of people never speak without thinking beforehand what they are going to say. The wonder is to find a person who says the right thing all in a moment without thinking about it. Talk about second thoughts being best, I would alter it to sudden thoughts are best. All my best thoughts come to me in flashes, Oh, Mab!"

Here she abruptly broke off. A sudden thought had that moment come to her, which the next found her giving utterance to.

"What if the subject of the man's meditations at the present moment is to get round mother and make her marry him? Oh, it would be too dreadful!"

Mab's color went to a russet-red. She did not flush so becomingly as Joyce did. She was lighting a candle at the moment to seal a letter by, and her hand shook so much that the lighted match fell to the ground.

Joyce put her foot on it.

"Well, there's one comfort," she went on, "I know how to put a stop to that little game very quickly, by a reference to dear papa's will." She gave a second energetic stamp on the extinguished match, adding, "I wish that were Captain Buckingham. I should like to stamp on him and put him out in exactly the same fashion."

She had not heard the door open, and a light step across the room, or she might have slightly modified her expression. Sylvia Buckingham had a very quiet way of opening doors, and her footfall might have been that of a beetle for all the noise it made upon the carpet.

Once more Joyce came to the conclusion that her words had been heard, and registered on the debtor's side of Sylvia's memorandum book, although the fair, immobile face made no sign.

"How dare she come creeping into rooms in this way? This is the second time!" thought the girl; and she looked across at Sylvia and gave another emphatic stamp on the defunct match.

"Am I intruding?" Sylvia asked, patronizingly and amiably as usual.

Joyce made her manner as much a reflection of the other's as possible.

"Not in the least," she answered, coolly; "Mab and I always lock the door when we wish to be alone."

Sylvia lifted her large steely blue eyes, giving Joyce one steady look. Translated into speech it might have run somewhat as follows:

"The time for paying off debts has not yet come. When it does, you may trust to the goodness of my memory."

Aloud she said: "I'm looking for a book to read to Mrs. Shenstone. Now, can you recommend one?"

Joyce pointed to the bookshelves.

"If you want to read mother to sleep, there are no end of books there admirable for the purpose. Darwin, Tyndall—ever so many. But, if you want really to interest her, I should recommend one of the society journals." Then she turned to Mab, and, àpropos of nothing, brought out the following surprising remark: "Mab, I do think our dear father was the best and wisest man that ever lived. He couldn't have taken better care of mother if he had tried. It was so sensible of him only to leave her a life-interest in all his property. Only fancy, on the day she gets married again she will have nothing left her but a paltry five hundred a year for her life!"

Her words launched themselves like a thunderbolt on her two listeners. Mab's face was a picture of confusion and distress. Sylvia suddenly found the volume she wanted and left the room.

"Oh, Joyce! how could you?" cried Mab, her eyes filling with tears, her cheeks aflame.

"How could I what, dear?" asked Joyce, calmly. "I have said nothing Miss Buckingham need take to herself or convey to her brother unless she is so disposed. I have only done my best to take care of mother on the lines dear father laid down."

"I do—do believe you are mistaken," cried Mab, excitedly, clasping her hands together."

"Perhaps."

"I'm sure you are hard on them, hard on mother, too!" Mab went on, vehemently. "Why shouldn't she choose what friends she pleases for herself? We left her so much alone, you and I being always together, no wonder she felt dull and thought she would like some nice companionable person to be in the house with her."

Joyce ended the discussion with a reminiscence of their recent seaside trip.

"Do you remember the hermit-crabs we used to catch at Rhyl, Mab?" she asked, "They were a delightful study. Such voracious creatures! And so thoroughly at home in their friends houses."

Mab thought it wiser to say no more.

XI

"Mother is actually developing a will of her own," said Joyce to Frank, as they sat in the back drawing-room, confidentially talking over the small details of the wedding-day. "When I said to her, the other day, how much I should like to be married from our dear old home in Gloucestershire, she said, right out, that nothing would induce her to go back to that 'hole of a place;' she loved dear London, and would like to live and die in it."

Frank's lips formed to the name that was in Joyce's thoughts at the moment.

"The Buckingham's," he said; "it's all their doing. I fear mischief will come of this intimacy before we succeed in getting rid of them."

"I've done my best," said Joyce, looking toward the larger room, where Sylvia sat embroidering by the fire, while her brother played an energetic game of *bézique* with Mrs. Shenstone. "Is it bravado, or thick-skinnedness on their part; or did I dream that I had spoken out plainly, and shown unmistakably how unwelcome they are in the house?"

"Change your seat, dear, for this sofa. I can't sit facing that man without wishing to—well, never mind, perhaps I may have the chance some day. What does Mab say to it all?"

But Mab, after that one morning of vehement championship had never once opened her lips on the matter. A new phase of thought was evidently beginning to take possession of her now. Her "practical beneficence" had come to a halt, her housekeeping duties were laid on one side If Joyce had not contrived to step into her sister's shoes just then, domestic arrangements would have run down generally, for morning, noon, and night found the girl shut up in her own room poring over books.

Joyce considered this a subject for congratulation, and wrote gleefully to Uncle Archie that Mab was at last growing into what Nature had evidently meant for her to be—a student. She had taken up with literature, and she felt sure would, sooner or later, blossom into an author.

Had Joyce known what sort of literature was occupying Mab, and who was supplying it, she might have told a different tale. But, one way or another, Joyce had her hands very full at that time. What with interviewing dressmakers, milliners, sempstresses, regulating the household, and, as far as lay in her power, keeping her mother within the borders of sanity, Joyce had no spare moments for peeping over Mab's shoulder at her books.

Then, too, there were Frank's leading articles for the *St. George's Gazette* which he always insisted she should glance over and criticise freely before he sent in.

The *St. George's* just then was making for itself a fine reputation for old-fashioned, red-hot Toryism, by the high-handed vehemence with which it discussed various leading topics of the day in certain of its articles.

These articles were signed "Stentor." People were beginning to ask who this man was; what right he had to lay down the law in that vigorously audacious fashion, as though from another altitude he looked down upon the miserable, groveling crowd, and saw panaceas for mundane ills that were hidden from their limited vision.

The question of women's suffrage was discussed; Stentor laughed it to scorn.

"Give women votes—no," he wrote; "I would take them away from nine hundred and ninety-nine of every thousand of the men, and the country would be all the better for the freedom from the clamor of ignorant tongues, for the silence in which men could take in the situation, reason, and act upon it. I would vote in the voters, and so simplify the whole machinery of electioneering. Let every town in the country return one voter for every thousand of its inhabitants, then we might expect intellectuality and commonsense to be brought to bear upon the return of members. To suppose that one person in a thousand is competent to have a voice in the election of a member is a generous computation."

This was bad enough. The Liberal papers poured vials of wrath upon the unlucky Stentor's head. But when Irish politics in their turn came on for discussion in the *St. George's* columns, the vials were turned into buckets. Weak hands have held the reins too long," he wrote; "now is the time to show sinew and muscle." Then he gave his absolute and final panacea for troublesome Ireland in three words: "Colonize the country. Reconquer it, if need be, but let the conquest and the colonization go hand in hand. England has unbounded resources, and overflowing population; let them both find their outlet in Ireland. Pour wealth, trade, soldiers, farmers, fighting-men, workingmen, in a flood into Ireland, from ten, twenty, thirty, fifty, a hundred, if need be, centers at once. In a word, colonize and civilize it: the terms should be synonymous in the nineteenth century."

This was like throwing a match among gunpowder to the Irish press. The journal was burned in solemn procession in Cork and Dublin, and the Saxon writer freely anathematized. Threats of dynamite and other disagreeable things began to find their way into the office of the *St. George's Gazette.*

A word of warning came from Scotland Yard, advising that the incognito of Stentor should be strictly preserved.

Frank laughed the warning to scorn.

"If they'd let me, I'd sign my name and address in full to the next dose I give them," he said, with a ringing contempt, to Joyce; "this is the liberty the democrats advocate—'freedom of speech for me, my friend, but a gag for you and every one who differs.'"

Joyce grew timorous, and counseled prudence. Her thoughts flew to her mother.

"I wish you hadn't scribbled your name to that one article you sent mother about 'patriotism as an investment,'" she said, referring to as hort, spirited sketch of Frank's, detailing how the Irish movement in New York had been turned into capital by American agitators. She made up her mind that the very first time she could get Mrs. Shenstone alone she would impress upon her the importance of not betraying Frank's identity with the writer of these fiery effusions.

It was not, however, easy to get a quiet five minutes with Mrs. Shenstone in those days. One or other of the Buckinghams seemed always in attendance upon her—within doors the sister, out of doors the brother.

Sylvia and Mrs. Shenstone had by this time grown to be all but inseparable, and had appeared to form one of those rapturous friendships rarely met with outside the walls of young ladies' boarding-schools.

Mrs. Shenstone, toward the end of October, had recommenced her weekly receptions. It was to Sylvia, not Joyce, she carried her appeals for advice as to the decoration and arrangement of her rooms, the entertainment of her guests during the momentous evening.

Joyce felt sure that Sylvia's eye had run over the invitation list, and that not a few cards were sent to personal friends of her own, for the rooms soon began to fill to overflowing, and the Irish-American element was unduly conspicuous. Joyce had never before in her life known that she had a temper. Now, she was being perpetually reminded of its existence by sharp twinges something like those of chronic toothache or headache.

There was some excuse for her. Sylvia, for some reason or other, seemed intent on feeding and developing every one of those foibles and follies of Mrs. Shenstone which Joyce had all her life long tried alternately to laugh or to trample out of existence. They certainly were becoming painfully apparent. Never before had her ridiculous love for notoriety at any price, her absurd attempts at juvenility and ingenuousness of manner, been so pronounced and conspicuous. Joyce felt sure that, though Sylvia with scrupulous exactitude set herself to applaud and gratify every one of Mrs. Shenstone's foolish whims as they showed themselves, in her heart she was laughing at her, and saying to herself: "See how easy it is to twist a weak-minded woman round one's little finger, if one only knows how to set about it."

Joyce began to lose a little of that confidence in herself and her own resources which Uncle Archie had so severely reprimanded. The dogged obstinacy that a shallow-brained person can develop under certain conditions came to her as a positive revelation. Not so very long ago she would have laughed to scorn the idea of her mother having a single name on her visiting-list through which she—Joyce—had decided to put her pen. But here was she compelled to stand a silent and helpless witness to an intimacy not only distasteful, but absolutely repugnant, to her.

She made up her mind that, before her wedding-day came round and she said her good-by to her home, she would take Uncle Archie fully into her confidence. The little interest that Mab appeared to take in what went on about her just then made it doubly necessary some one should come forward and look after her happiness in life.

Uncle Archie had written a short letter to Joyce, grumbling over the ills of life generally, but stating his intention of coming up to London the first week in December, so as to have a word to say respecting the wedding arrangements.

"Why I'm to be dragged up to town at this uncomfortable time of year is more than I can understand," he wrote, bluntly enough. "Your father's wish would have been that you should have married from your old home in Gloucestershire, and I certainly think his wishes on the matter should be respected. Don't ask me to stay in your house, I would as lief have lodgings in the County Asylum at once. Besides, Aunt Bell wants to be as near as can be to the big West-End shops so that she can get rid of her money as fast as possible, and if I don't humor her I shall have a life of it, so I'm bound to go to our old quarters in Clarges Street."

"Poor Aunt Bell, it's she who has the 'life of it,' I'm thinking," said Joyce, as, with the letter in her hand, she made her way to her mother's sitting-room, intending to found another appeal for a return to Gloucestershire upon Uncle Archie's blunt statement of her father's wishes.

For a wonder she found her mother alone. Mrs. Shenstone gave a great start at Joyce's approach, and looked nervously toward the door. No doubt she thought that a lecture was impending, and that it would be very much better to go shares in it with Sylvia.

Joyce noticed her nervous apprehension, and felt indignant, sorry, and pitiful all in a breath, to think that any one should dare in this way to come between her mother and herself. Those odious Buckinghams, to set such a condition of things going! That poor mother to allow it! Her thoughts flew to Frank's rashly-signed leading article, and she saw what seemed to her a better way of utilizing a five minutes' talk with her mother, than by reading aloud Uncle Archie's letter.

"Mother," she asked, "have you any spare numbers of the *St. George's Gazette?* I'm collecting the year's issue for reference. I'm looking for one dated September 15th; do you happen to have it?"

Mrs. Shenstone breathed again. It was not to be a lecture, then, after all.

"There are ever so many, Joyce, at the bottom of that cupboard," she answered, pleasantly. "Look them out for yourself."

Joyce went down on her knees and rummaged among the newspapers at the bottom of the cupboard.

She counted them up carefully, number by number. The one for the date September 15th was missing.

"Do you remember one that Frank signed in pencil, mother, and sent to you while we were away at the sea?" she asked, a little anxiously.

"What was it about, dear? Politics, you know, I never read. I'm not sensible and clever like you and Mab."

Oddly enough, following some inverted process of reasoning, Mrs. Shenstone, ever since her daughters had arrived at years of discretion, had been in the habit of founding a claim to distinction among her friends upon the plea: "They are so sensible and clever, I am such a goose," as though it were a disgrace to own to a fair amount of brain-power.

"Have you lent or given away any of the papers, mother?" asked Joyce, her thoughts flying naturally enough to the dear friend and alter ego.

"Ah, yes, dear, now you remind me, I did lend one number to Sylvia, with an article by Frank in it. It was all about Fenianism in America, I think. I didn't read it through, but I remember thinking it would be sure to interest Sylvia, as it was all about her own country."

"Did Miss Buckingham return it?" Joyce asked, feeling the farthest limit of silliness had been reached now.

"No. She asked me if she might send it to her brother. She said she felt sure he would be deeply interested in what a very young Englishman thought of their national character. Dear me, Joyce, how you stare at one! I'm sure she meant it as a compliment to Frank. She laid such an emphasis on the word 'young.'"

Forty-five naturally welcomes a compliment that twenty-five turns its back upon.

Joyce got up from her knees, and hastily left the room. The mischief, whatever it was, had been done. There was no use making a moan over it. In fact, more harm than good might be wrought by laying stress upon the circumstance. She could only hope that the Buckinghams had by this time forgotten all about the unlucky article, or, at any rate, had not associated its writer with the "Stentor" of aggressive politics.

She would keep her eyes open, however, she resolved, to all that was going on about her, and endeavor to ascertain a few particulars about these all but strangers. What was their position in their own country? What was their occupation, if any, in life? Above all, what was their object in thus making themselves free of a house where they had more than once been made to understand they were unwelcome?

No one but a mere baby in worldly knowledge could have supposed that their conduct in this respect was dictated by personal liking for Mrs. Shenstone. Joyce was no baby, but a woman, with a clear head and a fair amount of common-sense. Both refused to be satisfied with such a supposition. At one time she had been inclined to think that a comfortable income and an easily-ruled wife had been the object of Captain Buckingham's endeavor, and that his sister, so to speak, held the ground for him to make his advance. As time went on, however—notably, after her frank statement of the provisions of her father's will—she was compelled to dismiss this idea, though she could find no other to replace it.

Sylvia Buckingham had now been for about two months an inmate of the house. The brother, on an average, spent three or four hours out of every twenty-four in Mrs. Shenstone's society. If he did not lunch with her, he dined, or *vice versa;* if he did neither, he walked or drove with her, or chatted away his mornings, or even on occasions wrote his letters in some quiet nook in the house.

The smaller drawing-room had been all but converted into Sylvia's sitting-room. Here she transacted her correspondence, received any friends who might chance to call upon her, or read Mrs. Shenstone to sleep after luncheon or dinner.

In spite of that lady's openly-expressed liking, Sylvia and her brother must have felt their intimacy with this family stood on an oddly-strained footing.

Joyce, after her first daring attempt to dislodge the pair, had subsided into a freezing politeness. Mab's attitude toward them was that of a nervously repressed interest. It was a matter for congratulation that Frank's occupations at that period prevented his passing much of his time under Mrs. Shenstone's roof. His professional work was rapidly growing upon him; his hours at his chambers were proportionately lengthening. In addition there were sundry visits to be paid to his own people in Gloucestershire relative to certain business transactions that required settlement.

The selection and the furnishing of the London house which he and Joyce were to occupy after their marriage naturally enough was the occasion for many pleasant meetings and excursions together. Had things been otherwise, and he had spent as much of his time as formerly in Mrs. Shenstone's household, the chances were that the smoldering animosity between Captain Buckingham and himself must have been fanned into a flame. As it was, by tacit consent the two men, when they occasionally met, ignored each other as much as possible. Joyce could only hope that this condition of things might continue until Uncle Archie came upon the scene, and, speaking with authority, might induce her mother to put her household on a more comfortable footing.

XII

Mab, with three quarters of her senses absorbed by her books, only got at what went on around her in glimpses and whispers. Those books appeared to have an altogether magnetic attraction for her; morning, noon, and night found her shut up in their company.

Joyce—accustomed to her spasmodically enthusiastic fashion of following now one pursuit, now another—was in no wise surprised at her sudden, eager passion for study at a time when most young girls would have thrown themselves heart and soul into the preparations for the approaching wedding-day. Perhaps if she had chanced to follow her sister into her room, and had noted the method of their study, she might have found food for astonishment. She would have seen Mab first carefully lock her door, to secure herself from intruders, take invariably one book from her shelves, fling herself on the hearthrug, open her book, read one or two lines, then sit motionless with clasped hands gazing into the fire for hours, until, in fact, the clanging of the dinner-bell or the summons of her maid aroused her to the consciousness of the commonplace routine of life.

And had Joyce taken up the book lying open on Mab's knee, she would have seen that it was the autobiography of Marie St. Clair, the Boston seer, and that the name of George Ritchie Buckingman figured on the title-page.

The book was a small, cheap edition of one that had appeared in America in more pretentious form. It was written in the form of a diary, and bore distinct marks of abridgment, and a not too artistic editing. The early days of the girl, her home surroundings, and term of service in the draper's shop, were told in curt, bald language, but with a straightforward simplicity that vouched for the truth of the narrative. The latter portion of the story, that dealing with her public career as a professional clairvoyante, had a touch of artificiality in it, a straining for effect, and expanded here and there into transports which fell little short of hysteria. A critical eye would have detected in this portion of the narrative distinct marks of interpolation by another and a coarser pen.

Mab's eye, however, was not critical, but illuminating. It transformed hysteric flights of fancy into high-souled enthusiasm, supplied links to shallow logic, filled in misty outlines with grand truths born of her own spirituality.

One page had a strange fascination for her. The book opened at it with a touch now. It recounted the manner in which Marie St. Clair had had what she believed to be the secret of clairvoyante trance revealed to her.

It was a wierd and fantastic story, told in evident good faith, of a certain luminous appearance seen by her, which she hastily, but honestly, concluded to be that of a girl-friend asleep in her bed at the time.

"Astral doubles" were not talked about at that time, or at any rate were unheard of by Marie St. Clair. She christened her apparition "a luminous replica," and honestly believed she had struck the keynote of a great truth by starting the theory that every human body owned to "a luminous replica" of itself, possessing similar but more finely-developed senses and powers of motion. She followed up this theory with another, namely, that the soul, the "I," the "me," had the prerogative of dwelling either in the material or in the spiritual body, making use of the senses of that body, provided that, for the time being, the senses of the body out of use were sealed either in sleep or trance; but furthermore that this prerogative could not be exercised at will until after a long course of training in self-mesmerism had been gone through.

At this point the writer broke off from her narrative to give many and minute instructions as to the system of training to be adopted by the aspirant to honors in clairvoyance.

These were the pages on which, day after day, Mab's eyes were riveted.

Away from the solid earth, over the mountain-tops into cloudland, they carried her; men and women, with their trivial, everyday round of occupation, seeming to grow remote and dwindle in the distance.

Fancy a born musician shut up in some wilderness, knowing nothing of music save what the bird's notes gave him, and totally ignorant of all mechanical mediums for harmony. Imagine him suddenly transported to a concert-room where the violin is being played by a master's hand: imagine the instrument transferred to him with the message that by dint of study and practice he might create these sweet sounds for himself!

Mab felt herself in much such a case, as she sat there beside the fire with Marie St. Clair's book upon her knee.

"Claim your birthright," had been Captain Buckingham's counsel to her. The words seemed to have a deeper and larger meaning in them now. She coupled with them another sentence of his: "Through want of knowledge one may burn oil in an Aladdin's lamp." In it she seemed to read the record of her past life, her struggles against the ideal, the spiritual; her snatchings at the commonplace, the actual, which somehow had always managed sooner or later to slip through her fingers.

XIII

Joyce, returning home with her mother and Miss Buckingham from a tedious afternoon's shopping, was met by a circumstance which startled and pained her.

She was getting through a prodigious amount of shopping just then. Naturally enough she would have liked Mab's opinion on the yards of Valenciennes lace and cambric she was buying. Mab, however, had cried off, and retreated to her solitude and her books.

Failing Mab, Joyce had begged her mother to make the circuit of Piccadilly, Bond Street, and Regent Street with her. Mrs. Shenstone jumped at the idea, shook her little fluffy poodle out of her lap, and rang the bell at once to order the carriage.

"I'm wanting everything myself, I'm almost destitute of evening dresses," she said; "and, you know, Joyce, I'm so glad to get your opinion whenever I can. I'm such a goose about choosing things for myself."

This was like the sunshiny old days before the Buckinghams had set up a prickly hedge between the mother and daughter Joyce at once expanded into cheerfulness and animation. She as speedily relapsed into silence and gloom when she descended the stairs to find Mrs. Shenstone and Sylvia seated side by side in the carriage awaiting her.

"Sylvia is kindly going to show me where I can buy some lovely walking-boots; boots are always such a trouble to me," murmured Mrs. Shenstone, insinuating an apology.

"Boots always must be a trouble to any one with such a tiny ankle and high instep as you have," murmured Sylvia, insinuating a compliment.

Joyce sank back in the carriage, registering a vow that next time she went shopping, if she could not tear Mab away from her books she would choose her Valenciennes lace and cambric muslin alone.

So she sat confronted with Sylvia's flaxen head in her violet velvet bonnet, her steely blue eyes, her semi-satirical conversation or semi-satirical silence for the space of three solid hours, returned home in a state of mind in which a grasshopper would have been a burden, and was met by an annoyance by many ounces heavier than a grasshopper.

This was nothing less than the sight of Mab and Captain Buckingham coming side by side round the corner of the square.

"I must have this carriage relined. Everybody has drab lining, or myrtle-green, or navy-blue. I want something distinctive, quite out of the common," Mrs. Shenstone was saying as the carriage drove up to the door.

Joyce, with her eyes fixed on Mab and her companion advancing toward them, made no attempt at a reply.

"An apricot-velvet or satin lining would be something quite out of the common, and very becoming to a fair complexion," suggested Sylvia, with never a glimmer of fun in her eyes.

"The very thing! Backgrounds should always be most carefully selected," said Mrs. Shenstone, enthusiastically.

Captain Buckingham's hand opened the carriage-door, and assisted the lady to alight.

"We live in an age when backgrounds are very wisely accentuated. A generation back such things were left to chance. We, in these later days, have discovered the importance of the minutiæ of daily life," he said, didactically, ready, as usual, to lay down the law at a moment's notice.

"Mother," said Joyce, jumping out of the carriage without even a glance at Buckingham's still out stretched hand, "when people are as handsome as you and I are they can afford to despise even backgrounds." Then she caught at Mab's arm. "Mab, dear, how is this? Why are you out walking alone? I should have been glad and thankful for your company this morning."

Mab's face was the color of a flamingo's wing.

"I had a headache," she began, stammering over her words.

"I came in to see Mrs. Shenstone, found Miss Mab alone, and, looking so white, I persuaded her to come out for some fresh air," said Captain Buckingham over all their bonnets.

Joyce did not so much as turn her head toward him. She held Mab's arm tightly all the way up the stairs right into her room. Then she shut the door, and stood facing her.

"Now, dear, what is it? What does it mean? How came you to be walking alone with this man, about whom we know next to nothing?"

Mab was not one to tell Joyce that really she was old enough to look after herself; that assuredly it was no affair of a younger sister's whoever she might choose to go out walking with.

She stood in front of Joyce nervously unbuttoning her gloves, her eyes downcast, her hands trembling.

"I scarcely know how it happened, Joyce," she began, in jerky sentences; "I was in the drawing-room when Captain Buckingham came in—"

"He ought not to have come in when mother was out. Who did he expect to see?"

"I suppose they told him I was in; I don't know. I hadn't been a minute in the room before he came in; I only went down because my room was icy cold—and—and—my head ached—I felt half dazed," Mab went on, still more nervously and apologetically.

"Icy cold with that fire!" cried Joyce, pointing to the grate, where the flames made merry with the piled-up logs.

It really seemed as if Mab, who had a fine reputation for truth telling, were bent on annihilating it in a moment by minute and pitiful fibs.

Her confusion was painful to witness.

"I don't know how to make you understand, dear; I can't explain—it is impossible to explain," she said, helplessly.

Joyce felt bewildered. She looked all around the room as though for some solution to the mystery. Had her eye chanced upon the autobiography of Marie St. Clair she might have got nearer to the heart of Mab's secret. That book, however, with one or two others, had been returned to Captain Buckingham that very afternoon. The only thing in the room that attracted her attention was an easy-chair, with a pillow in it and a foot-stool in front, as if some one had been reclining there. It had been pushed into the darkest corner of the room away from the firelight or the wintry twilight that crept in through the panes.

She got an idea from this chair.

"Had you been asleep, dear?" she asked, eagerly: "one often wakes up shivering after a nap."

Mab gave a deep sigh.

"You might call it sleeping, Joyce; I'm not sure whether I slept or not. I only know—" Then she broke off again.

Joyce grew alarmed.

"Did you faint, Mab? Really, I think you ought to see a doctor. You must have felt weak even to get into that chair at this time of the day," she said, speaking out of the fulness of her own vigorous health.

Mab walked away toward the fire.

"Do, do let me alone, Joyce," she pleaded; "I can't explain—you couldn't understand even if I did."

And then she sighed again. Joyce followed.

"Darling, you know I always did hate mysteries!" she said, putting her arm lovingly round Mab's waist "I wish you would tell me all your thoughts, no matter whether I can understand them or not; but, anyhow, tell me just this: why, if you must go out, did you let Captain Buckingham go with you?—better by far have gone alone."

"He is a friend of mother's. Why should he not go out with me?"

"Mab, darling!" This in a voice full of pain. "If father were alive, do you think he would have allowed any of us to call such a man as that, friend?"

Mab's answer struck her dumb on the spot.

"Yes, I do, Joyce," she said, steadying her nerves, and looking her sister full in the face; "I think, if father were alive now, Captain Buckingham is the man he would choose before any one else in the world to be his own friend, and mother's, and yours, and mine."

Then, evidently to end a discussion for which she had no inclination, she freed herself from Joyce's arm and left the room.

Joyce followed, speechless, bewildered, feeling that another brick had been added to the wall which was gradually being built up between Mab and herself.

XIV

J oyce had made a hasty resolve that she would take Frank as little as possible into her confidence concerning the Buckinghams, fearing lest a declaration of open war between the two men might be the result.

On the day after her bewildering talk with Mab she broke this resolve, telling Frank fully all that had passed.

It was the night of one of Mrs. Shenstone's receptions; it might be more correct to say of Sylvia's, judging from the Irish "r's" and American "n's" which bayoneted the queen's English in all directions.

Frank had endured the atmosphere of the drawing-room for a dreary ten minutes, then had fled for an ecstatic ten minutes to the deserted dining-room, whither Joyce had somehow managed to find her way before him.

"One thing is clear," she said, speaking with a fine air of decision, but nevertheless quaking in her black satin slippers at her won temerity, "our wedding-day must be put off; I can't go away with you thinking only of my own happiness, and leave Mab here to the mercy of a pair of adventurers."

Frank's answer did not surprise her.

"No," he said, and not a doubt he meant it, "I'll stake my life we won't do that. I tried that game once, we won't start it again. I'll undertake to say our marriage will come off on the 21st, not a day later."

"But, Frank, be reasonable. What is to be done? We must do something. What are we to do?"

"Give me time to think, dear. I confess I was not prepared for such a thing as this. Your mother, you see, is sufficiently protected by your father's will; but Mab, unless we can take care of her, is at the mercy of any fortune-hunter who comes along."

Joyce's conscience here asked the unpleasant question, what if it were to her plain-speaking on the matter of her father's will that Captain Buckingham's attentions had been transferred from her mother to Mab?

"I will talk to Mab again," she said; "she is difficult to manage in some things. In small matters she always lets me rule her, but on some things she won't listen even to a suggestion, and of late her manner has puzzled me more than I can say. I'll talk to my mother too, and tell her she must—must drop those people, and at once—"

"Talk to whom you please, dear, but never again speak a word about putting off our wedding by so much as an hour," interrupted Frank, vigorously.

"And I'll talk to Sylvia, and tell her she must prevent her brother coming to the house. And I'll talk to the brother and tell him—"

"Wha—at!"

"I mean it. I'll tell him he must consider himself on strictly formal terms with us, and not presume to put himself upon the footing of a friend."

"You'll do nothing of the sort. If there's any talking to be done to that man, you'll leave me to do it, please."

"Ah, but you'll do it unpleasantly, and there'll be a scene."

"I'm bound to do it unpleasantly sooner or later, and I'd as soon do it tomorrow as any other day, if any good could come of it. But it would do more mischief than anything else just now. Between your mother and me the present condition of things is an armed truce, nothing more. If it came to a question between me and that man, she'd side with him, not a doubt, and forbid me the house."

"Mab, too, isn't a log—she will have something to say if it comes to open war."

"You might talk to your mother tonight, Joyce, when all the people have gone—I've heard you speak very effectively to her more than once," said Frank, after a moment's pause; "and you can write to Uncle Archie, telling him he must come up at once, and take Mab back with him into Gloucestershire while we are away in Paris. When we return, of course she'll be with us, and we can shut our door upon all undesirable intimacies."

There could be no mistaking the under-note of pride in his voice as the young man alluded to their joint possession of a front door. Joyce's fun-loving ear detected it.

"Ah! with what an air of authority we will draw the bolts against the dubious," she said, mischievously.

"Won't we! and I'll back up your letter to Uncle Archie with one by the next post; but in any case leave the Buckinghams to me. I'll speak to the man before long, but I will choose the moment for speaking, not allow him to do so."

There came the sound of doors opening, and movement along the hall outside.

Joyce gave a start.

"I must go back to the drawing-room at once. How dreadful! I've been talking here with you for half an hour instead of ten minutes—that was all the time I promised you—"

"Oh! these good-bys," groaned Frank, taking his farewell—a long, slow, sweet one, "thank Heaven they are nearly at an end now."

Joyce went with him to the front door, and picked out his hat from forty or fifty others of all sorts and sizes.

"Ah! the heads those hats represent," she said, with a lively recollection of the platitudes, bombast, and trivialities which had been doing duty for conversation up-stairs during the greater portion of the evening.

The night was pitch-dark, November was justifying its reputation in its usual braggart fashion. A man leaning against the railings of a darkened doorway, higher up the square, came forward as Frank left Mrs. Shenstone's doorstep, and accosted him, in a voice slightly above a whisper, with the words:

"What time is it, friend?"

Frank stared at him for a moment, but the inky fog conspired with the high coat-collar and hat which the man wore low over his brows to hide his features effectually. Frank could only make out that he was a tall, powerfully-built man; and his Irish accent was unmistakable.

"I haven't the remotest notion—time for idlers to be in bed, at any rate," was his reply in brusque tones, for somehow, he scarcely knew why, his suspicions were aroused.

The man, with never a word, drew back to his former position against the railings.

Strange to say, at the further corner of the square, the circumstance, with a slight difference, was repeated. A man—a fine, stalwart, soldier-like fellow—came along with rapid strides, and, in a louder voice than the other had used, asked the question: "What time is it, friend?"

Frank laid his hand on the man's shoulder. The voice was one easy to identify.

"Why, Ned Donovan," he asked, "what pranks are you up to now? What on earth has come to you, that you are dodging about the streets in this way, asking mysterious questions as to the time of day?"

Donovan shook off Frank's hand hurriedly.

"I beg your pardon, sir, I mistook you for some one else," he answered; and, before Frank could say another word, he was gone.

Frank got to his rooms without further hindrance, let himself in with his latch-key, turned up his gas, took off his hat, and was about to hang it on its peg, when, to his surprise, on the inside lining, on a scrap of card, he saw inscribed the name, "George Ritchie Buckingham."

For a moment or two he stood silently scrutinizing the hat. It bore a certain resemblance to his own hat, sufficiently, at least, to justify Joyce's mistake in handing it to him, and his own—with his mind seriously pre-occupied—in putting it on. But it was indubitably American, of a broader brim and rougher in make than one is accustomed to see in London streets.

He put it on again, walked to the looking-glass, and stood there taking stock of his personal characteristics. He discovered that he was close upon Captain Buckingham's height, that his shoulders were about the same in breadth, that he carried his head in a manner that, to a casual observer on a dark, foggy night, might suggest Buckingham.

These points of resemblance, slight though they were, struck a vein of thought in his mind, and suggested a possible solution of the mystery of these unexpected midnight greetings.

XV

M other, dear, let me into your room tonight, to act maid for you," cried Joyce, taking her mother's arm as she went out of the drawing-room that night on the heels of her departing guests. "Let me carry your train for you—so—up the stairs. I want to talk to you about the evening. What a number of people you managed to get together!— the rooms were packed from wall to wall. I never felt so near suffocation in my life before."

"Ah!" answered Mrs. Shenstone, complacently, as she subsided into a comfortable easy-chair beside her dressing-room fire. "Lady Cranbury need not have been so terribly afraid of my worrying her for introductions; I have got on very well without them, haven't I?"

"Lady Cranbury was a goose, and, if you had been an author, might have kept you going in quills from year's end to year's end," said Joyce, curling herself up on the opossum rug at her mother's feet. "Mother, who were those girls in green, with yellow complexions and pink mittens, who sang at the top of their voices about the 'Far, far West; the land I love best'?"

"Oh, those were Americans—friends of Sylvia's—I've forgotten their name."

"And that nice-looking old gentleman who paid you so much attention?"

"Ah, did you notice it, Joyce?" said Mrs. Shenstone, looking pleased and flattered. "Sylvia said it was so. But I've such a horror of seeming vain that I told her it was all her imagination. That was old General Bullen."

Joyce stifled her annoyance at finding herself for once in her life running in couples with Sylvia by asking another rapid question.

"And that tall, thin man, bald and bearded, with eyes like a ferret's and ears like a bat's, who was he?"

"How you describe people, Joyce! He was another friend of Sylvia's, also an American. I've forgotten his name."

"And that beautiful girl all in blue, with a dove's eyes and the walk of a peacock?"

"I didn't see her, Joyce. To my way of thinking, all the girls in the room tonight were remarkably plain, not to say ugly."

"Didn't see her! Why, I saw you write down her address and promise to call on her."

"That woman! You call her a girl! Why, she looked years older than I do, and as for good looks—"

"Was she a friend of Sylvia's, and also an American?" interrupted Joyce, anxious to get to the subject she had at heart, and feeling she had introduced it very diplomatically.

"Yes, dear, she was. But as for beauty! Dear me, you couldn't have looked at her very closely to describe her in that fashion. She hadn't a good feature in her face."

"I daresay you're right, mother; I didn't study her much, I'll admit. But, do you know, it seems to me there were a great deal too many American who were 'friends of Sylvia's' in the room tonight."

Mrs. Shenstone's reply to this for the moment made Joyce think she must be hearing with another person's ears, and after all did not understand her own mother tongue, so totally unprepared was she for the sentence.

"Well, dear, that is exactly what occurred to me, and, between ourselves, I'm beginning to think I've had nearly enough of Sylvia and her brother, too."

Joyce felt as if she must jump up, clap her hands, and sing as loud as any skylark. She answered, however, tranquilly enough, as though from its very beginning she had foreseen this satisfactory ending to the intimacy.

"I felt sure, mother, you'd sooner or later get tired of the pair of them. Sylvia may be all very well for a day, but for two whole months—oh-h!"

And the shudder which accompanied her "oh was suggestive of east winds and a black frost, at least.

"Well, between ourselves, Joyce," said Mrs. Shenstone, unclasping her bracelets and pulling off her gloves, "I think she has presumed a little on my kindness to her. It is true I gave her permission to invite one or two of her friends to my evenings, but I did not expect to find the room full of them."

"And the brother is every whit as bad as the sister," Joyce went on; waxing bold in her attack. "I'm sure, when you told him you'd be pleased to see him now and then, you didn't expect to have him morning, noon, and night in the house."

"Captain Buckingham has annoyed me once or twice lately, and I've spoken of it to Sylvia"; here Mrs. Shenstone fell into a slightly aggrieved tone. "At one time he showed me marked and unmistakable attention, but of late I have noticed he seems to have eyes and ears only for Mab."

The thought flashed through Joyce's mind that here lay the secret of Mrs. Shenstone's change of feeling toward her friends. Solicitude for Mab chased this thought away.

She caught her mother's hand in hers.

"Mother, dear, how long have you noticed this? Tell me."

"I really can't. Two, or three, or four times I have remarked when you have been out with Frank, and Captain Buckingham has come in, that he has shown Mab a good deal of attention. Oh, Joyce, how red your hand looks, and how fat, too, beside mine!" Here Mrs. Shenstone spread out her small fingers advantageously beside Joyce's, which had caught a glow from the fire-heat.

"Mother, yours are the whitest and prettiest hands I have ever seen," cried Joyce, delighted to be able to pay a truthful compliment. Then she went back to the danger threatening Mab. "Of course, now you see so clearly what the man's intentions are, you'll end the intimacy at once, won't you?" she queried.

"Well, no, dear; I don't see how I can very well. Mab is quite welcome to Captain Buckingham's attentions so far as I am concerned," she said, not intending sarcasm. "It's really time she thought of getting married. She's older than you, and when you are gone she'll be for ever moping in corners or breaking out into new eccentricities."

And if she had spoken out all the thoughts in her heart Mrs. Shenstone would have added, "And, with both my daughters married and gone, how delightfully free and unfettered my own movements will be!"

Joyce jumped up from the opossum rug horror-stricken.

"You don't mean to say, mother, that anything would induce you to consent to Mab's marrying that man!" she cried. "An adventurer we know nothing at all about, except that his manners are domineering, and objectionable, and insufferable, and that there is nothing whatever of the gentleman about him."

"Well, Joyce, if you are going to lecture as usual, I shall go to bed; I'm dreadfully tired. I declare you never come in for a quiet talk but what you end it in a lecture."

But Joyce was not lecturing now, simply storming; walking hurriedly up and down the room meantime, just exactly as Uncle Archie did when things went crookedly and a fit of gout was coming on.

"I would sooner see her laid in the grave at once—a hundred thousand times sooner," she said, in one corner of the room. "My dear, darling Mab to be sacrificed to a man of that sort!" she said, in another.

"Mother, you must turn Sylvia out of the house tomorrow, and tell the brother we will none of us ever speak to him again," she said, finally, going close to her mother, and taking her hands in hers once more.

"I can't very well, Joyce," said her mother, a little nervously. "I've asked Sylvia to stay on over your wedding-day, and I've asked Captain Buckingham to come to the evening party I intend to give the night before the wedding. You see, they are great friends of the O'Hallorans and the Kearneys and ever so many other people I'm on pleasant terms with, and you can't expect me to quarrel all round."

"I'll quarrel all round for Mab's sake," said Joyce, desperately. "I'll tell Captain Buckingham he sha'n't make love to Mab—he sha'n't even look at her. I'll tell Mab she sha'n't ever speak to him again. I'll tell Sylvia and 'the O'Hallorans and the Kearneys and ever so many other people' that we don't want their friendship or their friends' friendship. Yes, mother, I will, if you can't get your courage together to do it."

Mrs. Shenstone somehow managed to release herself from Joyce's tight fingers, and made straight for her bedroom door.

"Well, Joyce, tell anybody anything you like, so long as you don't expect me to do it and make myself ridiculous in the eyes of my friends. Dear me, what fiery tempers you two girls have!"

Then she got the other side of her bedroom door, and made sure her retreat by bolting it.

Joyce felt the time had come for action.

XVI

I t was a relief when, two days after this, crusty Uncle Archie and placid Aunt Bell made their joint appearance in the family circle, bringing common-sense with them as a welcome third.

"Told you so," said the old gentleman, sitting in conclave with Joyce and Frank over the library fire. "From the first day that I heard of your harum-scarum plan of a year in London, I prognosticated that mischief would come of it; and here's about as much mischief as three women with thirty idle fingers could manage to set going."

Mab had retired early to her room that night Mrs. Shenstone, Sylvia, and Aunt Bell were at the play. Aunt Bell, among other harmless proclivities adored the pantomime, and never missed a chance of seeing "Whittington and his Cat," or "Mother Goose."

"Thirty idle fingers, that includes thumbs," said Joyce, saucily, taking up the challenge thrown down. "In my young days elderly gentlemen used to express themselves with exactness, and knew the difference between fingers and thumbs." This in a manner fairly imitative of Uncle Archie in his aphoristic mood.

"In my young days, retorted Uncle Archie, raspingly, "young women were accustomed to treat their elders with marked respect, not to say reverence."

"Ah, but what elders they were!" This said softly, by way of interjection.

"And let me tell you, young lady, and you too, young man," here he jerked a sideways nod at Frank, "that, instead of spending all your time making eyes at each other, I think you might have troubled yourselves to use your common-sense to look after those who had none."

"Poor Uncle Archie!" said Joyce, patting his hand soothingly, "every one knows he doesn't mean half he says."

After this they fell to discussing "the situation" amicably and frankly.

"It's not mother I'm afraid of now," said Joyce, taking the lead in the talk; "she's bound, sooner or later, to get tired of the whole set—the O'Hallorans, and the Kearneys, and the Buckinghams, and all the rest. She always gets tired of people she sees much of. Then they quarrel, and don't speak, and everything settles down all right. But it's Mab, my darling Mab, I'm trembling for. If once she falls in love with a man of that sort, it'll be something awful; she is so true and steadfast in her likings."

CATHERINE LOUISA PIRKIS

"But things can't have gone so far as all that, surely? She doesn't see him on the sly, does she?" interrogated Uncle Archie, sharply.

"Oh, no; she has not exchanged two words with him since the day she went out walking with him. Whenever he comes in, I jump up and sit next to her, put my arm round her waist, and when he speaks to her I answer him, and—look at him. But that sort of thing can't last, you know."

"No, that can't last," assented Frank, vigorously, thinking how near the 21st of December was.

"But it's she herself who troubles me most of all—her manner, her ways, her looks even. It was bad enough in the old days to have her doing housekeeping and district-visiting in that feverish, defiant sort of way, as if she did it to spite herself; it is far worse now to have her shut up in her own room for hours at a time, and then, when she is dragged out of it, to have no thoughts for anything about her."

"You told me she was growing into a student, and you were delighted at it."

"Yes, but I made a mistake; she isn't. There is not a single book to be seen in her room. I looked yesterday."

"She's scribbling, perhaps. One can expect any amount of eccentricity from a scribbler."

"No, nor that either. She has not a pen nor ink in her room. It is altogether inexplicable. I haven't an idea as to what she does with her time when she's shut up."

Here she looked inquiringly at Frank, as though to get at his idea. But Frank, though he had an idea, and a strong one, on the matter, did not choose to give it to her. Instead, he said:

"Will you mind, just as a matter of experiment, running up-stairs and seeing what she is doing now, Joyce? It's exactly ten o'clock. She has been shut up in her own room for an hour at least; something she must have been doing all that time, if she is not in bed."

Joyce departed. Then Frank turned to Uncle Archie gravely enough.

"I hardly dare ask the question," he said; "but will you mind telling me if there has ever been insanity in your family?"

The old gentleman began to fret and fume immediately.

"Insanity!" he cried. "I don't know how you do dare to ask the question! Do you want to insult my nieces and me?"

Frank apologized profusely.

"Insult them, no!" he protested. "I love Mab as though she were already my sister. You know I am a sort of alien from my own people; beyond Joyce and Mab, I have no one in the world."

But Uncle Archie was not to be easily appeased.

"I ought to know something of my own family!" he said, irritably. "Will you take my word for it, there has been nothing worse handed down from father to son or from mother to daughter than gout on one side and folly on the other."

Joyce came back quickly enough.

"What an unusual combination!" she said, catching at the old gentleman's concluding words. "Gout and wisdom one can realize, or even gout and bad temper; but gout and folly! No; is such a thing possible?"

Then she turned to Frank.

"Mab is asleep in her easy-chair beside the fire. She looks beautiful— Mab always looks heavenly when she's asleep. I kissed her and covered her over with an eider-down quilt, because she felt a little chilly; but she did not so much as stir."

Frank and Uncle Archie exchanged glances.

"We'll have a doctor in tomorrow," said the latter, pushing back his chair from the fire to end the discussion. "If she wants to go to sleep, why can't she get into bed first, I should like to know?"

"A doctor!" cried Joyce. "Mab's not ill. I'm positive she can't be. If you had only seen her just now as I did, looking so sweet and tranquil, I'm sure you wouldn't let such a thought enter your mind."

But, though she spoke with a grand air of assurance, the mere whisper of such a possibility sent her creeping back to Mab's room in a state of nervous apprehension as soon as Frank had said his good-night and departed.

On her way up-stairs she had to pass the door of a small room given up to Kathleen and her dress-making. Voices from within fell upon her ear.

"Do you think I would marry an O'Shea?" said Kathleen's voice. "No, not if I had promised a hundred thousand times over."

"You shouldn't make promises you don't mean to keep," said a man's voice, which Joyce readily identified as Ned Donovan's. "And let me tell you I've found out your secret, and know well enough why you are breaking your promise to Brian O'Shea. Let me give you—"

"Secret—I've no secret!" interrupted Kathleen, shrilly.

"Let me give you a word of warning," Ned went on. "Brian is beginning to have an inkling of the truth, and it'll go hard with the man—you know who I mean—if he crosses Brian in his lovemaking."

Joyce went on to Mab's room.

"The foolish little flirt," was her mental comment on Kathleen's conduct.

Later on she read Ned's words by a fuller light.

XVII

"Mab darling, only three more weeks and I shall be gone," said Joyce, kneeling beside Mab's chair and putting her arm round her waist. "I'm going to ask you to do ever so many things for me before I vanish from the scene. In fact, I'm making my last will and testament this morning, and leaving commissions to be executed all round."

"What things do you want me to do, Joyce?" asked Mab, looking down with troubled eyes into Joyce's sunshiny brown ones.

"Well, dear, first and foremost I want you to promise that on the very day after my wedding you'll go back with Uncle Archie into Gloucestershire, and stay with him there the whole time I am away."

"Oh, that was all settled yesterday. I told Uncle Archie I would, and mother is going to stay with the Wheelers at Brighton meanwhile. Didn't you know?"

Joyce drew a long breath of relief and said a mental thanksgiving. Then she went on to request number two.

"And I want you, dear, during the short time I shall be at home, to take up with some occupation. Go into housekeeping again, or take some music lessons and practice hard."

"Joyce, I daren't touch music."

"Well, then, take up with something else—painting, embroidery; occupation of some sort you ought to have."

Mab grew nervous and distressed.

"I don't feel fit for anything just now, Joyce," she pleaded.

Joyce looked at her anxiously.

"You ought to see a doctor. Uncle Archie—" she began.

But Mab interrupted her vehemently.

"No, I will not see a doctor. There, my mind is made up. It is of no use you or any one else talking of such a thing."

"Dear, if you won't see a doctor you must let your friends prescribe for you. Now my prescription is occupation, steady, regular occupation from morning till night."

Mab sighed.

"What am I to do, Joyce? Will you tell me that?"

"Well, dear, why not re-commence your district visiting? Don't you remember how interested you were in those poor people at Pimlico, in the streets leading off the Embankment, I mean."

Mab shuddered, as though mentally she shrank from "those poor people at Pimlico in the streets leading off the Embankment" Joyce went on.

"It always seemed to me a little—yes, a little unkind, dear, for you to take up so hotly with them, lavish flannel and babies' clothes and books and coals on them, and then suddenly to drop them altogether and never go near them."

Mab grew thoughtful.

"I suppose it was unkind. Yes, Joyce, I'll go and see them all tomorrow, and make a point of calling upon them at least once a week till I go away with Uncle Archie," she answered, resolutely.

Once more Joyce sent up a mental thanksgiving. After all, things were arranging themselves far better than she had at one time thought possible. Here was Mab meeting her wishes as soon as they were uttered; and, as for her mother, ever since Uncle Archie had been in the house the shadow of his common-sense appeared to have fallen upon her, and nine-tenths of her whims and vagaries had retired into the background.

With regard to the Buckinghams a compromise had been effected. Sylvia still remained in the house as Mrs. Shenstone's guest; but it was an understood thing that on the morning of the wedding-day she was to depart to other friends across the Irish Channel.

Joyce had stipulated for a quiet wedding-day.

"Mother," she had said, "ask crowds and crowds of people over-night to the house, and I'll kiss them all round, and exhibit myself and my presents to your heart's content, but I won't have a soul at the church to see me married, except you, Uncle Archie, Aunt Bell, and Mab."

Mrs. Shenstone had fallen in with Joyce's wish; the party on the eve of the wedding was planned on an ambitious scale. Joyce, thankful to have secured a general peace, gave hearty and willing assistance. Sylvia also lent a more gracious aid than was her wont in matters where Joyce was concerned. Uncle Archie looked on, grumbling and austere, while placid Aunt Bell smiled serenely on every one generally.

Captain Buckingham seemed a little shy of the house now that Uncle Archie had taken up his abode in it. He and Mab never met, save in the society of others; and then Joyce took care that they should not exchange half-a-dozen words together. Sylvia's demeanor toward the family was that of formal politeness. Toward Mrs. Shenstone it was affability, slightly colored with reserve. Joyce, in her own mind, translated her manner into words somewhat as follows:

"Now, you foolish woman, that I have got all I want out of you and your surroundings, I mean, quietly and without any fuss, to drop you."

Mab was as good as her word. Each of the three weeks that elapsed between her talk with Joyce and the wedding-day found her making her rounds among the "poor people in the streets leading off the Embankment." Right glad they were to see her shy, thoughtful face among them again. They gave to it every whit as hearty a welcome as they accorded to her yards of flannel and tickets for coal.

Even the day before the wedding found her, with a packet of books in her hand, rapping with her knuckles at knockerless doors, and climbing ladder-like staircases that seemed expressly contrived for thinning the population. She worked very hard that day out of doors, just as hard as Joyce was working within doors at writing letters of thanks for her numerous presents, and arranging the details of her "packing up" with Kathleen.

Those two sisters had not dared trust themselves alone together for three consecutive minutes, lest their self-control, already strained to its limit, should utterly collapse. Joyce dashed off feverish, brilliant little notes of thanks, telling all her friends how light her heart was, and how sunshiny was everything about her. And Mab worked away with a will among her squalid, slatternly poor, staying out till long after luncheon-time, until, indeed, the gray winter twilight hid the sunless sky, and a light, drizzling rain began to fall.

Coming out of the narrowest and dirtiest of the streets she had been visiting, she was met by a woman who importuned her to go at once to see a neighbor of hers, who, she said, was lying dangerously ill in a blind alley—"Chandler's Alley," she called it, pointing in its direction with her forefinger.

Mab hesitated only a moment. It was late, it was damp and cold; but still, if a half-crown of hers and a five-minutes' cheery talk could lighten a fellow-creature's sufferings, she felt bound to run the gauntlet of dampness, late hours, or any other personal inconvenience.

So, refusing the woman's proffered aid as guide, she retraced her steps, feeling confident she knew exactly in which direction lay Chandler's Alley.

She had been too hasty in her reckoning, however. So, at least, she concluded when, as she took the narrow turning which was the only blind alley she knew of in the neighborhood, she found that it consisted of some twelve or fourteen neglected-looking houses which had evidently been condemned to be pulled down in order to make way for the large and handsome buildings which were just then springing up in all directions.

One only was tenanted—the last house on her left hand. It exhibited a sign over its blistered and battered door, informing the public that "John Johnson, plasterer," had therein taken his abode. It somewhat retrieved its generally dingy appearance by a trim muslin curtain and a row of flower-pots at the parlor-window.

"Was it worth while," Mab asked herself, "to knock at the door, and inquire whether the sick woman lived there, and if this were Chandler's Alley?"

She lifted the door-knocker. Some one turned the corner of the alley at this moment, and, with rapid strides, came toward her. It was Ned Donovan. She recognized him immediately. He, however, did not see her till he was within a yard or so. Then he stopped abruptly.

"Miss Mab!" he exclaimed, in tones of blank surprise.

She met surprise with surprise.

"Have you friends in this place?" she asked. "Kathleen told me you had gone back to your work at Woolwich."

The man's face darkened.

"They gave me my dismissal there, Miss Mab, and from another place afterward; because I am an Irishman, I suppose." His voice was not pleasant as he said the words. It altered as he added; respectfully: "This is not a place for you to be in, Miss Mab, at this time of day at any rate; if you'll allow me, I'll see you through these streets to your own door, or will call a cab for you at the corner?"

Mab chose the latter. She must, she felt, give up her errand of charity for that day. The rain was coming down briskly now, she was rapidly getting drenched, and felt generally tired and out of sorts.

Nevertheless, dreary and depressing as her morning had been, it was blue sky and sunshine itself by comparison with the one she could picture passed in Joyce's company, with the shadow of the morrow's farewells deepening upon them.

XVIII

Every one decided that Mrs. Shenstone's reception on the eve of Joyce's wedding was more brilliant than any to which they had before been summoned by that lady. It had been planned on a more ambitious scale, and had had more time, thought, and energy bestowed upon it.

Mrs. Shenstone, in the most elaborate of blush-rose tinted robes that a Parisian modiste could contrive, surveyed herself in succession in four full-length mirrors, and came to the conclusion that every one's first exclamation on entering her drawing-room would be, "Dear me, she looks young enough to be the bride herself."

Joyce acted as maid to Mab, and helped to attire her in a dress as dead white as her own. Then she arranged her thick brown hair so to shadow her anxious, thoughtful face, and so crowned and bedecked her with jewels that people saw in the girl a dignity and beauty they had never before noted.

As for Joyce herself, she decided that for that night at least she would be radiant; and radiant she was.

"Tomorrow," she confided to Uncle Archie, "Frank and I will creep into church silently and demurely to the sound of muffled drums, but tonight, at any rate, the drums shall not be muffled."

Uncle Archie muttered something to the effect that in his young days weddings and funerals alike were conducted decorously and without ostentation.

"People didn't make such fools of themselves then as they do now," he grumbled.

"Then it was by special interposition of Providence," laughed Joyce, patting the old gentleman's shoulder as if he were some big Newfoundland dog, to be kept for a given time from snarling and showing his teeth.

Sylvia comported herself with a good deal of unobtrusive tact that evening. She put on dark colors, and placed herself at Mrs. Shenstone's elbow as that lady received her arriving guests.

"You look as though you needed a chaperon, Tiny," she whispered, insinuatingly, into her ear.

And Tiny was instantly mollified, and every one of Sylvia's misdeeds was pardoned on the spot.

Frank felt himself to be on the very pinnacle of happinness that night.

"It's more than I deserve, a hundred thousand times more," he soliloquized, over and over again thanking Heaven that he had had the common-sense to make his pride give place to his happiness. It made him giddy to think of the years of bliss of which he seemed at the moment able to command a bird's-eye view.

He stood a little way apart from Joyce, watching her in her bright beauty so prettily humoring old Uncle Archie, so protective to Mab, so forbearing to all her mother's follies and affectations.

"It's worth living on prison diet all one's days to get such a night as this," he thought, "and to think that my whole life will be a succession of such nights, or rather of something infinitely better!"

Then somehow he felt his eyes were wet. He threw himself with energy into the stream of guests, found occupation by volunteering to bring ices to some elderly dowagers, who, ensconced in a quiet corner, did not feel equal to daring the crowded staircase to procure them for themselves.

The refreshment buffet was in the dining-room. As Frank entered only two persons were in the room—a maid who had come in for a gossip, and the man who was serving the ices. The former fluttered away at Frank's approach; the latter, an elderly, serious-looking man, to all appearance of the respectable butler class, held up a warning finger and whispered:

"Not a word, sir, if you please. I knew you would recognize me, so I've been waiting here to have a word with you on the quiet."

Then Frank, to his amazement, recognized in the serious-looking butler a detective, a man of a superior and thoroughly confidential stamp, with whom of late he had had dealings in connection with some intricate law business.

"Morton!" he cried, indignantly, "what in the name of fortune are you doing here? I've a great mind to—"

"Not a word, sir," said the man, again. "I've had my orders from Scotland Yard. There's a lot been going on here that you know nothing at all about. All sorts of dubious people have been making free of this house."

"Good heavens! But, whatever your information may be. I'm sure it isn't necessary for me to tell you that the lady of the house is perfectly ignorant of their dubiousness."

Naturally all his suspicions fastened at once upon the Bucking-hams and their Irish intimates.

"Ah!" said Morton, confidentially. "A nice lot the lady of the house has surrounded herself with! Fenians, sir! The house is getting quite a reputation as a sort of head-center. Appointments have been made, meetings called at the lady's receptions—under her very nose, I might say. Hush, sir! Here they come for ices. Raspberry, or strawberry, or vanilla did you say, sir?"

Frank had only time to whisper a word.

"Come to my rooms direct when you leave here, I shall be up all night. I've a great deal to say."

Then he took his ices and departed, but by this time all recollection of the personality of the elderly dowagers had faded from his memory. Whether they were attired in cœrulean blue or sulphurous yellow he could not for the life of him have said. He only knew they looked very hot and red in the face, and were making a perfect gale with their fans. But, possibly, that by this time was the condition of every elderly dowager present.

With an ice in either hand he went peering into all the corners of the room, so far, at least, as he could approach them for the crush. He pushed on one side the curtain which half-draped the small conservatory leading off the drawing-room, thinking the ladies might have retreated thither for a pleasanter atmosphere.

But there he saw a sight which made him start back a step in astonishment, and put down his ices on a small table briskly enough—nothing less than Mab and Captain Buckingham seated side by side in confidential talk.

"You should make the attempt daily, spasmodic effort is useless. The habit should be steadily persevered in," Buckingham was saying, in an authoritative tone that set Frank's blood boiling. As for Mab's face, it looked thoughtful, spiritual, dead white as her dress.

"Mab," said Frank, taking her hand, "will you go at once to Joyce? She is looking for you. She is in the music-room."

Mab rose instantly. Captain Buckingham rose also.

"Won't you put your cloak on?" he asked; "you pass a window on your way to the music-room. Here is a wrap some one has left behind."

Frank had to stand still and see Mab wrapped in an Indian shawl by Captain Buckingham.

"Good-night," she said to him, softly, when the operation was over. "I shall remember."

Then, without so much as a look at Frank, who stood there steadily watching her, she went straight out of the room. She made no attempt to seek her sister. Straight up the stairs to her own room she went.

Mab's bedroom was large, and luxuriously furnished. It looked comfortable enough as she entered. Candles were lighted on the toilet-table, a big, blazing fire crackled up the chimney, and threw a lurid light on the figure of a girl kneeling on the hearthrug, with her head buried in Mab's easy-chair.

"Why, Kathleen, what is it?" cried Mab in wonder, for muffled sobs seemed to come from out the cushions of the chair.

Kathleen's pretty, pouting face was all red and tear-stained, as she jumped up from her knees to answer her young mistress's questions.

"Oh, it's nothing—nothing—nothing—Miss Mab," she cried, vehemently, finding occupation meantime for her fingers in making up the fire, getting out brushes, lighting superfluous candles.

"But there must be something to make you sob like that," insisted Mab, going to the girl, and laying her hands kindly on her shoulder. "Come, tell me; I may be able to help you."

Kathleen stood still, with the match-box in her hand. She did not like to say that her tears arose from the fact that Ned had given her another terrible scolding, and had vowed he would have nothing more to do with her to the end of her life, unless she kept her promise and married Brian O'Shea. No, that would not do at all; disagreeable cross-questioning might follow.

"It's about Ned, Miss Mab," she answered, steadying her voice, but not looking Mab in the face; "he has changed so lately. He's in with a lot of people who are no good at all to him, and he'll end with getting into the hands of the police, I'm afraid."

"Ah—h! Do you know the names of any of these people?" asked Mab, recollecting her unexpected meeting with Ned that morning on John Johnson the plasterer's door-step.

"Oh! there are ever so many. Miss Mab, all Fenians or Nationalists. A bad set they are," answered Kathleen, still busying herself at the toilet-table.

Mab sighed. Thoughts came in a rush to her mind. After all the time, all the thought she had bestowed on this man, it was pitiful to think that he should thus determine to rush headlong to ruin. What could be goading him on to such mad folly? Here there came a conscious flush to her face, a stab of pain at her heart.

She knew his secret it would have been folly to pretend even to herself that she did not. What if, instead of being the good angel she had intended to be to him, she had been his evil one, and had darkened and cursed his life for him! What if it were his desperate love for her that was driving him to throw his life away in this reckless fashion? Could she do nothing, absolutely nothing, to save him?

She clasped her hands together and sank into the chair into which Kathleen had wept out her sorrows.

"Leave me, Kathleen; put out every light in the room. I want to think," she said, leaning back in her chair and covering her eyes with her clasped hands.

Kathleen did as she was bidden. At the door of the room she paused giving one backward look at her young mistress. It seem to her that she had suddenly fallen into a sweet, sound sleep.

For one instant the two men in the drawing-room below faced each other.

"Is this intended for an insult?" asked Captain Buckingham, his boots almost touching Frank's, their eyes on a level.

"You may take it so, if you like," answered Frank, carelessly turning on his heel, and with a look on his face that has ere this cost a man his life.

"The place is not convenient, or—" began Buckingham, but broke off abruptly. He made a moment as if about to pull out his watch, but checked himself. "I leave here at one—"

Frank's temper broke its bounds now.

"Do you want to know what time it is?" he said, his low, strained tones showing that he was at white heat. "It's a question, I believe, you are rather fond of asking. Well, I will tell you: time to give adventurers and conspirators a word of warning, and, if they don't take it, to hand them over to be dealt with by the law."

His temper had fairly vanquished his common-sense, or he would never have spoken such words as these. The instant they were out of his lips, common-sense asserting itself told him he had as good as sounded a reveillé in the man's ears which would give him and his possible confederates the start of the police, and render their detection and capture proportionately difficult.

Captain Buckingham, to all appearance, left him master of the situation. He grew ashen white, his eyes flashed.

CATHERINE LOUISA PIRKIS

"You may find another answer given to the question before long," he said, in a tone so low that the elderly dowager who stood at his elbow gesticulating to Frank for her ice did not hear a syllable.

Then he made straight for the door, and the sound of the front door closing a minute after told Frank he had quitted the house.

"What a consummate fool I've made of myself!" thought Frank. "I had better find Morton, and confess to him at once."

But though he hunted high and low for the man, and questioned every servant he came upon as to his whereabouts, he could not light upon him. He had disappeared, possibly to report to Scotland Yard certain proceedings which had excited his suspicions, or—Frank could only hope so—it might be that he had departed on the traces of Captain Buckingham.

Frank stood thoughtfully for a moment at the head of the stairs, just outside the music-room door. What had he better do? Slip away quietly, take a cab to Scotland Yard, and find out how much mischief it was likely his hot temper had wrought? He took out his watch; the hands pointed to a quarter to one. People would soon be leaving now; his absence would not be noted. He had better possibly frame some word of excuse to Joyce.

There was she radiant still, just within the music-room, which had for the evening been converted into a show-room for the brilliant silver and jewelry, which had been presented to her under the guise of wedding-presents.

Her clear, joyous tones came to him over the heads of the guests pressing in or out of the room.

"Now, this is the treasure cave, you must say your 'open sesame' before I let you in. This is it—'Joyce, my dear, I think you're the happiest girl alive.'"

With red lips parted, cheeks flushing, eyes brilliant, bright hair gleaming in rivalry with the jewels that crowned it, the long trailing white robe throwing all into bold relief, no artist who ever held pencil would have scorned Joyce Shenstone that night as the impersonation of his ideal Hebe.

She caught a glimpse of Frank as he paused irresolutely outside, and whispered the hurried question:

"Have you seen Mab anywhere? She has not been near me all the evening."

Frank's answer was intercepted by the appearance of Mab herself, descending the staircase from the upper floor. She still had on the Indian shawl which Captain Buckingham had wrapped around her. Her face was white as before, her eyes looked fixed and unseeing.

Joyce made sure she would come straight into the music-room for a passing word, and drew back a little into the room to make way for her. To her surprise she passed on and down the second flight of stairs. People were beginning to depart; a stream soon flowed in between Joyce, Frank, and the staircase. A sudden terror seized Joyce. She caught at Frank's arm.

"Oh, follow her; what is she going to do?" she whispered, for the look on Mab's face had fallen like a chill shadow upon her.

It was easy to say, "follow her;" a bird's wings over the heads of the departing guests might have done it easily enough. Nothing else.

Frank dived in and out, with and against the stream, as best he could. He got somehow to the drawing-room, had a tolerably fair view of it, thanks to two inches more of stature than most of the people there owned to. Mab was not there. Sylvia Buckingham was standing in her dark dress at Mrs. Shenstone's elbow, and that lady, looking a little tired and jaded in her blush-rose garments, serenely smiled her good-bys to her departing guests.

On to the dining-room, thence to the supper-room, Frank went. Not a sign of Mab anywhere. Thence out into the hall, on to the doorstep even, where stood a crowd of great-coated footmen, waiting for their respective masters and mistresses.

"Are you looking for any one, sir?" asked one of these, seeing "where has she gone?" plainly written on Frank's face. "A lady in an Indian shawl came out five minutes ago. We thought she was making for one of the carriages, but she passed them all and took the first turning to the right.

Mechanically Frank took a hat, which some thoughtful hand held out to him, and dashed out into the darkness. The bright, fitful lamps of the line of carriages, which reached from the door to the corner of the square, made patches of shifting light on the damp pavement. Beyond the line the dingy vista of the street which ran off the square showed dimly through the gloom. Down the turning the man had indicated Frank went at the top of his speed. It seemed to him, as he turned the corner, that a figure resembling Mab's disappeared at the further end. Faster and faster flew his feet over the ground. This by-street leading down to the river was deserted and silent. A crawling cab, two slip-shod girls, a belated street-minstrel were the only representatives of the bustling life which tided along the wider thoroughfare.

He turned sharply round the narrow street where it seemed to him Mab had disappeared. A gas-lamp at the corner of an alley leading off the street lighted up a gleam of gold in the shawl of a small figure which passed swiftly beneath it. Frank was running now, and, almost breathless, he gained the corner of this alley to see Mab, or, at any rate, a small, dark figure that might be Mab, standing on a door-step at the farther end.

Either the door must have been innocent of bolt or bar, or some one from within must have opened it, for Frank, to his dismay, saw it swing back on its hinges, and the small, dark figure disappear.

"Mab! Mab!" he shouted, frantically, and the dark, empty street and deserted-looking houses threw back his cry at him in hollow, mocking tones.

The whole thing seemed to him like some hideous nightmare, in which, against his will, he had been suddenly forced to bear a part, side by side with dream creatures, amid dream surroundings.

"What, in Heaven's name, is she bent upon?" he asked himself, desperately, as he gained the doorstep and pushed back the door through which the girl had disappeared.

He found himself in a narrow, dark passage with a door at the farther end, from beneath which struggled a yellow gleam of light.

There was Mab in front of him sure enough; there was also a man who had seized her by the arms, and was saying, in loud, rough tones:

"How now, young woman! What's your game, I should like to know?"

"Let her go!" shouted Frank, with all the breath that was left in his body.

"Who are you?" began the man, still holding Mab fast, for her aim was evidently to pass by him into the room beyond.

Frank had not learned boxing for nothing. One well-directed blow sent the man reeling backward, and crash he fell, bursting open the door of the room whence the light streamed. There came a sudden hubbub of voices from a table at which three men were seated. One sprang forward and seized Mab, dragging her toward the door of the house. It was Ned Donovan. Frank was surrounded, the light on the table was put out, but not before he had time to recognize Captain Buckingham's dark face and broad shoulders. He felt himself seized from behind, there came a heavy blow on the back of his head, then all was darkness and silence to him.

XIX

The slowly-breaking dawn of the winter's day that was to have heard the wedding-bells of Joyce Shenstone, found her standing beside Mab as she lay on her bed, chafing her hands, bathing her ice-cold forehead, trying to force wine between her colorless lips.

Mab had been brought back to the house, about half an hour after she had quitted it, in a cab. The cabman had stated that he was on his way to Mrs. Shenstone's house, on the chance of picking up a fare, when a man standing with the lady at the corner of a bystreet had hailed him, telling him the lady's address and bidding him drive carefully. The lady appeared to be in a half-fainting condition, and had to be almost lifted into the cab.

She had altogether fainted when they opened the cab door, and had had to be carried up the stairs to her own room. There she lay inert, lifeless, on her bed, her features, ashen gray against her white pillows, mocked by the glister of the jewels which still hung about her brown plaits and sparkled on her arms.

Joyce's face was only by one degree less deathlike in its pallor as she bent over her. It was by many degrees more anxious and bewildered. Wonder and anxiety halved her heart between them. By-and-by Mab might awaken to both, but for the nonce blessed unconsciousness held her.

Joyce had at first, naturally enough, imagined that the man who had called the cab and lifted Mab into it must have been Frank, and had, also naturally enough, wondered greatly why he had not jumped into it after her, and himself brought her safely home.

A few questions addressed by Uncle Archie to the cabman quickly proved the surmise incorrect.

"Did the gentleman give any reason for not driving home with the young lady?" he asked.

The man answered, with a knowing look:

"He wasn't a gentleman, nohow, sir. Whatever he was, he wasn't that It was too dark to see what his face was like, or what his clothes were either. But I haven't druv a cab for fifteen years not to know a gentleman's 'hi' from a workingman's 'hi.'"

The speech wanted translating. Uncle Archie was at first inclined to believe that the organ of sight was referred to. Little by little, however, the man's meaning made itself plain to him. The old gentleman grew suddenly abrupt and abstracted. He gave short, sharp answers to Joyce, bidding her be off and look after Mab, and not bother him. Then he dispatched one of the servants to Frank's rooms to see if he had returned there, another to the nearest police-station to request the immediate attendance of the superintendent.

The candles had burned low, the gray dawn had deepened into the dun yellow of a London sky before the faintest sign of returning life showed in Mab's face. Her heavy lids lifted a moment, drooped again, lifted once more, and the deep, wondering eyes fixed themselves on Joyce's face.

"Joyce, tell me what has happened," she whispered, faintly.

But the doctor interposed. He would not have so much as a word exchanged between the sisters till half an hour of rest had intervened, till tonics or food had been taken, and the patient's recovery assured.

So Joyce had to endure half an hour of bewildering suspense with the unanswered question, "Where is Frank? what occurred to separate you two?" held back with difficulty, and her sense of hearing straining to its utmost limit to detect the sound of Frank's ring at the door, his step on the stairs.

When at length the weary half-hour had counted out its thirtieth minute, and Mab, still with that white, puzzled look on her face, had repeated the request, "Joyce, Joyce, tell me what has happened," Joyce met it with the counter-question, "Mab, darling, tell me, first of all, what has become of Frank? Where did he and you separate?"

Mab stared blankly.

"Frank! Frank!" she repeated, "I have not been with him, have not seen him ever since—since—" here she broke off, putting her hand to her head as though the effort to think pained her—"since the night of the party, that was, oh! I don't know how long ago."

At this moment the doctor was summoned by a message from Uncle Archie to attend on Mrs. Shenstone, who had been running the gamut from hysterics to swoons, and back from swoons to hysterics for the past hour and a half.

Joyce, left alone with Mab, did her best to help her collect her scattered senses.

"Yes, dear, the party was last night, you know. You left the drawing-room rather suddenly. Kathleen says you went up to your room and fell asleep in your easy-chair. After a time you came down again, and—"

A sudden gleam of renewed recollection swept over Mab's face. She caught eagerly at Joyce's hand.

"Did he come back with me—Ned Donovan, I mean?" she asked, excitedly.

"No one came back with you, dear, not even Frank, who followed you out of the house to look after you. Where did you go, Mab? Try and think. We are all anxiety to send and inquire about Frank, whether he has met with an accident, or what has detained him."

Again Mab's hand went to her head.

"Joyce, I will try to tell you everything; but so much is misty to me I don't know how to get hold of it. I came up-stairs; yes, I remember, and found Kathleen sobbing because Ned had joined some dreadful secret society. I thought I would try to get him to give it up, and I sat down in my chair to think how I could best get hold of him. He always used to listen to me, you know, when his father could do nothing with him—"

"Go on, dear; you sat down in your chair."

"Yes." Here Mab grew painfully confused, and her words began to halt. "I sat down in my chair; I don't know how to tell you—you wouldn't understand, Joyce."

"You fell asleep, dear."

"Ye—es, you would think it sleep, I daresay, and I don't know indeed where sleep ended, and—and vision began—"

"Mab!"

"It's true, I can't help it—it's true. I saw—yes, I saw, but I could hear nothing. I saw Ned Donovan going up the steps of a house outside of which I had seen him in the morning. I saw him seat himself at a table with two other men, but who they were I did not know. And I thought 'That is their secret place of meeting—that is where their wicked plots are laid. Ned must shake himself free of them at once.' But, after this, everything is confusion to me. Whether I went really and tried to make him leave the house, or whether I think I did and only fainted on the bed, I have not the vaguest idea."

Joyce's bewilderment vanished now, swamped in an agony of apprehension for Frank's safety, in what might prove to be a nest of Irish conspirators.

"You know the house, darling, outside which you saw Ned Donovan yesterday morning!" she cried, breathlessly, trying to piece together Mab's facts, so oddly coherent in their incoherence, that they recalled the "stuff that dreams are made off."

"Yes, I know the house," answered Mab; "but I can't tell you the name of the street or the number of the house. I could take you to it easily. Give me your hand, Joyce; help me to get up at once."

But the mere effort to lift her head from her pillows threw her back into heavy, death-like unconsciousness once more.

XX

Silence and darkness seemed to fall upon the house that day. In the early morning the wind had sharply changed to the north; the heavy rain-clouds came down in soft, sleepily-floating snow. It heaped itself on the door-ways and window-ledges; it put distance between the street-voices and Mrs. Shenstone's warm, yet, withal, desolate rooms. For all the world it seemed to Joyce like the day of a funeral—the day on which one sees carried out of the house all that one holds most precious in life, coffined and ready for burial. From room to room she wandered restlessly. Now she would be bending over Mab, anon she would make her way into the library to consult Uncle Archie as to what was next to be done, or would stand staring blankly from the drawing-room windows at the rapidly-whitening streets. That soft, sleepily-whirling snow cut a notch in her memory sharper than any that graver's tool could have made. In after years Joyce never saw a snow-cloud thickening and rounding in a dun sky without a shudder.

Uncle Archie, although he had quickly enough communicated with the police, expressed his opinion stoutly and loudly that Frank would "turn up right enough before the day was over."

Mr. Morton, the solemn-looking detective, with large, expressive eyes, small nose, and mouth with drawn-down corners, who had ladled the ices of over-night, responded promptly to Uncle Archie's summons. He was frank and communicative as to the undesirable circle of friends with which Mrs. Shenstone had surrounded herself.

"If she'd been O'Donovan Rossa himself she couldn't have made a better center for the dynamiters and Fenians. There's nearly a dozen of the fine ladies and gentlemen who were here last night we shall keep a strict eye on for the next twelve months or so," he said.

Uncle Archie alluded to the Buckinghams.

"Of course they're about the worst of the whole lot?" he queried.

Morton shook his head.

"We know all about that pair," he answered, knowingly. "Of course they're adventurers, and the sooner you get clear of them the better; but they're not the worst of the lot by a long way. He's the open, loud-mouthed Fenian, the sort of man who knows the police have their eye on him, and, though he swaggers a good deal, takes care to keep within the law. He has lived by his wits, one way or another, for the past fifteen years. He played the part of showman to that poor girl in Boston who died about seven years ago, through mesmerism or clairvoyance."

Uncle Archie grew scarlet. He pulled the bell furiously.

"And do you mean to say a man of that sort has been made free of the house, associating with my sister-in-law and nieces! he cried, the words coming out very like the gobble, gobble of a turkey cock.

Then he turned to give an order to the servant.

"Captain Buckingham is never again, under any pretext whatever, to be admitted to the house. I will explain to your mistress."

"I would advise discretion—prudence," began Morton.

"Confound your discretion and prudence, we've had too much of it already," interrupted the irate old gentleman.

"Captain Buckingham has called twice already to inquire after Miss Mab, sir," said the servant putting fuel on the fire.

"Impertinent scoundrel! If he calls again tell him your orders; and, if that doesn't send the sister flying out of the house after the brother in double-quick time, I don't know what will," he added, turning to Morton, who had crossed his knees, folded his hands complacently, and sat staring into the fire as though he meant to give himself up to a pleasant morning in Uncle Archie's society.

There was no need, however, to take any trouble about sending Sylvia "flying out of the house." Her boxes had been packed over-night, and she was at that very moment saying a characteristic good-by to Mrs. Shenstone in that lady's sitting-room.

Mrs. Shenstone, between her fainting-fits, reclined in a rocking-chair fanning herself with a big ostrich-feather fan.

"If I could think myself of any use to you, Tiny dearest, I wouldn't start today," Sylvia was saying, sweetly enough, though the curves of her mouth seemed invariably to give the lie to her sweet words. "As it is, however, I can not but feel myself in the way. Your daughter has given me plainly to understand she will be uncommonly glad to get rid of me."

It may be surmised that Sylvia had not chosen to read Joyce's manner until it suited her convenience so to do.

"Oh, Joyce is so peculiar. We are never of one mind in anything. Ah-h, my head. Give me my vinaigrette, darling."

Sylvia handed the vinaigrette.

"And you won't forget, dearest Tiny, what I told you about the distress of those poor people in Connemara—you know you promised me a hundred pounds for them, and I had your name entered on the subscription-list at once."

"Oh, did you? Well, I can't write a check today, my hand shakes so," and flutter, flutter went the fan, faster than ever.

"Ah, but you know you always keep a good deal of ready money in your davenport; it isn't locked. Look here, Tiny, here's your pocket-book stuffed."

But it was not stuffed when it went back to the davenport, and Sylvia's purse had proportionately increased in bulk.

Then there had followed showers of kisses, sobs, farewells between the two.

But Joyce, meeting Sylvia on the stairs ten minutes later, could not have detected the ghost of a tear on her cheek, even had she called a field-glass to her aid. Only the briefest and most formal of good-bys passed between these two.

"I hope you'll have good news before night; an interrupted wedding is so painful," Miss Buckingham said, on her way out through the hall.

"Thank you," was Joyce's cold reply, as she went into the library, where Morton and Uncle Archie were still in consultation.

"I don't mean to say that anything very terrible had been concocted in this house," Morton was saying, as she entered the room; "but, if our information is correct, a new branch to an old society, or a young society itself, has been organized at this lady's evening receptions. It appears to consist of a council of three and a small executive; but at present we know but little of its special aims and objects, and what we do know, my dear sir," this with the air of one who had grand professional secrets intrusted to his keeping, "you may be quite sure we shall not divulge till the right moment."

"H'm, one doesn't need to be told that dynamite is at the bottom of all these conspiracies."

"Or boycotting in Ireland on a systematic scale. You, my dear sir, as an outsider, will hardly credit the time, the thought, the funds that are expended to bring about some small piece of boycotting in a remote corner of Ireland—a thing we in London read in a ten-line paragraph in our morning's paper, and forget all about the next minute."

All this time Joyce had been standing listening. She broke silence now.

"Do you mean to say you think Mr. Ledyard has fallen into the hands of any of these people, these Fenians and dynamiters?" she cried, feeling that now the ghost of her fears had suddenly taken definite shape and confronted her.

Uncle Archie turned upon her sharply.

"I wish to Heaven, Joyce, you'd stay up-stairs and look after Mab and your mother, instead of coming fussing in here, interfering in matters that don't concern you."

"There is really no cause for anxiety," said Morton, with a grand air of superior knowledge; "we shall hear of Mr. Ledyard long before the day is over. We are in London, my dear young lady, not in St. Petersburg."

"And why on earth have you your hat and cloak on, Joyce?" broke in Uncle Archie again. "Whatever whim have you in your head now?"

"Mab is better, and has been able to describe minutely to me the house outside which she saw Ned Donovan yesterday, and where most likely she went last night. I can take you to it at once if you will come," was her reply, which sent the two men looking for their hats at once.

The alley of condemned houses was little more than a quarter of a mile from Mrs. Shenstone's door. A swift, silent tramp of about five minutes through the snowy streets brought the three face to face with the sign-board of "John Johnson, plasterer."

The house was the ordinary six-roomed house one sees so often in London back streets. It consisted of a parlor, with kitchen behind, and four upper rooms, two on each floor. It bore much the same neat appearance as it had yesterday, when Mab had rapped at its front door. Signs of life were nowhere, and Mr. Morton's repeated knockings brought no response, save hollow echoes from adown the deserted alley.

Uncle Archie turned to Joyce.

"Now, Joyce, you've shown us the way right enough, you had better turn back and go home as quickly as possible," he said, raspingly.

"I'm going in with you, Uncle Archie," answered Joyce, growing very white, but withal as calm as, or calmer than, the old gentleman himself.

"That you're not. Of all things in the world I detest to have a young woman for ever forcing herself where she's not wanted."

"Hush, dear, don't scold, I can't stand it today; but I am going in with you," answered Joyce, in a voice that silenced Uncle Archie at once.

"The door is too tight to force," said Morton. "I know the landlord of these shanties, I'll go and get the key from him—it's only a stone's-throw from here—and ask him a question or two as to Mr. John Johnson, plasterer."

Uncle Archie and Joyce paced the blind alley for a long ten minutes while Morton departed on his quest. Here the snow was fresh and crisp. There was nothing to attract the busy life that tided along the larger thoroughfare.

A few children with red, dirty faces loitered a moment or two at the corner to stare at the unwonted apparition of a lady and gentleman in these unaristocratic quarters; but it was too freezingly cold for any one to loiter long, and Uncle Archie and Joyce pursued their tramp, tramp over the snow uninterruptedly.

That ten minutes prolonged itself to as many hours to Joyce's imagination, which peopled the empty, silent house of "John Johnson" with all sorts of terrors. Traces of Frank they must find here, it seemed to her. Perhaps they had shut him up in some cellar or hiding-place; perhaps they had left him lying bleeding and dying on the floor. The houses began to swim before her eyes, the snow to dazzle her. Would the man never come back? It was growing beyond endurance.

"Uncle Archie, I know I could get in at that front window if you helped me up," she said, desperately, clutching at the old gentleman's arm.

Morton turned the corner of the street at that moment and saved Uncle Archie the necessity of a remonstrance.

He came along with a brisk tread, his nose very much in the air and a big bunch of keys dangling in his hand.

"One of these will be sure to fit, the landlord says," he said, as he began trying one of the biggest in the lock.

Joyce could scarcely keep back her impatience; her fingers were clenching into the palms of her hands beneath her fur cloak, her feet were scattering the crisp snow into ridges and pits as she stood waiting a step below Morton with his big bunch of keys.

He, good man, blandly sought to entertain them with scraps of information he had just picked up concerning "John Johnson," while his leisurely fingers tried the keys in succession.

"Dixon, that's the landlord of these houses, he keeps an oil and color shop round the corner, says John Johnson came to him about six weeks ago to hire this house, stating he had a job of work on near, and the place would suit him for the next three months. He paid three months rent in advance, which Dixon was uncommonly glad to get, as he had taken it for granted that after the houses had been condemned to be pulled down, no one would be likely to make an offer for any one of them. He says the man looked like a decent mechanic, but there was nothing remarkable in his appearance, and he shouldn't know him again if he saw him."

"Oh, I am confident that key must fit!" broke in Joyce, imploringly. "See, it is the exact size. Ah, thank Heaven!" she added, as the key creaked in the lock and the door turned on its hinges.

Naturally they went first into the little front parlor which opened off the passage on their right hand. Bare walls, an empty fire-grate, and thirteen feet by twelve of bare floor met their gaze. Nothing else.

Mr. Morton took out his note-book and pencil to report—that there was nothing to report.

Joyce's impatience refused to be longer restrained.

"While you are writing I will run up-stairs and look through the other rooms," she cried, half-way up the first flight. "Don't trouble to come up, Uncle Archie, unless I call."

In succession she opened and shut the doors of four desolately empty, cupboardless rooms.

She came down-stairs swiftly enough to find Uncle Archie and Morton entering the small kitchen which flanked the front parlor. This was closely shuttered and dark as night. Uncle Archie paused on the threshold, fearful of running the gauntlet of possible stumbling-blocks with that tender old right foot of his.

"Oh, I've cat's eyes, I can see where the window is!" cried Joyce.

She and Morton together contrived to unbar the shutters and let in the white, frosty daylight. It revealed three wooden chairs—one overturned—a common deal table, with a lantern upon it. Nothing beyond.

"Ah!" said Morton, giving a low whistle, and beginning to scribble again, "we're getting on their traces, are we!"

A door to the right of the window caught Joyce's eye. She opened it. The light from the larger room revealed an empty oblong of red-brick floor.

"This must be the wash-house of the establishment," said Morton, leading the way into the little out-building.

Joyce followed on his heels. Her eyes followed his too as they went piercing into every corner. There was not a splinter of furniture here nor anything to lead one to think that there had been a scuffle, or that a life-and-death struggle had been fought out on the red tiling. Not so much as a crushed button or tattered rag, and, thank Heaven, none of those dark, wine-red splashes which men of Morton's profession know only too well.

Joyce drew a long breath of relief. She had not yet reached that stage of misery when a terrible certainty is welcomed as a desperate ending to a still more terrible suspense.

Morton proceeded to lift the latch of a little door at the farther end of this out-building; of bolt or bar it knew nothing.

A dreary picture in black and white met their gaze. A small square of yard, covered with untrodden snow, bounded by a low wooden fence with many gaps in it. Beyond this fence lay a stonemason's yard with several out-buildings. A big board announced the fact that it was "to let." Its frontage looked on the river; its further side was bounded by a narrow canal; its rear found its limit in the high wall of a factory.

The blackish river, with the yellow fog settling down upon it, set Joyce shuddering.

"We must go through that fence, we must search all those out-buildings," she said, trying hard to keep her failing heart from showing in her voice.

"My dear young lady," said Morton, composedly, "it will all be done before night thoroughly, much better than you or I could do it. We'll have men in here to remove the snow, dig the yards up if need be—"

Joyce felt as if her wits were leaving her.

"Dig, dig for what?" she asked, vaguely, almost unmeaningly.

When ten minutes later, as they three went silently out into the snowy streets, she heard Uncle Archie give a husky order to Morton, "We must have the river dragged without delay," she had no voice wherewith to ask the question, "Dragged! for what?"

XXI

J oyce, why don't you curse me?" moaned Mab, as she and Joyce sat alone together in their sorrow and desolation. "It is my doing—all mine."

A month has passed since the day that was to have been Joyce's wedding-day. During that month Joyce has gone through every phase of passionate grief; in it she feels as if she had lived a lifetime twice told. She is older, she says to herself, now than her mother, than white-haired, placid Aunt Bell, even than that wrinkled, crooning old body she saw the other day at the window of an almshouse as she went by. Like the old face she saw at that window, she feels she has said good-by to all the bright young things of life, to all the hopes, pleasures, desires which used to set her eyes sparkling, her cheeks glowing. Only yesterday she found herself looking longingly at a widow's cap in a shop window. If only she could have had the right to wear it, how thankful she would have been! If only some grim churchyard could have held for her a stone with Frank's name upon it, she knows she could go down on her knees even now, thank God, and call herself a happy woman.

"Hush, Mab, you pain me when you say such things!" was her quiet reply to Mab's moan; and then the sisters, clasping hands, sat in silence once more.

Uncle Archie came in while they were thus sitting.

Uncle Archie had of late found his rasping, incisive manner difficult to keep up, toward Joyce at any rate. So he had dropped it, and spoke to her in soft, tender tones that came strangely from his cross old lips. Sometimes he would take her in his arms, and smooth her head and curly hair as he used to when she was a little child.

His manner cut Joyce to the heart. She could feel his wordless pity for her, just as he could feel her unspoken despair.

"Don't sit there moaning, with your hands before you, child," he said, as he came in, "or you'll drive me foolish."

"Uncle Archie, I am not moaning, I am trying to think—my hardest," was Joyce's reply.

The old gentleman shook his head sadly.

"That is what I am trying to do from morning till night; but, Heaven help me, I am at my wits' end now."

At their wits' end! that was where they all were just then. Everything that human intelligence could conceive, that labor or money could execute, had been done, and yet not the faintest trace of Frank, dead or alive, had they come upon. The river had been dragged, the canal likewise: they had yielded up their usual treasures of mud, old boots, and other rotting *débris*, but never a vestige of Frank or Frank's belongings.

Every police-station in the kingdom had been communicated with. Every newspaper held conspicuous advertisements, offering large rewards for his recovery, smaller rewards for the slightest intelligence of him.

But, though imaginary clews and false trails had been started by the score, not one of them came to anything, or answered any purpose under Heaven, save that of buoying Joyce's heart up with hope for a day or two, in order that she might the better afterward sound the depths of her despair.

Mr. Morton still informed everybody in grandiose fashion that "we are in London, sir, not in St. Petersburg." But, beyond full assurance of that fact, his acumen did not appear to extend. He had traced Ned Donovan down to his lodgings, questioned him, and also his landlady, closely as to his movements on the 20th of December. The statements of the two were in accord.

Ned stated that, on the afternoon of the 20th, he chanced to be passing at the end of the blind alley known as Brewer's Court, when he saw Miss Shenstone standing on the door-step of one of the houses. He did not consider that it was a neighborhood for a young lady to be waiting about in alone, so he immediately turned the corner, and asked if he should fetch a cab for her, or see her to her home. On the night of the 20th, returning late from the house of a friend at Battersea, Bryan O'Shea, he saw, to his great surprise, Miss Shenstone in evening-dress, standing at the corner of a street leading into Eaton Square, She appeared to be in a half-fainting condition. He immediately hailed a cab that was coming in sight, placed her in it, and directed the driver where to take her. Of Mr. Ledyard he had seen nothing.

This statement, in effect, he repeated calmly and unhesitatingly to Uncle Archie and Joyce, and no cross-fire of questioning on their part could induce him to swerve from it.

The explanation seemed straightforward enough. At any rate, no testimony was forthcoming to controvert it. There was really no charge to be preferred against the man; no excuse, whatever, as

Morton explained to Uncle Archie, for taking him into custody. There was nothing, so far as appearances went, to connect him in any way with Frank Ledyard's disappearance. Furthermore, even supposing that Ned were in some post connected with possible Fenian meetings held in the suspected house, there was no proof whatever that Frank had so much as crossed its threshold. The last authentic information they had of the missing man was that he had turned the corner of the square in pursuit of Mab. After that everything was dubious.

Morton had cross-questioned to his heart's content every member of Mrs. Shenstone's household in succession. To Mrs. Shenstone he had devoted a scanty five minutes, had shrugged his shoulders, and got out of the room with speed, although the lady could very easily have entertained him for half a day with her tags and rags of reminiscences of passing events. To Mab he had given a long hour, and left her convinced that she had gone at least three parts of the road to a lunatic asylum. To Kathleen, the pretty waiting-maid, off and on he had devoted a good deal of attention, in fact, had seemed to take an especial pleasure in her society.

Uncle Archie had bewildered the police authorities generally by the forcible fashion in which he had insisted that Ned, the Buckinghams, or at any rate somebody somewhere should be taken up and prosecuted.

"You don't treat my opinions with common respect," he had informed Morton, hotly. "You simply ignore my suggestions, just as if I were some irritable, unreasonable old man, with gigantic prejudices, who didn't know what he was talking about."

Morton's eyes had showed a passing twinkle.

"Well, sir, you see we've no case against any one of the parties you name," he had tried to explain.

"Get your case, then. Whose business is it, if it isn't yours?"

"Now, there are the Buckinghams. We know they are a pair of adventurers, but at present they've done nothing to bring the law upon them."

"The man writes inflammatory articles for the Irish press. Isn't that enough to bring the law upon him?"

Morton had shaken his head.

"Those aren't the dangerous ones, sir. English law very wisely lets the loud-mouthed democrat alone. He makes a center, so to speak, for the dangerous ones to congregate to. Let him alone, and we know where to find them, and can put our hands upon them at any moment."

"Yes, but you don't put your hands upon them at any moment."

"We give them rope enough, sir, and they hang themselves." Here Uncle Archie had jumped up boiling over.

"Confound you," he cried, "I'll take your word for it. If they do get hanged it isn't you they'll have to thank for it." And Morton bad very wisely bowed himself out of the room.

Mrs. Shenstone had characteristically comported herself as the one on whom the household sorrow had fallen heaviest.

"Look at me, Joyce; I look ten years older," she had said, when her sobs and hysterics had died of a severe cold and sore throat, which did duty for them fairly well.

"Oh, mother, what do looks matter?" Joyce had replied, wearily, shrinking from her mother as she never shrunk from her before.

"And Joyce—oh, don't be in such a hurry to run away from me, child—I really think we ought, every one of us, to put on half-mourning—gray and black or gray and white. You see, if poor Frank isn't dead, something dreadful must have happened—Dear me! She's gone out of the room. How extraordinary! I meant it kindly, too."

So Mrs. Shenstone, in becoming gray and black *toilettes*, had sat in her drawing-room every afternoon receiving condoling visitors by the score, telling everybody what an awful blow she had sustained, how fond she had always been of Frank Ledyard, and how she had been looking forward to Joyce's wedding-day as the one, bright spot in her own very clouded and troubled career.

With evident enjoyment she would retail to Uncle Archie, Mab, Joyce, any one who would listen, the remarks of the said sympathetic visitors in response to her confidences. She seemed to think whenever Mab, Joyce, Aunt Bell, or Uncle Archie got together for a quiet five minutes that they were bent on excluding her from their conference. The idea ruffled her temper at times, sent her to hunt them up, and generally rout them out of their peaceable corners whenever there came a lull in the whirl of her afternoon callers.

On the very afternoon that Uncle Archie had confessed himself to his nieces to be at his wits' end, she swooped down upon them with capacity for a good half-hour's grumble plainly written on her face, and an open letter in her hand.

"Nobody comes to me now, saying: 'Mother dear, who are your letters from this morning?'"—here she looked at Joyce. "Nobody ever says to me now: 'Mother dear, let me answer your letters for you; I know you detest pen and ink'"—here she looked at Mab.

"Mother dear, who is your letter from?" asked Joyce, mechanically, feeling that the sooner she went through the expected formula the sooner she would be allowed to get back to her somber thoughts again.

Mrs. Shenstone's voice changed from plaint to pleasure.

"Well, dear, since you ask, it's from Sylvia Buckingham, telling me how glad the poor people at Lough Lea are to get the money I've sent her from time to time."

"Heavens and earth, ma'am!" cried Uncle Archie, jumping up in a towering rage, "you don't mean to say you are keeping up a correspondence with that wretched woman?" he began.

Joyce laid her finger on his lips.

"Oh! pray, pray don't make a scene, Uncle Archie," she whispered, with something of a shudder, for her nerves were not what they had been a month ago.

Mab intervened with the question:

"Where does she write from, mother?"

"From the Abbey House, Lough Lea," answered Mrs. Shenstone, looking down at her letter. Here Mab abruptly left the room—"And," the lady went on, in a voice that suggested approaching showers, "she sends all sorts of kind messages to all of you. To Joyce especially, she says, 'She never pitied any one more in her life, and she hopes your brain won't give way under it all.' There, that is what 'the wretched woman' says."

And all this in spite of Uncle Archie's thunderous frown, which most women would have felt at a dozen yards' distance.

But one might just as well have leveled a frown at a parrot or a butterfly as at Mrs. Shenstone.

XXII

M ab went straight up-stairs to her own room, and wrote down Sylvia Buckingham's address on a scrap of paper.

She was in a complex and miserable state of mind just then. She credited herself, and herself only, from first to last with all the sorrow that had of late visited the household—with Ned Donovan's reckless career, which incidentally it seemed might be laid to her charge; with whatever of mischance had befallen Frank in his endeavor to follow her unconscious footsteps. Worst of all was the fact that she did not see one single thing she could do to remedy the evil she had indirectly wrought.

"It was all very well," her sad thoughts ran, "for her to be saying to Joyce from morning till night, 'My darling, I would lay down my life to get back your happiness.' Her life laid down a thousand times over would do nothing for anybody, so far as she could see."

She threw herself into a chair, and covered her face with her hands, as though she meant to give herself up to steady, concentrated thought.

But Mab's thoughts as a rule were the reverse of steady or concentrated. One half at least of her brain-work was done unconsciously. Her best ideas came to her suddenly, disconnectedly. Seemingly, they were what people are pleased to call "inspirations"; in reality they were the definite product of unconscious cerebration.

Of late—notably since her careful perusal of Marie St. Clair's autobiography—she had become cognizant of the fact that, when her bodily powers seemed inert and drowsy, her brain was working its hardest and best. She did not fight against the idea. To say truth, to admit it and act upon it, seemed to her one step—the first possibly— toward the perfect attainment of the habit of clairvoyante trance which she was cultivating with such evil effect. Where other people would put their hands to their foreheads—as Joyce so often did now—and try to think their hardest, Mab would simply shut her eyes, nurse her drowsiness, make herself as nearly as possible a blank. Then, when renewal of bodily energy told her that her brain was craving its turn for rest, she would jump to her feet, seize her thoughts as they presented themselves, taking it for granted that they were the brightest and best she was capable of.

Half an hour's dreamy quiet in her chair left her with a suggestion which, from its mischievous malevolence, might have come straight from the Prince of Darkness, viz., why not write to Captain Buckingham, craving his assistance on a matter wherein it seemed permissible to think he had power to help her? Sylvia's letter to her mother had in the first instance suggested the idea, her half-hour of dreamy inertion left it paramount and irresistible.

She had surmised the possible enmity that existed between Buckingham and Frank, careful though the two men had been to conceal it in her presence. But it seemed to her that all enmities must die before the terrible sorrow that overwhelmed them now. She knew that of late, for some unexplained reason, her mother's interest had cooled toward Buckingham, that Uncle Archie had for bidden him the house, and was constantly alluding to him as "that scoundrelly American adventurer."

Neither fact counted for much. No one had ever laid stress upon Mrs. Shenstone's weather-like changes of taste, nor upon the blustering of old Uncle Archie, who was in the habit of consigning large portions of the human race from time to time to condemnation for comparatively light offenses. Her own repugnance to the man had died utterly, nay, rather had been pushed out of existence by an opposite feeling, which, as time went on, was rapidly gaining in strength.

In justice, however, to Mab, it must be said that no thought of self was in her mind when she took up her pen to write the letter on which she had resolved.

Never before, it seemed to her, had that pen had so difficult a task set it. There was so much ground to go over, and it had to be trodden so lightly if she did not wish to flounder in the mud.

It is not easy to tell a man in one breath that you know he hates a certain person, and in the next bespeak his help for that person. Also, her whole appeal for help was based upon a supposition she had no apparent right to form, the supposition that Buckingham was one way or another connected with those secret societies with which she had but little doubt Ned had linked himself.

Her letter took hours to write. When finished, it was scarcely the one she had planned. Somehow her pen, once set going, seemed to run away with her fingers, and brought in another and distinct theme, which a firmer hand would have kept in the background.

Mab was not a brilliant letter-writer; she lacked Joyce's power of terse idiomatic expression. Her written, like her spoken, sentences were given to halting and mistiness. She generally picked up her subject in its middle, and let it slip through her fingers before her correspondent could well get hold of it.

"You know our sorrow here," she wrote; "nowhere do we see a door of hope. My own fears, I confess, point all in one direction—a direction concerning which I would like to ask of you advice and assistance. Do you know—have you heard—the history of that terrible night of the 20th of December? How that with sealed senses I went wandering out into the dark streets, seeking for one who I feared had joined a gang of conspirators. How I went straight to a house that was probably used as a meeting-place for a secret society; how that some man there seized me by the arm, another lifted me out of the house, and after that all became darkness and confusion to me till I awoke to find myself lying on my own bed. Thoughts crowd into my brain as I write." This was where her pen began to wander. "You, who have taught me to claim as my birthright a power not granted to the generality of mankind, will you not also help me to make use of it now in our great extremity? You told me the last time I saw you—on the night of the terrible 20th December—that I had a gift which might be lacking to the angels of God. But, alas! what avails such a gift if I know not how to make good use of it? I followed implicitly your directions, similar, I suppose, to those you gave to Marie St. Clair. I have attained, in some measure, to the power of trance at will as she did, though not to the like extent. With her, however, the result was clairvoyance in its highest, purest form; with me it has been a mischievous sort of somnambulism which has brought misery upon those I love best in the world. I want the higher, better gift. I do not care what trouble, labor, self-denial I practice, so long as I attain it. And quickly, too, for it seems to me I might exercise it now for the lightening, if nothing more, of the terrible suspense which hangs over our home. You have helped me so far on my road; will you not help me to take yet another step?"

Though she shook her head over her letter, she at once sent it inclosed under cover to Sylvia Buckingham, feeling it was not in her to write a better.

Nearly a week passed before she received any reply. Then it came, dated from a London hotel, and ran as follows:

Dear Miss Shenstone:
  "You pay me a very great compliment in consulting me in the trouble that has befallen your family. Assuredly I can

help you in the way you wish, and assuredly I will do so. But I must see you. Your letter covers too much ground for me to go over in a sheet of note-paper. Your door is, for reasons with which I am unacquainted, closed against me, but I am glad to say there are other houses in London where I am always a welcome guest. Mrs. O'Halloran's is one of these, and she is good enough to place her drawing-room always at my disposal for receiving the ladies I have the privilege of counting among my friends.

"She is a friend of your mother's, and a most estimable person. Any time, any day, you may like to appoint, I will meet you at her house with a great deal of pleasure.

I remain, very sincerely, yours,

G. R. BUCKINGHAM

XXIII

Captain Buckingham stood, with his watch in his hand, at Mrs. O'Halloran's drawing-room window, in a tolerably contented frame of mind.

For to this man, in the midst of his storm-tossed adventurous course, there had seemed to come land in sight, and the promise of a haven at last.

His career had been a chequered one from boyhood till the verge of his fortieth year—his standpoint now. His father's course in some sort had determined his. A beggared Buckinghamshire farmer, he had crossed the Atlantic with his son and daughter, the only survivors of a large family. In succession he attempted a variety of callings, failed in all, and died in middle life, bankrupt once more, leaving his two children, George at twenty, Sylvia at ten, with his large ambitions and roving tastes for sole legacy.

George's thirst for notoriety and love of adventure drove him into the ranks of the Northern army, then at war with the South. Prior to this, however, he had dropped his English patronymic, adopted the name of his county for surname, and become a naturalized American subject. One or two brilliantly brave things he did during the campaign, for the man had plenty of animal courage; also one or two detestably brutal things, for his moral nature was about on a par with that of a stoat or weasel. Under the latter head must be classed his elopement with the daughter of a rich Southern planter, and his abandonment of her afterward, when he found that the family estates had been confiscated. She, poor child, died broken-hearted within a year of the marriage. Nemesis fell asleep, and George Buckingham heard no more of his girl-wife.

Soon after this, traveling through Boston, chance threw him across the path of Marie St. Clair, then an assistant in a glover's shop. He speedily detected in her the hyper-sensitive organism which lays its possessor at the mercy of the mesmerist.

Mesmerism and clairvoyance just then chanced to be the rage in Boston. In this girl, duly trained and "developed," he saw the prospect of a good income. Toward her he played the part of a gentleman Barnum, with a fair amount of pecuniary success, When eventually the girl's health and intellect collapsed, under the artificial conditions of life imposed upon her, his biography of her, written with the occasional help of her pen, brought him in dollars enough to start him on a new career.

He had left Sylvia a child, in New York, living as an adopted daughter with some homely tradespeople. He returned thither to find her grown into an attractive young woman, the center of a second-rate and somewhat fast set. Her ambition had probably kept her clear of perils that would have wrecked a weaker woman. This set numbered among its members not a few loud-voiced ultra-Democrats, and George Buckingham at once took up the *rôle* of scribe to them, for which a ready pen qualified him.

Among sparrows a chaffinch is a brilliant bird. Buckingham soon became king of his coterie, and, wielding a certain amount of power, attracted the attention of a political society connected with the Irish Nationalistic movement. He was speedily enrolled first a member of the executive, subsequently a member of temporary councils appointed for specific purposes. With a purse frequently at a low ebb, and principles on a par, he was precisely the man to have dangerous or difficult enterprises entrusted to him. In Sylvia he found a willing coadjutor. A capable one also.

Her qualifications for the work she undertook were wariness, a quick eye for character, and the weak side of human nature, a good manner, a clever tongue, a capability for adhering to the letter of given orders.

The brother's stock-in-trade consisted of an infinite audacity, a love of adventures with a spice of danger in them, and a strong sympathy with the rowdy side of everything, Republicanism included.

All successful villainy is more or less based on the sanguine assumption that the unit is swamped in the million. Captain Buckingham, when he endeavored to combine with his political work in England the equally interesting task of finding a wealthy bride for himself, must have taken it for granted that his early career had been outshone, and consequently thrown into oblivion, by the careers of more brilliant adventurers. And this notion Mab's eccentric conduct at the moment assuredly tended to confirm.

XXIV

No, Aunt Bell," Joyce had said, in response to the kind old lady's sobs and kisses, "it won't kill me, I'm too strong and healthy. I shall most likely live on for another forty years."

It was not said hysterically, passionately, between outbursts of wailing and tears, but quietly, assuredly, as a simple statement of a simple fact.

It was none the less pathetic. St. Simeon Stylites, "a sign betwixt the meadow and the cloud," as he looked up at the keen bright stars in the frosty night sky, might have said the same words in much such a tone. Possibly the cellar walls of the old Bastille echoed to them times without number.

Yet hope dies hard in young hearts. On the slightest of diets it nourishes a tough, strong life. In Joyce's heart it kept itself alive on nothing at all, for weeks and months after it had died in every one else's.

It was all very well for her to say to herself night and morning, as she did: "My darling, I know nothing but death would keep you from me." She never turned the corner of a street without her head turning right and left, seeking, inquiring, expecting; never heard the postman's knock without a throb at her heart lest a line of news of Frank might come in some letter; never bowed her knee in prayer without Frank's name being first and last on her lips."

The blank silence, the agony of never-lifted suspense, the comparatively enforced idleness at a moment when perhaps gigantic effort was needed were something awful to bear at times. It was not to be wondered at if Joyce looked, as her friends were in the habit of saying she looked just then, "the very ghost of herself."

What she had said to Aunt Bell in effect she kept repeating to herself, from the time she lifted her head wearily from her pillow in the morning, till she laid it there wearily at night.

She was just twenty-one years of age. There was nothing unreasonable in the supposition that she should live to be past sixty. That meant forty years more of a life which, if the choice had been given her, she would not have prolonged for as many days.

It meant long years of ceaseless, yet always futile effort, of agonized suspense, of a desperate clutching at phantom hopes till fingers were too weak or old to clutch at anything. It meant a heart vibrating to every passing rumor of calamity or mischance till, like a slackened stringed instrument, it lost power to vibrate at all.

Only physical incapacity in this world ever gets a day of its sentence remitted. Of physical incapacity Joyce knew nothing, so the weary treadmill of life went on for her. Petty cares, duties, annoyances had to be carried in addition to the weightier burdens. Business matters had to be discussed with Uncle Archie, in order to the proper management of the Gloucestershire estates; frivolities had to be entered into with Mrs. Shenstone. She had to be amused, played with, petted like any captious child, so as to be induced to remain contentedly in London instead of setting off to the Continent in search of new excitement and amusement, which of late she had seemed to consider a necessity to her health.

Beyond signing her checks, Mrs. Shenstone could not be persuaded to do anything in the way of business.

The check-signing, however, she performed with remarkable ease and pleasure. She would sit for ten minutes at a time gazing admiringly at her own signature.

"Ernestine Shenstone!" she would repeat, complacently. "I don't believe there's a prettier name to be found in the kingdom."

It had had to be broken very gently to her that her house had been made a rendezvous for members of Fenian and other associations. Even then the consequences were, to say the least, uncomfortable. Hysterics went on for half a day, all sorts of wild and foolish plans were propounded during the other half. She would put advertisements in all the newspapers, saying how she had been imposed upon by her friends; she would never, no, never, shake hands with an Irishman or an American again to the end of her life; never so much as enter a room where one was seated. She would call at every police-station in London, and put herself and her family under the protection of the police; that is to say, if she were compelled—here she threw a bitterly reproachful look at Uncle Archie and Joyce—to stay on in this terrible city of dynamite and conspiracies, when she would give worlds—yes, worlds—to be in lively, delightful Paris, beautiful Rome, or Florence.

The only course with any approach to wisdom in it, which the lady at this time decided upon was at once and forever to drop her correspondence with Sylvia Buckingham. But even this, so far at least as Mab was concerned, was a shutting of the stable-door too late to save the mare.

The immediate result of the cessation of those weekly big packets between Sylvia and Mrs. Shenstone, was to send the latter once more to Joyce with her confidences and cravings for sympathy.

CATHERINE LOUISA PIRKIS

"Mine is a clinging, dependent nature," she would say. "Sympathy I must have or I shall die. Come up-stairs, Joyce, to my room, and help me to read and answer my letters."

A revelation to Joyce's astonished brain was to follow the reading and answering of these letters. Her mother was developing into that pitiable specimen of womanhood, the middle-aged flirt.

In Sylvia Buckingham's sympathy with these ridiculous flirtations had possibly lain the secret of her influence over Mrs. Shenstone; also they afforded a ready explanation of the lady's easy indifference to the transfer of Captain Buckingham's attentions from herself to Mab.

Joyce in the old days would have scented the fun of the whole thing, seen naught but the humorous side of it, and would have given her mother no rest until she had made her, to some extent, see it also. She would have caricatured (verbally) every one of the lady's admirers, hit off their weak points with a fine pencil, emphasizing likeness by exaggerating it. Today, however, she had no heart for such doings. Everything in life seemed to her now to have more of pathos than of fun in it.

To think that her mother, after twenty years of dignified married life with such a man as her father, should condescend to listen to the inanities of some juvenile subaltern, or the platitudes of an ancient club *habitué*, seemed pitiful to the last degree.

"Mother, is it possible?" she cried, in her indignation, letting fall to the ground a letter from an elderly general who addressed Mrs. Shenstone as "my dear child" once or twice in the course of his brief epistle, and paid her a succession of those high-flown compliments which, with elderly gentlemen of a past generation, were the coin current in their intercourse with women.

"Is what possible, Joyce?" asked Mrs. Shenstone, in that much aggrieved tone in which she generally rebuffed her daughter's rebukes. "Do you mean, 'Is it possible' for a gentleman with eyes in his head to see that my hands are white and slender? or, having ears to hear with, to discover that my voice is like Cordelia's, soft, gentle, and low?"

Joyce's voice was not like Cordelia's as she answered:

"Mother, is it possible that you don't know when you are insulted? Why, even a child of fifteen could tell you that flattery and respect don't come hand in hand."

They were fated to hear more of this elderly general later on.

XXV

S o the year grew older. Brown winter greened into spring, spring grew golden under summer's magic touch, but there came never a word of Frank Ledyard, never a sign of him, living or dead.

Mab, in jerky, troubled fashion, contrived to keep up a series of uncomfortable meetings with Captain Buckingham unknown to any of her family.

Mrs. Shenstone made the golden hours fly with a continuation of her small epistolary flirtations and a round of trivial amusements; and Joyce made them linger with the dreary load of thought, profitless speculation, or wild surmise she put into them.

Uncle Archie's pastime just then seemed to consist in dealing out a series of snubs with fine impartiality to everybody—Joyce alone being excepted. Aunt Bell naturally came in for the lion's share of these favors; Mrs. Shenstone's claims being admitted next in order. Even Mab at times had to stand still, be lectured, threatened with a doctor and physic, as though she were a school-girl of thirteen instead of a young woman of three-and-twenty.

Frank's step-step-father—if that degree of relationship be allowed to him—coming up to London at that time to put in his claim of distant kinship to Joyce's lover, thought that outside Colney Hatch there was not to be found such another cranky, irritable old gentleman. Uncle Archie compelled him to remain seated while he stood over him, like a schoolmaster with a switch in his hand haranguing a refractory pupil.

"I tell you, sir," he said, rounding his periods in true pedagogue style, and making his forefinger beat time to his periods, "that I charge myself with my friend, Mr. Ledyard's, debts and responsibilities; I also charge myself with the safe keeping of his private and personal property. His rooms are locked up. His banker's book is in my desk. Not a soul shall lay a finger upon it."

It was possibly the words "debts and responsibilities" as much as Uncle Archie's oratory which sent the step-step-father back again into Gloucestershire, and kept him there.

Morton, the detective, took his share of Uncle Archie's benefits stoically enough. Off and on, Morton was a good deal about the house in those early summer months. One never knew when, or where, his white face and solemn eyes would make their appearance. He buzzed

CATHERINE LOUISA PIRKIS

about the kitchen quarters, made himself free of the housekeeper's room, and once or twice visited the breakfast-room, where Mab and Joyce as a rule spent their morning hours. Nothing inside or outside the house seemed to escape his eye.

It was about this time that a circumstance occurred which greatly troubled Joyce, and which left behind it rankling a miserable feeling of a chance just missed.

In her morning's packet of letters there came one addressed to her in an unknown hand—evidently a disguised hand also, for it was rounded, even, and regular until individuality it had none.

The letter was brief, containing only one or two lines, as follows:

"Will Miss Shenstone meet the writer of this letter on the Albert Bridge, Chelsea, at ten o'clock tonight. Please come alone."

No initials were added. There was nothing to indicate whence the letter had come. The paper was simply schoolboy's quarto, all in keeping with the handwriting. The post-mark was merely "London, W. C."

Joyce hid the letter hurriedly and carefully away. A wild rush of hope for the moment filled her heart. She was possibly on the verge of some clew, it might be of some valuable piece of information. Meet the writer alone! Not a doubt she would. There was no man living she would not have met alone at any hour of the day or night, on the chance of getting the news for which her heart ached. How she got through that day she did not know, it seemed of interminable length. She could not eat, drink, talk, nor remain in one place for five minutes at a time. Directly dinner was over she made an excuse and went up to her room. Then, putting on a dark cloak and simple hat, she crept down the stairs and let herself out by a side gate at the back of the house. Her movements were slow and cautious, and she satisfied herself that they were unnoticed.

It was a fine night, the streets were crowded. King's Road was especially so, and Joyce, unaccustomed to the evening traffic of the streets, felt herself jostled in all directions. She attempted no side thoroughfares, but went straight along the busy road to the broad street which leads direct to the Albert Bridge. Here the traffic seemed suddenly to cease. There was a long, quiet cabstand, a few well-dressed passers-by, a policeman, one or two respectable-looking workmen.

Joyce knew she was before her time, so it did not surprise her to find no one waiting on the bridge whom she could with any show of reason identify with her correspondent of the morning. She walked up and down the length of the bridge two or three times before the Old Church clock struck ten.

After that, every five minutes had its length doubled by her impatience and anxiety.

Could it have been nothing but a hoax after all? she asked herself, wistfully scanning every passer-by, or gazing drearily into the black shadows lying athwart the murky river. Yet it seemed hard to believe, in spite of her lately-increased experience in the world's wickedness, that any one could be base enough to find a pleasure in playing off even the mildest of jokes upon her at such a time of sorrow. No, it was not to be thought of. So she waited patiently, her hopes dying one by one as the church clock chimed the quarters and eventually tolled the hour—eleven o'clock. During the last half-hour of her waiting, she became aware of the fact that a hansom cab was pulled up on the embankment close to the bridge, so that its occupant, if there were one, could get a complete view of her as she waited out the weary hour. How long the cab had been there she did not know, but it was only during the last half-hour that she noticed it.

When at length, tired and sick at heart, she turned her steps homeward once more, it was to see the same hansom driving away from the doorstep of their house.

The back gate was locked when she tried it, an emergency for which she was unprepared. To say truth, her appointment and its possible results had so filled her mind, she had taken no count of any difficulties that might lie in the way of her getting back unnoticed to the house. So she was compelled to ring at the front door, which to her surprise was opened to her by Uncle Archie. He showed no astonishment at her appearance outside at this unusual hour. He only kissed her, and shook his head at her as she went past him straight up to her own room again.

But Joyce, as she passed the library door, had a glimpse of Morton seated within, and in a moment, with a pang of bitter disappointment, guessed the possible reason why her unknown correspondent had failed in his appointment. He had probably seen Morton on the track of her footsteps, and, dreading detection, had himself remained in hiding.

Had she heard Morton's words when Uncle Archie re-entered the library, she would have found her surmise confirmed.

"I see every one of the household letters, sir, before they leave the postman's hands," the detective said, "and this morning I noted one addressed to Miss Joyce in a disguised hand. I noted, also, the young lady's disturbed manner throughout the day, and, putting two and two together, concluded that she had received a piece of information she was keeping to herself, and that an appointment would be the probable result. Now, sir, amateur detectives are all very well in story-books, but out of story-books—" Here an expressive shrug finished the sentence. "Consequently I had my eye on Miss Joyce all through the day. When she left the house by the back door, I followed her through the front; when she arrived at Chelsea Bridge, I called a hansom, and sat in it watching her all the time, and if any one had turned up I should have had my hand on him in a moment. No, sir, I haven't served in my profession for twenty-five years for nothing. He must be a cute one who'll take John Morton in. Now, sir, if you'll get the young lady to hand over that anonymous letter to me, I may be able to read between the lines, and something may come of it."

But though Joyce, in helpless, weary fashion, gave over her letter into the detective's hand, nothing ever came of it beyond that long hour of waiting on the dreary bridge.

XXVI

K eep the family in London, sir," Morton had said to Uncle Archie. "Keep the condition of things as far as possible unaltered, and then—" he broke off abruptly.

"Then what?" Uncle Archie had cried, in a fume.

"Then wait and you'll see," the detective had calmly finished.

But patient waiting for what the months might have in store did not at all suit Uncle Archie's constitution. Gout began to threaten, his irritability grew upon him.

He caught Morton on the stairs one morning in what seemed to him a most frivolous flirtation with pretty Kathleen. He felt inclined to box their respective ears, restrained himself with difficulty, and ended with summoning Morton to immediate conference in the library.

"Is this what you call 'giving 'em rope enough'?" he demanded before the astonished Morton had time to get his wits together for his defense. "Is this what you call keeping an eye on things? Confound it, sir, I could have twisted a dozen ropes in the time you have been bungling over one. And as for eyes! I could have made them generally at everybody all round in less than half the time you have spent in making eyes at one pretty servant-maid."

Morton shut the door quietly.

"Servant-maids are suggestive sometimes," he said. But he said it in such a tone that Uncle Archie dropped his bluster at once and prepared to listen.

"Tell me right out, if you've anything to tell," he said; "Heaven knows, we've had suspense enough to last us to the end of our mortal lives."

"Sometimes suspense is better than certainty."

Uncle Archie shook his head.

"No; I think not, now," he said, wearily; "I might have thought so once, but I think now, for every one in this house, old or young, the cruelest certainty would be better than what we have had to go through during the past few months. Speak out."

"Speaking out is embarrassing sometimes."

"Don't fumble, man; out with it!" cried Uncle Archie, bringing his fist down upon the table with a crash that set the ink-bottles jingling.

"Well, sir, I've come to the conclusion that we are in London, not in St. Petersburg—"

"Heavens and earth, man, you've said that before."

"And that, consequently, being in London and not in St. Petersburg"—here Uncle Archie's foot came with a crash on the carpet—"it is impossible for a man to disappear and not leave a trace behind, unless he himself is a party to the transaction. It is easy enough in London—no place in the world like it—for a man to keep himself hidden; but simply impossible for him to be hidden without his consent."

And as Morton finished speaking he gave an uncomfortable look at the door, as though he would rejoice to be the other side of it when the full meaning of his sentences dawned upon Uncle Archie's brain.

But, strange to say, the old gentleman did not take his words one whit in the manner he expected. He grew suddenly white, he put his hand to his forehead for a moment, shading his eyes. Then he turned and faced Morton again.

"So you're the one to say it out first," he said, in a husky, uncertain tone; "I knew it would come, sooner or later—I've been expecting it," he broke off and put his hand to his head again, as though his thoughts pained him.

Morton felt reprieved, and drew a long breath.

"It is the opinion of my superiors at Scotland Yard, it is the conclusion at which we had arrived there," he said, in a voice that suggested apologies for the repellent truth it had to convey.

Uncle Archie began to recover himself.

"Give me the reasons, the facts from which your conclusions are drawn," he said, making his voice as hard as possible.

"Facts we have none, or next to none, to go upon. Our conclusions are based entirely upon experience. Of that we have enough and to spare at Scotland Yard."

"Well!"

"Mr. Ledyard is not the first bridegroom-elect who has disappeared on the eve of his wedding-day, and he won't be the last, take my word for it, sir, he won't be the last."

Uncle Archie gave a great start, though he said, "Go on!" calmly enough.

"Sometimes they disappear for one thing, sometimes for another. Sometimes they are being pushed into the marriage by their friends. Sometimes their affairs are on the verge of bankruptcy, and they are ashamed to confess that they are not in a position to marry. But, oftenest of all, another passion has taken possession of them—as a rule, a misplaced, ill-judged passion."

Uncle Archie's face showed a sense of relief.

"None of these causes could by any possibility have operated in Frank Ledyard's case," he said, quietly.

"Generally speaking," Morton went on, "they seek, in the first instance, to defer the marriage upon some apparently reasonable pretext. This, I am told, is what Mr. Ledyard endeavored—"

Uncle Archie jumped to his feet.

"Stop!" he cried, in a voice that made Morton think of the other side of the door again. "All this is slander, the blackest of slander and lies."

Then he stopped himself all in a hurry. If once he let himself go, and began to bluster, the colloquy must come to an end, he knew, and good-by then to any chance ray of light Morton might have to let in on the mystery. So he mastered himself with an effort, seated himself in another chair—this time with his back to the light—muttering something of an apology.

"Tempers don't improve as one gets older, and mine has been tried a good deal of late," he said, wearily.

"I have no wish to force my opinions on you, sir," said Morton, respectfully; "but we think, at Scotland Yard, that it is time you knew what we consider to be the true solution of the mystery."

"Go on," said Uncle Archie; "and then, leaning back in his chair, he prepared to hear Morton out, without further interruption.

"Common-place solutions to apparently impenetrable mysteries are the rule, not the exception, so far as our experience goes," Morton began, in dry, professional manner; "any member of my profession would bear me out in that. Inexperienced outsiders wander far afield searching for motives of action which the experienced detective finds lying ready to his hand."

"Get to the point, man—get to the point."

"When I first began to make myself at home in your house, sir, I said to myself, 'To the winds with the Irish Fenian business! we shall find the secret of the gentleman's disappearance within these four walls, or nowhere.' Then I took to questioning the ladies of the family."

"Confound your impudence!" muttered Uncle Archie.

"From Miss Mab I elicited—with due circumlocution, sir, be it noted—the important fact that, during the illness of Miss Joyce, toward the end of last year, that pretty maid, Kathleen, saw fit on one occasion to take up hot coffee to Mr. Ledyard, who was watching through the night, without any order having been given to that effect. She might have done so on more than one occasion for aught Miss Mab knew to the contrary. From Miss Joyce I elicited a no less important fact, viz., that the said pretty maid has a man in love with her whom her brother wishes her to marry, but whom she will not marry on account of another lover. From Kathleen herself I get unintentional confirmation of both these facts. She detests Irishmen, she tells me, and a life of poverty in a cabin. Now, sir, if you'll be good enough to put two and two together—"

But here Uncle Archie's impatience refused to be longer restrained.

"Are you a lunatic quite, sir," he cried, furiously, "or only a detective without an ounce of common-sense in your head? Supposing Mr. Ledyard has a dozen or more pretty servant-maids in love with him, is that to say he is to be in love with them in return? In any case, he has adopted a queer way of showing his love for a girl by running away and hiding from her."

"What—if—the—girl—follows—him—in—due—course?" said Morton, bringing out his words like so many raps from a carpenter's hammer. "Look here, sir, you are paying me handsomely for my professional advice. I will give you the best I have to give, and it is based on an experience of over twenty-five years, remember. Keep your eye on that girl, Kathleen. Take my word for it, before long she will disappear. Hunt her down, and wherever you find her depend upon it Mr. Ledyard won't be far off."

The door opened at this moment, and Joyce looked in. Her cheeks were very white, her hand shook as it rested on the handle of the door. Not a doubt but that she had heard the detective's concluding words.

Uncle Archie read the fact plainly enough in the wan face he had learned of late to read like the pages of a book. It would be useless to gloss it over.

"Tell him it's a lie, Joyce, the vilest of slanders. Anathematize him, denounce him—you'll do it much better than I should," cried the old gentleman, hoarse with mingled emotion and anger.

But Joyce's smile of scorn was her only anathema. To her way of thinking, to anathematize Morton for his inuendoes would have been something equivalent to "anathematizing a school-boy for throwing paper pellets at a Greek marble."

Without a word she turned to Uncle Archie.

"Will you please go up at once to my mother," she said, "she has something of importance to tell you."

XXVII

M rs. Shenstone's important piece of intelligence had been communicated to Joyce before any one else in the house. Going into her mother's dressing-room to ask a question as to certain details of money expenditure, Joyce found her in front of her looking-glass with her morning cap removed, in the act of arranging her hair in an intricate and very juvenile fashion which had lately come into vogue.

"Ah, put a few hair-pins in for me, Joyce, there's a good girl," petitioned Mrs. Shenstone, "I've a very strong motive for making myself look as pretty as possible now."

Joyce's wits at once jumped to the inevitable conclusion.

"Tell me, mother, are you thinking of getting married again?" she asked, quietly, as she fingered the hair-pins and brown plaits.

But Mrs. Shenstone did not think it right that so momentous a fact should be communicated without some little graceful prelude.

"How do you like the name of Bullen, Harold Bullen, Joyce? Don't you think it has a fine old English ring in it? It seems as if it should have a 'Sir' before it, instead of plain 'General,' doesn't it? Your dear father was always fond of old English names. He chose your name because his great-great-grandmother had been a Joyce."

Her father's name in this connection set Joyce shivering.

"Mother, I would let my father's likings alone if you've made up your mind to forget him," she said in cold, hard tones.

Of course Mrs. Shenstone lapsed into plaintiveness at once.

"There, I knew how it would be. I told Harold only yesterday, when I met him at Mrs. Haggard's, that I should have you and Mab grumbling at me from morning till night. It is very ungenerous of you, Joyce, because you can't have your own happiness to begrudge me mine."

Joyce kissed her mother.

"Mother dear, it is because we want to secure your happiness for you that we say the things we do," she said, apologetically.

But Mrs. Shenstone was not to be appeased.

"I wish to goodness you'd let me be happy in my own way. I never interfered in any way between you and Frank, did I? If Frank were here he'd tell you all the kind things I used to say to him about you both. I wish to goodness he was here, then he could have given me away on my wedding-day; a nice, handsome young fellow like that would have looked like my brother. Now Uncle Archie will have to do it, and every one will think he is my grandfather at the very least. I wish your dear father—"

But Joyce here fled from the room, fearing her mother was going to say she wished her dear father were alive, so as to have the privilege of giving her to her second husband.

She felt herself to be incapable of deciding the question whether the step her mother was about to take was likely to result in her happiness; so straight to Uncle Archie she went, feeling he ought at once to be made aware of the condition of things.

Uncle Archie's explosions were terrific all that day, and gout came nearer by a good many paces. Toward evening he calmed down a little, got Joyce alone, and talked the matter over with her.

"Things are gone too far, I suppose, now, for any amount of quiet reasoning to do any good," he said, unconsciously satirizing his own argumentative powers. "I know General Bullen slightly; he is a gentleman, and your mother might do a great deal worse, not a doubt. I shall make a point of giving him full details of your father's will, and, if after that he perseveres in his suit, I shall conclude he knows his own business best."

And to Aunt Bell that night the old gentleman said, as he pulled on his night-cap and put out the candle:

"After all, I am not sure but what it's the best thing in life that could happen. That woman wants a keeper if ever a woman did. Bullen may be able to do what nobody else has done—keep her out of mischief. So long as she's with the girls, she's bound to get them into hot water, and we shan't be always here to get them out of it, for I take it, you and I, Bell, are going down hill a little faster than we like to own, even to ourselves."

XXVIII

S ing a song very loudly, and very often, and some one will be sure to catch up your notes and play the echo to them. Uncle Archie's repeated assertions that "the police authorities at Scotland Yard were noodles to a man, sir," had found general acceptance among the friends of the Shenstone family. Every one had decided that, so far as Frank Ledyard was concerned, their work had been done in an uncommonly sleepy fashion. Yet it is possible that a fairly plausible brief for the defense might have been made out. "Experience and known laws," the police authorities might have said, "explain alike the mysteries of the universe and the trivialities of common life. Both point to one simple solution of the mystery before us, viz., an unwilling bridegroom seizing upon a chance opportunity for escape from an unwelcome marriage." The case could be paralleled over and over again.

The suspicion that Fenian or secret society machinery had been at work in the matter, was scarcely worthy of a second thought. The discovery that the house of John Johnson had been used as a place of meeting for possible conspirators was a thing apart, and to be treated entirely on its own merits. There was no tittle of evidence to show that Frank had so much as crossed the threshold of that house.

The private information which had sent Morton to ladle ices at Mrs. Shenstone's evening party was, in one sense, important, in another trivial. Important, in so far as it marked out for the observation of the metaphorical detective "eye" one or two supposed peaceful and respectable citizens; trivial, in so far as no distinct plot was unearthed, and consequently no arrests were made. Captain Buckingham was still looked upon as a clever adventurer, whom chance had made the mouth-piece of the advanced Irish party; who was most useful to police authorities when at large, and forming a center for the more headstrong democrats.

Ned Donovan, in company with another hot-brained Irishman, Bryan O'Shea, was regarded as one of the active organizers of systematic boycotting in Ireland.

"But that," as Morton informed Uncle Archie, "was a matter to be dealt with by the Irish authorities whenever law-breaking chanced to be the result of the boycotting, a by no means inevitable consequence. Let the brother go; it's the sister you should keep the sharp lookout on."

The latter half of the speech, let it be noted, was not spoken until Uncle Archie was out of ear-shot.

Although Morton had not summed up the Shenstone family so epigrammatically as Uncle Archie had summed up him and his colleagues, he had, nevertheless, in sufficiently graphic style, sketched their portraits.

"Knives, scissors, grape-shot, cannon-balls, vinegar, ginger-beer, pepper, crab-apples. You may select from that list to describe the old gentleman," he had been heard to say, "an oil-flask might represent the old lady"—Aunt Bell—"milk and water, or let us say sugar and water, out of politeness, the middle-aged one"—Mrs. Shenstone!—"As for the two young ladies, they're not a bad sort as young women go. The younger one isn't made of wash-leather, and she isn't made of buckram, but of a sort of something between the two. But the elder—" Here a protracted shake of the head did duty for a sentence. "She might as well be perched on top of the Monument in the thick of a London fog for all she knows of what goes on about her."

Mab might certainly have had a more poetic portrait drawn, but scarcely a truer one. Little by little her life had seemed to be separating itself from the lives of those around her. How it came about no one quite knew, but certain it was that she was never consulted now on any matter great or small in the household arrangements. Had she been qualifying for a convent, she could not more effectually have cut herself off from all mundane affairs. Yet withal of late she had seemed to put more of purpose and order into her daily routine of life. Its detail ran somewhat as follows—breakfast early, sometimes before any one else was down-stairs, then the morning service at the Abbey, afterward an hour or so of visiting among her poor people; the rest of the day, allowing the intervals necessary for meals, was spent alone in her own room.

A silent, dreamy, but not an unlovely thing, her life seemed becoming now. Could one of the sweet maiden-saints of old time have been suddenly recalled to life and placed amid nineteenth century surroundings she might have kept much such a course. Joyce, in spite of the intense pre-occupation of her own thoughts just then, could not keep the question out of them. "What is transforming Mab in this way? What does it mean? Where will it end?" She felt at times as though little by little, slowly but surely, Mab were being dragged out of her loving grasp by some hidden magnetic influence.

At one time she had urged upon her sister the advisability of resuming her ministrations to her poor people, now she felt as if those ministrations must be too spiritualizing—if the word be allowed—for Mab's temperament.

"Don't you think, dear, it would be wiser not to spend so much time among your poor people? Wouldn't it be better to visit them, say once a week, instead of every day?" she queried, gently, tentatively.

Mab aroused to a sudden energy.

"Oh, don't ask me to do that, Joyce!" she said, earnestly. "They are so terribly wretched, poor souls! The misery in the world is something appalling!" She paused a moment, then added, with deep feeling: "Oh, Joyce, I can understand Christ being glad to lay down his life for the world. I would cheerfully lay down mine for any two of the wretched people I know."

Her whole soul seemed spending itself just then in an infinite pity for every one around her.

"Poor, poor mother," was all she said, when the news of her mother's intended second marriage was told her. "Poor, poor Uncle Archie!"— not Joyce's mocking "poor Uncle Archie," be it noted—was her only acknowledgment for half an hour's steady irritable lecturing. And once Joyce, going suddenly into her room, discovered her with her arm round Kathleen's shoulder, comforting her and drying her tears as though she were a sister instead of her maid.

"Kathleen's tears come so readily; she is always crying now," Mab said, turning apologetically to her sister.

"What can Kathleen have to cry about?" asked Joyce, eyeing the girl coldly and suspiciously.

The question and look combined sent Kathleen with a downcast face out of the room.

It was, however, an incident occurring on the night before Mrs. Shenstone's wedding that thoroughly awoke Joyce from her preoccupation, and made her resolve that Mab's health, mental and physical, should have immediate professional attention.

June was drawing to an end now, the London season was working its hardest, knowing that its days were numbered. Outside in the streets sounded a perpetual whirl of coming and going carriages. The Shenstones had dined quietly. Mab had crept out of the room immediately after dinner. General Bullen had retired with his bride-elect to the back drawing-room, where, across a chess-board, an uninterrupted exchange of compliments for simpers did duty for love-making between the two.

Joyce dared not sit still and think. She and tranquil meditation had months ago said good-by to each other. She thought she would follow Mab up-stairs and sit with her till weary bedtime came round once more.

Only in the lower portion of the house the lamps were lighted. On the upper floor there lingered enough of June twilight to guide her to Mab's door. It was not locked, and turning the handle softly, she went in.

There was Mab, as usual, reclining in her high-backed chair, with eyes closed and folded hands. The chair stood against the window. An iron-gray sky with a smirch of red across it, where the sun had gone down, formed the background. Mab's face showed white in the twilight, but tranquil and placid enough. The nervous frown that perpetually contracted her forehead in her waking moments had disappeared, the full white lids veiled the troubled, weary eyes, the mouth seemed almost smiling in its perfect tranquillity.

Joyce stood looking at her for at least five minutes, scarcely daring to breathe lest she might awaken her from what appeared to be the calmest of sleeps. Then she seated herself near in a dark corner, patiently waiting for her eyelids to lift.

"Joyce, how beautiful you are—how strong and beautiful!" said Mab presently, in slow, dreamy tones, but without opening her eyes.

Joyce went and knelt beside her.

"I did not think you knew I was in the room, dear," she answered, speaking softly, for she half thought Mab was talking in her sleep.

"I have been looking at you for the past half-hour," said Mab, still with her eyes shut.

"My darling, I have only been in the room for about ten minutes."

Mab opened her eyes with a sigh.

"All the same I have been looking at you." And, as it were, unconsciously she laid marked emphasis on the two pronouns.

"Oh, Mab, with eyes shut; and you up-stairs and I down!"

"I see better with my eyes closed, dear. Our senses shut out as much from us as they let in; they are our limits as well as our lights."

"Oh, Mab, Mab!" and Joyce gave a startled, bitter cry. "Am I losing my reason, and don't know what you are saying to me, or is it you—you who are losing yours and slipping out of my grasp?"

Mab leaned forward in her chair, putting her arms round Joyce's neck.

"No, dear, I am not going mad. Once I feared I was—about three months ago—" she broke off, abruptly.

"Go on, dear," implored Joyce.

"So I went all by myself to the lunatic ward at the Penitentiary you know, Joyce, where I went to visit some of my poor people once. I asked the matron if any of the poor creatures who had felt themselves going mad had ever described their sensations to her. She told me that one woman had said to her that she felt as though a thick black curtain were being let down slowly, slowly, an inch at a time, between her and her fellow-creatures and the bright, beautiful outer world; that she knew that by-and-by it would be altogether let down, and she would be shut in alone in the darkness."

Joyce hid her face in Mab's lap.

"Oh, Mab darling," she cried, "you don't feel like that—you can't—it isn't possible."

"No, Joyce, I don't feel like that," answered Mab, solemnly, her face aglow with some intense hidden feeling. "I feel day by day, with every breath I breathe, as though on every side of me curtains were being drawn up, not down; as though veils were being rent, mists rolled away; as though the souls of my fellow-creatures were being revealed to me; and the secrets of the universe were being whispered into my ear. Oh, Joyce, I see, I hear with closed eyes and sealed ears fifty thousand times more fully than you do with every one of your senses working at their hardest."

Joyce lifted up a face white as Mab's own.

"Mab, Mab!" she cried, vehemently, "death will seal all our senses sooner or later. While we have them, let us use them."

Mab turned away with a weary sigh.

"You don't understand, Joyce," was all she said.

It was a simple statement of a simple fact. Joyce to Mab was an open book, written in words of one syllable; but Mab to Joyce was a page of problems, for whose solution a loving, sisterly sympathy supplied guesses in lieu of key.

XXIX

So the house in Eaton Square once more put on a smart and festive appearance, as became a house whose mistress was about to forget her widow's weeds and don bridal attire.

"Mind," Uncle Archie had said to his sister-in-law, in a voice that recalled a rusty gate creaking on its hinges, "there's to be no wretched parade of wedding finery. The first sign of cake or favors will send me back in a trice to Gloucestershire, and you'll have to find somebody else to give you to the happy man."

So Mrs. Shenstone, after much bemoaning, was forced to content herself with a marriage in a traveling-dress, a quiet family luncheon, and a departure immediately after for the nearest railway-station *en route* for Paris.

"No satin slippers, no flowers, no rice, no anything delightful!" she lamented to Joyce, as she kissed her at the hall-door; "creeping out of the house for all the world as though we were ashamed of what we were doing!"

"As you very well might be, both of you, at your time of life," grumbled Uncle Archie to himself, as he shut the door on the departing carriage. "Of course it's your own business, and you are each of you old enough to know what you are about; but for the life of me I couldn't say what you can see in each other to take a liking to."

Perhaps the newly-wedded pair might have been driven into a corner with the question. Possibly Mrs. Shenstone, if she had been compelled to a truthful answer, would have said:

"He is fifteen years older than I, and he calls me 'my child.' The combined facts take at least ten years off my age. Also he will take me the round of all the delightful watering-places and cities in Europe, and I shall return with a semi-foreign air of distinction which will enable me to throw open my doors in London to my friends with increased *éclat*."

And the old general, had the magic flute compelled his candor, might have answered somewhat as follows:

"I certainly thought her fortune was in her own hands; but still, after all, five hundred a year, added to my own six hundred, won't make a bad income. The daughters are easy-going, generous girls, and will be sure to let the mother have the old home to live in whenever she wants it, and as much of her old income as she requires for life. Also, she won't make a bad sort of companion for a man at my age. One can't get all one wants in this world; I've a horror of strong-minded women and 'ladies intellectual,' and, whatever her faults may be, they won't carry her that way, at any rate."

The old general was right in his estimation of the course of conduct Mab and Joyce meant to pursue toward their mother. They steadily refused to draw any benefit from her second marriage, as from the conditions of their father's will they very well might have done. Joyce was spokeswoman, as usual, and told Uncle Archie of their resolution not to touch one penny of their mother's income.

"If the dear old home in Gloucestershire is to be kept up again, mother will spend her money over it as she did before, no doubt," she said; "and living quietly, as Mab and I do, we have more money than we know what to do with."

Any one would have indorsed her statement. Living a life of conventual seclusion, with every girlish outlet of enjoyment cut off, she and Mab might have lost one-half their incomes without having to alter their daily routine in any one particular.

After her first little outburst of indignant remonstrance, born of reverence for her father's memory, Joyce did her best to make things sunshiny and smooth for her mother. She threw as much heart as she had to throw into the trousseau and wedding arrangements. All her mother's whims and wishes—and their name was legion—she endeavored to meet half-way.

"I should like, dear," Mrs. Shenstone had said, "for you to lend me Kathleen for a traveling-maid. She arranges hair so much better than Price—has a better eye for a profile. Also in appearance she accords so much better with a wedding-trip; she is, in fact, exactly the kind of maid a bride should have."

Joyce, though a little surprised at her mother's request, had assented readily enough.

Kathleen of late had fallen out of her favor. To her mind there was a suspicion of underhandedness about the girl, of some strong feeling at work in her mind which for certain reasons she was keeping hidden. She did not believe in her repeated asseverations that she knew nothing whatever of her brother's whereabouts; nor did she think the fact of her disinclination to become Mrs. O'Shea fully accounted for her dejected appearance and frequent red eyes. Mab, it is true, steadily refused to countenance any suspicion concerning the girl, but then Mab's conduct could scarcely be taken as a guide for any one else's, her Christian charity had of late so far outstripped in growth her common-sense.

"You may have her, mother, and welcome," Joyce had said, in reply to her mother's request; "only, don't let her go out alone, or she'll be sure to get into mischief."

The evening of the wedding-day found Joyce and Uncle Archie sitting in council once more in the library.

"This is the exact state of the case, Joyce," the old gentleman was saying: "gout is coming, coming, as fast as it can; and unless I can get to Cheltenham, and my old doctor, before it sets in, well—the consequences may be something awful for everybody."

"Oh, Uncle Archie, go tomorrow; why not?" cried Joyce. "I can look after Mab. I am never going to lose sight of her now, and mean to get in the best doctors in London to see her, one after the other."

"Cheltenham is a famous place for doctors; you have the pick and choice of doctors there," said Uncle Archie, as snappishly as he could make up his mind to speak to Joyce.

After this there followed a brisk argument between uncle and niece, as to the rival merits of London and Cheltenham as health resorts. Joyce showed a doggedness of purpose to remain where she was, for which Uncle Archie was unprepared.

"I am not young, Uncle Archie," she said, and, as she said it, in very truth she felt as though she had seen old Time's wheels go round for half a century at least. "We shall live so quietly; we shall go nowhere, we shall see no one. Some day we'll run down to Cheltenham and spend a month with you, but just now pray leave us alone here to do the best we can for ourselves."

But the real, though unavowed, reason that chained her tight to her London home was the thought, the instinct, the hope—so vague, so half-formed it was not possible to clothe it with words—that here, in the thick of the stirring life, where she had looked her last at her young lover, she would get news of him, living or dead, if ever such news was to be had.

People forget sometimes how useless it is to stand watching the curl of the water where the brave swimmer sank; and how the rocks far out at sea may get tidings of him sooner than the shallow river-bed.

CATHERINE LOUISA PIRKIS

XXX

Joyce was as good as her word. On the very day after her mother's wedding, that is to say, on the day of Uncle Archie's departure for Cheltenham, she set to work to turn herself as nearly as possible into Mab's shadow. It was a difficult part to play, this of a hybrid between a mother and a maid. Joyce set about it with diffidence. The buoyant self-confidence which at one time had carried her so smoothly over contrary currents was altogether lacking to her now. It had been born of a joyous heart and sunshiny experiences. It died with them. In its place there had come an apprehensive diffidence—that timid touching of stinging-nettles which tells the tale of the sharply-stung hand.

It must be admitted that Mab's demeanor was not calculated to inspire confidence. On the morning of Uncle Archie's departure, she came down early as usual, ate her breakfast hurriedly, and prepared to set off as usual for her morning's service.

Joyce demurred to this.

"Uncle Archie and Aunt Bell will be starting in an hour or so; can't you give up your service for one day to see the last of them?" she pleaded.

Mab hesitated only a moment. Then she shook her head.

"I must, must go to the Abbey today—you will understand why later on, Joyce. I will go now and say good-by to Uncle Archie—it can't make much difference."

Joyce met with a second repulse later on in the day. Uncle Archie had departed. Luncheon laid for two in the big dining-room did not look a cheering or inviting meal. Mab, as usual, ate next to nothing, and Joyce seized this as an opportunity to introduce the wish of her heart, viz., that Mab should go with her that very afternoon to consult an eminent physician, whom she and Uncle Archie over-night had decided to be the man in London most likely to understand the peculiarities of Mab's condition.

Mab did not give the suggestion a welcome.

"I will go to see any physician in London you like, Joyce, if it will make you happy, but I tell you most positively, as I shall tell him, I will take no drugs of any sort. Nor will I follow any directions he may choose to give. My lines are laid down for me."

Joyce, in her amazement, craved an explanation.

"What lines, dear, and who has laid them down? You talk enigmas," she said.

Mab flushed a deep red.

"It is of no use my explaining, you couldn't understand, Joyce. By-and-by, when you know more, you will forgive me, I am sure, any pain I may have caused you. Only let me alone now, I beg; I implore."

"Couldn't understand—let you alone," repeated Joyce, vaguely in a voice full of pain, and with a rush of hot tears to her eyes.

Mab grew vehement.

"No, you couldn't understand if you tried your hardest from morning till night. Could I understand, do you think, if an angel came down from heaven and talked to me in heaven's language?"

And here she hurriedly pushed away her plate, quitted the table, and quitted the room.

Joyce, left alone, felt as one in an oarless, drifting boat might feel who suddenly looked up and measured the space between himself and the receding shore. There were leagues between her and Mab now, not a doubt. A servant coming in with a telegram made her for the moment bury her heart-ache out of sight. Her thoughts naturally flew to the traveling bride and bridegroom. Could any ill-adventure have befallen them?

The telegram was dated from Calais, and ran as follows:

"Dispatch Price at once to Hôtel Bristol, Paris. Kathleen has disappeared."

Later on in the day, the telegram was supplemented by a letter from the General. Kathleen, it should be said, had been dispatched to Victoria Station with Mrs. Shenstone's huge dress-boxes and baskets there to await her mistress's arrival after the wedding ceremony. The General in his letter stated that they found her there right enough in the midst of the baggage, but that on arriving at Dover though the baggage had been deposited in the luggage van. Kathleen was nowhere to be seen. They had naturally concluded that she had, through some mischance, lost her train and expected her arrival by the next. However, up to the departure of the mail packet, there had been no sign of her. In the circumstances, he strongly advised that the authorities at Scotland Yard should be communicated with.

Joyce immediately carried out this suggestion.

"Only, however, for the sake of her father and mother. It can not possibly concern any one else," she wrote back to the old general by return post, indignantly resenting what seemed to her an inuendo leveled at Frank behind the words "in the circumstances."

XXXI

"Captain Buckingham wishes to see Miss Shenstone."

This was the announcement that fell upon Joyce's ears, as she and Mab sat together on the day after the news of Kathleen's disappearance had been received. Anger and indignation sent the hot blood in a rush to Joyce's cheeks.

"How dare he?" she cried, jumping up from her chair and the letter she was writing. "Tell him—"

But Mab interrupted, with a self-assertiveness that sat strangely upon her.

"I am Miss Shenstone; Captain Buckingham wishes to see me," she said, with a rush of hot blood to her face that most assuredly was not caused by anger or indignation.

Then to the servant she added:

"Tell Captain Buckingham I will come down at once and see him."

Joyce sprang at her, as the servant closed the door, and folded her hands over her arm.

"Mab, Mab, what is this? what does it all mean?" she cried, vehemently. "Tell me; I insist, I must know. How dare this man come to the house in this way, asking to see you? Have you given him any encouragement to do so? Have you seen or spoken to him since Uncle Archie forbade him the house?"

Mab answered, calmly enough:

"Yes, Joyce, I have seen him many times since, and always by appointment. Sometimes in Mrs. O'Halloran's drawing-room, sometimes in my morning walks."

"Mab!"

"Don't judge me harshly, Joyce. I had, ah! such a strong reason for wishing to see him—a reason which you yourself could not help approving. Our talk has been always of you—your lost happiness, and how to get it back for you. But yesterday—"

"Yesterday!"

"Yesterday he startled me a little by suddenly breaking off from our talk and telling me he loved me, and wanted to marry me. I could not find words to answer him then, so I told him to come here today for his answer."

Joyce's reply to this was a cry of pain so bitter, it told of a breaking heart. But she still clutched at Mab's arm.

"Mab, Mab, my darling Mab! it can not be, it shall not be. You marry a man of that sort! I could hold you against him, against the world—! This man shall not drag you away from me!"

In very truth, a doughtier than Captain Buckingham might have essayed in vain to unlock those convulsively clasping fingers!

Mab suddenly took to trembling under their touch.

"Joyce, I will speak out plainly to you. I feel I have only a 'No' to give him—I felt it from the first. I have put away all thoughts of that sort from my mind—"

"All thoughts of what sort?" questioned Joyce, holding Mab tighter as she felt the girl trembling more and more.

"All thoughts of love or marriage. In the life I have set myself to live, one sees the end as soon as the beginning. One has to put away the things of sense to grasp the things of soul—"

But with the last word her voice faltered. She grew heavy in Joyce's arms; her head sank back, her face grew white.

Joyce laid her on the sofa, and rang the bell for the servants. One she dispatched for a doctor, two she left with restoratives, bidding them sit by Mab's couch till she came back.

Even a disabled war-horse will fall into step at the sound of the bugle. Joyce went, with head erect, straight to the drawing-room, to meet and dismiss Captain Buckingham.

"It would not take many minutes to do this," she said to herself. "A few cold, decisive words, a touch to the bell, a look he should carry away and remember, and the thing would be done."

There was no sign of surprise on Captain Buckingham's bold, handsome face as she entered the room. From the first, when he had made his reckoning of the difficulties which lay between him and Mab Shenstone and her fortune, he had given foremost place among them to Joyce, with her vigorous animosity.

Well and good, he had said to himself; he had his weapons ready to combat alike vigor and animosity. And they were stouter and crueler than those with which, later on, he intended to do battle to Mab's convictions and fancies, so fine in their substance, so intense in their fervor, they might fitly be called religious.

He rose from his chair, but made no attempt at hand-shaking.

"I wish to see Miss Shenstone," he said, with a formal bow.

Joyce returned the bow with equivalent formality.

"I have to decline for her the honor of receiving you now, or at any future time," she said, coldly, laying her hand upon the bell to expedite his departure.

This was a rushing into battle without preliminary proclamation with a vengeance.

"I must hear that sentence from her own lips before I accept it," he said, loudly, defiantly.

"That you will never do. Captain Buckingham, I must ask you to understand that your visits to my sister, and every attention, small or great, you are wishing to show her, are at once and finally declined by her and by her family."

"That also I must hear from her own lips, or I must decline to accept as final."

"Captain Buckingham, I wish you good morning"; and again Joyce's fingers rested on the bell-handle.

He laid his hand on hers.

"Don't do that; don't make yourself ridiculous. There are no ten men who could turn me out of your house if I chose to stay here. I have come this morning expressly to say something to you—to your sister. Say it I will—listen to it you shall."

An electric battery could not have sent the blood coursing at a more rapid rate through her veins. She drew back a step, though not in fear.

"Shall—will," she repeated. "Those are not words to be spoken to me—by you."

She was speaking to him, but she was thinking of Frank, and how summary would have been his method of dealing with such impertinence.

Buckingham went on, in his loudest and most emphatic manner:

"I shall use none others. I repeat, you shall listen to what I have to say, and they are words that will send you down there on the carpet at my feet, praying me to tell you less or to tell you more."

Joyce's hot indignation was swamped now in a dread that chilled her cheeks and lips. His words could point only one way. Her fears had always suggested dark suspicions of this man. His words confirmed her fears.

She strove to command herself, and answered calmly, with a question:

"Are you referring to Mr. Ledyard? Let me understand what ground we are on."

"Supposing I decline to answer your question, what then?"

Her hot indignation came back to her.

"There are ways of making the unwilling speak. There is law in the land," she cried, vehemently.

He laughed contemptuously.

"Ah, English law has done so much for you already, no wonder you put your trust in it."

He paused for a reply. Joyce for the moment felt herself suffocating. Words would not come.

He went on:

"Send at once to your favorite detectives at Scotland Yard. Say to them: 'Here is a man who knows the secret you are hunting for.' Shall I tell you what their answer will be?"

Joyce clenched her fingers into the palms of her hand, and held back her words tight between her teeth.

"They will say to you: 'My dear young lady, we know that man, not you. He is not to be believed on his oath. Don't you know that the business of the loud-mouthed democrat is to set the police on false scents from year's end to year's end? That is the chief way in which he serves his cause. Take it for granted he knows no more than you or I do.'"

Joyce, as she listened, could almost have believed the man must have heard Morton's own words to her, when once she had spoken to him as to Buckingham's possible complicity in Frank's disappearance; so faithfully were they reproduced.

"You know I am speaking the truth to you," Buckingham went on, reading easily enough conviction in the girl's face. "Now come to me instead and say to me: 'Give me your secret, it is life or death to me.' Shall I tell you what my reply will be?"

He paused a moment, then dropped into a lower and less defiant key.

"I will say to you: 'My dear Miss Shenstone, on the very day that your sister becomes my wife, I will repay your congratulations with the information you are desirous of.'"

A rush of passionate words came to her lips.

"You—you can lift in a moment this awful load of agony from our hearts, and you are standing here making a bargain out of our necessity?"

"Ay, and a good hard bargain I mean to make of it, too. No shiftiness or double-dealing about it, I assure you.'

She drew back a step, wonder, incredulity, bewilderment, all showing in her face. In her most somber conceptions of villainy she had never pictured such blackness as this.

Buckingham went on:

"Don't let us waste time in question and answer. Let us get to the point at once. I want something done that you can do; you want something told that I can tell. In other words, I want you to use your influence with your sister, so as to induce her to become my wife, and you want me to give you a piece of information in which you are greatly interested. Very good; let us simply agree to an exchange of favors, and all contention comes to an end."

White and tottering, she crossed the room, and laid her hand upon his arm.

"Are you a man, or what are you?" she said, in low, unnatural tones, her eyes repeating the question to his, which, bold as they were, for one moment quailed and drooped.

Only for one moment; the next, confidence, and something akin to derision, came back to them. He laughed lightly.

"Are you insinuating a compliment? Am I to infer that you consider I am exhibiting superhuman devotion and heroism in the very simple and lover-like request I made just now, that you would do your best to bring about a marriage between me and a woman I am devotedly attached to?"

Then he contrived to free himself from the pressure of her hand, which yet rested on his arm, and made one step toward the door, adding:

"But you are disturbed, agitated, this morning, and unable to see things from a common-sense point of view. In a day or two I will call again, and talk this matter out with you. You will then have had time to think it well over."

Joyce sprang forward, putting herself between him and the door.

"No," she said, in the same low, dissonant voice as before; "there shall be no talk of tomorrow. Having said so much, you shall say more. You are bound to!"

"Shall! Bound to! Those are words with a nice sound in them. Suggest the rack, *peine forte et dure,* and all that sort of thing."

"I repeat, bound;" and here her voice grew firmer, louder, though white, whiter her face was getting. "Bound by honor, by conscience, by humanity."

He folded his arms across his chest, and looked down on her.

"Ah!" he said, mockingly, "what if I confess that these things—honor, conscience, humanity—are names to me, nothing more?"

"Yet, as he stood there, mocking her agony, an overmastering admiration for this young girl, so bold in her weakness, so defiant with her lack of resources, took possession of him. It added a fine, pungent flavor to his enjoyment of the part of semi-royal barbarian he intended playing; put him on a level at once with those ducal or kingly savages who had struck hard bargains with wives or daughters, and had sent back for their share of it a husband or a father with a dagger through his heart.

Joyce struck her hands together passionately.

"And you, who own this to me, ask me to get Mab to be your wife. I wish I had a thousand tongues, so that every one of them might answer 'No' to you."

He kept his head cool, in spite of her passion.

"Then there is no more to be said," he answered, calmly. "I will, if you like, consider the thousand tongues have spoken their 'No' to me. I will take it as final so far as you are concerned, but whether I shall take it as final so far as your sister is concerned is another thing. Now I will bid you the 'good morning' you so politely bade me at the beginning of our interview."

He looked at her as though expecting her to move from her leaning posture against the door. She did not stir.

"No," she said, her voice dropping into her former low, unnatural tone, "you do not leave this room with your secret untold. There must be a power in heaven or earth that will make you speak out."

He interrupted her with a scornful laugh.

"I should amazingly like to make acquaintance with it. Those who think to whip, drive, hound me into a thing I'm not inclined for, are terribly out in their reckoning."

"Then, Captain Buckingham, I entreat," and here Joyce suddenly left her position at the door, clasped her hands, and stood in front of him. "If you will not be driven, be entreated; I will go down into the very dust at your feet; I will retract every bitter, bad word I have ever said of you; I will beg your pardon for them a thousand times over; I will speak of you to the very end of my life as the one to whom I owe everything, if you will tell me just this, nothing more: Is he living or dead?"

There was no need to say who "he" was. Only one man's name was in their thoughts at that moment.

She was trembling from head to foot now; her face ashen white, her eyes glowing. A colder heart than Buckingham's might well have caught her fire and grown yielding. He made no sign, however.

CATHERINE LOUISA PIRKIS

"Go on. What else would you do?" was all he said.

"What else?" she cried, in a wild whirl of hope that her words had touched his heart. "What one human being could do for another that would I do; my gratitude all my life long would be yours. Ask what you would, I would strive to get it for you."

"Go on."

"How can I go on? What more can I say?" and now her wild whirl of hope changed to a wild whirl of dread. She made one step nearer to him, caught his hands in hers, clutching them tight in her agony. "Oh, Captain Buckingham!" she cried, piteously, "you must have a heart, hide it though you may from all the world. You must have had a mother once who loved you; there must be some one in the whole world who would lay down her life for you. Think—would you have had either tortured inch by inch as you torture me? Have mercy on me! It is only one word I ask of you—a 'Yes' or 'No' to my question: Is he dead?"

A marble mask could not have been more impassive than Buckingham's face, as he answered:

"And it is only one word I ask of you, a 'Yes' to the request I made a moment ago. Speak that word, and you get the answer to your question. Refuse to speak it, and I exercise a similar discretion. There is no more to say."

Then he freed his hands from hers, strode past her, and left the room.

XXXII

Joyce had not Mab's aptitude for slipping into unconsciousness whenever affairs neared a climax, and a tumult threatened. Only a white, haggard face told the tale of the storm she had just passed through, as, quaking and tottering, she made her way back to Mab's side.

Mab had been restored to consciousness, but still lay, with closed eyes, on her couch. Joyce dismissed the maids, and took their place beside the sofa. Mab's eyes opened instantly.

"Is he gone, Joyce?" she whispered, nervously.

When Joyce, making a gigantic effort, gave in reply a calm "Yes, darling," there came a long, weary sigh of relief and another question, this put a little eagerly:

"He won't come back again, will he?"

Joyce was all unprepared for this question.

"No, darling, he won't come back again," she answered, boldly enough; but her heart gave the lie to her words as she spoke them. It said, with no uncertain conviction, "He will come back again, and again, and again; he will test his strength against your weakness day after day, day after day, till how it will all end Heaven only knows."

"I don't want to see him, Joyce," Mab went on, presently. "I don't think I could say 'No' to him, if he really begged for a 'Yes.' But I feel 'No' is the only word I ought to say." She ended with another deep sigh, and a pathetic emphasis on the "I."

Joyce felt she must get to the bottom of this hideous mystery, no matter at what cost.

"Tell me, dear," she asked, gently, "how is it you have learned to—to—like this man in the way you do?"

Mab for one instant lifted her eyes to Joyce's face. They showed deep and shining as Joyce had never before seen them.

"Oh, Joyce," she said, in a low, impassioned voice, "if one walked into the room this very minute, bringing you glad news of Frank, how would you feel toward him?"

"I—oh, I should fall down and worship him! I would lay down my life for him, inch by inch, as he wanted it—I can't say more."

"Ah, you will understand, then. Well, listen! Captain Buckingham came to me bringing me glad news, the gladdest news in the world. He made me see how that I, who had been all my life long fighting against one half of myself, thinking it was the base, bad half, had in reality been fighting against the best, noblest part of my nature. He taught me it was my duty to loose it—let it go free, so that I might live here a life beside which an angel's might show clouded and dim."

Joyce's bewildered brain made vain efforts to solve what seemed to her a string of enigmas.

"Go on, dear; how did you set about it?" she asked, hoping the question might bring a ray of light in its answer.

"I studied deeply books of all sorts on clairvoyance and trance vision. I acquired the habit of self-mesmerism. I learned the art of throwing one's self into a trance—at will."

Joyce started. Here stood the mystery of Mab's life explained.

"Go on, dear," she contrived to say calmly enough, but all the time fearing that the revelations of this terrible morning were never coming to an end.

"I learned to know who, what, the 'I' of existence is. How that it is not the soul, not the body, but by dint of habit, by practice, by strong exercise of will, can reside in either."

"Go on, dear. And then—"

"Oh! the sweet things, the beautiful things, I have learned to see, Joyce. I know now what '*I* was in the spirit' means. If I lived long enough, like Swedenborg, like the prophets of old time, I know I should taste beforehand the glories of the world to come."

"And then, dear—"

"Oh! and then—why, then, darling Joyce, of course I should finally, eternally enter into them—after death, I mean."

"Shan't we all do that, Mab, if we lead true, patient lives here, without any straining after gifts and powers wisely put beyond our reach?"

But, the instant she had said the words, she would fain have caught them back. Mab turned her face wearily to the wall with a deep sigh, saying:

"I thought you would have understood, Joyce; I wanted so to tell you everything."

"Darling, tell me everything," pleaded Joyce, getting up from her chair and kneeling beside the sofa. "I will listen quietly, oh, so quietly; I won't interrupt you again."

But it was some minutes before Mab spoke again. Then there was something of pain in her tone as she said:

"Joyce, I don't want you to think I have been utterly selfish from beginning to end in the—the gift I have been cultivating."

"You selfish! Oh, my darling!".

"I have thought of all my friends throughout. It seemed to me if I trained myself to use this gift of seeing—it is nothing else—I might do great things for all my friends."

"Yes, dear, I understand."

"You know how I failed over poor Ned Donovan. Captain Buckingham explained to me how it was I did so fail. The thing haunted me—nearly drove me mad. I felt—I feel all your unhappiness was of my bringing—"

"No, no, no, Mab."

"Yes, it was, Joyce. I think the thought would have killed me outright, if Captain Buckingham had not shown me how my gift might be the means of repairing the terrible evil I had wrought."

A flash of lightning, all in a second, will reveal miles of night-hidden landscape. All in a flash Joyce seemed to see the double game Buckingham had played; how he had adapted his bait to his victim, and how desperately fatal it was likely to prove.

She wisely kept her indignation from her tongue, however, knowing how meaningless it would be to Mab's clouded brain. Mab went on:

"So, night and day, I shut myself up in my room, with but one thought in my mind, 'Frank, Frank, where is he; where shall I see him?' Oh, Joyce, how your hand trembles! Do I distress you? Shall I leave off?"

"Go on, Mab, quickly; for the love of Heaven tell me what you have seen!" cried Joyce, all vibrating with another feeling now.

"Alas, darling, so far I have seen nothing. And this is strangest of all, for I could fill volumes with the wonders and glories I have seen in the world that seems so commonplace to commonplace eyes, and yet leave the greater part untold."

There came a long, deep-drawn sigh from Joyce, nothing more.

"Yet whenever I close my eyes and say to myself, 'I will go feel after Frank in the wide, wide world,' strange to say, an odd noise fills my ears, a sound like the rushing and surging of an ocean. I see nothing but a great gray stretch of sky, a great gray stretch of sea beneath, not a sign of life anywhere—nothing but desolation all around."

Joyce's face was hidden in her hands now. This vision of desolation seemed in very truth an apt picture of her own empty, aching heart.

Mab tried to speak words of comfort.

CATHERINE LOUISA PIRKIS

"Darling, do not grieve so; I do not believe he is dead. If he were, I should have seen him, I know. It would take too long to tell you how I know it—and you wouldn't understand. Oh, and there's one thing, Joyce—one thing has been forced upon me in these long, silent hours. I am sure, I have felt it, I know it; wherever he is, he is true to you. By-and-by people will be trying to make out that Kathleen has had something to do with his disappearance. I have heard them whisper it already. But you'll never believe this, Joyce, will you?" Here she sat up on her couch, and put her arms all round her sister. "And in my long hours of—of vision this thought has come to me always first and last, strong and clear, 'Wherever he is, he is true, he is true, he couldn't be otherwise.'"

Joyce drew her hands from her white, stricken face, with never a tear on it.

"He couldn't be otherwise," she repeated, slowly, and the mournful scorn of her smile as she said it was a thing to remember. "Oh, Mab, has it taken you hours of trance to find out what is simple matter-of-fact to me, to every one who ever touched Frank's hand, or looked in his face? Dear, you have made to yourself wings to carry you over a plain, straight road that your feet could have trodden more easily by far. Oh, Mab, take to your feet again, let the wings go. The angels want them, not we!"

Mab sank back again on her couch, answering nothing. Her eyes closed wearily once more. Was it sleep or trance? Joyce asked herself.

XXXIII

There is an old legend of a knight whose brave heart was exchanged for that of a hare, and who ever afterward trembled at and fled from the dangers he before had courted. Joyce felt herself in much such a plight now.

Her terrible interview with Captain Buckingham had left her with but one thought paramount—a longing for instant flight. In it alone she felt lay Mab's safety, her own only chance of a successful resistance to an appalling temptation.

She dared not risk another interview with the man. In her last she had expended all her resources, had drawn upon her utmost reserves. Were they to meet again, she knew she must lie weaponless at his mercy.

She at once consulted the doctor, who had been hurriedly called in to attend Mab in her fainting-fit, as to the expediency of immediate change of air and scene for his patient. The doctor pronounced a decidedly favorable opinion on the matter.

"Nothing could be better for her," he said. "Her nerves were, so to speak, unstrung, her system generally lacked tone. For this condition there was no better tonic to be found than sea air."

Then there was Mab to consult, and here Joyce's heart misgave her sorely, lest Mab, following the dictates of one of her unaccountable impulses, should steadily refuse to be dislodged from her present quarters.

Her misgivings, however, were not verified, for Mab gave the heartiest welcome to the project.

"The very thing, Joyce!" she cried, excitedly. "Oh, I can't tell you how often lately I have longed to get to the sea. I feel—" but here she checked herself abruptly.

"But, dear, why did you not say so, it could so easily have been managed?" queried Joyce, astonished.

"If only we knew where to go!" Mab went on, with a sigh, a curious, wistful expression passing over her face.

"How would you like a quiet little village in Switzerland among the hills and lakes?" asked Joyce, eager to put first the ocean, then the Alps, between Buckingham and herself.

Mab shook her head.

"I don't think the place I want to go to is in Switzerland."

Then she drifted into apologies and explanations.

"It's just this, Joyce: the sea haunts me night and day. How can I make you understand? There is for ever in my ears the rush and roar of a mighty ocean, and when I close my eyes, and you think I am sleeping, I see nothing but big brown rocks, steep and bare, and a grand sweep of murky, dashing sea."

Joyce gave a great start. Mab's visions after all might be something other than the picture-parables of mystic truths which she had deemed them. What if they were to throw a clearer light on the miserable darkness than any that their vast expenditure of time, thought, money had been able to throw.

"Oh, Mab darling, can you not give the place a name?" she asked, breathlessly.

Again Mab shook her head.

"When I was a child," she said, "and went with Uncle Archie across Scotland, I remember spending a day in much such a place. I think it was in Ayrshire, on the coast looking across the North Channel. I would like to go there first, Joyce, if you don't mind, although it isn't quite the place I see in my—my dreams."

So their preparations for flight were at once begun, Joyce urging them forward with an eagerness which told tales of her failing courage.

In spite of her haste, however, she did not forget to take every precaution to keep their destination a secret. Two days after Buckingham's visit to the house saw them ensconsed in an hotel in Carlisle. Here Joyce took the opportunity of dismissing their London maids and engaging others, thereby cutting off all communication with the London household. From Carlisle they went direct to Newton Stewart, the little town where, in the old days, Mab had stayed with Uncle Archie.

Here they heard of a little sea-side place which seemed in every respect to fulfil Mab's descriptions. Tretwick-by-Sea it was called. Joyce found she could engage a small furnished cottage there for herself and Mab. Other accommodation for visitors there was none.

This little cottage had been built by a wealthy inhabitant of Dumfries, as a last hope of saving the life of an invalid son. The hope had proved futile, and since the death of the lad the little house had remained unoccupied. It was well furnished, and fitted with many invalid comforts. It stood half-way up the cliffs, and was consequently sheltered from rough land breezes. In addition, it commanded without interruption a view of a grand sweep of coast and the great rolling North Channel. The coast-guard station stood on a level with it, about a quarter of a mile away. A few fishermen's huts clustered on a lower level at about five minutes' walking distance. These were the only habitations that Tretwick could boast on the coast-line. Above, on the cliffs, a landscape scarcely less desolate met the eye. The bastion of a ruined castle on a hill made a bold, sharp outline against the sky. Beneath it in a hollow stood an ancient church with ivy-covered tower, surrounded with a mossy, sunken church-yard. The few cottagers who attended service in this old-world sanctuary had their homes on the farther side of the castle-crowned hill, and their humble roof-trees were consequently hidden from view. In the foreground stretched an apparently illimitable heath in its full glory of purple heather and golden gorse, but with never so much as a stunted Scotch fir to break its picturesque monotony.

Joyce, as she and Mab posted their last few miles across country into the heart of this solitude, said to herself that if they had searched England from corner to corner they could not have found a better hiding-place.

It was burning August weather, and the vivid sunlight threw every feature of the landscape into bold relief.

Mab awakened to sudden animation at her first glimpse of the narrow beach, great brown rocks, and restless ocean flashing into all sorts of brilliant shifting tints in the effulgence of sunshine.

"It was something—something like this I saw in my—my dreams, Joyce," she cried, enthusiastically. "I feel now we are nearer—" She broke off abruptly and ended with a sigh.

Joyce sighed, too. She never heard Mab speak of her dreams without a thrill. Vistas in cloudland though they were, they seemed to suggest possibilities of a glimpse of hope now that all orher possibilities were cut off.

But were they possibilities of which she dared take advantage? she asked herself, gazing sadly at Mab's pallid face, and thin drooping figure.

CATHERINE LOUISA PIRKIS

XXXIV

During the two days that elapsed before Joyce and Mab took flight for the sea-side, Captain Buckingham did not molest them, either personally or by letter.

This line of conduct he had deliberately planned, his reasoning running somewhat as follows:

"This resolute young woman will be bound sooner or later to meet my views. She is not one, I take it, to stick at a trifle, and stand shilly-shallying, when words of hers can end a suspense which must be worse than any certainty. In a day or two there will come an imploring little note, begging a second interview. Well and good. She shall have her second interview, and I'll undertake to say it'll be a somewhat less stormy one than the first. By hurrying matters forward I may simply retard them; better let them alone to take their course. It's a bold game I'm playing, a desperately bold one; but when has audacity, joined to skill like mine, ever failed of a triumph?"

The motto of Danton, "De l'audace, encore de l'audace, et toujours de l'audace," aptly enough expressed the principle on which this man had governed his life.

Put a grain of sand under a microscope, you will see it clearly, not a doubt. At the same time you will be apt to look it out of its proportions, and exaggerate its importance in the scheme of the universe. Captain Buckingham had spent so many agreeable hours in the contemplation of his own prowess, that he had grown to overlook the fact that there were such weapons in the world as truth, honesty, and honor, by which it might be successfully combated.

He gave rein to his thoughts, and let them career freely among the pleasant probabilities the future might have in store for him when once Mab became his wife.

The work of his society had of late been pressing and important. A running fire of urgent orders was being received from head-quarters by every mail. Boycotting and moonlighters' work were being carried on briskly enough in Ireland, where Sylvia was proving herself a very efficient agent. But the impression seemed somehow to have arisen at the New York center that the work of the society was beginning to flag in England. The ugly word dynamite had begun to be whispered from one to the other of the council, and the scheme for the destruction of certain public buildings in London—set on foot about a year previously, but abandoned out of deference to cooler heads and clearer judgments—was once more hinted at.

These whispers, of necessity, had reached Buckingham's ears before they resolved themselves into the form of a definite order. He had shrugged his shoulders over them; had said to himself that he was getting older, and less inclined to risk his life and liberty than he had been in his old harum-scarum days.

"Now," he soliloquized, as he allowed his fancy to run riot in the benefits an alliance with Mab might confer upon him, "married to a rich wife, comfortably settled in New York or London, things would be altogether different. I should take higher standing at once, and they'd let me off these risky ventures for the sake of the money and influence I should draft into the league."

It may be conjectured that this man had no intention of playing the part of a Barnum toward Mab, although it had suited him well enough to fill this *rôle* toward Marie St. Clair. She, a poor, illiterate girl, could only have been of use to him as a professional clairvoyante. With Mab Shenstone the case was different. As a tractable, rich wife she would benefit him infinitely more than in any other guise. The clairvoyance, he had from the very first decided, could be useful only in so far as it helped to form another and closer link. That securely forged, let the lighter and temporary bond be snapped at once.

Hand in hand with these thoughts came another not one whit less exultant, having in its substance more of the barbaric chieftain than of the nineteenth century republican. It painted the hour of triumph when, on the day that made Mab his wife, he would turn to Joyce and say: "Here we are, brother and sister at last. Now, as a brother, let me give you a little piece of advice: Forget that hot-headed lover of yours as quickly as possible. He met his death on what would have been his wedding-day." That would be a speech worth making. It would be triumph and revenge at one blow. It would pay back, with a fine touch, a score of petty slights, insults, inuendoes which these two had seen fit from time to time to launch at him. He could picture the girl's face as he said the words; the beautiful eyes uplifted, first in expectancy, then in agony, to his. He could fancy the cry of pain that would break from her lips as the full meaning of his words struck her brain. Why, it would be every whit as good as bringing in the young fool himself, and laying him down at her feet, with a dagger through his heart.

He admitted readily enough that the game was not without its risks—whenever was there a game worth playing that did not include risks? But the risks here were small, the triumph large. There would be certain small details that would require nice adjustment, such, for instance, as how to couple his certain knowledge of Frank's death with his perfect innocency in the matter.

Joyce was a vehement, passionate woman, he knew, but, after all, vehemence and passion would naturally become diluted when directed against a sister's husband, and that sister as much doted on as Mab was. And even supposing she were to carry matters so far as to set on foot a police inquiry, there was absolutely not one tittle of evidence to be brought against him.

So in a thoroughly contented frame of mind he reposed for nearly a week upon his resolve to take matters quietly, and not run the risk of spoiling the whole thing by rushing at it "like a bull at a gate."

As the days went on, however, and there came no sign whatsoever from Mab or Joyce, his resolve grew weaker. A slight feeling of uneasiness took possession of him. He began to think that it might be as well to change his tactics and take the initiative.

He accordingly penned a brief note to Mab, asking her to grant him an interview, and then, to make sure of its safe delivery, he decided to be his own messenger.

Captain Buckingham's quarters in Bloomsbury saw a good deal of Ned Donovan's handsome Irish face just then. On the very day on which Buckingham penned his missive to Mab, he sat waiting in Buckingham's sitting-room, with dispatches from New York in his breast-pocket.

Into this young Irishman's demeanor there had come of late a dogged sullenness and reserve which sat ill upon him. Buckingham, keeping a steady eye upon him, had noted it.

"He's doing good work, and work that no one else could be found to do just now," he thought; "but he's doing it at the sword's point. By-and-by there'll be a question or two he'll have to answer, and it'll go rough with him. But that won't be till we've got all the work we want out of him."

And forthwith he had sent Ned upon missions that were hourly becoming more distasteful to him, and had treated him with an arrogant brusqueness which at times set the Irishman's blood boiling.

Naturally the relation between the two men was somewhat strained. Fellowship in a cause is not omnipotent to swamp all minor enmities and discords in life.

The individual must wither before "the world," or in other words "the cause," can become "all in all." In this young Irishman the "individual" was very strong; in spite of disappointments, mortifications, and all sorts of hardships, it showed as yet no sign of withering.

"Why I love my life Heaven only knows," he would sometimes say to himself; "but not a doubt I do love it, and it won't be long before I claim my right to do what I please with it."

Possibly Captain Buckingham read these thoughts, or something akin to them, in the man's face as he entered the room. They added additional fuel to the discontent which had taken possession of him, when on arriving at Eaton Square he had been told that the Misses Shenstone had left town, and that all letters were to be forwarded to Mr. Archibald Shenstone at the Grand Hotel, Cheltenham, as they had not yet made up their minds as to their destination.

With a brief nod to Ned he held out his hand for his dispatches, opened and read them in silence.

"There is nothing here to make me alter my present arrangements," he said, when he had run his eye over them. "The work in County Down can be well carried through by an inferior officer. It will most likely devolve upon you."

Ned frowned a deep, ugly frown.

"The rick-firing and cattle-staking business is not the work I'd choose to set going—" he began.

"Since when has it been the custom of the Society to ask its members what work they would or would not choose?" interrupted Buckingham, curtly.

"Nor was it the work I was led to believe would be given to me, when I joined the society," Ned went on, doggedly.

Captain Buckingham looked up at him, a curious expression passing over his face.

"I suppose you know the penalty attached to insubordination?" he asked, meaningly.

Yes, Ned knew well enough, none better; and silence fell on him at once.

"I shall have more to say to you by-and-by on this head," Buckingham went on; "meantime, you had better start for Cork at once. At the end of the week, full directions will be sent to you at your old quarters there. On second thought, it will be better for you to cross by way of Milford. You can branch off from Gloucester, and run down to

Overbury. A day will be allowed you off duty to spend with your father and mother."

Ned's face brightened. Work in Ireland was rough and risky just then, it would be cheery to get a glimpse of the old couple in the gardener's cottage before he set about it. But what could have put such kindly forethought as this into the captain's head? he asked himself.

He was soon to get his question answered.

"While at Overbury, I wish you to ascertain the Miss Shenstones' present address, and at once telegraph it to me here," Buckingham resumed. "Through your father and mother, no doubt you can easily get at it. If they fail to know it, go on to Cheltenham, and find it out through the servants at the hotel who post the old uncle's letters. You've done that sort of thing neatly enough before now."

Ned's face fell again, the dogged, sullen look came back to it. He bit his lip, answering not a word.

Of Captain Buckingham's attentions to Mab he had had hints from Kathleen, long before they had been so much as suspected by any member of the family. These hints had roused the wild beast in him, and had had, moreover, the practical effect of making him set on foot a few special inquiries concerning Buckingham's previous career. The result of these inquiries had not been inspiriting, and had contributed its quota to the distrust with which the man viewed his chief.

Captain Buckingham noted his silence and read it correctly. To himself he said: "That man must be brought to book before long, with a good strong hand too." Aloud he said, as he drew his chair to his writing-table and spread his papers before him:

"These are all the instructions I have to give. When next you hear from me it will be at Cork. Good-morning."

But Ned did not stir.

"I have a question to ask," he said, and Buckingham's quick ear once more detected the ring of rebellion in the man's tone. "Is this—this address you desire me to get for you required for the work of the society, or is it required for your own private use."

Buckingham jumped up from his chair—the commanding-officer to his very backbone.

"Look here, my man," he said, setting his teeth over his words, 'you've had one warning against insubordination, I take it you won't get a second. You've had your orders, they will not be repeated. I've no more to say." Then he went back to his writing-table.

Ned went silently down the stairs and out of the house. Outside, in the open air, he drew a long breath.

"It won't be for long—it can't be for long, now," he muttered, clenching his fingers into the palms of his hand. "Let me get breathing-time, that's all, and I'll pay off my debts to the last farthing."

XXXV

A fter all, the police had not to bring any extraordinary amount of ingenuity to bear upon the task of discovering Kathleen.

They went a little far a-field at first; having learned that a young woman answering to her description had taken ticket for Liverpool, they immediately concluded that she was to be found in America, and set the Atlantic wires going; only, however, to discover that she was not, at any rate, to be heard of at New York.

A detective, dispatched on second thoughts to her father and mother in Gloucestershire, returned with the tidings that she had sent for a box of her clothes, left behind at Overbury; that she had married Bryan O'Shea, much to the disgust of her parents, who "hadn't much opinion of the O'Shea family," and that her present address was at the O'Shea Farm, Lough Lea, County Down.

This news circuitously reached Joyce and Mab in their sea-side cottage.

Mab, as usual, had a kind word to say for the girl.

"I don't think, on the whole, we treated either Ned or Kathleen fairly," she said; "we did our best to give them notions beyond their station; and then, when most they wanted our help, we let them slip through our fingers."

Joyce characteristically dismissed the matter.

"She was a weak little goose," she said; "if she meant to marry Bryan O'Shea, why didn't she do it without any fuss?"

With the tragic anxieties that pressed upon her at the moment, a sentence seemed more than enough to expend upon this girl and her ridiculous love-affair. But the chances were that, if Joyce had given to her a true account of the facts of the case, she would considerably have modified her epithets. If, for instance, she had seen pretty Kathleen's white, forlorn face throughout the whole of that long stolen journey to Liverpool, on the day of Mrs. Shenstone's wedding, or had heard her talk with her brother Ned, when close upon midnight she had succeeded in unearthing him from his lodgings somewhere in the slums in the heart of the town.

The brother and sister had walked together up and down the dark side of a quiet street, talking in low, constrained tones.

This in substance was their conversation:

"I think you must be out of your mind. I never thought you had much, but what little you had is wanting now," Ned said, in a hard, gruff voice.

Kathleen's reply came in muffled tones.

"Ned, tell me what I have come all these miles to ask you, and I'll go back home, or to the Shenstones, or anywhere else in the world you like. Where is Mr. Ledyard? What have you and the captain and Bryan O'Shea done with him?"

"What has any one of us to do with Mr. Ledyard, I should like to know? And also what have you to do with the gentleman? Will you tell me that, my girl?"

"I? Nothing whatever. Only this may interest you perhaps. Miss Joyce is breaking her heart after him."

"You were not always so particularly fond of Miss Joyce. I've heard you wish her in her grave more times than I could count," sneered Ned.

"Oh, well, she'll be there soon enough without any wishing on my part—and," this added with emphasis on each syllable, "Miss Mab, too, for she's breaking her heart as fast as her sister."

"Is that true, Kathleen?" he asked; and there came a softer note in his voice now.

"Gospel truth. Send me back with a message to her."

Ned resumed his walk. His steps at first were hurried, and Kathleen could barely keep pace with him. Presently they flagged, and she laid her hand upon his arm.

"Look here, Ned—" she began.

He turned upon her furiously.

"Look here, my girl. The best thing you can do is to be off to Lough Lea as quick as possible, and marry Bryan O'Shea as you promised. Otherwise it may go harder than you think with one or two you care most for."

Had there been moonlight enough to show Kathleen's face, Ned might have noted an odd, resolute look come into it—a pallor and rigidity which seemed to turn her into the marble likeness of herself.

"Very well," she said, slowly, "I'll go to Lough Lea and marry Bryan O'Shea; and, whatever comes of it, I shan't forget 'twas you gave me the good advice.

XXXVI

Joyce was no sooner safely shut in in her sea-side solitude than she fell to measuring the distance she had put between herself and possible hope. Here was a man who held in his hand the secret she would have paid for cheerfully with her life, and here was she fleeing from him and stopping her ears, as though she had neither part nor lot in the matter.

It had been easy enough—comparatively, that is—in the height of her passion to wish she had a thousand tongues to speak their "noes" to the hideous temptation; it was not so easy in a cooler moment to echo the wish. At a crisis her instincts had saved her; now, when she took to reasoning on the matter, her brain grew bewildered, her moral sense confused. A hundred thoughts and plans in turn suggested themselves, only in turn to be dismissed as impracticable.

Joyce sorely needed a counsellor in this emergency, but where was one to be found? Mab, for obvious reasons, was unfitted for the part; Uncle Archie, with gout threatening and his irritable temper at its worst, was scarcely the one to handle so delicate a matter. The police authorities, except as a last resource, were not to be thought of. Joyce knew that, if she attempted compulsion in any form, the man would simply throw himself into a defiant attitude, and her chance would be at an end.

Of course, there was always the supposition that Buckingham's words might have been mere bombast to force her to favor his suit to Mab. But it was a supposition she did not for a moment dwell upon. Her only thought was how to get at the knowledge he might hold without striking an unworthy bargain with him.

It was scarcely strange that in this connection Ned Donovan's name should suggest itself. Although she had no facts whereupon to base the conjecture, there had always been present to her mind the possibility that Ned and Buckingham were members of the same political organization. If such were the case there might be means of information common to both, which Ned might work advantageously for her now. Also there was the possibility that, as comrades in a league, Ned might have some influence over Buckingham, which he might bring usefully into play.

In addition to all this, there was his devotion to Mab, which, naturally enough, was an open secret between the two sisters. In other circumstances, Joyce would have been reluctant to trade upon a devotion whose unobtrusiveness and unselfishness years had tested, but had not shaken. Now, however, in this her sore extremity, she felt justified in appealing to it.

Whether direct good to herself might result from it or not, of one thing she felt confident, viz., that no unworthy concessions respecting Mab would be made by him.

So she sat down and wrote a long, passionate, pleading letter to the young Irishman, giving him, in outline, the account of her interview with Buckingham, beseeching him to see this man for her and get What terms he could out of him.

"To no man living but you would I intrust such a mission," she wrote. "I speak the simple truth when I say I would rather it should be in your hands than in mine; for, alas, that I should have to write it! I feel that your devotion and loyalty to my sister are at this crisis more to be relied on than mine."

Then she concluded with an entreaty that he would use judgment and caution in the matter, remembering how much they all had at stake. Furthermore, she added a postscript imploring him on no account to let Buckingham have her present address; "for, see him again in this world," she wrote, "I never will, or my chance of Heaven will be gone."

It was a desperate appeal to make; but affairs were in a desperate condition with her. When it was done, she knew not whether it had been well or ill done.

She inclosed the letter under cover to Kathleen, at Lough Lea, for of Ned's whereabouts she was totally ignorant. Then she set herself to fill up the terrible gap of waiting that must ensue, as best she might, with the common-place and the trivial.

The common-place is one of the few things in life of which the supply is in excess of the demand. It will never be elbowed into a corner by tragedy, let it try as it will. So, at least, Joyce found, as she waited impatiently for letter or message from Donovan. There came the usual flow of letters to read and answer.

Like this from good Aunt Bell:

"Do spare your uncle as much painful correspondence as possible, Joyce. Poor darling, his temper was always an irritable one, and it doesn't improve under this long attack. If I didn't give in to him in every matter, great or small, the house wouldn't hold us two."

Or this from Uncle Archie:

"I'm a little out of pain today, and hope to keep so if your aunt will only let me have my own way as to medicine and diet. It's a little late in the day to complain; but you know she was always inclined to be despotic, and, to keep the peace, I simply have to knock under to her in everything."

And finally, this from her mother, on her wedding-tour:

"We have had a desperate—desperate quarrel, darling Joyce. I'm coming home at once. Ah, my good looks have been my bane all my life through. If I had been a plain woman I might still have been happy Ernestine Shenstone. It all began yesterday because I told him some people in the hotel where we are staying thought I was his daughter, not his wife. Now, I ask you, was that enough to put him in a tearing rage, and make him call me "madam," instead of "my child," all the rest of the day? And he does look like my father—no one who saw us together could deny it. The bald patch at the back of his head gets bigger every day, and he goes to sleep in his easy-chair whenever I begin to talk to him, and, if this is not a sign of old age creeping on, I don't know what is. Oh, and do you know, Joyce, he wears a horrible red cotton night-cap at nights, and sometimes he forgets and comes down to breakfast in it. If I had only seen him in it before we married! But there, it dosen't matter; only expect me at Overbury almost as soon as you get this. By-the-way, dear, there's one thing I should like to ask you to do for me. He is always asking me—at least he asked me once or twice lately—if I know anything of the interior of a place called Earlswood. Now, between ourselves, Joyce, I don't, but I don't want him to know my ignorance; so if you could just find out a little about the place, and let me know, so that I could give him an answer which might imply I knew a great deal, I should be very much obliged to you. I mean only, of course, if you don't see me back in a day or two. Perhaps, after all, I may alter my mind; one never feels quite sure of one's self in such matters."

And a postscript to the letter, added the next day, showed that Mrs. Bullen had very much altered her mind:

"Darling children," it ran, "we've kissed and made it up again—it was nothing more than a lover's quarrel, after all. We are off to Venice tomorrow, and most likely sha'n't return to England until next spring, we both hate the cold weather so. I send you the letter just as I wrote it yesterday, so that you may have all our news.

Your loving mother,
ERNESTINE BULLEN

XXXVII

N ed received Joyce's letter at Cork just as he was on the point of starting for Lough Lea with a sealed packet for Sylvia Buckingham, who was still enjoying her comfortable quarters at the "Abbey House" with a pair of vigorous Nationalists for host and hostess. It raised in him a riot of tumultuous feeling, adding fuel to his slumbering fire of discontent with his work, of animosity to his chief. He anathematized himself for his folly in swearing allegiance to a league that reckoned the unreasoning obedience of a dog among the cardinal virtues. Cranmer-like, he could have burned in slow fire that right hand of his which only overnight had telegraphed to Captain Buckingham Mab's and Joyce's address.

She, the woman he had worshiped from afar with such true, unselfish devotion to be handed over to the cruel keeping of a man like Buckingham!

"See him!" he muttered, "ay, that I will, and to some purpose too! I knew the day of reckoning wasn't far off, but I didn't think it was at my door."

Then he had started on his journey to Lough Lea, forming his plans as he went; but it was not until Lough Lea was reached, and he was making his way in the dawn of a golden August morning through the green lanes to the Abbey House, that his plan of action definitely and finally arranged itself.

It was simply this: He would follow on his chief's footsteps, forestall his arrival at Tretwick; if such a thing were possible meet him within a stone's throw of the house where these sisters had taken refuge, and have a few sharp, strong words with him there. Yes, he knew well enough what those words must be. Chief or no chief, for a brief five minutes he would speak as man speaks to man, when the full heart dictates the words, and give him to understand that these young ladies were not now, nor at any future time, to be molested. Should the captain laugh his words to scorn and order him back to his duty, well, then he would have a few words to say to him about duty also, and would remind him that on one occasion he had somewhat stretched his prerogative which compelled his subordinates to an unreasoning obedience, and that an impeachment to that effect laid before his superiors at New York might be attended with unpleasant consequences to himself.

Had Sylvia Buckingham read the man's thoughts in his face as he presented his sealed packet to her, she could not have treated him with a more repellent harshness. Possibly she took her cue from her brother. This Irishman was evidently out of favor at headquarters.

Ned kept his discontent to himself. His thoughts were too busy with the course he had mapped out for himself, and its minor difficulties of detail, to allow him to be much disturbed by superficial annoyances.

From the Abbey House he took his way straight to the O'Shea farm, separated from it by two or three fields and an occasional bog. It was an antiquated and ill-kept edifice, flanked on one side by an untidy-looking potato-field, on the other by an equally untidy-looking poultry-yard. A few gaunt cattle grazed in an adjoining field, whose gaping, torn hedges betokened the fact that it had known nothing of repair or hurdle since the last hunt had ridden through.

Whatever revenue the O'Shea family might enjoy, this little ragged homestead most assuredly could not be credited with the responsibility of being its fountain-head.

An old woman smoking a short pipe sat on a bench at the front door. She had a bright yellow cotton kerchief tied over her head, but beyond this her costume inclined to the dusky and ill-mended. Occasionally she withdrew her pipe to exclaim an "Arrah thin, be off wid ye," to the cocks and hens who came straggling in from the poultry-yard, making frantic efforts to slip past her bare feet into the house. This exclamation, alternating with another, a muttered Irish anathema, whose modified English equivalent would be, "'That's a fine wife for an O'Shea to bring home! Look at her and admire her." The said anathema following the shadow of a girl down the garden path to the gate, where Ned stood waiting for her.

"Look at her and admire her!" assuredly not a difficult task for an eye undazzled by O'Shea ideals. Kathleen O'Shea is not the Kathleen Donovan of a year ago. That Kathleen was a good ten years younger to look at, and about her there hung such a glamor of bewitching smiles, fun, and arch glances that one never stopped to criticise the shape of her mouth, the color of hair or eyes. Now that the glamor has gone, the fun, arch glances, bewitching smiles together disappeared, it is possible to take calm stock of her face and features; to discover that her eyes are large, deep blue, that dark rings around them accentuate their look of haunting melancholy, and tell the tale of weary days and sleepless nights. One wonders whether it is the pale face that throws the blue-black hair into such bold contrast, or whether it is the black hair that makes the face show so deathly white in the glinting morning sunlight.

In one respect only is the Kathleen of today identical with the Kathleen of last year, and that is in the matter of pretty and neat attire. That bygone Kathleen had been known to spend an hour in front of her looking-glass, arranging her glossy hair, before she saw fit to present herself to her young mistresses, to perform for them a similar office. Her mother had been wont to assert that the only way in which to get housework done by those dainty fingers of hers would be to banish all looking-glasses from the house, when not a doubt she would set to work to scour the pewter plates on the kitchen dresser, in order to make them do duty as mirrors.

Whether Kathleen through necessity had been driven to perform such an office for the O'Shea pewter plates might be doubtful, but certain it was that those plaits of dark hair, which shone like a raven's wing in the sunlight, must have had abundant aid from a looking-glass, in order to their present elaborate arrangement, as likewise the prettily-tied knot of ribbon which held her collar in its place.

The brother and sister talked in low tones, with many a furtive glance toward the old woman and her pipe. Ned's words, though all but whispered, were vehement and emphatic.

"I tell you," he said, breaking abruptly into Kathleen's queries as to the health and well-being of the old father and mother in Gloucestershire, "life isn't worth a brass farthing to me. I'm hunted, dogged from morning till night, in spite of all the hard work I've done for them."

Kathleen laughed, not the pleasant laugh of old days, but a harsh, scornful laugh. Her voice, too, was harsh and scornful as she answered:

"You work hard, but you don't work well. They say you're not to be trusted—you're too tender-hearted."

"Tender-hearted! I'll give them proof of my tender heart if I get a chance."

"When they set you to stake Mike Kearney's cattle, didn't you let them all slip through your fingers, so that the beasts came back to their sheds as soon as the boys had left plowing up the fields?" she went on, not heeding the interruption.

"The poor dumb things! I would have cut off my right hand sooner than torture them! If those men had any sense they would—" He broke off for a moment, as if he dared not trust himself to speak his mind.

Kathleen looked warningly over her shoulder toward the house.

"Don't forget you are on the O'Shea property at the present moment," she said, sarcastically.

"Confound the O'Sheas, every man of them! Now, what good has your marriage with Bryan done for me, I should like to know, after all the fine talk he and Maurice made over it?"

"Ah, were you fool enough to expect any good for yourself out of that?"

"I don't expect much from any man or woman, let them be brother or sister a thousand times over; but I don't look to have my footsteps watched and dogged by a man who has married my sister, and that man's own brother."

"They're set to do it."

"I know that. Now, look here, Kathleen." Here Ned's voice took a softer tone. "Just get those two off my heels for the next twenty-four hours—I don't want more. Tell them I'm off to Milford on the captain's business—special business. Swear it, if you like. Tell them I shall be back again in Cork tomorrow night at farthest, and shall report myself there. Tell them any lies you like—you used to be famous at that sort of thing once."

"I may be again when the right time comes."

"Well, the right time has come, take my word for it. Don't you see my necessity? It's a matter of life or death, I tell you."

"I spoke those words to you once before, but you shut your ears to them. I told you Miss Joyce would die, Miss Mab would die, all for a secret you might tell, but wouldn't."

Ned's face grew white.

"Give over fooling, Kathleen, for the love of heaven. I tell you this is a matter of life or death to me; that perhaps in this world you and I may never set eyes on each other again. Now will you do what I want you—get me free of those two men, Maurice and Bryan O'Shea, for the next twenty-four hours?"

"It's easy to say 'get me free of those two.' How am I to do it, I should like to know?"

"Do it any way that comes uppermost. Don't stick at a trifle so long as it's done, and that before I'm out of sight of the house. Get them into a row with the O'Gormans—you used to be a capital hand at setting men by the ears at one time. Make it a shillalah business if you like, and then bring the whisky and deal it out liberally all round. Do it anyhow, so long as it's done. I tell you it's a matter of life and death; not only to me, but perhaps to some others." This added with a significance that must have set the girl's thoughts ranging.

"I'll do my best," she promised; but the promise was given sullenly and grudgingly enough.

"Very well, then, take care that it is your best, or it may be worse than useless to me. Now I'll go. Remember it's to Milford, on the captain's business, that I'm going. Stick to that, whatever else you're doubtful about."

He turned on his heel and left her. Possibly it was the bright August sun which made him draw his hat low over his eyes, and choose the shadow of the hedgerow to walk in rather than the open road.

Kathleen stood watching him out of sight, leaning over the gate and shadowing her eyes with her hands. Suddenly, to her surprise, he stood still in the pathway, then came back with steps as hurried as those that had carried him away.

"What is it?" she asked. "I've no money—no, not a penny; so it's no use asking me for any."

"I don't want money." He looked right and left to make sure there were no listeners, and his voice sank to a whisper. "It's just this—if anything happens to me—I mean if I'm found one day lying in the road with a bullet through my brain, I want my watch—my old silver watch"—here he laid his hand upon it—"given to Miss Joyce—to Miss Joyce, do you understand?"

Then, before she had time to make her reply, he did a thing she had never known him do in all his life before—leaned over the gate and kissed her.

XXXVIII

After all, the sea-breezes did not do so much for Mab as Joyce had hoped they might. Without any definite illness, there was yet that in her condition to cause Joyce serious anxiety—a muscular weakness so great as at times to incapacitate her from walking, or even from lifting her hand to her head. She appeared to have a disinclination for bodily exertion of any sort. She would spend the whole day, if allowed to do so, lying with closed eyes on her couch, or listlessly reclining in a high-backed chair at the open window.

Joyce, as she sat beside her, watching her in silence, could only wonder over a certain mystic beauty that seemed so to overspread Mab's face as to render it difficult to identify that face with the pained, anxious countenance of a year back. A feeling akin to the awe that one feels in the presence of the unknown and supernatural, took possession of her, It was second only to another feeling, that of apprehensive terror lest her darling might be plucked out of her hand by another and a stronger one than Captain Buckingham's—the iron hand of death itself.

She began to think it would be as well to get Mab nearer home, or at least near some big city, where, in case of need, good medical advice could be readily had,

She hinted as much to Mab as they sat together two days after she had dispatched her letter to Donovan. Mab did not seem to hear her. As usual, she was leaning back in her easy-chair, with closed eyes.

The window was open. The sun had just sunk into the sea, amid flames of violet and ruddy gold. The waves lay steeped in all the changeful glory of the after-glow. Not a sound, save the lapping and soft dashing of the waters on the beach, broke the outside stillness. Joyce never allowed Mab to spend this sunset hour in solitude. She had learned from experience that this was the time when her visions took strongest hold on her, and the world seemed to let her slip.

Joyce was just then fighting a far harder battle than ever Mab had fought against the voice of her own heart. "Those dreams of hers may cost her her life," the doctor had said, when called in to attend Mab in her fainting-fit. And those dreams seemed now to Joyce's fancy the only door which might chance to open and let in a ray of light.

She sometimes felt herself to be in the plight of a man who, having been denied a life-boat and a plank as a means of safety from shipwreck, says, "Now I'll die sooner than touch the rope you fling to me."

She had shut her ears, and had fled from Captain Buckingham's temptation; now she was as good as putting her right hand across Mab's eyes, and saying, "You, at any rate, shall not pierce the darkness!" her left hand, as an afterthought, across Mab's mouth, adding, "or, at least, whatever you see, you shall not tell me."

She dared not reason the matter out with herself. Instinct, nothing else, guided her in her extremity just then. She seemed to be living out her life in painful jerks, snatching at what was right, but holding it slackly, and praying it might slip through her fingers; fleeing from evil, as she had fled from Buckingham, but all the while, as it were, with her head looking over her shoulder, hoping that evil might overtake her.

These still, sunset hours, which seemed to bring naught but peace to Mab, always found Joyce at her worst. All her doubts, terrors, misgivings, regrets, seemed then to swoop down upon her like so many evil birds in a mighty clamorous flock.

Suddenly Mab's soft, uncertain tones broke in on her thoughts.

"Joyce," she queried, "do you ever feel people to be near you before you see them?"

Joyce started, for at that very moment, chancing to lift her eyes to the open window, she had caught sight of the figure of a man on the beach below, whose outline recalled that of Ned Donovan.

"Whom do you feel near you tonight, dear?" she asked, eagerly, still keeping her eye fixed on the man on the beach.

She had a reply she did not expect.

"Captain Buckingham," answered Mab, in slow, clear tones.

Joyce's impulse was to cry aloud:

"Oh, Mab, don't let that name pass your lips! That man is temptation incarnate, and he will turn us both out of the road to heaven if he can!"

But she held in her impulse, biting her lips till they blanched.

She rose from her chair, went to the window, and looked out, shading her eyes with her hand. What if that were Captain Buckingham on the beach, and in another five minutes she should be called upon to face him and go through a second fiery ordeal!

With a great thrill of thankfulness she saw her fears were groundless. The man was Donovan, not a doubt. Most probably he was coming to the house to answer her letter in person, and not knowing the exact geography of the place had come along the coast instead of by the cliffs.

She would not have him shown into the room where Mab was, she decided. It would take him a good five minutes to get to the house; presently she would creep out of the room quietly and see him alone down-stairs.

Mab's voice again broke the silence.

"Last evening, just at this hour, Joyce," she said, her eyes still closed, her voice growing more and more soft and slow, "I had a sweet, strange vision. I feel I must tell it to you."

"Dream, you mean, darling," interposed Joyce, nervously.

"Call it a dream, if you like, Joyce. I thought I was crossing the heath in the dead of night. It was pitch-dark, but somehow I did not miss my way. Suddenly, looking up, I saw straight ahead of me, shining out of the darkness, a clear, soft, white light. I thought it must be the moon rising from out of the trees in the little churchyard in the hollow."

She paused. Joyce went over to her side, putting her arms round her. Mab's dreams at such a moment were not to be put on one side unheeded.

"As I drew nearer," Mab went on, in the same slow, faint tones as before, "I saw there was no moon, that the light, instead of coming from the sky, came from the churchyard itself, and was streaming upward, a full, clear, quiet blaze of light in the dark heavens."

"Go on, dear."

"I wondered what could be the source of this light. But not until I had entered the little gate, half hidden by those two dark yews, did I know. Then, Joyce, an awful and wonderful sight lay before me, On every grave—every mound, every tombstone—stood an angel clothed in light begirt with light. Upward, downward, round about them streamed this light; every dark tree, every pebble in the path, every cloud in the sky was boldly, beautifully outlined by it."

Joyce's heart was beating wildly, she trembled for what was coming.

Mab went on softly and dreamily still.

"And what struck me most was the intense stillness that prevailed. There was this mighty host—for it was a mighty host, on some graves stood two or more angels—and yet never a sound. The silence was in itself grand and awful. I felt fascinated, yet I was not afraid. Step by step I went nearer, till I could feel—yes, feel—their light falling upon me, and could see their marvelous and beautiful faces. Some were old, noble and stern-looking; some were young, like lovely girls or boys; some were mere children; others like cherub babies. Some stood as though praying, with arms outstretched to heaven; some were kneeling on the graves, with bowed heads; one or two had drawn swords in their hands, which flashed golden-bright in the white light. For the moment I thought it must be the day of resurrection, and that these were the souls of the dead rising out of their graves."

"Oh, Mab!" broke in Joyce, in an awe-stricken voice.

"But the next moment it was borne into my mind that the dead were lying quietly sleeping beneath in their graves, and that these bright, beautiful beings were their guardian angels, those who had watched over them and taken care of them in their life-time, and who had not given them up now that they were coffined and hidden out of sight."

Again Mab paused, and now her voice sank to a deep, solemn tone.

"And suddenly, as I stood there gazing and wondering, I saw in the midst of all this radiancy one dark, blank space; it was a grave with no angel upon it. It made my heart ache, and I thought I would make my way through the light to this forgotten grave, and say a prayer for the poor soul lying beneath. The air fell upon me chill and damp as I drew near the spot, the darkness was so dense I could feel it, just as I had felt the light. I could not see the name graven on the stone, so I traced it out with my finger. And it was the name of George Ritchie Buckingham."

Joyce gave a great start, but words would not come.

"And as I knelt there I heard a voice, a sweet, strong, sad voice, speaking out of the stillness, and saying, "Who will come and be the angel of this grave?" I looked up as I knelt and said, "Here am I, Lord, take me!"

Her voice, low as it was, vibrated with passion as she finished speaking. And, as she lay back in her chair, pallid, with upturned, luminous eyes, Joyce's wildly-aroused fancy could almost believe that her offer of herself was at that moment being silently accepted, and that the translation from body to spirit was being wrought. She clasped Mab tightly in her arms.

"My darling, my darling," she cried, "stop, stop, or you will break my heart! You, you to be—"

Then she broke off, thrusting back her words unspoken, fearful of the uncouth note of contrast they might strike to Mab's brain. She made a great effort to steady her nerves, which Mab's eerie talk had shaken. She scarcely felt fit to face Donovan and his possible revelations. He must be almost at the door now. She got back as much self-control as possible, and rang the bell for Mab's maid to stay in the room during her brief absence.

She gave one long, steady look out of the window as she passed. There were no signs of Donovan anywhere now. The after-glow had faded, one or two faint twinkling stars shone out in a pale green sky; the grayness of early night was settling down upon the sea.

XXXIX

Joyce waited in vain for Donovan. Neither on that night nor on the next day did he make his appearance. She grew wildly impatient, and made every possible inquiry concerning him of the coastguard-men and fisher-folk. No one, however, appeared to have seen a man answering to his description.

Joyce felt she must start for Lough Lea there and then, and find out for herself whether Kathleen had faithfully delivered her letter. She would have done so, not a doubt, had not a sudden change for the worse shown itself in Mab. Without any apparent cause, there had come to her so great an accession of muscular weakness as to compel her to keep her bed during the early part of the day. It set Joyce measuring once more the distance between herself and good medical advice. She dispatched a messenger to Newton Stewart for the best doctor to be found in the place. By the same hand she sent an urgent telegram to Kathleen, at Lough Lea, asking whether her letter had been given to Ned, and what was his present address.

Then nothing remained to do but sit still and stare at the blank wall which once more seemed to confront her.

In the afternoon the doctor arrived. Mab's condition seemed to puzzle him. He prescribed for her rest, quiet, and a tonic, and departed, promising to come again on the following day.

An answer to Joyce's telegram arrived in due course from Kathleen. It briefly stated that the letter had been delivered to Ned, but that where he was at the present moment she had not the slightest idea, nor had she any means of finding out.

Then Joyce, at her wits' ends, telegraphed to Morton, requesting him to do his utmost to discover Ned's whereabouts as quickly as possible.

To find him, she felt was an absolute necessity. If he could not be found, and induced to face Buckingham for her, what alternative remained?

Here Joyce's heart supplied the inevitable answer, an answer that had been growing into definite shape during the last few days of impatient waiting:

"You must see him yourself! And then Heaven help you, that's all!"

Joyce covered her face with her hands and sank into a chair beside

Mab's bed. For the last twenty-four hours, which had magnified themselves into as many days, she had felt herself drifting to this point.

See Buckingham again! That meant concession on the one side, victory on the other; there could be no middle course. But on which side was victory likely to fall? Heaven help her, indeed!

She looked down on Mab's white, yet withal tranquil face, and thin hand lying on the coverlet. In fancy she saw the wedding-ring on the slender finger, through her instrumentality; Buckingham triumphant; her own agony of suspense at an end.

Then a sudden great terror fell upon her. She sank on her knees beside the bed, bowing her head on her hands. Surely never before did dry eyes and dumb lips plead so passionate a prayer!

How long she remained thus she did not know. The afternoon sunbeams gave place to the long, slanting shafts of evening. Still she knelt there in her dumb agony. Time stood still for her, as it does in sleep, as it may in death.

Mab's soft voice recalled her to consciousness.

"Joyce," it said, "I would like to get up now, and go down to the beach, and see the sun set."

Joyce did not oppose the wish. To say truth, there was not left in her much strength to oppose anything—least of all Mab's sudden impulses, in which of late she had learned to acquiesce without demur.

So they two went down and sat upon the beach together, watching the great sun sink low and lower till it disappeared, a burnished, fiery ball, beneath the waters.

It is all very well for the poets to say that Nature has a voice and speaks a message to every living soul. The truth of it is, the living soul first puts its message into Nature's mouth, then takes it out again, rings the town-crier's bell, and says, "Oyez, oyez, oyez! This is what great Nature has to say."

Mab, as she sat there with eyes upturned to the fading sky, said to herself:

"There is evening's rest after morning's toil for all creation. It must come; God sends it."

Joyce got for herself an altogether different message out of the grand, desolate seascape; the gaunt, brown rocks; stony beach; dashing surf. They seemed to laugh at her littleness, her weak resistance to fate, to bid her fold her hands and confess herself beaten at last.

"Compare your strength, your duration with ours, and what are you?" they seemed to say, in one mocking voice. "Oh, you, less than a speck on the folds of Creation's garment, find a Providence for yourself if you can!"

The crunch of feet on the pebbles broke in upon their thoughts. It was an old fisherman approaching. As he passed he said something in broad Scotch, pointing with his finger a little distance ahead.

Joyce could not catch his words, but her eye followed his finger. She saw a knot of fishermen, and one or two of their wives, gathered together under the deep shadow of the rocks, a little to the left of the footway that led up to their house.

Some bare-legged boys in blue jerseys were running up the cliffs, as though dispatched on messages. A coastguard-man was descending with a telescope under his arm.

"An accident—some one may have fallen over the cliff," said another fisherman as he went by. "It'll likely be a stranger."

A great and sudden dread seized Joyce, a dread that swamped every other thought, yet a dread utterly unaccountable and unreasonable. It did not follow, because the fisherman had said it was most likely a stranger who had met with the accident, therefore that stranger must be Frank Ledyard. Yet this was the fear that had taken hold of her now. "My darling, we must, must meet again somewhere, somehow," she had said to herself over and over again, even when her hopes were at their lowest, her fears at their height. Now the thought that chilled her heart was: "What if this be the meeting after all! What if, in the dead face lying there, I recognize the face I am hunting the world to find!"

The little knot assembled under the cliff's side had formed into something of a procession now. Four men headed it, bearing an improvised ambulance on their shoulders on which lay stretched the lifeless burden; the women and children straggled beside them and brought up the rear. The twilight was deepening rapidly into the gray of night; the shadows of the old rocks went stretching out nearly to the sea-line. Weird and shadowy looked the dismal little cortège as it moved along slowly, silently, save for the crunch of the pebbles underfoot, which told that the burden was a heavy one.

Joyce, the spectre of herself, tottered forward to meet it, her hands clasped, her face bloodless.

But it was from Mab, not Joyce, that there broke that low cry of pain, so like the cry of a wounded dumb animal that has had its death-blow dealt to it.

For in that "it," borne past on the men's shoulders, in that battered form and disfigured face, grayer than the gray twilight that was settling down upon it, she had recognized the face and form of Captain Buckingham.

XL

Thus, in sudden awful fashion, were Joyce's agonies and questionings forever set at rest. No need now to dread that mocking smile, that taunting tongue, nor to close her eyes and shudder over the wonder when and where she would be brought face to face with both again. She had but to open them, and there was the cruel face lying low, with no taunt upon its lips, no mocking glitter in its eye.

With her fears died her hopes also. Where was the chance now of getting at the secret this man held? Into his grave with him, not a doubt, it would go.

If it had not been for this recognition of Captain Buckingham's body by Mab and Joyce, he must have been buried under a nameless stone. Several persons, it is true, came forward stating that they had seen him walking along the cliffs two days previously. An innkeeper from Newton Stewart deposed to having supplied him with a "machine" which set him down within a mile of Tretwick. But to one and all he was an utter stranger.

Joyce gave to the authorities of the place Sylvia Buckingham's name and address. With this, her part in the tragedy came to an end.

The first feeling in the mind of the good people of Tretwick was, that Buckingham had met his death by mischance. The cliffs, below which his body had been found were treacherous and ill-protected, all sorts of gaps and fissures being hidden by the gorse and stunted bushes. A stranger attempting to find his way along them in the late evening, might easily enough, by one false step, lose his balance. There could be no doubt that Buckingham had fallen from these cliffs. He was a heavy man, his fall could be traced down the side by the uprooted bushes to which he had clung, the displaced crumbling sandstone, and a torn shred or two of clothing here and there in the gorse.

Joyce, with the thought of her desperate appeal to Ned in her mind, and of his sudden appearance on the beach, wondered whether a darker story might lie behind this.

It was an awful thought this—that incidentally, perhaps, this man's death had been brought about by her instrumentality. After she had written her letter to Ned, she had wondered whether it had been ill or well done. It seemed to her now that it had been very ill done indeed.

CATHERINE LOUISA PIRKIS

Later on, her wonder was to be changed into certainty. When Sylvia arrived, at her suggestion an inquiry as to the cause of her brother's death was duly held under the auspices of the Procurator-fiscal. Evidence was then brought forward which threw a new light upon the whole matter. Two or three men deposed to having met a stranger, tall, and in appearance like' an Irishman, walking rapidly in the direction of the sea. A woman stated that, going home late one night from the house of a sick relative, whom she had been nursing, she met a stranger of similar appearance, limping, with a handkerchief twisted round one wrist. It was dark, and she could scarcely see his face, for his hat was pulled low, and the collar of his coat was turned up. He had accosted her civilly, told her he had hurt his knee in scrambling up the cliffs, and injured his wrist; he asked if he were in the right road for Newton Stewart. The woman directed him on his way, and then thought no more of the occurrence, until the finding of Buckingham's body recalled it to her mind.

Posters giving as full a description as possible of this man, and offering rewards for his apprehension, were at once put into circulation.

The good people at Tretwich were not a little surprised at the calm and self-possessed manner in which Sylvia Buckingham comported herself, through what must have been a succession of trying scenes to any woman. She traveled alone from Lough Lea, crossing the North Channel at Port Patrick, took up her quarters at Newton Stewart, and thence drove daily to Tretwick. The kindly-hearted people in the neighborhood were prepared to receive her with warm sympathy, and offers of hospitality for so long as she chose to accept it. Somehow, when they saw her, their sympathy was chilled, and their hospitality not offered. Whether it was a certain preoccupied air, which seemed to imply she had weighty matters on hand, to which private feelings must yield place, that cut her off from their compassion; or whether it was the curt, business-like manner with which she went through all legal preliminaries, and ordered her brother's funeral, that jarred upon their sentiments, it would be hard to say. It is possible that both causes were in operation.

Sylvia made an apparently candid statement as to her brother's occupation, as member of a patriotic league, which she said numbered on its roll some of the noblest names in the land.

Whatever deep feelings she might own to, she certainly kept them well under control. The only matter on which she seemed to evince the slightest amount of anxiety, was the getting possession of the papers and other belongings found upon her brother. They were handed to her intact, and were after all of seemingly small importance. They consisted of a memorandum-book, every entry in which was written in cipher; a purse containing gold and American bank-notes; a gold watch, to all appearance a perfect, well-made chronometer, but from which, strange to say, the hands had been removed.

The Procurator-fiscal, in handing the property to her, commented on this fact.

Sylvia replied briefly that no doubt it could easily be accounted for, but that she herself was unable to offer any explanation of the matter.

Possibly the fact might have had a deeper meaning for these good people, could they have followed Sylvia back to her hotel at Newton Stewart; have gone with her into her room, and have watched her affix to the numerous letters she was just then dispatching, in lieu of her signature, a seal in red wax which bore the impression of a clock without hands.

XLI

All these details respecting Captain Buckingham's death came to Joyce only in whispers. Even these whispers were unasked for. Four walls now held for her all the best that life had given to her, in so much as they shut in Mab with her fast-waning life, and made a crypt-like sanctuary wherein she could eat out her own heart with her bitter-sweet memories of the past.

It had not needed the warning of the doctor from Newton Stewart to convince her of the fact that the herald-clouds of the great, dark, silent night were already gathering around Mab, and would soon hide her away altogether from the touch of loving hands the sight of loving eyes.

Naturally, Joyce's anxieties and responsibilities were doubled by her distance from her friends and the centers of the best medical advice.

She did a good deal of telegraphing. She telegraphed to London, then to Edinburg, for doctors. Then to Aunt Bell to break the news carefully to Uncle Archie. Lastly to her mother and the old General at their latest address, trusting that, sooner or later, the telegram would follow them and find them out.

After that nothing remained to do but to sit beside her darling, to hold her hand, and watch the white face; the face on which, slowly but surely, was settling the drawn, beaten look that comes to man or woman only once in a lifetime, and which seems to say plainly, as a voice could say it, "Oh, Death, we have wrestled it out together, and the day is yours."

In due course the doctors arrived, consulted together, and also in due course departed, leaving behind them multitudinous directions for the care and comfort of their patient; but nothing that could be construed into the faintest suggestion of a hope of her ultimate recovery. The shock to her nerves, they said, had shaken her very slender hold of life, and it was now a question not of weeks and months, but of days and hours.

She seemed to be in no pain whatever. From the moment when they had brought her into the room, and laid her insensible on the bed, never a question had passed her lips, nor any sentence that could however remotely be referred to Captain Buckingham, or her life in the past.

Joyce wondered sometimes whether that terrible scene in the twilight had niched itself in Mab's memory as an awful, immutable fact, or whether it had presented itself as one among the many visions which had helped to efface the border-line between the natural and supernatural to her clouded senses.

All day long Mab lay silent and motionless. At rare intervals her eyes opened, with a wandering, bewildered look in them, as if they held a question that refused to be put into words.

Sometimes her lips would part, and Joyce would eagerly bend down her ear in the hope of catching some word, some sentence, that might tell what were the thoughts the tired brain held. Generally, however, they would close again after muttering some incoherent, unmeaning phrases.

"She will most likely pass away in her sleep," the doctors had said. But was this sleep? Joyce asked herself, as again and again Mab's words would come back to her: "I know now what 'I' means; how that 'I' may be in the soul or 'I' may be in the body at will." She could almost fancy that Mab, her true, loving Mab, was standing beside her invisible; was wandering through space at will; was anywhere, in fact, rather than penned within that weak, weary form which lay so still on its pillows.

Painlessly and tranquilly the end came at last. Just as the dark night was beginning to creep out of the room through the leaves of the vine which shadowed the window, and the rush of bird-notes outside in the dimness told that day was at hand, Joyce, holding Mab's hand in hers, felt it suddenly grow colder.

Her eyelids trembled a moment, as though they would but could not raise themselves. Then the pale lips moved, and Joyce's straining ears could just detect the whisper:

"In the churchyard in the hollow, Joyce."

"Yes, darling," Joyce whispered back. Her own aching heart told her only too surely to what the words referred.

There fell five minutes of perfect, solemn stillness in the room. Outside there sounded the rustle of the light breeze, the soft wash of the sea on the pebbles.

Then Mab's faint voice whispered again:

"Always the sound of the sea, Joyce."

Joyce's heart was beating wildly. She bent her ear low, and lower. But, for all its straining, it could only catch a few muttered, incoherent sentences.

Once she distinguished the words. "Dieppe—getting dark." Then her thoughts flew back, with a sudden thrill of pain, to the last seaside trip they had taken with their father before his death. There came vividly before her one day, when she and Mab had gone wandering out alone on the shining wet sands at low tide in the twilight, and their father, coming out in search of them, had stood high on the beach calling them by name.

Evidently the same thought was in Mab's mind. A sweet smile for a moment parted her lips, although her eyes still remained closed.

"Coming, father," she said, softly yet distinctly, as though answering a sudden summons.

Then the smile slowly faded, the hand which Joyce held became gradually icy-cold. There came a sigh—and Joyce knew that her darling had gone to claim a better birthright for herself than any her occult religion could have brought within reach of her hand.

XLII

J oyce felt herself frozen into silence and insensibility. Her hopes were dead in her heart now, so likewise her fears. Nothing else, in very truth, of agony, of despair, she felt the years could have in store for her. She shrank from none of the sad duties which of necessity devolved upon her in the absence of near friend or relative. She herself chose Mab's last resting-place in the little churchyard, and followed her as sole mourner to her grave.

She scarcely realized her own identity as she went about her mournful duties; she felt battered out of all likeness to herself.

"Now you, Joyce Shenstone," she found herself saying one day, as she stood staring in the glass at the thin white face which called itself her reflection, "what do you mean to do with yourself for the next forty years? You'll never die, you know; you are made of cast-iron or marble, not flesh and blood, certainly."

Mrs. Bullen and the general arrived the day after the funeral. Joyce's telegram, after numerous mischances, had overtaken them in the north of Italy, and, though they had hastened their return as much as possible, wings alone could have brought them in time to say good-by to Mab.

The general was very silent, Mrs. Bullen as diffuse and hysteric as she could be reasonably expected to be.

Between her fainting-fits and floods of tears, she told Joyce a strange story which had met them on their way to Tretwick.

It was to the effect that a certain Irishman, by name Donovan, in the act of stepping on board a Greenock trader just about to sail for the north, had been shot dead by some one standing on the quay. The murderer was supposed to be an agent of some secret political society, and had not yet been arrested.

There could be no doubt of the identity of the man Donovan with their old gardener's son.

Mrs. Bullen had plenty of tears to shed for Mab, but her tears had never been known to clog her conversational powers, even in the early days of her widowhood. Side by side her tears and her gossip flowed together.

"My darling daughter," she sobbed, "we were such companions! I never wanted for sympathy with Mab in the house. Oh, and by-the-way, Joyce, only think! I met Sylvia Buckingham on the platform at Newton

Stewart station. She was in deep black. She looks horribly sallow in black; years older than I do. Take away her blues and her grays, and her good looks are gone. She was just as kind and affectionate as ever; kissed me again and again, and asked after everybody. She told me all about her brother's awful death through a fall over the rocks here, just when he was so kindly coming to see you and our darling Mab. Poor George! I always liked him, although it was very naughty of him to bring all the funny people he did to my house. I should have liked to have introduced him to you, dear." Here Mrs. Bullen turned to her husband: "He was an old admirer of mine, and such a fine, handsome man."

The General raised his eyebrows, but said nothing.

Mrs. Bullen went on:

"Sylvia is a most tender-hearted person. She spoke so kindly of poor Ned, and was going, she told me, straight to Greenock to save his poor father the long miserable journey. She said she should arrange all about his funeral, and take possession—for his parents, of course—of whatever property he might have about him. Oh, dear, what a tragedy it all is! It seems death, death, everywhere."

Here a flood of tears prevented, for a time, further speech.

Joyce's heart echoed her mother's last sentence."

"Death, death everywhere."

Here was a third door of possible hope shut in her face by Death's unmannerly hand.

XLIII

The gardener's cottage at Overbury was an altogether ideal place of abode. It might have been constructed of flowers and creepers only, for all trace of brick or woodwork that met the eye. Tea-roses framed the windows, and, trailing across the glass, turned commonplace squares into picturesque diamond panes. Honeysuckle defied the pruning-knife; and, after covering side-walls and roof, did its best to render ugly chimney-pots ornamental as well as useful. Boxes on the ledges, filled with the glories of the garden, contributed their quota of color and odor, while a luxuriant Virginian creeper, "fading here into yellow, kindling there into red," threw its wild drapery heedlessly, lavishly, in all directions.

So much for the exterior. Within all was in sharp, gloomy contrast to this blaze of beauty and color, for the only son lay in his coffin in the room which had once been his bedroom, and the old father and mother had wrung their hands, looked in each other's faces, and had sung their Nunc Dimittis, though to another tune to that in which Simeon had sung it in the days of old.

"If he had but kept clear of those secret societies, our brave strong boy might have been by our side now," was the burden of their lamentations; and then they would fall to weeping again.

Naturally, in their eyes, Ned figured as a martyr. Of his identity with the man for whose apprehension on suspicion of murder rewards had been offered, they knew nothing. Captain Buckingham's death had only touched them remotely. They knew nothing of him personally, only by repute, as the brother of a lady who had shown, steady, persistent kindness to Kathleen during her short married life, and who now, in their time of sorrow, seemed anxious to extend a like benevolence to them.

They accepted her kindness humbly and gratefully. The old father said a prayer for her as he knelt beside his son's open grave in the little country church-yard; the old mother sobbed out her wonderment over such unexpected beneficence, with her head on Kathleen's shoulder.

"To think the lady should take such uncalled-for trouble, for two old bodies like us that she never set eyes on," she moaned, between her bursts of grief.

Kathleen, who had come from Lough Lea to attend her brother's funeral, seemed to have no tears at command. She stood listening, like one in a dream almost, saying never a word.

Her father had a word to say, though, when he came home from the solemn service, with a wisp of crape round his hat, and a face aged by a dozen years.

"I heard from Miss Buckingham this morning," he said; "she sent Ned's purse, to which, she says, she has added a small amount that perhaps you may like to spend in planting our boy's grave. She asks permission to retain his old silver watch in memory of him. What say you, mother?"

Kathleen gave a violent start, and a curious look flitted athwart her face. She had not forgotten the promise she had given Ned as to the destination of his watch if ill-fortune overtook him.

"What say I?" cried the mother. "There is only one thing to say: let the lady keep it and welcome. It's only the kindest of kind hearts could ask for such a thing; I love her for her love to our boy."

Later on in the day, when Kathleen contrived to get her father alone for five minutes, she had a question to put about the watch.

"Wasn't it one of two, father?" she asked; "didn't my grandfather give you and Uncle Patrick each a watch on the same day? Uncle Patrick gave Ned his, I know, when he bought a better one. What became of yours?"

The father went to a drawer, and produced the facsimile of Ned's watch.

"I put it away," he said, "on the day my old master made me the handsome present of a gold one, when I won the first-class medal for our grapes and pines." The old man looked sadly at the antiquated, tarnished thing. No doubt it brought a rush of memories of pleasant days gone by. "I wanted to have given it you, child, years ago, but your mother said t'was not smart enough to go with your gay clothes, and laces, and ribbons, and you wouldn't value it."

Kathleen held out her hand for it.

"Give it me now, father. See, I've no laces, or ribbons, or smart clothes, and I should value it for your sake and Ned's."

The father could hardly believe his ears.

"The voice wasn't Kathleen's, the look in her eyes wasn't Kathleen's," as he told his wife afterward when recounting the incident; "but there— trouble had changed them all, no doubt," he concluded, "and possibly Kathleen found them as much changed as they found her."

The day afterward another surprise met them, in the shape of an announcement from Kathleen that she was going into service again.

"I shall never go back to Lough Lea," she explained. "I detest the O'Shea's—man, woman, and child. I can't live here to be a burden on you. I shall ask Miss Buckingham to take me as a traveling-maid. She is always moving about from place to place."

The mother had not the heart to utter reproaches, which at one time would have come readily enough to her lips, respecting the girl's folly in marrying a man for whom she had no liking. So she sighed, and said nothing at the moment; but to her husband she spoke freely afterward.

"I don't seem to know my own child; all her pretty ways and love of finery and smart things are gone," she said, looking back regretfully to the fault and follies for which she had soundly rated Kathleen times without number. "Her marriage with Bryan is a miserable one; he treats her badly, not a doubt; he's always away from home, she says, now at one place, now at another. If she can't stay here with us, I couldn't choose a better mistress for her than Miss Buckingham; but I expect, after she has been about the world a bit, she'll come back to the old home and settle down to cheer us up at the end of our days."

So spoke the mother's hopes—short-lived hopes, however. They died of the good-by Kathleen gave her—a long, strong, silent one— when, after a letter from Miss Buckingham expressing her willingness to accept her services, she set off for Greenock.

Sylvia welcomed Kathleen with more cordiality than she had ever shown to Ned. Nothing could have suited her plans better at the moment than this companionship of the girl under guise of maid.

"She is a silly little prattler," she thought, picturing to herself the trifler of days gone by, not a girl whom the experiences of life had embittered and hardened. "Her vanity lays her at the mercy of every one who cares to play upon it. She can only become dangerous by accident; under my eye no such accident can arise. If we want to make use of her as an unconscious instrument, she can be made to do good service."

So Kathleen received a hearty welcome to the Greenock hotel, where Sylvia had taken up her quarters. With great apparent candor, Miss Buckingham told Kathleen all she knew of her own plans, implying that she expected her frankness to be repaid with a similar confidence.

"I may go to France," she said, "or it may be to Vienna, or perhaps back to New York. I can't tell in the least till I hear from my friends across the water. Tell me, do you think you will like long journeys and short rests for a time? And what has become of your husband, and when do you expect to see him again?"

To which Kathleen replied, with a similar candor, that long journeys and short rests would suit her better than anything else just then; that she felt she needed change of air and scene after the terrible shock of her brother's death. As for Bryan, she had not the remotest notion where he was. Of late, his absences from home had been frequent and prolonged. She feared, but of course she could not be sure, that he had joined some Fenian society. If so, she knew his home would see but little of him, and as she hated old Mrs. O'Shea and the dilapidated O'Shea farm, she did not care if she never set eyes on the place again.

Sylvia looked long and steadily at the girl as she finished speaking. Kathleen bore the gaze without flinching. Whatever suspicions might have arisen in Sylvia's mind, not a muscle of Kathleen's face gave substance to them.

On the day after her arrival at Greenock, Kathleen fell into her maid's duties. Sylvia made the kindest of mistresses, putting Kathleen on a thoroughly friendly, confidential footing, and showing a sympathetic curiosity as to the girl's private affairs, which might have proved embarrassing to many in her class of life.

Not so with Kathleen. She reciprocated sympathy with an apparently frank confidence, and opened her heart freely to her mistress while she fulfilled the duties of the dressing-room. Every question as to her husband and her married life she answered with a candor scarcely to be expected in so newly-made a wife.

"The truth of it is, ma'am," she said, while her deft fingers busied themselves with Sylvia's crape gowns or bonnets, "Bryan got tired of me within a week of our wedding-day. It's my belief the O'Gorman girl has turned his head, and he'll be uncommonly glad to be quit of me."

For once, Sylvia's keen eye for character was baffled.

"The matter lies in a nutshell," she said to herself. "The girl is jealous of some attentions her husband has been showing a neighbor's daughter. A jealous woman is a dangerous woman while the fit lasts, and it is just as well she should be here under my eye, so that danger may be nipped in the bud."

After Bryan and the "O'Gorman girl," they passed in review the members of the Shenstone family.

Kathleen shrugged her shoulders and drew her pretty mouth down at its corners significantly when she spoke of Mrs. Shenstone and Uncle Archie. Sylvia alluded to Joyce and Mab.

"One would scarcely believe they were sisters, they were so unlike," she said, feeling her way to Kathleen's likes or dislikes.

"Miss Mab was all goodness and kindness, and all the world loved her," said the girl in reply; "but Miss Joyce was often hard upon me—sometimes I hated her."

As to the deaths of their respective brothers, neither mistress nor maid were disposed to be so confidential.

"Ned knew he was playing with edged tools," once Kathleen said, when the matter had been lightly touched upon. And Sylvia thought it wiser not to hunt the subject down.

While Kathleen's fingers and tongue were thus perpetually kept in occupation, her eyes also had never so much as a spare moment. Not a detail of Sylvia's daily life escaped them. Every square inch of every cupboard or wardrobe, as well as every corner of every trunk, was in due course laid bare to them.

Sylvia's morning visit to the post-office to fetch her letters was the time when Kathleen's most energetic explorations of hiding-places were carried on.

Within a week of her arrival at Greenock her work of investigation had answered its purpose, and had come to an end. Ned's old silver watch, discovered alongside of Buckingham's gold one in a small box within a trunk, lay in her hand, and the fac-simile watch, given her by her father, had taken its place.

To secure two days' holiday from Miss Buckingham, under pretence of seeing her father and mother before she set off on her travels with her mistress, was a comparatively easy task. The watch, not a doubt, must now find its way to Joyce's hand. What results might follow from its so finding its way, Kathleen had not the remotest idea. Loyalty to her promise to her dead brother had been the mainspring of her action in this matter, and had taught her treachery toward one to whom, judged by her inadequate moral code, she deemed that naught but treachery was due. Underlying this thought was the conjecture that Joyce might find a meaning in Ned's bequest which no one else could. It might be a necessary link in a chain of evidence, of which Joyce held fragmentary portions. Or, it might be the enigmatic answer to some question the young lady had once put to Ned. In any case, she had done her part, she said to herself, as she laid the dead brother's watch beneath her pillow at night, and closed her eyes to dream of the old bygone days when she and Ned played childish games of ball in the little cottage garden, or, later on in life, walked side by side in the gray-green twilight meadows, building castles in the air, of which, alas, there remained not one stone upon another now.

XLIV

U ncle Archie, rough weather is setting in, I can't leave Mab alone in the wind and the hail," wrote Joyce, in response to the old gentleman's entreaties that at once she would come to him in Gloucestershire and make her home there, or anywhere else in the world she might choose so long as it was in company with him and Aunt Bell.

Uncle Archie rubbed his eyes over the letter. Was this Joyce, the common-place, the clear-headed writing? Had the mantle of the dead sister fallen upon her? he asked himself, for, though the bold, free hand was Joyce's, the diction was none of hers; it was Mab's.

Off and on the old gentleman fussed a good deal that day—declared that his shoes were beginning to pinch him again; a statement which set Aunt Bell's heart fluttering with the possibility that the truce between him and his old enemy the gout had come to an end.

She grew anxious and sympathetic immediately. "It was that curry last night; I felt sure they had put cocoanut into it—I mean," she corrected herself, "it's all that new boot-maker—I said from the first those soles were too narrow."

Uncle Archie cut both sympathy and anxiety short by ordering instant preparations for a journey to the North.

"If it's on crutches I must go to her, since she will not come to me," he said, with decision.

And Aunt Bell, knowing better than to attempt a remonstrance, set about the packing at once.

Just for once in her forty-five years, Mrs. Bullen sang a song to the same tune as Uncle Archie.

"You can't live on here for ever, Joyce," she reasoned, "and, if you want to be quiet and not see a soul, you need only go down into Gloucestershire and stay with Uncle Archie. You can be just as wretched there as here, the only difference will be you'll have a few more comforts about you."

And then she launched into a tirade against the little Scotch watering-place, putting foremost among its shortcomings its lack of a dressmaker, who could lay down the law for them concerning the depth and the cut of their crape garments.

At this point the old general made his infrequent voice heard.

"Let her alone—for the present, at any rate," he said, pityingly; "don't you see she's broken?"

So they let Joyce alone. With this result: every "darkest hour before the dawn"—the last hour of Mab's life—found her crossing the heath which sloped down to the churchyard in the hollow; every day that broke, no matter whether sullen and stormy, or golden and gay, saw her hiding the ugliness of the newly-made mound which marked Mab's resting-place with masses of dewy purple heather, late marguerites, and flowing grasses; all the autumn glories left to the heath.

Then, this sweet, solemn task ended, she would sit in the long grass with one arm thrown across the mound, watching the night clouds beaten off the tops of the hills, the night blue—which held their base for some ten minutes after—little by little torn into shreds and swept into nothingness by the red flames of the dawn that came surging up from behind the cliffs—itself like some great glorified sea.

But though Joyce would sit there, still and silent, watching out the changes of the fleeting panorama of the morning, she had no eye for its glories, no ear for that wild rush and crescendo of bird notes which filled the dark air, and rose high and higher with the day. Only one thought held her heart, as she sat there in the mossy hollow, with unseeing eyes staring into the dimness or the radiance of the dawn: "My darling, would to Heaven you and I could change places; it would be better for us both!"

Unconsciously, disjointedly, her thoughts would paraphrase the bitter wail: "Better for you to have learned here among the shadows of Time how misplaced were your love and trust, than have to read it evermore in the light of Eternity! Better for me to go straight at once where true love waits me, than to sit moaning among graves over its dust and ashes."

For at last, after many sore struggles for its life, hope was dead within her. It had gone into the grave with Mab. If Joyce had tried she could not have made her heart thrill to any one of the chance clues, improbable or possible surmises which the day's post might bring. With limp fingers she would hold her packet of letters, with limp fingers she would lay them by. Despair held the day now. Frank's fate, whatever it was, must be a thing of the past, which perhaps only the light of Eternity would reveal to her. So the close of each day saw her laying her head on her pillow with the moan which sorrow and suffering have made common to humanity, "How long, how long?" and each day's beginning found her sitting among the graves with the bitter cry on her lips, "Would to Heaven you and I could change places, my darling."

XLV

Sometimes Joyce would lose count of time as she sat thus beside Mab's grave, and the sun would be high in the heavens before she would arouse herself to think of going back to the house. Mab's grave was in the loneliest part of the lonely churchyard. No village life ever strayed through the mossy paths. It was an island of silence in what was not a very stirring sea at its best. Its gray stone wall was completely hidden from view by some stunted yews and an undergrowth of wild rose bushes. Through a break in this tangled screen, Joyce could catch a glimpse of the wide heath stretching away to where the brown cliffs met the blue sky. The sea and the beach lay out of sight a couple of hundred feet or so below.

Once as she sat thus, her face turned toward the cliffs, her arm thrown across the heather-heaped mound, her hat beside her in the long grass, she saw, yet without seeing, a small, dark figure on the edge of the cliffs, making a silhouette against the blue sky. Anon it vanished. She was too much absorbed in her own thoughts to notice by which path it had disappeared, how, leaving the cliff's edge abruptly, it had followed the narrow sloping path which led straight to the churchyard.

Ten minutes after a shadow fell upon the grass at her feet, and a voice sounded in her ear, saying:

"Miss Joyce! Miss Joyce!"

She looked up to see Kathleen O'Shea—in deep black like herself—standing a yard or so on the other side of Mab's grave.

The voice was respectful, grave to solemnity. Joyce, however, was not inclined to give it a welcome. When Kathleen might have been of service to her she had held aloof; there was nothing at the present moment to render her presence anything but an intrusion.

"Yes, I am here," she answered, coldly, not rising, but merely turning her head toward the girl; "do you wish to speak to me? Have you come over from Lough Lea to see me?"

For an instant the two pale faces looked at each other, one either side of Mab's grave. The thought in each heart put into words would have run somewhat as follows:

"Is this the face so full of bright beauty which I knew something under a year ago? Why, then, Sorrow can beat old Time at his work with ease."

"I have not come straight from Lough Lea, Miss Joyce," answered Kathleen, I have been to Overbury to attend Ned's funeral. From Overbury I went to Greenock two or three days ago—" here Joyce looked up at her inquiringly, Kathleen went on: "I came over to Tretwick by coach from Newton Stewart the first thing this morning. They told me at your house where I should find you."

"Poor Ned! poor Ned!" said Joyce: and there came a softer note in her voice as she said it, wondering much over the mystery which lay behind the young Irishman's fate, and whether, in this life, it would ever be given to her to know it.

"I had a commission intrusted to me by Ned," Kathleen went on, "and I have come to you today to fulful it—it was to give you this, Miss Joyce." Here she drew out of the pocket of her traveling cloak the old-fashioned silver watch.

Joyce, however, did not offer to take it. Kathleen looked wistfully at her for a moment, but there came no gleam of intelligence into Joyce's eye. Evidently Ned's meaning in his last legacy was a blank to her.

"I had some trouble to get it, Miss Joyce," she began, falteringly. Then she broke off abruptly, and, as though moved by a sudden impulse, laid the watch beside Joyce among the heaped-up flowers on the grave.

"He must have meant it for Mab," said Joyce, sadly, thinking how fitly it lay there amid the heather, the dead Irishman's tribute of devotion to his dead benefactress. "Poor Ned! If only he had come to me that night instead of lying in wait—" she broke off hastily. It occurred to her that most probably Kathleen knew nothing of Ned's hurried visit to Tretwick, and the ugly suspicions which connected him with Buckingham's death.

But Kathleen flashed into a sudden fire for which Joyce was unprepared.

"Miss Joyce," she cried, with a vehemence that proclaimed all the Saxon in her dead, all the Celt rampant, "Ned did well to lie in wait for that bad, black-hearted man, and speak his mind to him. He did better when he fought him as they say he did, and thrust him backward over the cliff. He would have done better still if he had tossed his body out into the rough sea while he was about it, instead of letting it be brought in here for Christian burial."

Here she threw an angry glance toward the corner of the churchyard where a big white stone marked Buckingham's resting-place.

Joyce looked up astonished. Was this the Kathleen whom not so very long ago she would have summed up in her usual terse fashion as being "playful as a kitten, merry as a bird, and with feelings about as deep as a butterfly's?"

She put her astonishment into questions.

"Why did you—why did Ned ever have anything to do with the man, then, if you thought thus of him? Why did you not stay quietly with us in England instead of rushing off in that foolish fashion to marry a man who—"

Once more she broke off hastily. She had no right, she felt, to utter to this young wife the suspicions which filled her own mind as to Bryan O'Shea's complicity in Fenian conspiracies with Captain Buckingham.

A sudden change of expression passed over Kathleen's face. She suddenly came round the grave and stood beside Joyce, laying her hand on her arm.

"Miss Joyce," she whispered, scarcely above her breath, "do you want to know why I married Bryan O'Shea? Shall I tell you the whole truth now from beginning to end?"

Then, without waiting for Joyce's reply, she went on hurriedly, in the same low tone:

"It was because my heart was breaking—yes, breaking for news of Mr. Ledyard—I did it. I said to myself one of those four men know what has become of him—Ned, Captain Buckingham, Bryan, or Maurice O'Shea. Ned I had tried to move, and could not Captain Buckingham I knew was cruel and hard as death itself. Maurice was such a liar that I could not believe him on his oath. But Bryan—even if he would not tell me what I wanted to know for the asking—I knew I could get secrets out if I married him, and gave him plenty of whisky. There was nothing else in life for me to do. I meant always to marry him on your wedding-day."

A great rush of jealous pride swept over Joyce.

"You—you tell me this," she cried, drawing back a step and shaking Kathleen's touch from her arm.

But the next moment love had trampled her jealousy under foot. She caught Kathleen's hands in hers almost crushing them in her vehemence.

"Oh, Kathleen!" she cried passionately, her words coming all but incoherently, "You loved him; I felt it—I knew it. For the love of heaven tell me what you have found out! Don't keep me waiting while you spin out excuses for what you did. Out of mercy tell me all you know—in one word, if it be possible."

Kathleen's head drooped.

"Alas, Miss Joyce!" she said, brokenly, "not in one word nor yet in one hundred, can I tell you what your heart is aching to know. I've learned nothing—no, not one single syllable about Mr. Ledyard; though I've found out some other things I want you to know, and I've come here today on purpose to tell them to you."

Joyce let go the girl's hands and sank once more on the ground beside Mab's grave, bowing her head and hiding her face.

Kathleen knelt on the grass beside her.

"Miss Joyce," she said, in a voice that seemed to grow suddenly stern and harsh, "there are other broken hearts in the world beside yours. Think of my old father and mother! How they worshiped Ned, and how his miserable hunted life and dog's death must haunt them to their dying day. And think of me!" Here there came a ring of passion, or it might have been of self-scorn, into the hard voice, "tied for life to a man whom I hate, and whose hand I know is red with my brother's blood!"

Joyce drew her hands from her face.

"Is that true? Did Bryan O'Shea shoot Ned?" she asked, in a tone of horror.

"Ay, Miss Joyce, it's true enough. And, what's more, I knew beforehand he'd have it to do, and power I had none to stop him."

"Oh, Kathleen, Kathleen! what do you mean? You knew—yet had no power to prevent! Why, I would have moved heaven and earth to save a brother's life."

"Would you, Miss Joyce? Not if you knew what I know, and had seen what I've seen since I've been Bryan O'Shea's wife. I might have prevented Bryan shooting Ned, perhaps; but only one way, by taking Bryan's revolver and shooting him through the heart. Then I should have been handed over to the police to be dealt with. But all the same Ned would have been shot, and the man who shot him would not have been handed over to the police."

For a moment Joyce's face flushed with indignation.

"It is monstrous—justice ought to be done. It is my duty, your duty, to denounce this man as a murderer," she cried, vehemently.

"If we did, Miss Joyce, there's not a soul could be brought to prove our words, and a good score at least who would swear he was a hundred miles away when the deed was done. But all the same, he'll suffer for it." Here there came a sudden gleam in the girl's eyes. "He's too sure a shot not to have work of this sort given him again to do, and one day he'll get his death by it. But not yet—no, and I don't want it to be yet."

"You want to try and forgive him first?" questioned Joyce, a little doubtfully.

Kathleen laughed a bitter laugh.

"I try to forgive him! There's little enough of forgiveness he'll get out of me, Miss Joyce. No; he shall suffer, and just exactly as he made me suffer. The 'Red Right-hand of the League,' as they call it, has 'removed' my brother; the Red Right-hand of the League shall 'remove' his."

"Kathleen!"

Once more the two pale faces looked at each other. But the face of one was that of a strong soul compelled to the transient weakness of an inert submission; the face of the other, that of a weak soul impelled to the transient strength of a purpose of revenge.

"Ah! and he loves that brother, Miss Joyce, just as I loved mine. Weak, tipsy, and stupid though Maurice O'Shea is, Bryan loves him, and—" She broke off abruptly. For another moment there fell a pause. When Kathleen resumed it was in a more even tone. "I want to tell you this morning, Miss Joyce, all about this League. When you've heard it, you can make up your mind who you'll tell it to."

Joyce's heart began to beat wildly. After all, the girl had something to tell! True, it might be something to lead them down a blind alley straight to a blank wall again; or, possibly, might take them by a circuitous road to a hidden grave; but, in any case, it must be told, and must be listened to.

"Tell me everything you know, from beginning to end—everything," she implored.

But Kathleen had a condition to impose.

"Before I tell you one word, Miss Joyce, you must give me your solemn, sacred promise that my name shall not be mentioned to the police as an informer—no, nor to living soul!" she said, with decision.

Joyce drew a long breath. A promise might prove an embarrassment. Yet she dared not throw difficulties in the way of the girl's confidences.

"Tell me how you got this knowledge—how you found out what you have to tell," she asked, by way of gaining time for herself.

"How I found out? Didn't I marry Bryan O'Shea on purpose to find out?" Kathleen answered, excitedly. "He was fool enough to think I married him because I loved him, but he found out his mistake before the wedding-day was over. Then his love turned to hate quick enough, and—" She broke off a moment, then resumed. "Well, no matter. He thought he had frightened and mastered me. He did not know how I used to hide and creep about the house, and listen when he and Maurice were sitting up late and talking over their work, thinking I was fast asleep up-stairs. I never let a chance slip, not one, Miss Joyce. When Bryan used to take too much whisky, he would let fall hints which I took good care not to remind him of the next morning, but which were easy enough to fit onto something else I had heard before."

Here Joyce interrupted her impatiently.

"Tell me at once all you have to tell," she said.

"But I want your promise—your solemn promise, Miss Joyce—that my name shall not be mentioned to living soul," said Kathleen doggedly. "Remember, if my name gets whispered about, I am doomed."

Joyce thought again.

"You must let me tell Uncle Archie, or how can I make use of what you tell me? I will make him give me his word of honor that your name shall not pass his lips. Will that do?"

For a moment Kathleen remained silent. Joyce's impatience grew upon her.

"Come, Kathleen, do not keep me in suspense; you ought to know you can trust my word, Uncle Archie's word—"

Kathleen looked at her steadily.

"Yes, I know I can trust you, Miss Joyce, and Mr. Shenstone, too, but no one else."

"There will be no one else to trust. I give you my solemn promise your name shall not be mentioned by either of us to living soul. Now begin at the very beginning—tell me all about this League—all about your troubles and Ned's, which, I suppose, began with these miserable plots and conspiracies."

Kathleen drew a long breath.

"Mine began about three years ago. Miss Joyce, when I went to stay with father's people at Lough Lea, and I first met Bryan O'Shea. He was always fierce, and wild, and passionate, and half frightened me into promising to marry him. I was glad enough to get back home again, and would have forgotten all about my promise, only Ned wouldn't let me. Ned, Bryan, and Maurice had all joined one of those dreadful secret societies at the same time. Bryan was cruel and reckless, and did all that was wanted of him ruthlessly. He could turn the women and children out of their warm beds into the cold fields in the dead of night, and beat the old men nearly to death, particularly if he owed them a grudge for anything that happened years ago." She broke off a moment, then added: "Ah, if those Fenian leaders, safe on the other side of the ocean, only knew the number of small debts that are paid off under pretence of patriotism, they wouldn't be so keen to set the Moonlighters and Boycotters going."

Joyce shuddered.

"Go on," she said, again.

"Ned was altogether as tender-hearted. He used to cry off a lot of things that the O'Sheas volunteered for. Bryan and Maurice went up in high favor with the heads of their society; Ned went down. He and Bryan were soon in what they call different grades, and Bryan made things very hard for Ned, because he took it into his head he was preventing me keeping my promise to marry him. At times, I think Ned was half desperate, and scarcely knew what he was doing or saying."

"Poor Ned! Poor Ned!"

"It was poor Ned when Captain Buckingham came on the scene, Miss Joyce. He met him one day coming out of your house in Eaton Square, and thought he would be useful on dark nights for messages and that sort of thing, because he had no brogue whatever, and so couldn't be identified as an Irishman in the dark. Captain Buckingham was just then forming a branch association for some special work that was going on. It was to consist of himself and three other members. He and Maurice and Bryan were enrolled the first three; Ned joined as fourth.

"This branch society was pledged to do the hardest and the roughest of the Society's work. Captain Buckingham they called Joshua, because he had removed the hands from his watch, vowing that for him time stood still till vengeance was executed upon the oppressors of Ireland. The members had a sign and a countersign. The sign was the question, 'What time is it, friend?' as they lay their hands upon their watches; the countersign was the answer, 'Time stands still,' as they drew their watches out and showed that they had not been wound up. They used to meet once a week in Brewer's Court, till—"

Here she broke off.

"I know," exclaimed Joyce. "Go on, tell me, everything." She was listening breathlessly now to every word that fell from the girl's lips.

Kathleen resumed her story at another point.

"When they found that they had drawn the eyes of the police on them in London, they thought it better to remove what they called the center for correspondence to a quiet part of Ireland. So Miss Buckingham arranged a center for them in County Down—Miss Joyce, that woman is every whit as bad and heartless as her brother was."

"Ah!"

"She's worse in one way, for she never runs the slightest risk herself in any shape or form, though she throws plenty of danger in the way of others. No; she has her comfortable home at the Abbey House, and she goes to her balls and her dinners dressed in her silks and her satins. But wherever her shadow falls there follows misery for some poor soul. Say she dines twenty miles from Lough Lea one night; next day there come a troop of boys plowing up a decent farmer's land, and the farmer himself is found in a ditch nearly beaten to death. Or she dances at a ball at some far-away place, where everything is quiet and happy; within twenty-four hours there comes a Moonlighters' raid for arms, some one is shot dead, or the house and ricks are fired, and the poor people are left starving."

The girl's own vehemence compelled her to pause a moment.

Joyce said nothing. There was that in Kathleen's manner which puzzled her and made speech a difficulty.

Kathleen went on again, rapidly as before.

"And as for deceit and lies—ah, I've matched her at that just for once in a way! She thinks she's sending off to New York her brother's watch and Ned's watch. It's one of the articles of the League, that if a man dies in the work his watch is to be handed to the Council, who will pass it on to a man willing to be sworn in to take up the dead man's work. Well, she's welcome to her brother's watch; it's little enough good it'll do to any man who gets it. But as for Ned's—"

Again the girl broke off, then turning suddenly to Joyce, asked in a quieter tone:

"And you'll tell all this to the police, Miss Joyce?"

"Undoubtedly, word for word."

"Ah, they'll never form a timeless league again, as they used to call it—in England, at any rate. The captain's dead—"

"Where is Maurice O'Shea?" interrupted Joyce.

"Don't know, Miss Joyce. The League will find him out safe enough."

"The League! The police, you mean."

Kathleen laughed.

"Ah, there are some who do their work better than the police; but they'll be out in their reckoning for once in a way."

Joyce was troubled; bewildered also; some hidden meaning seemed to lie behind Kathleen's words; she felt herself at a loss.

"Where is Bryan?" she asked, wondering whether the girl's answer would let in a ray of light.

"I don't know, Miss Joyce. I dare say I shall soon enough when he sends for me to join him somewhere in America—New York, perhaps," answered Kathleen, in a bitter, careless tone.

"Sends for you! Could you live under the same roof with that man? Surely you would not go?"

Kathleen's face grew set and rigid.

"Yes, I should go," she answered, slowly. "I wouldn't have blood spilt on mother's doorstep. I shouldn't dare refuse to go, if he sent for me; but New York would never see me. There are some who start for it, but never land."

The last words were said in a tone so low, that they could not have reached Joyce's ear had they not been spoken with an emphasis which doubled their meaning.

They roused in Joyce that protective, defending instinct, always so strong in strong natures, but which, with her, had known no outlet since Mab had been laid in her grave. She made one step toward Kathleen, put her arm round her shoulders, drawing the girl close to her.

"Kathleen," she said, kindly, "you shall not go if they send for you a thousand times over. You shall stay here with me; I will take care of you. I blame myself for not having looked after you better. I might have kept some of this dreadful misery from you."

"No: not you, Miss Joyce!"

"I might, if I had not been so selfishly wrapped up in my own happiness that I had eyes for nothing that went on around me."

Kathleen suddenly freed herself from Joyce's arm.

"Miss Joyce!" she said, excitedly, "I didn't deserve looking after in those days, and I don't deserve it now. Do you know I used to hate you when you were so happy?—yes, hate you—and all because you were a lady, and young and beautiful, and—and Mr. Ledyard loved you."

"I know, I know; say no more about it," said Joyce, hurriedly, feeling that this was the point at which her indulgence for Kathleen failed her.

But Kathleen was bent on saying more. She went on, speaking even more quickly and excitedly than before, as though fearful lest her courage might give way.

"I think I could have killed you if I had had the chance sometimes when you used to come into the room, looking so bright and happy after you had been walking or talking with Mr. Ledyard. Once I tried to kill myself—"

"Kathleen!"

"I did, Miss Joyce; but my courage failed me—a little—little more courage and it would have been done. Then, when I found I could not do that, I made up my mind I would marry Bryan O'Shea, and get away from you and the sight of your happiness."

Joyce remained silent, steadily looking at the girl. Her memory was busy piecing together by-gone fragments of circumstances which, at the time, had seemed without meaning.

Kathleen misinterpreted her silence. She waited a moment, then went close to Joyce, speaking in slow, quiet tones:

"Miss Joyce, there's one thing I should like to say to you before I go. You must not think Mr. Ledyard knew anything of all this, or that he ever said a word to me that any gentleman might not have said to any poor girl."

The nearest approach to a smile of which Joyce was capable in those sad days, parted her lips, but still she said nothing.

"It all began as it ended, with my own folly," Kathleen went on, as though she were bent on making a full confession and leaving no dregs of suspicion in Joyce's mind. "I was going home from the village one day—Overbury, I mean—in the winter twilight, and a rough farmer's lad overtook me, and would persist in following and annoying me. Mr. Ledyard happened to be coming from the house and met us. He soon sent the man off, scolded me for being out so late, turned back, and saw me safe home. It was after that I used to say to myself: 'If I had only been a lady he might have married me;' and then it was I took to hating you. Oh! don't you see, Miss Joyce? Pray, pray believe me!" Here she clasped her hands together imploringly. "It was only my own vanity and foolishness, nothing else."

Joyce's ghost of a smile vanished. She looked Kathleen full in the face with clear, solemn eyes.

"Why take the trouble to tell me all this?" she asked, quietly. "Do you think if you told me a story exactly the reverse I should believe one syllable of it? Don't you see—don't you understand that nothing any one could say would ever shake my faith in his truth and honor?"

She seemed to be addressing Kathleen. In reality she felt as though she were saying the words to Frank himself.

While they had been talking, the early brightness of the morning had waned; a fresh breeze had risen, black masses of clouds came rolling up from the sea.

Kathleen had grown weather-wise during her brief sojourn on the Irish coast; she picked up Joyce's hat from the ground and handed it to her.

"There's a storm coming, Miss Joyce," she said; "you ought to make haste home."

But Joyce did not stir. Mechanically she put on the hat, saying never a word. Her brains ached with the load of thought Kathleen had put into them. Little by little the facts of that terrible twentieth of December began to piece themselves into the story of plot and crime she had been just listening to. Not a doubt rested in her mind now as to Frank's fate. Following Mab's footsteps, he had gone into the conspirators' meeting-place, and had there met his death. How they had done their work without leaving trace of it behind was the only mystery to be solved now.

She covered her eyes with her hands, shuddering. She scarcely heard Kathleen's words of farewell as the girl turned toward the churchyard gate.

"Good-by, Miss Joyce; I must go at once, I have to catch the coach at the other end of the heath. Thank you for listening to me so patiently this morning."

In another instant she was gone, making her way with swift steps across the heath, a small, dark blot between the gloomy stretch of dark purple and the iron-gray of the lowering sky.

Joyce looked after her between the parted boughs of the scant leaved trees, trying to gather her wits together. She wished she had not let her go so hurriedly, there were questions she would have liked to ask her. She essayed to call the girl back.

"Kathleen!" she cried, leaning over the low stone wall, and beckoning to her with her hand.

But the small, dark figure did not turn its head. The rough, salt breeze threw her voice back at her as it swept down the church-yard path, whirling and hurrying the dry, dead leaves before it.

There fell one, two large drops of rain on her hand. A white sun for a brief moment cleft the inky mountains of clouds, throwing one long, slanting shaft of light athwart the churchyard. It straggled in and out among the tombs, emphasized the newness of the big stone which marked Buckingham's last resting-place, and, found out the tarnished silver of the dead Irishman's watch as it lay among the heather on Mab's grave. It caught Joyce's eye.

"Poor Ned!" she thought. "He must have meant it for Mab. I will take it home and wear it for both their sakes."

She took it up reverently from the grave. It was a large, heavy thing, and owned to a solid outside case of silver. This showed on one side an ugly, russet-brown stain, which marked the sure course that Bryan's bullet had taken.

And as she stood there looking down on it, with eyes that had long since lost the trick of tears, a sudden thought came to her. What if, by means of this watch, Donovan had meant to send a message to her, which he had not dared to put into words while he lived his uncertain life, with Death for ever dogging his heels?

With trembling fingers she pressed the spring of the outer case. No; there was nothing there save the marks of daily wear and tear. Then she opened the inner lid which covered the mechanism.

The wind swept past with a mighty rush; the rain came down in a great drenching shower; but Joyce stood still, heeding neither wind nor rain, for a brief sentence, which fixed her eye, written in blue pencil within the inner lid.

It ran thus:

"Latitude N. 62. 32.
Longitude W. 7. 10."

XLVI

U ncle Archie, you may take off your overcoat while you eat; but you'll have to put it on directly after. I am going to Greenock tonight, and I'm sure you won't let me go alone," said Joyce to the old gentleman, as she kissed her welcome to him and Aunt Bell.

Uncle Archie arrived at Tretwick on the day that Kathleen had her interview with Joyce in the churchyard. He and Kathleen must have passed each other on the road.

"To Greenock!" repeated Aunt Bell. "My dear, do you know your uncle was sixty-five last week, and can't be expected to fly about the country like a bird?"

The old gentleman turned upon her sharply.

"Well, what if I did have a birthday last week," he said, raspingly, "I'm none the worse for it this week, am I? And if Joyce and I choose to start on a journey to the North Pole, whose business is it so much as our own, I should like to know."

Aunt Bell was silenced at once. Mrs. Bullen's exclamations died unspoken. She contented herself with taking possession of Aunt Bell and her wraps, and escorting her up-stairs to her room.

Uncle Archie looked grimly after the retreating figures of the ladies. Then he turned to Joyce.

"Now that the women are gone, Joyce, we can talk in peace: or rather, you can, for I see you have something to tell me."

He paused a moment. Years ago he had got into the habit of being aggressive in his talk with Joyce, and of making brief pauses at the end of his sentences in order to give her time to fire off her retorts. It was hard to get out of the habit, although these were days when retorts had ceased to be fired. She had no bright repartees lying in wait for him now.

So he filled in the gap himself with a sigh.

"I know you'll say, 'I'm a woman, just as much as the others, I suppose.' Well, I suppose you are; but somehow you're so clear-headed I'm apt to forget the fact at times."

Joyce's reply was to kneel beside him as he sat at the table, place Donovan's watch in front of him, and point to the sentence written within the lid.

A great surprise had met Uncle Archie on his arrival at Tretwick. He had expected to find Joyce transformed by her months of sorrow into some shadowy counterpart of Mab. From her letters, he had judged that her strong, brave spirit had collapsed at last, and that to him would be assigned the difficult task of preaching her into her old self again.

"I would sooner a hundred times over she should have deteriorated into her mother's likeness than into Mab's," he had said to Aunt Bell during the journey, "I could then have scolded the pair in one breath. But, as no doubt you remember, it was always just as useless to scold Mab as it would have been to scold the mist on the top of the Mendips; and I suppose it will be precisely the same with Joyce now."

But directly he had set eyes on Joyce he was driven to confess he was altogether out in his reckoning. Although, in the thin, pale girl who linked her arm in his and led him into the house, there was little enough of the beautiful, light-hearted Joyce of days gone by, there was yet in her nothing to recall the likeness of the shadowy, hesitating Mab.

"She has taken something into her head now, and whatever it is she shall have her own way about it, though nothing may come of it," the old gentleman said to himself, as he felt her grip on his arm, and noted the steady look of purpose in her eye. So her first words naturally did not take his breath away.

But the sight of Donovan's watch, introduced without a word of explanation, did.

"I don't understand—I don't understand," he faltered, rubbing his eyes and turning the watch from right to left, from left to right, as if somewhere in its tarnished silver sides he would get a hint for the solution of the mystery.

Joyce had to tell him the whole of Kathleen's story in the churchyard before he began to understand at all. Then he, too, as Joyce had done, began to feel his brain overweighted.

"Give me time to think, give me time to think," were his first words.

So Joyce leaned her head against his shoulder as she knelt beside him, clasped her hands over his arm, and gave him as much time as he cared to take.

Five minutes would have covered it. Then there came a question, gravely put.

"And I suppose, Joyce, the outcome of this is that you mean to start forthwith to Greenock, get a boat there of some sort, and go steaming away to latitude 62° 32′ logitude 7° 10′?"

"That is what I mean to do."

"And when you get there you expect to find—"

He broke off abruptly, not daring to speak the words which might cover Joyce's expectations.

"Uncle Archie, I expect nothing—hope for nothing; but go I must."

"Get me a map."

Joyce spread one before him on the table.

"I have already looked it out," she said. "North latitude 62° 32′, west longitude 7° 10′, is in the wide ocean. It is close to the Faroes; it may be an island not marked on this map. I don't believe half the islands are marked here."

Uncle Archie shook his head, frowning heavily.

"Mab's last words were 'always the sound of the sea, Joyce,'" said Joyce, in a tremulous undertone, as though groping in the dark for the hidden meaning of Mab's words.

Uncle Archie's frown grew deeper.

"Mab suffered from blood to the brain. No wonder she had always a rushing sound in her ears," he said, curtly.

Then, as though to prevent a recurrence to a topic which seemed to lift his feet from the solid earth and to set his brain rocking, he began asking a mulitude of questions concerning Kathleen and her story.

"You ought to have cross-questioned her rigorously, Joyce," he concluded. "There may not be more than a spice of truth in what she told you. She was always a good hand at fibbing. Her dash of Irish blood is quite enough to make her do her romancing easily."

Joyce shook her head.

"There was no romancing in what she told me this morning," she said; "if you had seen her you could not have doubted she was speaking the truth."

"I wish I had seen her. You should have kept her here till I came. It is all so wildly incoherent—inexplicable. Not so far as her story of the League is concerned—that may be true enough, in outline that is—but her own conduct. She vows vengeance against her husband, yet goes a fine roundabout way to get it. This pledge to secrecy, too—I can't understand it!"

"She may be afraid of the consequences if her name should be mentioned."

"Yet her conduct in telling the story is not that of a timid woman."

"A strong purpose makes cowards brave sometimes. Ah-h—" and here Joyce broke off abruptly, as though struck by a sudden thought.

"What is it?" queried Uncle Archie, turning sharply round and facing her.

"No, I will have nothing to do with it," she said, speaking slowly, half to herself. "I see now why she came telling me this story, and who she wants to have the credit of it."

"Who! what!"

"She wants the League to think that Maurice O'Shea, Bryan's brother, has turned informer, and then they'll take his life as they took Ned's and Bryan will suffer as she has suffered. No, I will have nothing to do with it."

"Upon my word, Joyce, I don't think you need be squeamish on the matter. They're a set of scoundrels, every man of them, and so long as they get paid out one way or another I really don't care two straws who helps them into their coffins."

"I will have nothing to do with it, Uncle Archie. I can't tell you why, but all desire for vengeance has died out of my heart now. I couldn't take it, even if it were offered to my hand."

Uncle Archie looked at her till there came a mist before his eyes.

"Don't get too angelic, Joyce," he said, huskily, "or I shall expect you'll get to heaven before I shall."

"Angelic! If you could have seen into my heart at one time you would have feared I should never get to heaven at all! Oh, Uncle Archie!" she added, tremulously, as her thoughts flew back to the hour of agony she had spent on her knees beside Mab's bed. "It was only lack of opportunity saved me. Nothing else."

"Joyce, Joyce," said the old gentleman, deprecatingly, "don't speak like that of yourself. It pains me."

"It's true, Uncle Archie. And what is more, Kathleen's little scheme of vengeance is weak beside those I have contrived and executed in imagination. But all those feelings are dead now." She broke off a moment, then resumed, in a low uncertain tone: "I didn't sit all those hours beside Mab's grave, with Captain Buckingham's tomb facing me, for nothing. I've learned to look at it without a curse rising to my lips. I feel now the sins of those men might have been mine if—"

But here Uncle Archie laid his finger on her lips.

"That'll do, Joyce, you shake my nerves when you talk in that fashion. Let those men be. As Kathleen said, Bryan will get his dues safe enough some day, and we'll leave him to get them his own way, while we think of something else." Here he laid his hand upon the watch which lay before him, with the map, on the table. "Now, so far as I understand you, your idea is to work out this clue—if clue it be—entirely unaided by the police. Now my idea is to telegraph at once to Morton, and set other brains—brains used to that sort of work—going on the same scent."

"Telegraph then, Uncle Archie, set their brains going. Let Morton go with us if you like. I'll see he doesn't do any harm this time," said Joyce, with a bitter recollection of her hour of waiting on the bridge, and her lost chance. "But, all the same, I go to Greenock tonight."

"Very well, then Morton shall have a telegram before night. Now about Greenock. What are we to do when we get there?"

"Do! there is only one thing to do there. Get a boat at once. You'll know best what sort of a boat it ought to be."

"No doubt I shall. And then—"

"Then we'll start at once for—for this place."

"Well."

"And—and—find out everything that—that is to be found out."

Uncle Archie did not reply. He leaned his head thoughtfully upon his hand. His brains were clouded. Joyce's plan, wild and hopeless as it seemed, was yet one not to be dismissed, unless a better could be substituted.

"The equinoxes are just setting in, I suppose you know that," he said, presently, by way of getting time for himself

"Equinoxes! What are they after what we've been through?"

"And, Joyce, as your aunt said just now, I was sixty-five last week, and if I fall ill you'll have to look after me. I sha'n't let Aunt Bell come; she's always fit for nothing at sea."

"As if I didn't know how to look after you just as well as Aunt Bell. She had better go back with mother and the general into Gloucestershire. It'll take two to look after mother when she hears we are going," answered Joyce, not intending sarcasm.

"And, Joyce, if I die you'll have to bury me in the sea, you will."

"Uncle Archie, if you're afraid, don't venture. I'll go alone."

"And, Joyce,"—and now Uncle Archie's voice took a deeper tone—"you mustn't build on this—this memorandum of Donovan's. After all, it may mean nothing—nothing at least so far as we are concerned. You mustn't build any hopes upon it."

"Uncle Archie, hope is dead in my heart as well as fear."

"And, Joyce,"—this yet more gravely and a little tremulously—"there is something else you ought to face, child, though it is hard for me to tell it to you. Remember, whatever in the shape of tidings we came upon, there can be little enough of joy for you to be got out of them. Our suspense can be solved only in one of two ways. Frank living, means Frank voluntarily in hiding from us. Frank honest, true loyal, as he left us, means Frank in his grave."

Joyce's voice was not tremulous as she answered, with never a tear in her sad eyes.

"Then, Uncle Archie, I am journeying from one grave to another; but still I must go."

XLVII

I t is all very well to say with a fine air of decision "I will," or "I must go here, or there." Solomon's carpet is a thing of the past; and, though we can swim easily enough on our wishes from world to world in the dreamland of poetry, for transit, in the waking hours of prose, ways and means have to be consulted. Joyce and Uncle Archie, having arrived at Greenock, drew as it were a long breath, opened their eyes wide, and took the measure of the road they had to go. A full purse will carry most things before it, but it can not quite lift old Time off its feet. It secured a good strong craft—in other words, a small coasting steamer—for the two, in which to undertake their somewhat visionary journey towards the Arctic Circle, an experienced captain for it, and a competent crew of some ten or twelve men; but it could not compress these achievements into the twenty-four hours which Joyce's eager heart would have deemed a liberal allowance of time for them; so a week from the day on which they had left Tretwick found them still at a Greenock hotel, with preparations all but, yet not finally, complete.

To Joyce's fancy that week at Greenock seemed to stand alone in the current of her life, isolated from the miserable past with its crush of sorrow and strain of suspense, isolated also from the dreaded future with its possible solutions of direful mysteries. It had a lull and a quiet all its own. It was like the brief breathing space on a battle-field, when the sullen roar of the enemy's artillery momentarily silenced, the general in commands asks himself, "Now, is the day over, or will they open fire again?"

Every day of that week of waiting and preparation, the feeling seemed to grow upon them that now they were nearing the end of their long, painful suspense; a feeling which Uncle Archie characteristically put under a bushel by exhibiting an extra amount of cynical irritability, and which Joyce, naturally enough, hugged to her heart, saying to herself, with every breath she drew.

"By so much nearer the end; one way or other it will soon be all over for us now."

She could not, with an amount of trying, have realized the picture of their little boat cruising fruitlessly in and out among those northern islands day after day, till stress of wind or weather beat them off into some sheltered harbor. It was of no use for Morton, when, in quick response to Uncle Archie's telegram, he made his appearance at the hotel, to shrug his shoulders, turn up his solemn eyes, and say, in an altogether superior manner, "Of course I'm willing enough, sir, to go cruising with you and the young lady anywhere you wish, but if you call a memorandum of that sort a clew, then I've followed my profession for five-and-twenty years for nothing. It was most probably a note scribbled by the Irishman, as an aid to memory of something that does not concern us in the slightest degree." Joyce did not so much as take the trouble to answer him; he might just as well have tried to persuade her that the solid earth on which she stood was nothing but vapor. One question, however, which the man put, set her thinking. "Had Kathleen, when she brought the watch, made any allusion to the handwriting within? Were there grounds for supposing that she was cognizant of any facts connected therewith?"

Joyce could not feel her conscience at rest on the score of Kathleen. She blamed herself bitterly that she had not made a stronger effort to detain the girl. On the day after her arrival at Greenock, Joyce had written a long, kind letter, begging her to come to them at once, and undertake with them this journey to the North. She wrote generously as well as kindly, intimating that her reasons for wishing this were two-fold. In the first place, should good result from the journey, there was no one she knew would share more heartily in her joy than the one who had gone halves with her in her sorrow. Secondly, if in the end their worst fears were realized, and nothing but fresh misery lay in store for them, there was no one in all the world to whom she would turn more gladly for sympathy than to Kathleen, her companion as well as maid in days gone by. This letter Joyce addressed to Kathleen at Overbury, totally ignorant of the fact that at that very moment the girl was fulfilling her duties as Sylvia's maid within a quarter of a mile of the hotel where she and Uncle Archie had taken up their quarters.

Joyce had received no reply to this letter. Morton's question rendered her doubly impatient of Kathleen's silence. She dispatched a second letter, even more kind and entreating than the first.

Morton shook his head gravely over it all, and expressed his opinion that everything was turning out exactly as he had anticipated from the very first.

To say truth, Morton could never quite bring himself to believe in Kathleen's honesty of purpose. To his way of thinking, everything she said, like a language of symbols, had a hidden meaning, everything she did was done with an ulterior motive which only an initiate—in other words, a detective—could divine.

It was possibly easier for the worthy man thus to magnify Kathleen's capacity for intrigue than to confess how completely he and his colleagues had been at fault as to the cause of her hurried flight into Ireland.

Uncle Archie, after giving careful consideration to the matter, had decided that no good purpose could be served by communicating to the police in their entirety Kathleen's revelations to Joyce. He had, therefore, adopted a mid-course. The girl's purpose of revenge, after Joyce had let in light upon it, could be easily enough read. No good end would be promoted by furthering it. It would be better, therefore, to leave the tale of the timeless league untold. It had been virtually dissolved by the deaths of the captain and one out of its three working members. It would be easy at any time to relate the story of its formation, should necessity for so doing arise. With regard, however, to Kathleen's statement that her husband had been Ned's murderer, matters stood otherwise. This was a piece of information the old gentleman's conscience would not allow him to keep back. So he handed it over to Morton as though it were a surmise evolved from his own meditations on the matter, or based on the description given of the man who had shot Ned, and had disappeared on the Greenock quay.

"Some one must be sent from Scotland Yard to ask that young woman a question or two. Her statements can hardly be taken for Gospel," was the remark with which Morton showed Uncle Archie that his innocent subterfuge had been pierced in a moment.

"No one would question her to such purpose as I should. She would tell me what she would tell to no other living soul," cried Joyce, suddenly rising from her chair to fetch pen and ink wherewith to dispatch a telegram at once to the Donovans' cottage. A great unspoken dread had suddenly arisen in her heart—what if Kathleen had received the terrible summons to join her husband and had not dared refuse to obey it?

She made the telegram as urgent as she could.

"Come to us here at once, we want you. It is of the greatest importance that you should come without delay," ran the message. In company with Uncle Archie she herself carried it to the office in the town. She would return by way of the quay, she thought, so as to give a passing glance to their little steamer secured alongside, and note how far its preparations for departure had progressed.

Morton had shown himself particularly interested in the outfit of that little steamer and the hiring of its crew. He had displayed a technical knowledge on these matters a little astonishing to Uncle Archie.

"You see, sir," he had said, by way of explanation, "my profession gives a man a wonderful facility for acquiring knowledge wherever it is to be had. An orderly brain, and keen powers of observation, I take it, are the first requisites necessary for learning the A B C of any calling. Now unless a man in our profession possesses both these admirable qualities, I assure you he is nowhere at all, sir—nowhere at all."

"Then there must be a great many of you in that delightful position," Uncle Archie had replied, snappishly, for Morton's platitudes never failed to irritate him.

Morton had objected strongly to the name of the steamer, *Frea*.

"It's a name of ill-omen," he had bluntly informed the captain, a bluff, good-tempered Dane, who spoke excellent English. "Now, if those English or Scotch sailors you are engaging to make up your crew knew a little of ancient mythology they'd refuse to sail in her."

Upon which the captain had laughed heartily, and had replied:

"Yes, but you see they don't know a scrap of it; nor do I either, for the matter of that. We Danes know nothing of your English superstitions. All I know is, my little craft had her first nail struck on a Friday; she was christened on a Friday, and so we called her *Frea*, who is the godmother of all the Fridays. And there's not a Dane on board of her who'll give the matter a second thought."

"Not that I'm superstitious," Morton had continued. "But I was born in Cardiff, where they think a great deal of such things. Now, if any man in Cardiff—"

Here Uncle Archie had interrupted him irritably.

"My dear sir," he had said, "we are in London, not in St. Petersburg—I mean, we are in Greenock, not in Cardiff. Be so good as to leave your superstitions in the place of your nativity."

Naturally enough the *Frea* saw a good deal of Uncle Archie and Joyce during that week of waiting. Not a day but what they might have been seen making their way along the bustling quay. More than ever crowded and bustling it seemed to be on this particular afternoon that Joyce dispatched her telegram to Kathleen. A big steamer was getting under weigh, its deck was thronged with passengers, who were waving their adieus to cheery or sorrowful friends and relatives lingering yet on the pier. Its prow was turned southward, and Joyce concluded from sundry expressions that caught her ear that New York was its destination.

"One would think," said Uncle Archie, snappishly, "from the fuss they're making, and the pocket-handkerchiefs they are flourishing in our faces, that America was the bourne whence no traveler returns, instead of a country which sends back to us our rogues and vagabonds—with one or two native specimens added to the number—almost as fast as it gets them."

Joyce made no reply. Her attention had been attracted by two female figures on board the steamer, whose outlines seemed strangely familiar to her.

They were standing near the wheel, one was tall and of good carriage, the other was short and slight. Both were dressed in neat, plain mourning, with heavy crape veils. The neatness, however, of the one dress was the neatness of a lady, the neatness of the other dress that of a maid.

As the steamer with one final pant and plunge put distance between itself and the quay, the taller of the two, suddenly turning, faced the shore, raising her veil.

The shifting September sun, playing hide-and-seek among the crowd on the deck, made plain to Joyce the pale face, fair hair, and satirical mouth of Sylvia Buckingham. Joyce's heart failed her lest the small figure beside Sylvia might be Kathleen.

There could scarcely be a doubt but what Sylvia had seen Joyce as she stood on the quay, for although the slight smile which parted her lips and showed her small teeth could scarcely be construed into one of friendly recognition, it had yet a word of meaning.

"See," it seemed to say: "you and I have had more than one tussle together, who do you think has got the best of it now?"

A letter received the next morning from old Donovan gave substance to Joyce's misgivings. He wrote, with many apologies, in reply to Miss Shenstone's telegram, that Kathleen had left home about ten days previously, having undertaken the duties of traveling maid to a lady who had shown him and his family great kindness in their time of sorrow—a Miss Buckingham. He thought the lady's name was not unknown to Miss Shenstone. It was a bitter blow to him that Kathleen could not rest contented in her own home. He had received a letter from her only that morning, stating that she was on the point of starting for America. When he would hear from her again he did not know.

"I am now bereaved of both my children," concluded the old man, in simple scriptural fashion; "and I am bereaved."

XLVIII

J oyce's fancy had drawn in somber colors many a dismal picture of the events of that memorable night of the 20th of December. Could it have painted truly, in detail, as well as in outline, the interior of the little outbuilding of the house in Brewer's Court, this is what it would have shown her; Frank lying on the red-brick floor, gagged, his feet bound together, his hands tied tightly behind him; a flickering lantern, on a level with his head, throwing fitful light on his gray, unconscious features; a man bending over him, with face only by one degree less pallid and rigid.

That man was Ned Donovan. He was trying with rapid fingers to unloose the knots of the gag which covered Frank's mouth and nostrils. His breath was coming thick and fast; he was muttering to himself in short sentences.

"If they had told me to stand up against him in fair fight I could have done it, but in cold blood—no; and I don't forget he was trying to protect her—"

He succeeded in loosing the tightly-tied bandage, but some minutes passed before the faintest sign of animation showed in the prostrate man's face. First the eyelids quivered, then lifted; and the eyes turned upon Ned with a vacant, bewildered look in them.

"Lift my head," he said, faintly, and then the eyes closed again.

There was nothing in that bare, little out-house—not so much as a brick-bat—that could be converted into a substitute for a pillow. So the Irishman knelt on one knee on the floor, raising Frank's head and shoulders by supporting them against the other knee.

Then Frank's eyes opened again, and there came a question in a stronger tone.

"Ned, why in Heaven's name am I tied in this way—what does it all mean?"

Ned's answer came in a low, constrained voice.

"It means," he replied, "that you've walked into the lions' den, and they won't let you walk out of it, if they have their way."

"Who are 'they'? Loose my arms, man, and let me see if I can get to my feet. There, help me to twist round on my side, you'll get at the knots better that way."

As yet he was unconscious that his feet were tied.

Ned in silence did as he was requested, and then busied himself with the knots that bound Frank's arms, moving his lantern so as to throw its light upon his task. But it was not one to be got through in a moment. The cord was strong whip-cord; the knots were hard and fast; the arms were doubly tied, at the elbows as well as at the wrists.

Frank repeated his question in another form.

"Does 'they' mean that scoundrel Buckingham and his colleagues? Where are they—the whole lot I saw sitting round the table a minute ago?"

"A minute ago! Close upon an hour ago, sir. I left you in their clutches to get Miss Mab into safety."

"Ah! you got her back all right?"

"I sent her home in a cab. Yes; she's safe enough, thank Heaven!"

"Who was it struck me behind? Hang it, can't you get those knots undone? Haven't you such a thing as a knife in your pocket?"

Ned kept his face bent over the knot.

"I've left off carrying a knife about with me. I daren't trust myself sometimes—"

He broke off abruptly.

"Try your teeth at them. Can't you get help of some sort? Where are those men? Great Heavens, if I could only get at them for a moment."

"You marked one of them for life, sir," said Ned, between his bites at the cord.

"Which one?"

"Maurice O'Shea," answered Ned. "He stood at the door watching while the meeting was held. He had only gone off guard for a moment to fetch a match for his pipe, and then it was that Miss Mab made her way in."

"Ah! Now be good enough to tell me who struck me behind, so that I may know the man when next I see him."

These questions must have sounded oddly enough in Ned's ears, put by a man for whose chances of life the boldest would not have given the toss of a half-penny ten minutes ago. It was time some glimmer of the truth was let into his brain. So he answered slowly, between his efforts at the knots:

"Bryan O'Shea it was who struck you behind; Maurice gagged you; the captain and Bryan together tied your hands and feet: then, when I got back from sending Miss Mab home, they told me it would fall to my share to do the rest."

"What rest?"

Silence was Ned's answer.

His strong teeth had by this time slackened the last knot which bound Frank's elbows. His wrists, however, were still held fast by the cords.

"So far, so good," Ned muttered, going straight at the other ligature.

"What rest?" again demanded Frank, impatiently. "Look here, Ned, if you've anything to say, out with it. Don't fumble over it."

Ned went a roundabout way to work.

"Our captain, in sudden cases of emergency, has the right to pronounce sudden and extreme sentences. This right is granted to him by our Articles of Association."

"What on earth has that to do with me?"

Ned still chose to get to his end by circumlocution.

"When I got back I found the captain had read aloud to the others the article giving him this right, and nothing remained but to pass the sentence—on you."

"On me! Ah, I see! And you were deputed to carry the sentence out, and you haven't done it. Well, I need not talk to you of my gratitude; but you shall feel it all your life long. To my dying day I shall never forget that I owe my life to you."

"Owe, sir! No; you don't owe your life to me yet."

Great Heavens! What was this man made of! Was love of life or fear of death unknown to him that murder had to be spelt out to him letter by letter, and then shouted into his ear, before he could be made to understand the dangers that beset him? To most men in his position there would have been no need even to whisper the truth; a failing heart would only too surely have suggested it.

"Well, if I don't owe it to you, I don't know whom I have to thank for it," answered Frank, heartily, still missing the mark. "If Maurice or Bryan O'Shea had been told off to execute the sentence, I take it they would have made but short work of it."

Ned tugged at his knots for a moment in silence. When he spoke next it was in short, brusque tones.

"You don't see, sir; you don't understand," he said, still with his face bent low and his fingers busy. "I've had a certain work given me to do, and my life must go for it if it's left undone."

Frank missed the man's meaning no longer.

There fell a minute's silence. A minute which held for Frank in its sixty seconds, the rush, the whirl, the turmoil of a lifetime.

CATHERINE LOUISA PIRKIS

Out of the darkness of the bare little room seemed suddenly to flash Joyce's bright, beautiful face; over the tumult in his heart seemed to sound her clear happy voice saying, as he had last heard it:

"This is the open sesame. Joyce, my dear, I think you are the happiest girl alive!"

When he next spoke his voice had changed.

"Well," he said, in odd, quiet tones "are you going to do your work?"

There came no reply from Ned.

"I can't prevent you, you know. I'm at your mercy, tied here hand and foot at your feet—and I'm not going to whine and cry for my life, I can tell you," Frank went on.

Ned's answer was the sudden release of Frank's hands.

"The feet won't take so long to unstrap, sir," he said, "they've not put quite so much strength in there. I daresay they were more afraid of your hands than your legs. They knew you'd be a better hand at fighting than running away."

Whether that was their reason or not, certain it was that Frank's feet were set free with but scanty expenditure of labor.

At first it was hard for him to stand upright; every muscle in his body seemed bruised and aching. His head whirled; he felt sick and giddy. He leaned against the bare wall for a moment. When he spoke again, it was with an effort.

"Now you must tell me everything, Donovan, so that I may see exactly your danger and mine, for I take it we stand much upon the same footing now," he said.

"Ay," answered Ned, bitterly. "There isn't much of a chance left for either of us."

"Where are those men now?"

"Bryan O'Shea is waiting at the corner of the court till I come out and report that my work is done. Maurice is stationed about a dozen yards ahead of him in case he may be wanted. The captain has gone back to his lodgings at Bloomsbury, where I shall have to report myself tomorrow at six—or rather this morning at six, giving full particulars."

"Why didn't O'Shea stay with you and assist you in your—your work?"

"He is on guard against interruptions. He will signal to me to get into hiding should the police come along. Besides, it is not the custom of the Society to set more than one man on at such risky work as this. If detected, the loss of one man is less than that of two to the Society, and there is also less chance of a betrayal of the Society's secrets. Of course, where there are two men at work there is more or less risk of one buying his life by turning witness against the other."

"And how were you supposed to do your work, may I ask, since they only half did it for you? I see no weapons of any sort—no knife, revolver, nor anything else."

Ned's reply was to open the door of the out-building leading into the little square yard. It let in a rush of cold bleak north wind. Overhead the black snow-clouds were beginning to pile in the night-sky. Not a ray of moonlight or shining of gas-lamp anywhere; only the windy flicker which came from the lantern behind the two men made here and there a fitful patch on the outside gloom. Not a sound broke the night-silence save the rush of the north wind as it swept past, and the lap-lap of the river against the sides of some belated steam-launch making its way along the receding stream.

Ned pointed down the narrow yard:

"That leads straight down to the river—at least there is only a low broken fence dividing it from an empty wharf which overlooks the Thames. I am supposed to make sure you are insensible—to use my fist if need be to keep you so, but on no account to shed blood, for 'blood spilt,' says the captain, 'tells tales.' I am then supposed to drag you down the garden, through the fence on to the wharf in the darkness. You can guess the rest. The tide is running out fast now. 'It'll be miles away before morning,' the captain said, as he went out at the door."

Frank was silent for a moment. It is a somewhat odd experience for a man, as he stands warm, breathing, sentient, to hear himself spoken of as "it." His next words had the whole of his heart in them, not a doubt.

"The scoundrel! My day of reckoning with him isn't far off, he may rest assured."

"What are you going to do, sir?"

"Do! What do you suppose I'm going to do but hand the whole lot of them over to the police?"

One long, low whistle at this moment came thrilling through the night air, followed at a short interval by one less prolonged.

Ned stepped out into the windy darkness and gave in response a short whistle on the same note. Then he came back, shutting the door behind him without a sound.

"What does that mean?" asked Frank.

CATHERINE LOUISA PIRKIS

"It means—any difficulties? Do you want help?"

"And your reply meant—?"

"No."

"Ned, that fellow won't be making off before we can get at him, will he? I feel all to pieces tonight, but still—"

Ned impatiently crossed the floor, and stood at Frank's side, laying his hand upon his arm.

"Look here, Mr. Ledyard," he said, roughly, "it's time you took in the whole thing, the risk I've run, the danger we're in. I take it you love your life—you've every reason to. I love mine, I know that, though why, Heaven only knows, I don't."

It would not have needed a philosopher to answer Ned's "why." At three-and-twenty the love of life is hard to kill, more especially when disappointments and crosses have made a man feel he has scarcely got his due of enjoyment out of those three-and-twenty years.

"Love my life! I should think I did," exclaimed Frank, thinking of what the morrow promised to bring him; "but I can't see how the love of our life can in any way interfere with our handing those fellows over to justice."

"Don't you know, sir, neither you nor I would be allowed to leave this court alive if we showed our faces together? Bryan has revolver in his pocket; he's a sure shot enough."

"Well, then, don't let us show our faces together. You go out first and draw the men off; I'll follow after. There's no difficulty that I can see."

"And when you left here I suppose you'd go straight to the police and make known the whole thing from beginning to end."

"Exactly; what else on earth is there to be done?"

"And—what—becomes—of—me?"

He put long pauses between his words, doubling his meaning by his slow emphasis.

"What becomes of you?" repeated Frank. "Why, of course, you'd be put under the protection of the police till those scoundrels were disposed of. You'd be safe enough then, I suppose."

Ned laughed a short, bitter laugh.

"You forget that those men and I represent not only a small branch association, but a big League pledged to—well, no matter about that. What I want you to understand, and what you don't seem able to understand, is that the moment your face is seen alive, here or anywhere else, my life is gone. As I stand here before you, I am a condemned man, and your appearance alive anywhere is the signal for my sentence to be executed. You may put yourself under the protection of the police, well and good, but there's no twenty bodies of police can protect me. Do you understand now, sir?"

"Ned, I am not likely to play the part of a cur or a coward."

And the tone in which Frank said this showed that at last Ned's words held their full of meaning for him. Then, for a minute, the two men stood staring into each other's faces silently, the flicker from the lantern showing one bitter, haggard look shared between them.

Frank was the first to speak.

"Whatever you propose I shall feel bound in honor to accede to. I won't take my life at the price of yours," he said, huskily.

Ned stood silent. Frank went on:

"I will remain in hiding where and for how long you please, until—that is—you can get away into some place of safety. Only one proviso I make; you must take a message from me to Miss Shenstone explaining matters. I can't have her dragged in for any of this misery."

Ned still did not speak; so Frank went on again:

"America, of course, would be no refuge for you; nor France, nor Belgium—"

"No, nor any corner of the earth, so far as I can see," broke in the Irishman, impetuously. "Heavens, that I should have sold myself into this state of bondage!"

And then in his wrath he lifted up his voice and cursed the day that he was born; cursed his Irish blood, which had found its kith and kin among traitors and cowards; cursed the tyranny of wealth and rank which called such a race of traitors and cowards into existence.

Frank subsided into coolness before the tumult.

"Don't let yourself go in that way, for Heaven's sake. Let's take counsel together and see what can be done for the best," he said, quietly.

But, think as they would, everything seemed for the worst, nothing for the best. They passed in review every corner of Europe where there would be a likelihood for a forsworn Fenian to dodge his destiny. Ned shook his head over it all.

"If I could be tossed out of the clouds into the heart of Norway, or even on the coast," he said, "I might be safe enough there; it's a little out of the track of Fenianism, but the thing is how am I to get there? Not tonight, nor tomorrow night, should I cross London alive with the work I have had dealt out to me to do. The Society gives a man his work

CATHERINE LOUISA PIRKIS

for each day, and, if they haven't perfect faith in that man, they appoint two men to look after him and see that it is done. When work slackens, as it may before long, then I can begin to think of my hiding-place. But at the present moment, it seems to me, the only thing to do is to hide you, not me, till my chance comes round."

The happy wedding-day, of which the morrow held the promise, seemed suddenly to disappear from Frank's sight into the dim distance. He tried to keep his head steady.

"As I told you a moment ago, I am prepared to go into hiding where and for how long you please, on the one condition I have named. So far as I can see, your safest plan will be to turn sailor so soon as you can get a fair chance of escape, and live upon the ocean."

"Yes," answered Ned, thoughtfully, "so long as I kept clear of the Atlantic highway, or the Australian steamers, I should be right enough. The life would suit me—"

"It would be a glorious life," broke in Frank, "and, after the bondage you've lived in the last two or three years, I should think you'd hail it with delight. If circumstances hadn't made me a lawyer, I should have been a sailor myself."

A long, low whistle once more broke in upon their talk. It was sounded on a lower note than before.

Ned made no attempt to answer it.

"What does that mean?" asked Frank.

"It means warning. I am not to stir till he signals again."

"The scoundrel! I'd like to signal him. Well, so far as I can see, it only remains now to arrange my hiding-place, the where and how long it is to last. Thank Heaven I have some money with me—ah, I suppose those men didn't rob me of my purse as a finish to their kind treatment?"

With an eagerness he had never before evinced on the matter of pounds or pennies, he ransacked his pockets, and, thankfully enough, came upon a roll of bank notes, with which, in view of the morrow's necessities, he had provided himself, and for safety had stuffed into his pocket-book over-night, as he had left his rooms to attend Mrs. Shenstone's evening party.

Ned eyed them.

"They wouldn't touch notes—they're too wary," he said; "but if it had been gold no doubt it would have been appropriated for 'patriotic purposes.'"

"Patriotic humbug! But I tell you what, Ned, you shall have half of whatever I've got here, so that we may each have an equal chance of fulfilling our share of our bargain. There's nothing like solid hard cash to tide a man over difficulties."

He knelt on the floor beside the lantern, so as to count over the store of "solid hard cash" he had to divide.

Ned stood looking at him, still thoughtfully turning over in his mind the ways and means that remained to him for redeeming his forfeited life.

"Whaling up in the North would suit me better than anything else in life," he presently said, with an energy which showed that, for all his love-lornness and wretched bond-service, the love of adventure and a reckless freedom was strong as ever in his heart.

Frank looked up sharply from his bank-notes.

"That reminds me of the trip I took about four years ago, when I broke down with hard reading. I took passage in a whaler from Dundee, and sailed out beyond the Faroes. A better hiding-place from Fenian Leagues, or any phase of civilized (or brutalized) humanity couldn't be found than the Faroes. For all practical purposes they are as far off from England as Australia."

Ned's face brightened.

"It would be giving me a chance, sir, if you'd manage to get out first to the Faroes and let me, later on, join you there. I should be safe enough on board a whaler, or anywhere up in those northern regions; but everywhere else I run the risk of a bullet through my head, or rather, should run the risk, if once it were known I had failed in my duty."

Frank got up from his knees with his bank-notes parceled into two lots.

"Here you are, Ned," he said, thrusting one lot into the Irishman's hand.

Ned took them a little doubtfully.

"Will it be safe to use them, sir? I mean, do you think their numbers have been taken?" he asked.

"No fear. A man who owed me a lot of money paid me these notes late yesterday as a first instalment. He's much too big a scamp to take the numbers of his notes, or have the faintest notion where he got them from."

"It's a mercy the captain didn't know that," muttered Ned, as he pocketed the notes.

CATHERINE LOUISA PIRKIS

"Ay. Well, now, I take it we stand on an equal footing, and we'll strike a cool, clear-headed bargain, leaving nothing to haphazard or chance. As I told you a minute ago, we put in at the Faroes on our way back to Dundee. I hired a small boat, and went coasting in and out among the islands. Several are uninhabited, and one, I remember, had lost its pinnacle, and was nothing more than a sunken rock. On this rock had been placed a beacon with glass prisms, which refracted the light thrown upon it from a neighboring islet. This islet was little more than a rocky headland jutting out into the ocean; and, beyond the old couple who kept the light-house, and their children, I don't believe it owned to a single inhabitant other than gulls or gair-fowl."

Ned's face brightened.

"The very place, sir," he began, enthusiastically, ready at one bound from the depths of despair to take the heights of hope.

Frank went on with his description in a tone destitute of enthusiasm.

"This old couple had lived there for twenty years. The man was a deaf-mute; his wife was an old Scotchwoman, deaf, but decidedly not dumb. She took it for granted that every one's first question to her would be for the name of the island, its latitude and longitude; so, whenever she saw a stranger, she dropped a curtsey, and said: 'Sir, this is Light Island, latitude 62.32 north; longitude 7.10 west.' I can hear her now. It impressed the latitude and longitude of the place in my memory; but you had better write it down—there may be a hundred or more Light Islands up in the North, for anything I know to the contrary."

Ned produced a scrap of paper from his pocket, but pencil he had none.

Frank had a blue-lead pencil at command, but he objected to the paper.

"You'll lose that," he said, eyeing it dubiously; "or perhaps light a pipe with it."

"Never fear, sir."

"But I do fear. A meeting-place like this ought to be tattooed on your arm or leg, if we had means at command. Have you a watch?"

Ned was not likely to forget he had a watch, over which he had sworn his impetuous oath of allegiance to a League that set time at defiance.

He produced it in its old-fashioned case, with the hands stationary at the memorable hour that his bond-service had begun.

Frank handed him his pencil and superintended the writing in the inner lid of the latitude and longitude of Light Island.

"It's a special Providence put that place into your head, sir," Ned said, his enthusiasm mounting high and higher. "It'll be easy enough for you to get away unnoticed, before the hue-and-cry is set up after you. When once you're missed, there's not a town or village in England could hide you; but out there on the Faroes I take it you'll be safe enough from newspapers or the detectives."

Frank was in no mood to play the echo to the Irishman's enthusiasm.

"Yes, it's a dismal enough look-out," he said, gloomily, "but I'm not going to shirk my share of the compact. I can get across London on my legs before dawn, take the first train to the North, be at Dundee before night, and on board a whaler or any other boat I can catch before the hue-and-cry, as you call it, has had time to begin. Once at Light Island, I remain there until you get free from your bondage and take my place. This is my share of the bargain, isn't it?"

"It is, sir. I wish I could make it lighter for you."

"Never mind about that. I am grateful enough to you that I am here to strike a bargain at all. Now for your share of it. Give me that scrap of paper you offered me a minute ago."

Ned handed it to him.

Frank, supporting the paper against the brick wall, wrote a hurried line, addressed to Joyce, Ned holding the lantern close to his shoulders meanwhile, to give him the necessary light:

"My darling," it ran, "don't be uneasy about me. I'm quite safe, and in a few days will be back again, and explain everything to you.

F. L.

More than this the paper would not admit of.

He folded it, and handed it to Ned.

"I trust to you to give this into Miss Shenstone's hands yourself," he said, emphasizing the last word.

Ned took the paper.

"It shall only pass out of my hands to go into Miss Shenstone's," he said.

"Yes. And it must be delivered at once—at once. Do you hear, Ned?"

Ned's face clouded. Mountains of difficulty rose up before him now.

"The when and the how must be left to me, sir," he answered, with a rough decision.

"No, they must not be left to you. This is a matter which concerns me more than anything else in the world. If you can't tell me definitely when this note will find its way into Miss Shenstone's hands, I shall deliver it myself before I go into hiding, no matter at what risk to my life."

An ugly change passed over Ned's open face.

"Look here, Mr. Ledyard," he said, gruffly, laying his hand on Frank's arm, "let me understand where we are. Are you trifling and playing the fool with me? Are you seeming fair and above-board with me, and meaning all the time to throw me over at the very first opportunity?"

Frank shook him off indignantly.

"Do you doubt my honor?" he cried. "Is there no such thing as gratitude in the world? Is it likely I should take my life at your hands, and then put yours in jeopardy?"

"That is precisely what you would do if you tied me down to time in this matter, or took it into your own hands. You don't know—how could you?—the network which hems me in at the present moment. You don't know how impossible it is for a man, who has once sworn allegiance as I have to a powerful League, to claim an hour to himself. Wherever he goes, eyes are on him; whatever he does, it is reported to his superiors. If I were to go from here to Miss Shenstone suspicions would be set afloat at once, and my life wouldn't be worth a brass farthing before the week was over."

Frank's face was growing white and whiter with the effort to keep himself in check. He asked another question:

"How long must I keep in hiding? Tell me."

Ned broke out again into vehemence.

"How is it possible for me to tell you? Ask a man who is crippled hand and foot when he means to use his limbs again. He'll tell you, tomorrow if power comes back to them; and I tell you, tomorrow would see me shake off this cursed bondage, if I could see my way to it. No, sir; time myself I can't, and won't pretend I can. A bargain without a date, it must be, or no bargain at all."

Three short, quick whistles came in succession at this moment from without.

Ned promptly took the lantern from the floor, and went toward the inner door of the room.

"That means I must come at once. I'daren't delay another moment, or they'll be down upon us. That cord must be hidden. Can you charge yourself with it, sir? I dare not. Better not leave the house for full half an hour after I am gone, then lose no time in getting away. You had better take my great-coat to cover your evening-dress, I shall say I 'marked it'"—this said with a meaning impossible to misconstrue—"'and threw it into the Thames.'"

While Ned had been speaking he had been quickly moving toward the front door, after depositing his lantern on the table of the inner room. Frank muttered an angry word. Twenty-four hours would have seemed but a scanty allowance of time for the striking of so momentous a bargain, and here was he begrudged an extra five minutes.

He followed Ned, laying his hand on his arm.

"A moment more. There must be no loose arrangement of these details—they are of vital importance. I have your word for it that that note goes into Miss Shenstone's hands as soon as possible?"

"As soon as possible. Yes, sir."

"Very well; I trust you, remember. Now, another thing, you must write to me directly you get a chance, and tell me how things go."

Ned thought a moment.

"Under what name, sir, shall I address you; I dare not use your own."

"Oh, some common name that won't attract attention. Better keep to my initials though, they're marked on my linen. Say Lee—Frederick Lee."

"Frederick Lee. I won't forget."

"And, Ned, there's one thing else. You run tremendous risks daily, should anything happen to you—forgive me for putting it so plainly—how on earth am I to know it? Or how is any one to know where I am, and send me word?"

Ned paused with his hand on the lock of the front door.

"I will provide against that, also—" he began.

"Yes, but how, man?" broke in Frank, impetuously; "tell me in what way. This is a thing of first importance—not to be left to chance or hap-hazard."

"You must leave the whole thing to me, sir, from first to last. It is impossible for me to say how I shall do this or that. If I laid down a settled plan, the chances are, it would be impossible for me to adhere to it. Circumstances, and the thought of the safety of both of us, must guide me."

Frank groaned. The whistle sounded again impatiently from without. Ned, with his last look, added another last word.

"Don't forget, sir," he said, quietly, "we have changed places now, and my life is in your hands."

Frank sprang forward impetuously, seizing him by the hand.

"I am not likely to forget," he cried, vehemently. "I tell you I am simply a dead man till you give the word."

XLIX

In the snowy dimness of the winter's dawn, Donovan crept back to his lodgings, after reporting to the "Captain" that his work was done, balancing in his mind the question, how it was possible for him to keep his pledge and inform Joyce of her lover's safety without risk to his own life.

Meanwhile Frank was putting distance between himself and all he held most precious in life. The whole thing, looked back upon, seemed to him like some wild, melodramatic dream in which he had lain quiescent while another man had played his part.

The over-night—the brilliant evening party, the tumult of expectant joy in his heart—had been real enough to him, not a doubt; the common-place life beginning to stir in the wintry streets was real enough also, with its suggestions of work-a-day squalor and grinding misery. But this midnight interlude which linked the brilliant overnight with the squalid dawn seemed less like a bit of his own actual experience than a fantastic nightmare, whose grip had set his brain rocking.

The bruises with which he was covered literally from head to foot, the ugly red rims round his wrists, the Irishman's coarse greatcoat were, however, evidences not to be disregarded of the reality of the experience of the past few hours. Without them he might easily enough have believed that his memory was playing tricks with him, and have gone about his day's work as usual.

He felt terribly shaken. The cold, fresh air of the morning, though it steadied his nerves somewhat, could not work miracles; some little vigor it put into him, although scarcely of the quality he was accustomed to have at command. It was a relief to him that he was compelled to keep moving; an enforced inactivity at that moment he felt might have annihilated what little reasoning power was left to him.

He had made no outward sigh to Ned how hard hit he had been by the weight and suddenness of his mischance. He was not disposed to set up a moan over it now; as a matter of fact, little power for moaning seemed left to him. His thoughts were all one confused, incoherent whirl, in which the events of last night mingled oddly enough with the earlier occurrences of the day. The only fact which he seemed to realize distinctly was that he was to go into hiding somewhere, skulk away

CATHERINE LOUISA PIRKIS

from the notice of men as though he were a criminal eluding justice. And this part of the compact he set himself scrupulously to fulfill.

He felt faint and giddy still. He would have been grateful enough for a stimulant of any sort. He looked enviously at the workingmen getting their early breakfasts from the itinerant coffee-vendors. But he dared not run the risk of getting a cup for himself. Then the snow began to fall. His teeth chattered, and he shrank from the northeaster in a way that seemed to him unaccountable.

When he reached the Great Northern station, an early train was about starting for the North. He had only just time to get his ticket and swing himself into it. It was a workman's train, and he chose a well-filled compartment, wisely reasoning that in a crowd he would be less likely to attract attention. One of his fellow-travelers chanced to be a British workman of "advanced" democratic opinions. These he proceeded to air for the benefit of those about him. More than once he appealed to Frank for confirmation—or the reverse—of his political notions. Frank's replies must have been given in odd, incoherent tones, for the British workman turned to his companions and openly expressed his opinion of the gentleman's condition. Then he addressed Frank again, advising him in kind, fatherly fashion to get home as soon as possible and "sleep it off."

He little knew, good man, how gratefully Frank would have welcomed the power to lie down in some quiet corner, and in heavy sleep toss into oblivion the whole hideous drama of overnight.

Three times he had to change trains on his way to Dundee. At each of these stoppages he contrived to get refreshments for himself, of which he stood greatly in need; without which, indeed, he could scarcely have arrived at his journey's end.

About nine o'clock at night he reached Dundee, with head burning, limbs aching, and thoughts, if possible, more chaotic than before, with his long day of rapid traveling. The bustle of the town bewildered him. The quay seemed one mass of moving heads, dancing lights, deep shadows, ringing bells. To his fancy every one seemed staring at him, and he could not divest himself of the feeling that presently some one would come up, lay a hand upon his shoulder, and tell him that, in spite of all the fine precautions he had taken, every one knew who he was. He slunk away from the busy thoroughfares, engaged a night's lodging in a quiet street leading off the quay, borrowed a razor, and, with a more unsteady hand than he had ever in his life owned to before, shaved off his mustache and whiskers.

Then he went out once more, trying his hardest to collect his thoughts, and plan step by step his temporary exile. He bought a portmanteau at one shop, which he filled with some necessary articles of clothing at another. Among other articles he purchased a low-crowned felt hat, rightly judging that his present hat showed somewhat incongruously against the Irishman's rough greatcoat.

Then he returned to the quay, and proceeded to make cautious inquiries as to outgoing vessels.

He scarcely realized his own identity as he went about these things. It was for him an altogether remarkable experience to be skulking in corners, shunning men's eyes, giving a false name, drawing his hat low over his brow, turning his coat collar as high as it would go; in fact, doing the utmost that lay in his power to elude every sort of observation. It would not have required a very strong stretch of his imagination to have persuaded himself that he had, in very truth, committed some crime, and was doing his utmost to escape the hand of justice.

Before he took himself to his night's lodging he ascertained that two or three small steamers were on the point of sailing for the Faroe Fishing-Banks.* In one of these he contrived to secure a berth. It was of a better build than most of the outgoing boats, and promised a quick passage. It was fitted with a large square tank in the middle for the purpose of bringing back live cod for the London market, and the captain, a Norwegian, readily consented at Frank's request to take a day's journey beyond the fishing-banks to Light Island, when he understood that he might put his own price on the passage. But best of all, at least for Frank's chance of a successful disguise, was the fact that the boat was to sail at sunrise the next day.

His night's rest in his quiet lodging of necessity was brief; also of necessity, it was troubled. Hideous dreams peopled it with all sorts of terrors. Now he was a murderer or some other criminal endeavoring to escape into hiding. Now it was Joyce who was trying to save him from prison; now it was he who was trying to save Joyce, for it seemed to him that she had shared in his crime; and through it all the noisy,

---

* The author desires here gratefully to acknowledge indebtedness to Sir Wyville Thomson, author of "The Depths of the Sea," and to the anonymous author of "Some Faroe Notes" in the May number of the "Cornhill Magazine," for their graphic descriptions of the Faroe Isles.

bustling quay figured as background, with lights swinging, crowds of heads, bells ringing, perpetual shoutings, jostlings, and confusion.

He woke, with a groan and a great start, about two hours before daylight, gathered together his few belongings, and hastened on board the little steamer.

Once on board, the inevitable physical reaction set in. He hid his face in the narrow, dark berth assigned to him, and, worn out with the heavy mental and physical strain he had endured through the past forty-eight hours, collapsed utterly. He felt himself alike incapable of thought or movement. With but brief interludes he slept at least half-way across the rough wild stretch of ocean that lay between Dundee and the Faroes. If the boat had added one to the nameless wrecks which the hurrying tides were busy burying under their swollen loads of tangly sea-weed, Frank would have gone down knowing nothing of that passionate longing for one more glimpse of loved faces, one more clasp of loved hands, which makes the bodily agony of poor drowning souls by comparison a thing of naught.

As the boat neared the Shetlands, however, youth and a good constitution, under the kindly influence of the sea-breezes, began once more to assert themselves.

He collected his thoughts together and strove to look the inevitable fairly in the face. He strove even to make the best of it, buoyed himself up with hope, and forced himself to believe that Ned's sturdiness of purpose to escape from his thraldom was not for a moment to be questioned. Ned would not shirk his share of the bargain, he assured himself, and he (Frank) had no wish to shirk his. Ned's last words, "My life is in your hands now, sir," were not words to be lightly forgotten. Of course, the man would as speedily as possible get his freedom, redeem his promise, and release him from his miserable exile.

These were the whisperings of his hopes.

The Shetlands passed and the Faroes in sight, however, other thoughts not quite of so bright a hue came to him. He stood on the deck, leaning over the side. The steamer was flying along easily before the wind with but little steam on. It was a bright winter's day, the white foam came dashing into his face with every plunge the boat made in the waters. The wind had a touch of ice in it. It seemed to tell tales of Norwegian glaciers and fiords, brightly-dressed, yellow-haired maidens, rough fisher-folk, strong-handed, sea-roving Norsemen.

Frank recalled with a pang one happy half-hour when he and Joyce had been discussing their wedding-trip together, and she had said, in her usual gay, frank manner, "Now, if it had only been July instead of December, how delightful it would have been to have packed a knapsack, and 'made tracks,' as the Americans say, for the land of the midnight sun!" And he had promised her that the very first summer holiday they took together should be in that delightful region. Here was he, well on his way to the northern latitudes, but it was scarcely in the holiday spirit he had contemplated.

The more he thought over things, the more discontented he grew with them. Why had he not arranged matters more definitely with Ned, and when he as good as gave his word not to send letter or message to Joyce, why had he not stipulated that she should be informed of his hiding-place, so as to be able to send letter or message to him?

Looked back upon now, his midnight interview with Ned seemed so hurried and confused that everything that ought to have been done had been left undone. It would have lightened the gloom of this dreary exile—would have turned it by comparison into a holiday—could he have looked forward to a line from Joyce telling him how things went with her, what sort of a stand she might make against Buckingham's insolence and her mother's foolishness.

For foremost among his anxieties, naturally enough, was the thought that this man was left free now to act according to the dictates of his audacity.

Frank had no wish to underrate Joyce's courage or strength of will, but he knew how limited her knowledge of the world was, and what feeble weapons after all a woman's courage and strength of will were when opposed to the unscrupulous villainy of a man like Buckingham. Uncle Archie at his best was a doughty antagonist, he readily enough admitted; but, unfortunately, the old gentleman's irritable temper and his frequent attacks of gout showed him more often at his worst than at his best. A fact, no doubt, of which Buckingham would take due cognizance.

"There'll be a heavy day of reckoning for him—the scoundrel—when once I get a chance," Frank muttered, shading his eyes with his hand, and momentarily shutting out the bright seascape of dancing waves and winter sky.

A sailor touched his arm, and offered him a glass wherewith to get his first glimpse of the Faroes. Frank put it on one side without a word of thanks. It seemed to him he would see enough and to spare of the Faroes before he had done with them. There they were, straight in front of him, treeless, sunless, their soft coloring and bold, fantastic outlines looming dimly out of a shrouding veil of clinging silver mist. He looked across the roughly dashing waters of the Sound, which rolled between him and Light Island, where the tall, round light-tower showed like some ghastly monument to the dead, and for the first time the whisperings of mutinous discontent with his own ethics made themselves heard in his heart.

"Now," he said to himself, "in the name of common sense, can it be expected of me to hide myself from my fellow-creatures like some escaped felon dodging the hangman just to save the life of a man who, no doubt in the eyes of the law, has forfeited it a hundred times over?"

Common sense held her peace. Possibly the matter was a little outside her domain; but honor and gratitude joined voices together, and in chorus preached his duty to him. They did it simply enough, too, just repeating his own promise over again in his ear; "I shall be simply a dead man, Ned, till you give the word"; and the question was settled at once.

L

Thus, when the hue-and-cry after the missing man was at its loudest; when Ned, like some hunted hare, was so sore beset with actual pressing dangers that he dared not trust himself to give a thought to Joyce's by one degree less urgent necessity; when Mab was striving her hardest to attain the seer's gift; and Joyce was looking longingly at widow's weeds and irrevocable tombstones; Frank, on his sea-bleached rock, was fighting with might and main to preserve a fortitude, which, in the circumstances, fell little short of the heroic.

Although it was veritable midwinter, and King Fog reigned supreme, it was a matter for congratulation that by comparison with the general run of winters in these northern latitudes it was mild in the extreme. Of necessity, Frank's life among these uncultured, though kindly, islanders promised to be a rough one, and climate became of proportionate importance.

Light Island, by comparison with Stromoe—the island on which Thorshavn, the capital, is built—was a desert. Its population, all told, was but a feeble company, consisting of the old lighthouse-keeper, and his children of a second and third generation.

Frank's intercourse with the people was at first naturally much restricted. He knew scarcely a word of Danish; they had but little English at command. The few idioms they knew had come down to them, strongly flavored with Scotch, from the old lighthouse-keeper's Scotch wife. She, poor soul! had been gathered to her fathers in the preceding year, and had been borne over-sea for burial in a Faroe whaling-boat to one of the Shetland Isles, where lay her dead kith and kin. Old Christian, however, the deaf mute, lived on to trim the lamps of the light-tower; a task which had been assigned to him by the Lag-Thing, or Faroe Parliament, some twenty years previously. Not once in all those twenty years had he been known, through illness or any other cause, to fail in his trust. Day after day did the old man make his way up the rough ladder into the round tower, there to watch out the long hours of the dreary winter's night, or the short golden ones of the summer night, which, in truth, had not much of night in them after all.

This round white tower, whose light fell athwart the sunken rock, was built on the very edge of a jutting headland, which stood nearly two thousand feet, without break or so much as an outstanding ledge,

CATHERINE LOUISA PIRKIS

above the sea. A plain, straight, awful fall of rock it showed from above or below.

The light, like the tower, was of primitive construction, and was fed by the whale-oil, which came so readily to hand in these islands. Of late years, however, since the toppling over of the pinnacle of the Monk Rock into the sea, it had been supplemented by a somewhat modern contrivance—a metallic reflector, which threw a parallel beam of light on the sunken rock. An apparatus—an arrangement of glass prisms—had been erected on a beacon on this sunken rock. This caught the beam of light and refracted it, giving the appearance of a flame springing up from the rock itself.

On his first arrival Frank threw himself heartily, if a little spasmodically, into the pursuits of the islanders. A man must do something with his days, even though they may consist of but eight hours at their longest. So in turn he fished, he trapped sea-fowl, or mended boats or nets.

After a time, however, this light-tower saw more of him than did any one of the grass-covered huts. He speedily made the calculation that two thousand feet of rocky height with forty feet of tower superadded, could command a noble view of the sweep of ocean which separated Faroe from the British Isles, and consequently of every northward-bound vessel.

Henceforward the old deaf mute became almost his sole companion, if, that is, a deaf mute who can neither read nor write can be dignified by such a title."

Three low cottages, roofed with growing turf and huddled on a sheltered, inland ridge of rock, sufficed for the little colony.

The good, kindly souls accepted without question Frank's statement, that he had made their island a place of assignation with a friend, who would shortly cross over from England or Scotland.

They made him heartily welcome to one of their huts, set apart for him the warmest corner by their peat-fire, and treated him to the best of the frugal diet they had at command—rye-bread, whale-meat, wind-dried sea-fowl—disdaining so much as to look at the English coin he ventured to tender in acknowledgment.

Among its scanty furniture the one room of the light-tower numbered an ancient telescope. It did little more than double the range of the naked eye; but that even was a gain not to be despised. The old man, as he came heavily up the ladder with his oil-can, would find Frank, with a sigh, putting on one side the rickety old thing for the night; and, long before the sullen red flush of the winter's dawn gave him warning that the night-watch was ended, Frank would come springing up the ladder, two steps at a time, eager to take up his post once more.

It made a pathetic picture: that drowsy old man nodding in his wicker-chair over his knitting-pins, with dumb lips, and ears locked against every sound, noisy or gentle, jubilant or sad; and that eager young one, with senses strung to highest pitch by an expectancy so intense that it was near akin to agony.

Facing the old man was another wicker-chair, high-backed like his own, and, like his own, blackened with age and the smoke from the peat-fire. On it lay a pair of rusty knitting-pins and a ball of sheep's wool. That was the chair whereon the old wife had sat, keeping him company through the long night-watches, and that was the last scrap of work wherewith her thin, feeble fingers had busied themselves. To this chair the old man's eyes would lift dreamily at times. In it, no doubt, he read a page of past history, or, perhaps, a line or two of blessed hope for a future meeting—who could say?

Facing the young man was the sweep of ocean without a sail and sky without a cloud—a great impassable barrier between him and all he held most precious in life—with no tender memories of the past written upon it, nor any golden promise for the future, so far as he could see—a wide, desolate blank, which pained his eyeballs to scan, and made his brain sick with its staring emptiness.

That was on bright, keen, frosty days. But when the northeast wind set in, and brought with it rolling masses of formless vapor, which compacted into one solid wall of fog, everything was changed. A great, wonderful hush seemed to fall alike on sea and land; it was as if some mighty power had held up its finger to all creation, imposing a sudden, awful silence. Even the rush and swirl of the waves at the base of the rock sounded muffled and far away; the cry of the gair-fowl came distant and stifled.

High up in that round tower, cut off from the land, shut away from a glimpse even of sea or sky, dense dun fog everywhere, with never a book within reach, nor soul with whom to exchange a thought, it was no wonder if Frank at times found it difficult to realize his own identity with that eager, energetic young man who had looked upon life as a big wrestling-ground wherein muscle and vigor were bound to carry the day.

CATHERINE LOUISA PIRKIS

"Great heavens!" he cried aloud once, in the extremity of his impatience, "a man might as well be shut up alive in a tomb at once and be done with it."

It mattered after all very little whether he cried loud or whether he cried low. That old deaf mute, with the knitting-pins in his hands, never moved a muscle nor bent the ear toward him.

It seemed as if Heaven itself had grown equally hard of hearing; as if that great dense wall of fog were playing the part of sounding-board to him, throwing back his cries in his teeth.

LI

I t was just about the time that Uncle Archie and Joyce, looking into each other's blank faces, confessed themselves to be at their wits' end, that Frank received his first message from Ned.

Frank might have confessed himself in much the same predicament as Uncle Archie, for he had been putting to himself one or two uncomfortable questions, to which his wits were incapable of supplying adequate answers. Such for instance as "Supposing mischance of some sort has overtaken Ned and he is dead, without revealing my hiding-place, how on earth am I to become aware of the fact? How long, in common reason, may it be expected of me to remain here waiting for some sign of his existence?"

It was easy enough to recall Ned's vehement promise that he would provide effectually for such an emergency; it was a more difficult task to feel the matter set at rest by it. Even Ned's hurried line only succeeded for a time in allaying apprehension. The note was brought by the little fishing-boat, which, in fair weather, coasted between the islands, bringing from Thorshavn cheeses and tinned meats in return for the sheep's-wool stockings knitted by old Christian's daughters.

Frank, with eager fingers, tore open the envelope. Perhaps it might contain a line from Joyce, he thought. A chill of disappointment fell upon him when he saw only the few following lines from Ned:

"Am hard pressed, dogged, and watched night and day—dare not attempt flight. Give me time."

Second thoughts, however, told him it was better than no message at all, and he tried to get his utmost of hope out of the few brief words.

It may be conjectured, nevertheless, that he would have read the lines with other eyes could he have known how Ned had failed in his share of the compact; how Joyce's terrible suspense remained unlifted; how his own brief note to her, instead of finding its way to her hand, had been held in the flame of a candle till it was burned to ashes, and the ashes even carefully scattered to the four winds of heaven.

Of all this, however, he was necessarily ignorant, and his trust in the Irishman's sense of honor remained unshaken. It seemed to him an altogether unworthy thing to harbor a suspicion against a man who had saved his life at the risk of his own, without exacting so much as bond or promise in return.

Old Christian's eldest son, who had acted messenger, eyed him as he read the letter.

"Your friend stays long," he said, in his composite idiom.

Frank put as cheerful a look on his face as he could command; and tried to make the man understand that everything was all right, and that people could not always keep their appointments to the day and hour.

The man trailed his fowler's net along the rock, and, on the strength of the cheerful look on Frank's face, forthwith invited him to join in a fowling expedition.

"The wind was favorable—a little sport would make the time pass more swiftly," he intimated.

So Frank threw himself heartily on the man for companionship that day, and in his newly-recovered buoyancy of spirit he equaled every one of the well-seasoned fowler's daring exploits over crag and chasm, in the teeth of a strong gale which, blowing shoreward, swept in the sea-fowl by dozens into the net. The exercise heightened his spirits. He began to read a world of meaning in Ned's few hurried lines.

"The man was heartily sick of his slavery," he said to himself, "not a doubt he would soon make a desperate effort and gain his freedom."

Then what a hey-day of gladness he and Joyce would keep together—why, the happy festival on the eve of what was to have been his wedding-day would be a funeral feast by comparison!

But this buoyancy of spirit was after all of short duration. A few days of sea-fowling, alternated with cod-fishing, saw the end of it. Back to the solitude of the lighthouse tower and the weary gazing through the telescope Frank betook himself once more.

"It's more than flesh and blood can bear," he would groan sometimes, feeling the young eager life within him well-nigh annihilated by the silence, the immensity of outside creation; of the vast rolling ocean, the empty sky, the bare, brown, awful rocks.

A solitude can be a prison or a paradise, according to the point of view from which it is regarded. To Ned, hunted, harassed, with limited ambitions, keen young love for life, above all, for a life of purely physical freedom, it doubtless would have figured in the latter guise. He would have gloried in the reckless daring of rough seas and rougher winds which the life of the Faroese whale-fisher involved. He would have outdone the boldest of the fowlers in their desperate clambering adown tremendous precipices in the teeth of a driving gale. If he could have reached this haven, the chances were he would have settled down a veritable Viking among Vikings, and, in the smiles of some yellow-haired, blue-eyed maiden, have learned to forget his first ill-starred passion.

Frank's notion of a paradise necessarily included higher ideals. Judged by these, the island solitude took but low rank. Quite apart from the special circumstances of his life at that period, there was in his nature but little that was congenial to solitude and inaction.

He had said to Ned, and had meant it, that if circumstances had not made him a lawyer, he would have chosen to be a sailor. That might be true, but the chances were that if he could not have seen straight ahead of him a prospect of stepping on board a flagship, he and salt water would speedily have parted company. Quite apart from his true, passionate love for Joyce, and his bitter disappointment at the postponement of his happiness, the very energy with which he had worked the lines of his life, rendered him intolerant of any interruption to it. A pause in his career at any moment would have been an agony to him. Silence, solitude, were for him synonyms for vacuity and extinction. To attempt to find a voice in either would have seemed to him something equivalent to putting his ear to a coffin and listening for speech from the dead man within.

So, gloomy and despondent, he set himself to bear his banishment as best he could, drawing largely upon his stores of fortitude to keep up even the appearance of equanimity before his kindly entertainers.

Old Christian's son tried in vain to tempt him on a second fowling expedition.

Frank looked down the black chasm of shelving rocks, shook his head, and turned his back on it. In the gloomy despondency which had succeeded the transient buoyancy caused by Ned's letter, he did not dare to test the strength of his grip upon good luck. He shrank from physical danger in a way he had never in his whole life known himself to shrink before.

"Everything was against him; good luck was a thing of the past," he said to himself now, as day after day went by and there came not another word from Ned.

Once, in the old happy time gone by, he had dared, as only the young and happy can dare, to trifle with and defer his happiness; now Fate, in her irony, had turned the tables on him, had brought his cup of happiness close to his lips only to snatch it away with the taunt: "See,

I have taken a leaf out of your own book, and it's a part that suits me uncommonly well."

It seemed to him that he and Joyce in this world were never to meet again. Death and mischance were forever stalking abroad on the lookout for targets for their darts. He had put himself in their way, and, so to speak, had flung defiance to them. "Come, stand straight and bow your head," he could fancy they said to him now.

It was scarcely to be wondered at if, in the extremity of his misery, he asked himself a few more questions—such as: "Supposing, throught his enforced inaction of his, Buckingham and a few other scoundrels contrived to elude justice, might he not be held morally responsible for the fact?" Or to put it another way: "Would not the guilt of a broken implied promise be less than that involved in leaving at large acknowledged traitors and criminals?"

Then when his conscience gave a sturdy "no" to sophistry, it shifted its ground and put its questions in another form, thus: "Would it of necessity be a breach of his implied word of honor to communicate with the police at London in some roundabout fashion, putting them on the scent of the timeless League? Would Ned's chances of escape of necessity be endangered? Could not the police be made to understand that Buckingham and the O'Sheas were first to be secured, and that Ned was in no sort a willing accomplice in their plots?"

But to these queries his legal knowledge, aided by his practical common-sense, gave a succession of most decisive negatives. What evidence had he to offer that would inculpate the three other criminals and leave Donovan unimpeached? Did they not all four, so far as regarded treasonable conspiracy, stand upon the same footing? What right had he to suppose that Ned, no matter how hard pressed he might be, would turn informer, and save his life to the hazard of his comrades' lives? Did not his previous knowledge of the man point to a diametrically opposite conclusion? Much as Donovan had owned he loved his own life, he had been willing to put it in jeopardy for one to whom he was in no sense bound by ties either of kindred or friendship.

And when Frank had reached this point in his self cross-questioning he started aghast at himself, and the sorry figure he had showed beneath it. He felt forced to admit that the seamy side of his nature had indeed come uppermost, when he allowed himself to balance questions of a purely personal nature, under the guise of impersonal benevolence, against his freely volunteered promise, "I shall be simply a dead man, Ned, till you give the word."

So the dark days of the northern winter went slowly by, at such a snail's pace indeed that Frank began to lose count of them, and would say to himself, as he got up from his straw mattress in the morning, or threw himself wearily upon it at night, "Now where are we? In the middle of January, February, or March? Great Heavens, was ever winter so interminably eked out as this?"

It was not until its very last hour was counted out, not until the fogs had begun to lessen visibly, the real breath of spring to make itself felt in the salt breeze, that another brief message came from Ned. It ran thus:

"Give me a little longer. For the love of heaven, remember your share of the bargain."

That must have been written and dispatched about the time that Uncle Archie, wincing under Morton's suggestion that Frank was in voluntary hiding, had bidden Joyce take up the cudgels she scorned in defense of her lover.

A little later on, just when Joyce, despairing of her own strength, was taking refuge in flight from Captain Buckingham's persecution, Donovan was dispatching a third letter to Frank, brief like the others, but a little more desperate, as follows:

"Hunted almost to death. Don't forget I lie at your mercy now."

After this, there came another long silence, which Frank made busy with the wildest hopes, fears, conjectures, despairs. Then, just about the time when Joyce, broken-hearted, was straining her ears to catch Mab's last words, "Always the sound of the sea, Joyce," Frank, on his ocean-washed rock, was reading, with dimmed eyes and bounding pulses, Donovan's final message. It was dated from Greenock, and contained only five words:

"Thank Heaven, free at last!"

Words which might aptly have been written on the Irishman's coffin-plate. Elsewhere they lacked meaning.

LII

The brief, sunless, Northern summer had come to an end. The islanders had cut their rye, and garnered it, dug their last crop of potatoes, and stored them. The women were busy carding their wool for their winter knitting, the men were organizing a cod-fishing expedition on a larger scale than usual. There had chanced to be that year a failure in the catches on their own coast, so this expedition was planned to go a little farther a-field, in hopes of a better find. It took all the men from Light Island, save and except only old Christian, the deaf-mute. Frank had of late again thrown himself—somewhat fitfully, it must be owned—into the daily pursuits of these worthy, simple-minded folk. One can not live out one's life at agony point. An active, healthy man, under thirty years of age, must of necessity find an outlet for muscular vigor. So he had helped the men in turns to catch their fish, or their fowl, or to farm their land.

As the little fleet of cod-fishing boats put off from the shore, he stood on a ledge of rock, waving a hearty farewell to the men.

"Now," he said to himself, with the ring of Ned's final message still in his ears, "this is the last I shall see of these men. When they come back, not a doubt I shall be half-way home."

It was a pleasant thought. It deepened the blue in the sky and the waters, turned the autumn haze into a summer's glory, put a tone of melody even into the harsh cries of the puffin and gull; in a word, set the whole fair picture of land and ocean smiling, as though with a hidden joy.

Long after the boats had exchanged the waters of the sound for the open sea, he stood there, indulging in a variety of pleasant speculations. He could picture Joyce's wild intensity of joy as a twin to his own; Mab's tender, troubled eyes, looking a greeting her lips had no power to speak; Mrs. Shenstone's possible rush of pretty speeches, to be succeeded no doubt by all sorts of ingenuous exclamations upon the sorry figure he cut in her drawing-room, with his quaintly-made garments and untrimmed hair; Uncle Archie grumbling a cynical yet hearty welcome; and Joyce making peace all round with her bright little speeches and happy smiles.

But alas for his expectations! The boats went out, and the boats came in, but there came never a sign of Ned nor message from him.

Rough weather set in. Strong gales blew persistently from the northeast; the good wives on Light Island began to speculate on the chances of a whaling expedition, which had started from a neighboring island in the spring and had not yet returned. This, and the possible hazard the incoming mail steamer to Thorshavn might run, were the staple topic of talk among the islanders.

Frank's fears, though they lay all in another direction, were not one whit less gloomy. He naturally enough concluded that Ned, on the eve of sailing from Greenock, had, through untoward circumstances, been compelled to delay his departure. It was therefore more than likely that he was on the ocean highway now. It was highly improbable that he would be able to secure a passage in a well-built, sea-worthy steamer; now what might be the fate of a small fishing-smack or trading vessel in the sea that was running then?

A whole train of gloomy possibilities suggested themselves. Back again trooped the string of uncomfortable questions he thought he had set at rest forever by the sturdy negatives he had dealt them. The ignobleness of the whole thing seemed to stifle him. He to be waiting quietly and patiently on this barren ridge of rock, with the best days of his life slipping past, when perhaps, if the real circumstances of the case were laid bare to him, he would see that quietness and patience savored less of the heroic than of the despicable! The mere thought was torture to him.

The bond of honor which held him must have been a tough one. It was strained to its utmost limit during those days of despondency and bad weather.

Then the fog set in. Light Island became once more roofed and walled with the dense ocean mist. Old Christian began wheezing and coughing a good deal; his eldest son took to sharing the lighthouse duties with him, turn and turn about.

Frank volunteered his services. He had naturally acquired some Danish idioms during his long stay on the island; the younger Christian had picked up some of his English. Their talk consequently was fairly intelligible to each other.

"I have been with you some time now; you know me and know you can trust me," Frank said. "Occupation is the first of blessings to me. I've caught your fish for you; and caught your fowl, too; let me now go shares with you in the lighthouse work."

So it came about that Frank was admitted to a third share in the dreary responsibilities of lighthouse-keeping. Perhaps it would be more correct to say to a half, at any rate while the rough weather prevailed, for old Christian gratefully fell in with the younger mens' suggestion, that while the fog and wind lasted he should remain quietly indoors, mend the fishing-nets and nurse his asthma.

With nights broken in this fashion, it might be supposed that Frank had a welcome to give to a whole night's rest whenever he had a chance of it. Not so, however. A great restlessness had fallen upon him. Anything in the shape of quiet or repose was an impossibility to him. Sleep shunned him at night; his days were passed in incessant wanderings from coast to headland, from headland to Light Tower.

He made desperate efforts at reconnoitering, through field-glass and telescope. They were all fruitless efforts. Not once while those equinoctial gales lasted did the fog lift sufficiently to show a patch of blue sky, much less a square mile of blue ocean. His brain begin to feel sick and giddy with the perpetual repetition of the one thought:

"Where under heaven is Ned now? Of what sort of strength is the boat that is bringing him?"

The torture of those hours would have been beyond even his tough powers of endurance, could he have known who was at that moment defying wind and wave for his sake.

LIII

There came one awful day, the like of which not one of those hardy fisher-folk could recall. It seemed as if all the winds of heaven had combined to pour their fury upon the rock in one ceaseless, roaring blast. The great sea was lashed into frothy hillocks; sheep were blown off the headlands into the Sound; the women and children prudently kept within doors lest they might share a similar fate; the men drew their boats high up on the beach in sheltered nooks. The gale brought the fog in great rolling masses from the ocean: brought it in, swept it out again, and brought it in once more. Never since Frank had set foot on the island had he felt himself so stifled and oppressed by the fog. It was like being packed in a box filled with feathers. He began to ask all sorts of questions as to the possible risks boats would run on the open sea that night. Were shipwrecks of frequent occurrence on the coast? How far out would the beacon on the Monk Rock be seen? Would it lose half its radiance, or would the fog quench it altogether?

He got, in reply to his questions, a longer list of casualities than he expected. One man counted on the fingers of his hands no less than eight shipwrecks he could remember within sight of the Faroes in less than half that number of years. Another began the narration, in glowing language, of a fog and wind-storm he could recall, when the beacon on the Monk Rock had not been visible a hundred yards out, and a big ship had struck upon the sunken pinnacle, and all hands had perished.

Frank, of necessity, lost many of the details of the terrible incident through his ignorance of the Danish tongue; but he understood enough to set him shivering, and to send him questioning the younger Christian as to what means of fog-signaling (if any) the Faroes had at command.

The man's reply was to the effect that none, so far as he knew, had ever been in use on the islands; that an imperfect method of signaling, such as horn-blowing or gun-firing on the beach, would be as likely to do harm as good, the fog, it was well-known, frequently making the sound to appear to come from an opposite direction. But he had unbounded faith in the beacon. The fog, too, might lift before night—why not? One could only hope for the best. He had lived through fog and wind in his little fishing-smack in the open sea before now. Others might have equal good luck, why not?

But Frank had, somehow, in these days, lost his faith in good luck. He found it far easier to say to himself, "This is a direful day; there's ill-luck in that wind and fog for me, as well as for the poor souls who have to face it," than to say a prayer for those at sea, and turn in an hour or so earlier to shorten the dismal black hours of the night, as he had done many a time of late.

In the morning he had contrived, by keeping close under the shelter of the overhanging rocks, to get down to the beach, and had come away awe-stricken with the sense of the incapacity of man when once the wild forces of Nature, uncurbed and unbridled, are let loose on him. Toward evening, however, although the fog had thinned somewhat, going down to the beach had become an impossibility. The sea had come rushing up the thoroughfares that led down to the coast, and showed beneath the windows of the little huts an angry torrent of white foam. The path over the rocks to the light-tower still stood high and dry, but Frank noticed that young Christian equipped himself in his waterproof overalls for the night-watch a full two hours earlier than usual, and that a good-sized basket of provisions was packed for him to take with him. It was not difficult to understand that he was facing the possibility of being cut off for a time from the little colony. Frank was on the alert to accompany him without delay.

"It will be my turn on duty tomorrow," he said to the man. "I had better take my chance of getting to the tower while I can."

So with lanterns and provisions the two men set off for the dismal night-watch, old Christian, from his fireside corner, nodding a sleepy approval to them between his fits of wheezing.

The pent-up coldness of the lighthouse seemed to meet and strike them on cheek and lip as they entered. Naturally, the light was their first thought. That attended to, they wrapped their rugs and cloaks about them, and made as big a fire as due regard to the quantity of peat fuel stored would allow.

Young Christian stroked his straw-colored beard, and made one or two monosyllabic exclamations, to which Frank replied by brief nods. Then the man lighted a pipe, drew a chair into a warm corner, crossed his legs, and indulged either in a brief snooze, or in meditation of a somnolent character.

As for Frank, chair, pipe, or meditation was alike impossible to him. Had the room been long enough to admit a backward and forward march, the chances were he would have got through close upon thirty miles that night. Young Christian suggested to him once that, as it would be his turn on duty tomorrow night, it would be as well for him to get as much rest as he could that night. Frank scouted the idea.

Even a brief half-hour of sleep seemed to him an impossibility with that uproar of furious wind and wave without, and that turmoil of hideous apprehension within.

Every blast of roaring wind that beat against their tower, every dash of wild waves against the rock seemed to come laden with ten thousand voices more terrible than their own.

Would the gale never die of its own fury? Would the blessed daylight never come and the dreary watch be over? It seemed to have lasted a decade of years already. Frank pulled out his watch. The hands pointed to half-past four. Why, then, another two hours at least must elapse before they could hope for the faintest streak of dawn to do battle with this inky fog!

With something of a groan he sank down on the floor beside the peat fire, supporting himself on one elbow and shielding his eyes from the smoke. An open boat on the wildest sea, he felt, would be paradise itself compared with the torture of this forced inaction.

LIV

H e might have fallen asleep, perhaps; or, perhaps, there had come a lull to the turmoil of his thoughts, and, by contrast, it seemed unconsciousness.

A dull sudden boom broke across the temporary calm, and sent him to his feet with a start. What was it? A crash, telling of some havoc wrought by the still furiously blowing gale; or was it a more awful sound still—a signal of distress from some foundering vessel?

Young Christian had sprung to his feet at the same moment.

"What was that?" one asked the other, each feeling he held the answer in his own heart, and that perhaps at that moment some score or so of poor souls were going to their death amid the terrors of the storm.

Frank went to the look-out window in the tower, peering out into the gloom; or, rather, trying to; for nought met his gaze save the "blackness of darkness" everywhere; the black, leaping waves showing like so many inky shadows springing from a Stygian gulf as far as they dared into the world above.

"We must get a boat; we must do something," he cried, desperately.

The other shook his head.

"We have no life-boat—no boat but a life-boat could live in that sea."

"They may be near enough for us to fire a line into them with one of your fowling-pieces, and so get a rope from them. We may do something with a rope," cried Frank, making his way rapidly down the ladder-staircase into the room below, where lamps, string, and fowling-pieces were stored.

Young Christian followed him.

"That gun was fired far out at sea," he said.

"The fog muffles sound," said Frank, busy lighting the strongest hand-lamp they had in store.

"It muffles sound, and also makes it seem to come from another quarter. Now, would you say that gun came from north, south, east, or west?" said the other.

"They'll fire again—we shall tell better next time," answered Frank, opening the door and making his way out upon the rock, lamp in hand.

But, for all the use it was, he might just as well have left the lamp behind him. A dense wall of fog barred them in; over the darkness came the roaring of the northeaster, bringing with, it the rush and swirl of the waters which swamped the thoroughfares running inland.

At the peril of their lives they ran along the edge of the rock, in the teeth of the driving gale. They fired fowling-piece after fowling-piece into the black fog, hoping for an answering gun to show that their signals were heard. But, though they waited out there in the cutting blast with straining ears for an hour or more, never an answering gun came athwart the racket of wind and wave.

"Heaven help them, whoever they are," said Frank, firing his last shot into the air, "they are beyond our help now."

LV

Out on the broad Atlantic, the little ship *Frea* had done brave battle with the tempest. She had got well away from the Scotch coast, had steamed past the Shetland Isles, and was almost in sight of the Faroes, when the storm had broken forth in its full fury. It had snapped the mast as though it were a willow wand, torn its one sail into ribbons, and swept it away like a handful of dust.

The little vessel had lumbered heavily from side to side, rolling like a log in the deep troughs of the sea.

Uncle Archie grew apprehensive.

"It's her way of doing things; she's like some people, you know— takes life heavily, but she's none the less to be relied on," said the captain, cheerily, jealous for the honor of his little craft.

But later on in the day as the gale, instead of abating, steadily increased in strength, he grew less cheery, and his voice was only heard giving short, sharp orders to his crew.

Once, toward midnight, Uncle Archie thought he heard the words "driven out of our course—we must go wherever the wind takes us now," but the deafening turmoil wind and wave kept up prevented his being certain.

Toward daybreak matters grew worse. The sky was wild, the rain came down in buckets. Big seas broke over the deck, rushing down the hatchway into the cabin where Joyce had been bidden to remain. The lifeboat hanging in the davits was swept away, and, worst fate of all, the skylight of the engine-room was smashed at the same moment by the fury of the blast.

After this all was consternation, though, thanks to the good seamanship of the captain and crew, there was no confusion. The engineer came up reporting that the fires were out, and that they were up to their middle in water below; another man rushed forward crying that the ship was filling through the openings in the deck.

The signal-gun was at once fired, in case help was to be had from some passing vessel. Then there came the hurried order to man the remaining boat. Joyce heard her name called desperately by Uncle Archie, and, rushing up from the cabin, found herself caught in some one's arms and lifted into the boat where some four or five sailors were already seated. Uncle Archie and Morton took their places beside her, the boat was lowered rapidly though cautiously, the remainder of the crew leaped in from the mizzen chains, followed last of all by the captain.

All was hurry, confusion, and bewilderment to Joyce. From the time that the order to man the boat had been given, to the time when the men, with their oars, pressed the boat off from the sides of the sinking steamer, only about five minutes had elapsed. In that five minutes they had been nearer death than ever they had been in their lives before.

They realized this as, carried away on the crest of a mountainous wave, they turned to give a farewell look to the battered steamer. She lay on her side now; the black line of her hull showed for one moment between the masses of madly-dashing waves; the next the black line was altogether gone, the funnel only showing dark between the white, foaming spray. Another big wave carried the little boat onward; and when they lifted their eyes next not a vestige of the *Frea* was to be seen.

After gratitude for their own present safety, came the anxious thought, if the big boat were unable to live through the gale, what about the little boat?

In good truth their danger was not fanciful. Out there in the open sea they had not the fog that begirt the Faroes—that began where the waters of the Gulf Stream met the colder waters of the ocean—but it was pitch dark; there were neither stars nor moon, the wind was furious, and every moment the big seas sweeping down upon them threatened to engulf them.

Without excellent seamanship the little boat could not have lived in that sea for twenty minutes. But excellent seamanship they had. The captain had a cool, clear head, every one of the sailors was an "old salt," and knew well enough what he was about.

The captain took his place at the helm, giving his orders distinctly. The men were to row in spells, and those who did not row were to bale out the water, which threatened every moment to swamp them. This was by no means light work; only one baler had been thrown into the boat on starting, and hats and caps had to be called into requisition. It was bitterly cold, the wind was piercing, hands and arms speedily grew benumbed and chill. After all, the rowing seemed the lighter work of the two. Morton worked away at the baling briskly and bravely, rolling up his shirt-sleeves to the elbow, making a scarlet pocket-handkerchief do duty for his fur cap, and earning such high encomiums from the captain that the worthy man began to think that, after all, he had mistaken his vocation, and would have made a better sailor than detective. Poor old

Uncle Archie did his best, but his limbs were stiff, and it was quickly evident that his task told upon him.

"Some one must keep a lookout for the big waves with the white crests," said the captain, looking at the old man. So he volunteered for the duty, sitting back to back with the others, and Joyce, taking from his hand the baler he had in use, possibly found the work lighter than he had done.

So they tossed about in the dark, at the mercy of wind and wave. Where they were they knew not. They only knew they were being driven before a strong northeaster, it might be toward the coast of Iceland, it might be toward the dangerous Shetland shoals. Their only safety, they knew, lay in keeping to the open sea. To be dashed upon the shore in that gale could mean but one thing for them all. Perhaps, when daylight broke, they might sight a sail or find themselves in happy proximity to land. If not, Heaven help them, with not so much as a flask of fresh water among them, nor tin of hard biscuit.

A sailor in the darkness asked if any one had an idea of the time. The captain pulled out his watch. Joyce thought it must be close upon day-dawn—that darkest hour she knew so well.

It was too dark to see the face of the watch; but, feeling for the hands, the captain said he thought it must be between five and six.

Suddenly Joyce dropped her baler, leaning back silently against Uncle Archie's shoulder.

"Poor child, poor child!" he said, pityingly, "You are worn out—shivering—wet through and through."

Even as he spoke, the backwater of a big wave, whose full force they had backed to escape, came over them, a great, furious shower drenching them to the skin.

For a few minutes the work of baling went on silently and vigorously, Joyce doing her best with the others. Then she leaned back heavily upon Uncle Archie, again whispering to him over his shoulder:

"Uncle Archie, tell me, do you see anything?"

"Anything! A light, or boat, do you mean? I wish to Heaven I could!" moaned the old man; "but, beyond the black outline of the big mountains of waves, I can see nothing."

"Nothing!"

"Do you mean the phosphorescence on the sea, Joyce? I can see that thankfully enough, for where we should be without it in this inky darkness I'm sure I don't know."

"Only that?"

Uncle Archie thought a moment. Joyce might have another meaning. His voice dropped as he answered:

"Do you mean the last pitiful sight we saw, child? The waves leaping and dashing over our poor little steamer as it rolled over and disappeared in the darkness! Ah! I shall see that sight, with my eyes open or shut, to the last day of my life."

Joyce said no more. She was still leaning heavily against Uncle Archie's shoulder. He could feel the full throbbing of her heart, the deep drawing of her breath.

He began to grow alarmed. Was she giving way at last? After all these months of heroic endurance, was she going to confess herself beaten, worn out?

"Child, child," he said, don't give way like this—for me, for my sake hold out a little longer."

But still Joyce said nothing.

"Speak, my dear," he went on, nervously. "Do you see anything? Has something frightened you? Have you lost your courage at last?"

Joyce roused herself with an evident effort.

"Frightened, Uncle Archie, no! I never felt myself safer in my life. Never for one hour since Mab died have I lost the sense of her presence; but I never felt her so near as I do now. A moment ago I felt her so close to me, I wondered at myself for not seeing her. I fancied you—every one in the boat—must see her beside me. I thought something must be wrong with my eyes—that they must be "holden" as once the disciples' were—"

"My dear, my dear!" moaned Uncle Archie, fearing that Joyce's brains were leaving her.

"It's true, Uncle Archie"—and now Joyce's voice, as it grew lower, grew strangely sweet and solemn, "and, if I saw a score of angels spreadings their wings over the boat, I could not feel safer. One way or another, I feel it is all ending now, and, whichever way it ends"—this even more solemnly than before—"I know it is all right."

LVI

Toward morning the wind lulled, dying hard in a succession of long, low, howlings. To Frank's fancy every one of those howlings were so many evil triumphant voices rejoicing over a night of havoc and distress. "We have done our work well," he could fancy they said, "wrecked a good ship or two, drowned a few score of souls; there's no earthly reason that we should not go to rest again."

There was no glow of dawn in the sky, none of that glad flush of color spread across the heavens, which seems like Creation's hymn of thankfulness to its Maker for night ended, day begun. Only the fog whitened a little, then thinned, and hung about the low ground in tattered folds.

Frank scanned the horizon with his old telescope. The hull of a wrecked vessel would have seemed all in keeping with that lashing, brown sea, and dismal, iron-gray sky. But no vessel, wrecked or otherwise, broke the dreary monotony of the seascape.

They got their boat out, intending to pull round the coast and out into the open sea, in case there might be wreckage of some sort to tell the tale of the lost ship.

Young Christian's son, a boy of twelve or thirteen, made his way at daybreak to the lighthouse, bringing dismal accounts of the destruction the gale had wrought inland overnight. The palings round the rye-fields had been carried away, the sheep-folds had been utterly destroyed, and some of the sheep blown into a gully. It would take a week to repair the damage wrought.

Frank wondered what would repair the damage wrought outside on the wild Atlantic, and whether it might so happen that he held a personal interest in the answer to the question.

For, reason with himself as he might, he could not divest himself of the notion that the winds of last night had held his fate in their hands; that somewhere beneath the murky, troubled waves was hidden away a message for him which perhaps only the Day of Judgment would reveal.

They enlisted the boy's services to steer for them. The two men pulled across the Sound out into the open sea. It was rough work; they had to row their hardest, for the waves, although they lacked the terrific force and volume of overnight, were still turbulent. Nothing but a drear expanse of sea and sky met their gaze, turn it which way they would.

They had left the remnants of the fog behind them in the Sound; the sky showed patches of bright blue here and there between the hillocks of fleeting clouds. Not a boat was anywhere in sight, not a vestige of wreckage to be seen—not so much as the splinter of a mast or broken floating hen-coop.

They rowed backward and forward aimlessly for an hour or so, young Christian repeating meanwhile that brief chapter from his experience, of how that within a mile of where they rowed now a big Russian bark had gone down with all hands, and not so much as a floating spar had been left to tell the tale.

But Frank scarcely heard him for the tumult his own thoughts kept up within, a tumult which one simple question had started and kept going.

"Now, supposing that Ned, on his way here, was drowned in the storm of last night, am I to wait on, trusting he has kept his promise to provide for that emergency? Or may I consider that I have fulfilled every claim that honor or gratitude can have upon me, and return to my friends?"

It was a complex question. He had at one time been quick in answering questions in a word, at cutting all sorts of knots with a single touch. But here was a knot that defied alike fingers or knife. Second thoughts suggested that perhaps, after all, it was a question he had no right to ask, and, when he fell to considering upon what grounds he had started it, he found they were unsubstantial enough. His mind was restless and ill at ease, he had heard a signal-gun fired in the height of the storm; on this slight foundation he had built a fabric sky-high. Ned was, of necessity, in that particular boat; Ned, of necessity, had been drowned, with every living soul on board. There was, evidently, nothing in reason to warrant such a conclusion.

With something of a groan he helped to run the boat in and pull it up on the beach. Then he offered to assist young Christian with his shattered palings and sheep-folds. Hard, incessant work, for that day at least, he felt he must have. To sit still with folded hands meant mental torture of the worst kind. Perhaps, while his hands were busy, his brain might clear.

With brief intervals for food the two men worked hard till close upon sundown. Then another mood fell upon Frank; he grew restless, distracted again, threw his carpentering tools down in a heap, strapped his seal-cap under his chin, and went wading through the receding waters down to the beach once more.

Why he went he could not have said, he felt too perturbed in mind to reason on this or any matter. His brain felt all on fire, his nerves unstrung. The anxiety and suspense of the past nine months were beginning to tell upon him physically as well as mentally, the grip of the terrors of overnight was on him still.

The wind had ceased entirely now; the sea, with many a sullen roar, was settling down to its usual wash and ceaseless lapping, at the base of the mighty headland on which the Light Tower was built. The fog was nothing more than a thin veil of silver mist, hanging here and there on the horizon in all sorts of fantastic clouds, which caught the wonderful Iris hues, thrown upward by the sinking sun. One cloud in shape was like a huge promontory, jutting out into a waveless sea of blue; another showed like a gigantic dolphin with fins of fire, and, like a dying dolphin, was flashing into marvelous, changeful tints, as minute by minute the sun sank lower. Sea-gulls flapped in front of it, catching momentary rainbow colors on their gray wings. The white-crested waves far out at sea caught here a golden tinge, there a dash of violet or crimson, at the will of the mist or of the dying sun.

Frank saw it all without seeing it, Great Nature will charm a man into speech, or awe him into silence, only in so far as the man's brain is calm enough to play the part of mirror to her brilliant lights or gloomy shades. Let that man's brain be turbulent with fear, remorse, passion, regret, and Nature will spread her glories before him in vain. She may pipe to him, he will not dance; mourn to him, and he will not lament.

Thus it was with Frank now. He was blind to the beauties around him; he saw nothing but the miserable tragedy of his own life being played out conjointly with that of another young life infinitely dearer to him than his own; saw himself here a prisoner chained to a rock, by chains none the less cruel that they were invisible; saw Joyce miles and miles away, stretching out empty arms toward him, with longing eyes and aching heart. He looked away from the brilliant sky-picture overhead, and saw naught but the cruel, crawling, merciless sea at his feet.

We talk about the grandeur of the sea, or its fury, or its cruelty, but you must put on one shore all that is most precious in life—love, happiness, home—and yourself, a lonely exile on another; then let the great sea roll in between the two shores, to know what a jailor it can be.

And as Frank stood thus, a forlorn, despairing man, a sudden thought of Mab came to him. Whence it came, what brought it, he did not know. During all these months of exile his thoughts had rung the changes on but one key-note—Joyce. Hers was too engrossing a personality to leave much room for another's beside it; and, to say truth, though Mab might have flitted at times like a shadow through his dreams, she seldom or never filled his waking thoughts. Yet here, in the midst of this silence and solitude, came a thought as entirely distinct from its surroundings as would have been the sudden carol of a nightingale on that seashore or the coo of a wood-pigeon.

One turns over the letters of a dear, dead friend, and tries to conjure out of the mists of bygone years the face we have known and loved; but we find that the sweet and once familiar features are not to be summoned at will. We tie up the packet of letters with their faded ribbon, put them by in a drawer amid sprigs of rosemary and dead roses, go out into the busy world, buy and sell in the market, or dance at our balls, when lo, of a sudden, the tender eyes look out at us, and among a hundred other faces, the sweet mouth smiles once more its greeting or adieu!

So it was with Frank now. Without effort of will, Mab's personality at that moment filled his thoughts; without strain to his memory, he could see her face as he had known and loved it in the years gone by. Not as he had known it of late, with that brooding look of dreamy pre-occupation perpetually clouding eyes and brow, but as he could so well remember it in the old, happy days at Overbury, before death had entered the house—an anxious, thoughtful face, perhaps, as one could fancy the face of a guardian angel to be anxious and thoughtful, with its vicarious sorrows, but a face that could withal shine out into an intensity of joy, as he could remember it did once in the gray dawn of a memorable day, when she had laid her hand upon his shoulder, and had told him the glad news that Joyce had passed the crisis of her illness.

This vision of Mab was so real to him that it would have scarcely startled his senses if, at that very moment, she had turned the corner of the big, jutting headland, under whose shadow he stood, and had come toward him holding out both her hands—as she had so often met him in the old days—saying: "Oh! I am so glad to see you; Joyce and I were just at that moment talking about you."

A gull wheeled low over his head, flapping its gray wings, and uttering its long wailing cry. Was it a presage of bad weather again for the night, Frank wondered, lifting his eyes anxiously to the quarter where the sun had sunk, and whence the wind now blew.

All the colors had faded out of the sky; inky masses of clouds hung low upon the horizon; the sea showed beneath a cold stretch of iron-gray, over which the night mists were slowly spreading themselves. From out the mists, far out at sea, the "white horses" ominously lifted and tossed their curling crests.

But presently, something else beside the "white horses" seemed moving in the distant dimness. Frank strained his eyes their hardest, shading them with his hand from the dashing spray. Yes, it was a boat, and a heavily-laden boat, too; for it sat low in the water, as though its burden were as much as it could manage. And it was also, so it seemed, making straight for Light Island.

But what of that? Frank asked himself. What was there in the fact of a heavily-laden boat making straight for the shore to set his pulses throbbing at fever heat? Had he not seen scores of such boats go out, and come in, all through the fishing season? What more likely than that it was a boat from one of the smacks off the Faroe fishing-banks charged, perhaps, with letters or light cargo for the Faroes, and anxious to run for land before a wild night set in?

As the boat came nearer, another thought succeeded. What if this boat's load were a remnant saved from the wreck of the vessel in distress last night? What if Ned?—but here, with a strong hand, he put an end to a thought that, bordering on hope, fell little short of agony. He would just stand still and wait patiently. He had strong, far sight. Five minutes would show him who were the occupants of the boat. He would know Ned's head and shoulders among a hundred. And what was a five-minutes' waiting compared with the months of miserable suspense he had lived through?

But as he stood and waited he was compelled to own that never before had five minutes spun itself out to such an unconscionable length. On and on came the boat, slowly but steadily, its occupants showing black against the gray of the sky and sea, above, below. Yes; it was the remnants of a wrecked crew, Frank decided; there were certain signs of distress about them there was no mistaking; some of them were hatless; one or two seemed leaning forward, elbows on knees, as though they had had a rough time of it and were well nigh worn out. Frank's eye strained painfully for the broad shoulders and head which were to bring deliverance to him.

"I shall see better in another minute," he muttered, trying to keep up the illusion of hope a little longer.

And in another minute he did see better, and the illusion of hope died utterly in its realization. For in that drooping figure, with head bowed and hands clasped, seated there in the stern of the boat, he recognized with a thrill of joy so intense it was near akin to a pain the face and figure of Joyce Shenstone.

He scarcely dared trust his eyesight.

"It's the spray that's blinding me," he said aloud, in a voice which none would have known to be his, it quavered so. But, nevertheless, he was in the sea in no time, and as nearly out of his depth as he could trust himself to go.

Uncle Archie looked up at the great, beetling crag.

"Lift your head, child," he said, turning to Joyce, "and thank heaven we're safe now. Here's Light Island."

The captain dropped his glass from his eye.

"Bravely pulled, well done, men," he said.

The men drew their oars into the boat, wondering much over the gaunt-looking figure with seal-cap and unkempt beard that had hailed them, and was helping to pull their boat high and dry on the beach.

But they wondered still more when, as they held out their hands to help Joyce land, the same gaunt-looking figure pushed past them, took her bodily into his arms and carried her to shore.

Thus these two sorely-tried lovers joined hands once more. There came for them one moment of rapture, of intense unutterable joy, such as no human soul can live through more than once in a life-time, a moment not to be counted by the hands of a clock, for in its brief yet immeasurable "now" a whole miserable past was gulfed and gone.

And, when tongue can find words to speak the joy of such a moment as this, Language will have reached its goal, and may fitly claim the right to halve the throne of Thought.

Frank clasped Joyce to his heart as he had never in his life clasped her before; and, as for Joyce, her breath came and went in gasps, she trembled in every fiber of her body, but words she had none.

"Is that the way they do things on the Faroes?" asked Morton, solemnly, for the moment not recognizing Frank, and giving the captain a nudge as he spoke.

But Uncle Archie, like Joyce, said never a word. He only stood still on the beach, quaking and shaking from head to foot as he watched Frank and Joyce a yard from him standing silent also, holding each other's hands, looking into each other's eyes.

"Perhaps," thought the old gentleman, "by-and-by, when we reach that far-off shore toward which we are all traveling so fast, just in that way we shall greet our friends of lang syne—hold their hands, look into their eyes, say nothing."

Then another thought struck him, to which he gave utterance at once.

"Men," he said, in a thin, trembling voice, looking round at his shipwrecked companions, "we have been through great perils the past few hours; before we go a step farther I should like to kneel down here on the beach and thank the good Lord who has brought us safe to land."

"Ay, ay, sir," answered the captain, "if you'll be parson, we'll all follow lead."

So Uncle Archie knelt down on the rough pebbles, and one and all knelt down beside him, those who had hats taking them off, and Frank and Joyce clasping hands still.

"We thank Thee," began Uncle Archie, in a choking voice.

"We thank Thee," faltered Frank, in muffled tones.

Then there came a pause.

"We thank Thee," began Uncle Archie again, turning upward his old face in the twilight with tears streaming down both cheeks.

But he could get no further, and no one else had a voice wherewith to follow him even so far.

And, as for the Amen, the great sea must have said it for them, for only its voice was heard as they rose from their knees.

LVII

When they found their voices, however, they had enough to do with them. Never before, surely, had the old brown rocks of Light Island echoed to such a buzz and hum of talk.

The sailors, both Danish and British, began telling of the rough time they had had out there in the Atlantic; how that, when day broke and the wind had lulled they had found themselves miles out of their course, well on their way to Iceland; how that the tiller of their boat had broken and the captain had been forced to steer with his hand in the water till his arm was half frozen; how that their lips were parched and dry, for, save a half-filled brandy-flask which one of them had in his pocket, drink there was none. Nor was food to be had either, even so much as a crumb of dry biscuit. And how that in this plight all through that raging storm their hard work of baling, of rowing, and of occasional desperate backing of the boat, to escape the breaking of the big waves upon her, had had to go on continuously.

All this was recapitulated again and again, as, in a body, they threaded the mountain thoroughfare toward the row of inland huts, where Frank knew a hearty welcome, together with food and shelter, would be offered to the shipwrecked party.

But Frank's and Joyce's stories were yet to be told. Uncle Archie ought, perhaps, to have been the one to demand an explanation of Frank, to rush at him with a whole catechism of "whys" and "wherefores." He did not, however. He contented himself with walking side by side with the young people, his arms folded behind him, his eyes cast down. He probably felt that the strain of emotion he had already to bear was enough for the present; the "whys" and "wherefores" had better be deferred for a time. He shook his head now and again, as though at his own thoughts, as he went along; and once or twice Frank noticed that he stumbled, as though his feet could hardly carry him. Physical hardship tells heavily on the down-side of sixty.

As for Morton, he threw himself heartily on the Danish captain for companionship; and, had any one followed close on his heels listening to his talk, such expressions as the following might have been heard of frequent recurrence:

"I knew how it would be from the very first. I always said he was alive and hearty somewhere." This said with a nod and sideglance toward

Frank. "A man doesn't serve twenty-five years in a profession like mine without knowing what's what."

Frank, like Uncle Archie, felt that it was better that his story and Joyce's should be kept waiting for awhile. The suddenness of the whole thing was overwhelming. The simple fact of walking beside Joyce in quiet, silent happiness was utterly bewildering. It was like giving a man too much food after months of famine. The mere thought of the agony that would have been his had he known who were outside in the darkness struggling with wind and wave for dear life was in itself a cruel torture. He tried to shut it out of his mind; it hurt him as the recollection of some awful calamity escaped by a hair's breadth will hurt a man for hours after the danger is past.

Something else hurt him even more grievously—the still, white tragedy of Joyce's face. The anguish and long patience written upon it were easy enough to read. No joy of meeting, however intense, could efface it.

Yet, though Frank said to himself, it was better for them both that his story and hers should remain untold for a time, there was one question which rushed naturally to his lips. It was:

"Where is Ned? Of course it was he who told you where to find me, Joyce?"

Joyce started.

"Poor Ned!" she answered, as calmly as he could. "You do not know— how could you? He was killed—shot at Greenock—no doubt by some member of the League he belonged to, anxious to avenge Captain Buckingham's death."

Frank almost staggered.

"Dead! Buckingham! Ned!" he said, in a bewildered tone putting his hand to his head.

Then a sudden, great fear took possession of him. Those past nine months held many a dismal secret, not a doubt; and one by one, in some quiet corner, they would be told to him. But there was one dread that must be set at rest at once; so he asked a question in a nervous, roundabout fashion, lacking courage to put it direct.

"Joyce," he said, "I feel as the old prisoners released from the Bastile must have felt when they began to ask after the friends they had left behind in the outer world. You and Uncle Archie I see before me alive and well, thank heaven! but tell me who else of those I cared for are alive and well also?"

Joyce's hand, held fast in his, began to tremble violently.

"All your people in Gloucestershire were well when I heard last," she answered, very quietly.

Frank made an impatient movement.

"I mean in your own home circle," he said.

"My mother and Aunt Bell are well also," she said, her voice now sinking very low.

"Go on."

But Joyce was silent. Then Frank knew that his great dread was realized, and that however many kindly voices might welcome him home, Mab's would not be numbered among them.

He said nothing; but he felt now that Joyce's story, when it came to be told, would hold its own against his for tragic gloom.

The sheep dogs on watch outside the huts raised a hubbub as the party approached. Young Christian, and one or two others came out to meet them.

"You did not tell me," he said, in his mixed Danish, wagging his yellow beard at Frank, "that the friend you were waiting for was a woman."

Then he welcomed the strangers heartily, entered into friendly talk with his compatriots, and, with the help of the women, a plentiful though simple meal was soon set before the weary travelers.

At meal-time they discussed the question of sleeping arrangements. How could they make room for so many within the small compass of their huts? Naturally the Light Tower suggested itself.

"It will be my last night on duty," said Frank. "Some one, no doubt, will keep me company through the watch."

And Uncle Archie and Joyce, feeling, in spite of their fatigue, what an impossibility sleep would be until confidences had been exchanged, hailed with delight the prospect of an eight or ten hours' quietude.

So, in the little room which had been prison-house, or catacomb, to Frank through so many dreary months, those three sat up through the night, talking and listening by turns, making each other's hearts ache over again, bringing tears to each other's eyes, words of pity to each other's lips.

Once Joyce bowed her head on the arm of the old wife's wicker-chair, and her tears fell in a shower on the rusty knitting-pins which lay beside it, as Frank told the story of the miserable night when he lay, tied hand and foot, at Ned's mercy. He would fain have glossed over this part of his narrative, but Uncle Archie would not have it.

"Go on," he said, "tell us everything. Let her cry; it will do her good. She has been dry-eyed for many a day past."

On parts of her story, Joyce touched but lightly. She dared not test her powers of self-control by going through the last day of Mab's illness, nor Frank's, by giving in detail the history of Captain Buckingham's persecution. By-and-by, Frank would have much to hear, not a doubt.

But once, in spite of her reticence, Frank sprang to his feet in overwhelming indignation and anger, as she told simply, without comment, her own and Uncle Archie's interview with Ned, and how that, through all those long months of suspense, the Irishman had not given them so much as a word of hope.

Frank's indignation refused restraint. Hot, angry words came in a rush to his lips.

"I can't forgive him—dead and gone though he is. He expected me to keep my faith, and he broke his! If I had but known! He had better by far have been the murderer he might have been than the coward he was."

Joyce pleaded for him, telling the story of her anonymous letters, and her long hour of waiting on Chelsea Bridge.

"He made the attempt, not a doubt, to let me know a part of the truth so soon as he could," she said. "I daresay he thought that, if he had told me at first, I should have relaxed effort to find you, and so have betrayed him. Also, no doubt, he saw always before him this happy end to all our misery. He was young; he loved his life—"

"Yes; and he lost it—as those deserve to who love life better than honor," interrupted Frank, hotly. "Don't ask me to forgive him, Joyce. I could forgive Buckingham almost sooner than him—though heaven knows that would be hard work enough."

But later on he made a concession; at least Joyce understood it to be such.

The day after this night-watch saw the whole party ensconced in an hotel at Thorshavn, the little capital of the Faroes, and two days after that saw them on board a homeward-bound steamer.

Frank and Joyce stood on deck looking their last at the little islands, at the staring white tower of Light Island; the steep, awful rocks, grand and terrible in outline, soft and tender in their green and brown coloring under the subdued Arctic light. They had stood in silence thus for a long time, while Uncle Archie, seated close at hand, turned over a packet of American newspapers which, just as the boat was on the point of starting, had been thrown on board by some good people for the old gentleman's especial delectation.

At last Frank spoke, words that could be applicable to nothing unless it were to the denunciatory judgments he had passed upon Ned, Buckingham, and one or two others, and to the easy fashion in which he had at one time been wont to solve the problems of life in a single word.

"The truth of it is, Joyce," he said, "we are all of us too ready to lay down the law and pass sentence on every matter under heaven. We think it a proof of our wisdom instead of our folly to have an answer ready to every question that presents itself. We rush in and talk, talk, talk, where angels would veil their faces and weep in silence."

Possibly Frank, like Joyce, had not watched out long hours in solitude for nothing.

"Ay," said Uncle Archie, solemnly, looking up from a paragraph he was reading, with misty eyes, "a prayer for mercy for ourselves, a cry of pity for the whole human race, these are the only words that come fitly from our lips."

The paragraph he had been reading appeared under the heading of "News from New York," and related how a young girl, in the act of landing at midnight from a Greenock steamer, had taken a false step, been precipitated into the harbor, and had been drowned, in spite of efforts made to rescue her.

The name of the girl was Kathleen O'Shea.

THE END

A Note About the Author

Catherine Louisa Pirkis (1839–1910) was a British detective novelist. Born into a middle-class English family, she was raised among eight siblings and moved frequently in her youth. In 1872, she married Frederick Edward Pirkis, with whom she raised two children. Between 1877 and 1894, she published 14 novels and contributed frequently to periodicals and magazines. Towards the end of her life, she dedicated her time to animal rights activism, helping to found the National Canine Defense League in 1891. A popular novelist of Victorian England, Pirkis is remembered for her character Loveday Brooke, a fictional detective dubbed the "female Sherlock Holmes" for her appearance in *The Experience of Loveday Brooke, Lady Detective* (1894), Pirkis' final published work of fiction.

A Note from the Publisher

Spanning many genres, from non-fiction essays to literature classics to children's books and lyric poetry, Mint Edition books showcase the master works of our time in a modern new package. The text is freshly typeset, is clean and easy to read, and features a new note about the author in each volume. Many books also include exclusive new introductory material. Every book boasts a striking new cover, which makes it as appropriate for collecting as it is for gift giving. Mint Edition books are only printed when a reader orders them, so natural resources are not wasted. We're proud that our books are never manufactured in excess and exist only in the exact quantity they need to be read and enjoyed.

bookfinity™

Discover more of your favorite classics with Bookfinity™.

- Track your reading with custom book lists.
- Get great book recommendations for your personalized Reader Type.
- Add reviews for your favorite books.
- AND MUCH MORE!

Visit **bookfinity.com** and take the fun Reader Type quiz to get started.

Enjoy our classic and modern companion pairings!

Classic & Modern

Printed in the USA
CPSIA information can be obtained
at www.ICGtesting.com
JSHW022214140824
68134JS00018B/1040